SIREN

Book Three of the Vinyl Trilogy

SOPHIA ELAINE HANSON

CALIDA LUX
PUBLISHING

D1598970

VINYL: *Book Three of the Vinyl Trilogy*

ISBN-10: 1-7321376-0-9
ISBN-13: 978-1-7321376-0-8

Editor: Katherine Catmull
Cover Design: Docshot
Printing: Createspace
Print and eBook Formatting: Heather Adkins

For those who find a home in music

Darius

Charlotte

Ronja

Larkin

Cosmin

SIREN

PART ONE: THE BURNING ONES

PROLOGUE: THE GIFT
Evie

There was a certain peace in giving up. Peace was not something Evelyn Wick was familiar with. On her first night in prison, she pounded on the door and rattled the bars of her window, trying to pry one from its niche. She cursed the Offs who delivered tasteless food. They did not appear to hear her. Maybe they didn't. Singers clung to their ears, pouring The New Music into their minds. Who knew what it did to warp their reality?

Eventually, her voice grew hoarse. A deep ache filled her lungs. She took to prowling the perimeter of her cell, searching for an exit that did not exist. All the while, her thoughts spun webs in her skull. Iris. Samson. Ronja. Roark. Henry. Terra. Mouse. Iris.

When the Offs came to collect her after what felt like weeks, Evie was ready for them. She fought dirty, going for the eyes and throat. Her knuckles were bruised and her lip split by the time they forced her to the floor. Two of them pinned her while the third regarded her with a detached expression, hemorrhaging from his busted nose.

She had first noticed it in the warehouse. The Offs with the red emblems on their uniforms did not react to pain. They were either the toughest bunch of bastards she had ever met, or The New Music was numbing them. That meant they would have to die if they were to be stopped.

That was perfectly fine with Evie.

They dragged her, writhing and swearing, from her cell and down a long corridor. The hall reminded her of Red Bay, only darker. Older. The stone walls leaked. There was no electricity, only gas lamps. Eventually, they reached a metal door marked XVI. Evie committed the number to memory.

One of the Offs opened the door with a screech. It was pitch-black inside, cold as the canals in winter. Her captors shoved her in and slammed the door. Evie stumbled, throwing her hands out in front of her. Someone caught her by the shoulders. She would know that touch anywhere.

"Iris!" Evie gasped, reaching out blindly to draw her to her chest. Iris melted into her, shivering. "Are you all right? Did they hurt you?"

The surgeon gave a wordless shake of her head. Evie exhaled in relief and allowed her knees to give. They followed each other to the ground.

"Are you okay?" Iris rasped. Evie could almost taste how parched she was. "Have you seen anyone?"

"No," the techi replied hollowly. "No one."

"Me either. I've been alone this whole time. I thought I was going to go crazy. I thought . . . " She choked on a sob.

"Shhh . . . " Evie rocked Iris back and forth, smoothing her stiff curls. They had grown since she last touched them. They had been apart for far too long. "I know, I know."

"Why are they keeping us alive?" Iris asked. "What are they playing at?"

Evie did not reply. They both knew the answer to that

question: they were insurance. As long as they were alive, Ronja would do whatever Maxwell said to keep them safe. Even if that meant becoming his weapon of conquest. "If we're alive, so is Ronja," Evie assured Iris in a low voice, keenly aware that the room was likely bugged. "As long as she's alive, we have a chance."

"A chance for what?" Iris whispered urgently. "It's all over. The Anthem, the radio, the revolution. All of it."

The door banged open, bathing the Anthemites in searing light. Iris stifled a scream. Evie drew her closer, snarling up at the silhouettes in the frame. Before she could climb to her feet, two figures were shoved inside and the door shut with a clang. "Who's that?" Evie demanded.

"Good to see you too, Wick."

The techi felt her heart stutter. "Terra?"

"And me," came a bored masculine voice.

"Mouse?" Iris squeaked, disentangling herself from Evie and scrambling to her feet. The techi followed suit, squinting into the void. She couldn't see an inch, much less across the cell.

"Unfortunately," Mouse replied.

"Are you all right?" Evie asked. She took a cautious step forward. "Are you hurt?"

Terra grunted. "I'll be fine. Just a little crispy."

Evie smiled tightly. The last time she had seen Terra, she had been unconscious on the floor of the clock tower, brought down by a stinger to the spine. She certainly *sounded* better, but Evie had learned not to take anything Terra said at face value.

"I ran out of toilet paper a week ago," Mouse told them glumly.

"Just be grateful you're still in good enough shape to worry about your ass," Evie replied. "What have you got, Terra?"

"Not enough," she answered tersely. "From the architecture I'd guess we're somewhere in the core, maybe beneath the palace.

Dozens of guards, all under The New Music. No exits in sight."

"The Offs," Iris spoke up in a small voice. "They act like machines, like they're not even human."

The space grew colder in the wake of her words. Someone sniffled forlornly, probably Mouse. Evie hugged her arms to her chest. She had never doubted the claims Ronja and Roark made about The New Music, but seeing it in action was more terrifying than she could have imagined.

Dulling emotions was one thing. Obliterating them was another.

"Guys," Mouse asked. "What are we doing here?"

The earsplitting screech of an intercom coming to life answered before they could. "An excellent question, Mr. Constantine." A chill lanced through Evie at the sound of the strange, loping voice.

"Maxwell Bullon," she growled. "Show yourself, you coward."

"Are you really in a position to be demanding things of me?" the disembodied voice of the tyrant inquired silkily. "But I suppose I would like to be able to see your faces. It will make this so much more interesting."

Evie felt her pupils contract as bright light flooded the space. She shielded her eyes, blinking rapidly to gather sight. They had been crammed into a claustrophobic cell made entirely of glass. A large speaker was mounted in one corner, a whirring video camera in the other. Beyond the translucent walls was a featureless room with a domed ceiling and curved black walls. There was not a soul in sight.

Iris pressed closer to Evie, who looked down at her in vague wonderment. A part of her had begun to believe she would never see her again. Even covered in grime, her features shaded with exhaustion and fear, Iris was the most beautiful thing she had ever seen.

"What the hell is this?" Terra snarled up at the camera. She had lost a considerable amount of weight. Her long blond hair was stiff with grease and bluish circles had formed under her sharp eyes. "Where are the others?"

Evie felt her stomach clench. How had she not noticed? Roark was not with them. She had expected Maxwell to keep his precious Siren locked away, but if he wanted all his bait in one place, why had he left out the most important piece?

"Your comrades are otherwise occupied," Maxwell finally answered, his voice brushed with static and something else. Something Evie could not place. Before she could dissect it, Bullon continued. "I have brought you here today to present you with a gift."

"A gift?" Iris spoke up bitingly.

"Yes, Ms. Harte, a gift. Specifically, a piece of information. You will be pleased to know that my soldiers have yet to capture the Belly."

Evie felt her heart leap into her throat. Her eyes darted first to Iris, then to Terra and Mouse. The albino boy was acting in accordance to his nickname. Terra was quiet, calculating. Evie returned her gaze to the camera. She could feel Maxwell watching them through the lens.

"Thanks to Mr. Romancheck, we learned the location of your headquarters months ago," he said. A wave of nausea rolled over Evie at the mention of Henry. Her friend. Her brother. A slave to The New Music. Was he behind the camera too, watching them with lusterless eyes? "We have them surrounded, but it appears they have sealed themselves below ground."

The Anthemites looked at one another with a mixture of hope and dread. Evie kicked her mind into high gear. "If you try to dig them out, you'll hit gas lines," she warned him. "You'll blow everything within a five block radius."

"I am aware of this," Maxwell replied. She could have sworn she heard a twinge of irritation in his voice. "Believe it or not, I would prefer your people survive this ordeal. They will make valuable soldiers."

"Well, seems like you have a problem there, mate," Evie said with a snide laugh. "What will you do?"

"I will do nothing," Maxwell answered, unruffled. "I am far too busy to deal with the four of you. I will leave you in the capable hands of my colleague."

"Who?" Terra snapped.

Evie knew the answer before the door beyond the glass rolled open, revealing a handsome young man with dark skin dressed in white. Henry.

1: BLACK SHORES

The sea was a machine unlike any Ronja had encountered. There were no gears spinning beneath its dark waves, no coal to stoke its engine. It was mad. It was cold. It was relentless. But she was safe, tucked into the Tovairin ship like a message in a bottle. She wanted nothing more than to stay. Unfortunately, the black shores of Tovaire were approaching fast. They would run aground in minutes. Beyond the charcoal beach were craggy cliffs like thunderheads. There was no vegetation in sight, no city on the horizon. The sky was a muted shade of silver.

Pressure around her fingers.

Ronja looked down. A soft brown hand was wrapped around her own. She lifted her chin. Her pulse stumbled the way it always did when their gazes locked. His gold-shot eyes were embers against the dreary scene, his mouth pressed into a worried line.

"You all right, love?" Roark asked.

"Fine."

"I think you've taken my place as the master of deflection."

Ronja felt her mouth quirk into a smile. "I've learned from the best." Silence grew between them as the northern wind howled. Ronja tugged the fur cloak Jonah had given her tighter around her shoulders. The shoreline crept closer. They were less than two city blocks from the sand.

"How's your jaw?" Roark asked after a while.

Ronja reached up to touch the fading scars that ran from the corners of her mouth to her jaw, the ghosts of the cruel bit Maxwell had forced her to wear. The healing wounds felt as if they belonged to someone else. Revinia, The Music, the Anthem, Maxwell, the clock tower, the radio station. They all belonged to a girl who no longer existed.

"Better," she said.

"I can barely see the marks anymore," Roark went on. "They'll be gone before you know it." He brushed his thumb across her freckled cheekbone. She mustered a weak smile to appease him. "How are you doing . . . besides that?"

Ronja passed him a glance, then flicked her gaze back to the imposing cliffs. "What do you mean?"

"Well." He cleared his throat, raking his fingers through his dark hair. "You've been through a lot."

"We all have."

"You especially. Not to mention what Jonah told you."

The Siren bit the inside of her cheek. This was not the first time Roark had tried to illicit a response from her about the bombshell theory. It was just a *theory*, she reminded herself for the thousandth time. It could all just be a coincidence. Stranger things had happened.

"If you ever want to talk," he started.

"I'm fine, Roark."

A shout from aft drew their attention. Jonah was fifteen feet in the air, clinging to the mast with his legs and grasping a thick length of rope. Despite the bitter air, he wore nothing but a loose tunic and leggings. His first mate Larkin was shouting up at him in Tovairin, her tattooed hands gesturing madly.

Jonah barked a curse and released the line. The main sail crumpled. The ship slowed. Ronja turned back to the bow. Her stomach plummeted like an anchor. The black cliffs loomed so high they seemed to dive forward to greet them. The soaring clock tower burst into her mind. The city going dark in waves. The shot echoing through a marble room.

"*Allae!*"

Ronja was knocked aside. She glowered at Larkin who hoisted herself up onto the bow. Since the start of their voyage, the Tovairin girl had been nothing but standoffish. She seethed each time Ronja entered a room, purposefully elbowed her when they passed each other in the narrow corridor. The Siren had tried several times to bridge the gap, but it was rather difficult seeing as they did not speak the same language.

Larkin lifted a thick coil of rope over her shoulder, the lean muscles of her arms rippling, her bare toes clinging to the rail. She brushed her smooth black braids out of her face. They were almost blue in the silvery light. With the grace of a dancer, she rose up on her tiptoes and leapt into the waves.

"What the hell is her problem?" Ronja muttered, wiping droplets of frigid water from her face. Before Roark could answer, a shudder ripped through the ship, its belly grinding against the sand. She peered over the edge anxiously. Larkin was waist deep in the surf, working with the tide to guide their vessel onto the beach.

"Happy to be back on land, princess?"

Ronja rounded on Jonah, bristling. He had dressed again in his fur-lined jacket and waterproof boots. His dual swords were strapped to his back, his black hair knotted near the top of his head. "I told you to stop calling me that," she replied sullenly.

The captain cracked a lopsided grin. "Whatever you say, princess."

"Oi," Roark warned him, slinging an arm over her shoulders. "Watch it."

Ronja shrugged him off gently. The last thing she wanted was to be caught in the middle of a testosterone fest. She lifted herself onto the bow and swung her legs over the edge. Below her was an infinity of midnight sand. With a deep breath she let herself drop. She hit the ground harder than expected, tripping forward. Her fingers sank into the cool, malleable sediment. It felt different than she expected, softer. She shivered as the surf rushed in like a great exhalation, pouring over her knuckles. She had never seen a beach before, but was fairly certain the sand was supposed to be white.

"Ro?"

Ronja clambered to her feet, wiping her palms on her thighs. Jonah and Roark stood before her. She had not heard them hit the ground. Roark was watching her tenderly. Jonah looked amused. He had shouldered a heavy pack in addition to his broadswords.

"*Yessan!*"

They followed the voice to Larkin, who was already some fifty paces inland. She beckoned them, her agitation radiating. Ronja had only picked up a few Tovairin words during her stay on the ship, but she was pretty sure *yessan* meant *hurry the hell up*. "Best not to keep her waiting," Jonah said. He hitched up his pack and started after Larkin.

Ronja and Roark were left alone at the shore. The wind tugged at their clothes and hair. The surf lapped at their feet hungrily. "Ronja," the boy began as soon as Jonah was out of earshot. "I—"

"We don't have time for this," she cut him off. "Maxwell's carriers will arrive in Revinia any day now, if they're not there already." She tucked deeper into her furs as the wind swelled again. "We have a week at *best* to convince the Kev Fairla to invade a city they barely know exists. Every second counts."

Before Roark could reply, Ronja walked off toward the cliffs, her heavy cloak flapping in her wake.

2: BURIED
Ito

Ito drummed her fingers on the oak surface of the conference table, her chin cradled in her hand. The vent above her hummed noisily, pumping recycled oxygen into the Belly. The techis told her they would run for a few months at best. But if she could not get the man sitting opposite her to see reason, they would remain sealed beneath the city for much longer than that.

"Tristen," the lieutenant tried again, leaning toward Wilcox. "Walk me through your logic."

The commander scowled at her like a petulant child. The expression clashed with his aging face and silver buzz cut. "I don't owe you an explanation, Lin," he growled.

"No, but you owe them one," she hissed, jabbing her finger at the door separating them from the rest of the Belly. "When Roark radioed he told us to evacuate, not bury ourselves alive."

She had been dozing in her quarters when her portable radio had crackled to life. At first there was only static. It was so faint she thought she had imagined it. Then, a voice. *This is Drakon. Does anyone read me? The Siren has fallen. I repeat, the Siren has fallen.*

The Siren.

That name had been slithering through the streets of Revinia since Roark and the others disappeared. Wherever it went, unrest followed. For the first time Ito could remember, civilians were resisting their Singers. Food was stolen from government stockpiles. Monuments immortalizing The Conductor were defaced. There had even been rumors of citizens murdering corrupt Offs in the middle ring.

Only two weeks before Roark's distress call, dozens of topside Anthemites radioed to report a phenomenon the likes of which they had never seen. Every window was blazing. Torches held aloft to scatter the night. A citywide march toward the core. A rallying cry loud enough to drown The Music in their ears. *Passion is paramount. Disobedience is due.* It was the start of the uprising the Anthem had tried and failed to spark for decades.

Then all at once, silence. Utter, deafening silence. Anthemites had radioed the Belly, the wonder in their voices replaced with terror. "No one is talking," one agent had breathed into his microphone. "They're in the streets, all of them. They're walking like they're a unit. Like they're all one body. I think—"

Ito never learned what he thought. Wilcox had shoved her out of the way and emptied his gun into the dashboard of the communication hub. "The New Music is here," he had said quietly, his slate eyes fixed to the smoking piece of junk before them. "Rally the stationary guard. We're going dark."

Hours later, they had been buried. On Wilcox's order, the elevator was destroyed using the explosives originally intended to breach the rubble that guarded the six emergency exits. Without the aid of C4, the massive boulders were impossible to budge. The entrances to the sewers were welded shut. Even the air vents had been plugged with steel plates. The only grates that remained open were those connected to the CO_2 scrubbers.

"The Conductor is at our door, Ito," Wilcox insisted, bringing her back to the present. "If we open it, they'll flood the Belly with The New Music. We'd be better off dead."

"You may believe that, but you owe your people a choice," she replied steadily.

"Even if we were to get out, how would we survive The Air Song, hmmm?"

"We'd find a way, we always do," Ito said firmly. When Wilcox did not react, she pressed on. "We owe them a chance to escape. Dozens of our own are still out there. Evie, Iris, Terra, they're still in the hands of The Conductor."

"Those traitors can rot," Wilcox spat. Ito flinched despite herself. "Westervelt and his pet mutt started this mess. With any luck it will finish them."

"Sir—"

"Enough, get out!"

"Tristen—"

The commander slammed his palms into the conference table, sending a shudder rippling through the wood. It took everything Ito had not to shrink back into her chair. Instead, she did what she always did. She lifted her chin and hardened her gaze. Across from her, Wilcox was panting like a wounded animal, his eyes shifting and his face the color of red wine. "Speak one more word of this and I'll strip you of your rank," he said. "Question me publicly and you'll never speak another word."

The vent coughed above Ito, one of the air scrubbers tripping over itself. She pushed her chair back and got to her feet swiftly. Her heart thundered in her ears. Everything was brutally sharp, clear. "Your cowardice is going to get us all killed, sir," she said softly.

The commander tore his gaze from hers, his upper lip curling. "So be it."

3: THE EDGE

The cliffs were considerably further from the waterline than they appeared. The trek was made more difficult by their heavy winter clothes and the uneven sand. It took them a good ten minutes to reach the base of the mountain. By the time they did, Ronja had worked up a sweat. "Now what?" she asked no one in particular, craning her neck back. Large white birds circled overhead, lolling about in the airwaves.

"We climb," Jonah answered as he adjusted his pack.

"What?" Ronja yelped. Jonah and Larkin smirked at each other, then strode off toward a large boulder near the bottom of the cliffs. Roark and Ronja exchanged a glance. When they looked back at the Tovairins, they were gone.

"Uh," Roark said. "Do you think . . . "

"Hurry up, *beveks!*" Jonah called. His voice had a strange echoey quality to it, as if he were shouting at them down a long corridor.

"*Bevek* means foreigner, right?" Roark asked, eyeing the spot where their guides had disappeared.

"More or less," Ronja replied absently. She was pretty sure it was some sort of slur, but was not in the mood to analyze it.

"Come on," she said. She stuck out her hand for Roark to take. His eyes ignited at the offer. She knew she had hurt him by refusing his help earlier. That was the last thing she wanted to do. That did not mean she wanted to sit around talking about her feelings. She wanted blood.

Roark laced his fingers with hers as they approached the boulder cautiously. Ronja traced its damp surface as they rounded the bend. It was smooth and shone like a record. They found themselves in a cool sandy aisle between the cliffside and boulder. Carved into the mountain was an arching entryway, roughly six feet high and fringed with drooping moss.

Ronja swallowed, her eyes trained on the entrance. She felt Roark watching her, scanning her features for signs of a breakdown. Irritation reared in her. Her mind was as cold and sharp as the rocky shores behind them. There was no room for weakness. There was no time to mourn those they had lost.

She disentangled her hand from his and marched on, her boots whispering across the sand. Brushing aside the curtain of moss, she ducked into the mountain with Roark on her heels. Cool, surprisingly fresh air washed over her.

"Took you long enough," Jonah said. Ronja squinted ahead into the semi-darkness. The only light came from the weak electric lantern the captain held aloft. From what she could tell, they were in a dingy tunnel with rough walls. "Come on," he continued, turning on his heel and marching into the unknown. "Larkin is probably already halfway up."

"Up?" Ronja asked. She jogged after him, Roark still trailing her. The sound of their footsteps rebounded off the walls of the tunnel, meshing with the pings of dripping water. "Where exactly are we going?"

"You'll see," Jonah answered. She got the sense he was being mysterious on purpose, which soured her already deteriorating mood.

"I'd rather you just tell me," she tried again when she reached his side. The lantern painted imposing patterns on his handsome face. "If you could just skitzing—"

The world was pulled out from beneath her feet.

Before fear could take hold of her, before she could blink, she was falling. A scream ripped from her throat as a hand snatched her by the forearm. She dangled like a pendulum over a bottomless maw. Panting, she looked up. Jonah stood above her. He had thrown the lantern aside, they were lucky it had not gone over the edge of the cliff with her. "Watch your step," he said lamely.

"Pull me up!" she screamed, her voice reflecting back at her. Her legs kicked uselessly, the tips of her boots scuffing against the rock. Roark shot into the ring of light and crashed to his knees, skidding to the edge.

He reached down, his fingers straining. "Here!"

With a grunt of effort Ronja reached up her free arm and grasped the offered hand. Working as a unit, they dragged her back to solid ground. As soon as her knees struck the stone, Jonah released her and went to retrieve the lantern. Roark yanked her into a desperate embrace. She mumbled that she was all right, but he just held her tighter. She could feel his heart thundering through his cloak. Closing her eyes, she surrendered to his arms.

"What the hell is wrong with you?" Roark demanded, shouting at Jonah over her head.

"How much time do you have?"

"You let her walk off a pitching cliff!"

"What, am I supposed to be babysitting her?"

"She—"

"Can speak for herself," Ronja cut in, peeling back from Roark and glaring at Jonah. She got to her feet shakily. "What the hell kind of mountain is hollow?"

Jonah arched a condescending eyebrow at her. "Who said this was a mountain?"

"Wait . . . is this a volcano?" Ronja choked out.

"Not an active one." He raised his finger in the air. "The ancients sealed off the top, the rest is still hollow. It makes for a pretty good base."

Understanding dawned on the Siren. "Is this the headquarters of the Kev Fairla?"

The Tovairin grinned, revealing stark white teeth. "Patience, princess."

"If you call me that one more time, I swear—" Ronja cut herself off with a gasp, backpedaling toward the exit as a rattling crash exploded above her. Before the echoes had faded, Roark had drawn his borrowed knife, aiming it at the void. Jonah laughed, holding the lantern higher to scatter the shadows.

"Larkin gets faster every time, I swear," he said. Ronja took a cautious step toward the ledge. A rope ladder with metal rungs had descended from above. It swayed back and forth, creaking like the branches of an old tree.

Jonah stepped up to the edge of the abyss and steadied the ladder with his free hand. "Ladies first," he said.

Ronja shook her tangled hair out of her face and flipped her cloak over her shoulders. Refusing eye contact with either boy, she grasped the closest rung. The ladder trembled more than she had expected it to, which did little to quiet her nerves.

"Climb around to the other side," Jonah directed her as she put her other hand on the rung. "Or you'll bash your head on the—"

"I get it."

Ronja secured her first foot on the ladder, then the second. Jonah continued to hold it steady as she navigated to the other side, scarcely daring to draw breath. The darkness seemed to reach up toward her, nipping at her ankles and wrapping around her calves.

"Be careful," Roark called from the edge. She locked eyes with him through the window of two rungs. His eyes glinted with concern, or maybe it was just the light of the lantern. She offered him a brief nod, not trusting herself to speak, and began to climb.

4: GODS AND MONSTERS
Evie

"Henry," Evie breathed. She released Iris and approached the sheet of glass that separated them. "What the hell is going on?"

Physically, he appeared in excellent health. He looked even stronger than he had when they last crossed paths in the clock tower. When he had hurt Ronja. When he had murdered Samson with a headshot, right in the center of his brow. Evie had watched his face when he pulled the trigger. There had not been a flicker of doubt. She gritted her teeth as rage boiled in her gut. The urge to fly at him swelled in her, but she knew her anger was misplaced. Her gaze flicked to the camera, then back to him.

His dark features were as blank as the curved walls beyond their cell. He was not bored. He was not even apathetic. He was nothing. Every inch of his beautiful mind had been stripped by the gold Singer that clung to his ear. "Henry," Evie tried again, keeping her voice low to prevent it from shaking. "Do you know who I am?"

"Yes," he answered. The techi could not help but flinch at the sound of his voice. It was as if she were hearing him speak on a recording captured a long time ago. Familiar, yet somehow foreign. "Evelyn Wick. Techi, sharpshooter, lifelong member of the terrorist organization known as the Anthem. Wanted for at least six counts of murder and high—"

"Okay, okay, I get it," she snapped. To her surprise, he shut his mouth at once. His lusterless eyes roved across her face, searching for something. Her skin prickling, Evie peeked over her shoulder. Iris had scooted back to stand between Terra and Mouse. Her lower lip quivered, but she still managed to hold her head high. *That's my girl.*

"Evie."

She cut her eyes to Terra. The blonde was watching her intensely, a warning blazing in her hazel eyes. Evie gave a subtle nod, then returned her attention to what remained of Henry. "What do you want, Henry?"

"The Conductor has tasked me to collect intel from you," he answered.

"The Conductor is dead. You were there."

Evie was still grappling with the weight of the events at the clock tower. Seeing the crippled form of Atticus Bullon hunched in a wheelchair, sucking oxygen down through a tube, had turned her world upside down. The man she had fought her entire life was nothing but a puppet, a remnant of the dictator who had created The Music.

Now he was dead, murdered by his own son. The game had changed, and she was a soldier without orders.

"The Conductor has been reborn in his son and rightful heir of this world, His Excellency Maxwell Sebastian Bullon," Henry answered smoothly.

Evie barked a mirthless laugh, her breath clouding on the glass. "Reborn? Are you skitzing kidding me? What, do you think that bastard is some sort of god?"

The techi flinched when Henry slammed his powerful fist into the glass. The wall shuddered, but did not crack. He leaned in, his nose nearly brushing the window. "Do not speak ill of The Conductor," he whispered. "You will live to regret it."

"Doubt it," Evie snarled.

"I had planned to give you a chance," Henry said, taking a step back and straightening his pristine suit. The red badge on his lapel hooked her gaze. Three crimson pillars that formed a perfect square. The white eye of Atticus Bullon had been retired. This was a new symbol for a new age. The age of Maxwell Bullon. "I guess we'll have to do this the hard way."

Henry snapped his fingers, the little pop echoing through the cavernous room. Evie took an involuntary step backward and collided with Iris, who had scrambled up to stand beside her. Their hands found each other as the door to their cell was wrenched open, revealing a team of Offs brandishing crackling stingers. Evie counted six men, all twice her size. The four Anthemites drew into a tight knot, backing toward the far wall. "You won't kill us, Henry," she called out, her gaze fixed on the encroaching Offs.

"Perhaps not," Henry replied tonelessly.

Evie gritted her teeth against her terror, scanning the clot of Offs. They were outnumbered and outgunned, but they had faced worse odds. Terra cracked her knuckles.

"Guards," Henry said in a cold voice. "The redhead."

Evie did not think. Her body worked without her consent. She whipped Iris behind her and launched herself at the nearest Off, kicking out his knees. As he went down, she spun to nail another in the face with her elbow. He fell into his comrade and they went over like dominos. Someone was screaming. They sounded very far away. Evie cranked her arm back and punched another Off in the trachea.

Then there was nothing but white light and agony.

5: INTIMIDATION

*F*ifty-one. *Fifty-two. Fifty-three.*

Ronja counted the beats of her ascension. She could have squeezed her eyes shut and it would have made no difference. Jonah had stowed the lantern in his pack for safe keeping. The world was at once unimaginably vast and unbearably claustrophobic. Her nerves were fraying, her teeth creaking under the strain of her grimace.

Fifty-six. Fifty-seven. Fifty-eight.

"How much further?" she called down to Jonah. He and Roark were some ten rungs below her. The ladder shuddered and swayed with each step they took.

"Not much," the captain yelled back. "Just another minute or two."

Wincing, Ronja forced herself to climb faster. Her soles whined against the metal rungs. Her thoughts wandered, her obsessive counting faded.

The last time she had scaled a ladder like this was to escape Red Bay. Her feet had been bare, her body bruised, her mind still reeling from the series of impossible events that had slammed into her with the force of an auto. Looking back, everything then was so simple. Save her family. Get out.

Now she was the fulcrum of a war bigger than she could have possibly imagined.

A burst of light from above caused Ronja to freeze. Relief flooded her. A month ago she could not have imagined being enthusiastic about meeting the Kev Fairla. They were at best an unknown and at worst their enemy. Now she was desperate to be in their presence, especially if it meant getting off the flimsy ladder. She sped up, keeping her eyes fixed on the blossoming pocket of light.

By the time she reached the top, Ronja was panting with exertion. Digging her callused fingers into the rock face, she heaved herself up with a grunt. She crawled forward until she was certain she would not fall again, then got to her feet. She scanned her new surroundings apprehensively.

The light that had guided her to the top of the rock face was a large electric bulb sheathed in a metal grate. It dangled from the natural ceiling, its wires burrowing through the stone. An arched entryway that led to a tunnel similar to the one at the beach was carved into the rock, and . . .

"Ah!" Ronja yelped. "Skitzing hell, Larkin." The Tovairin girl skulked near the entrance, draped in shadow. She was as still as the wall she leaned against and twice as unforgiving. Terra and her perpetual grimace popped into Ronja's mind. A dull ache filled her bones. Ronja never thought she would see the day she missed Terra Vahl. "How did you get up here?" she asked, not at all sure the girl would understand. "Did you climb?"

Larkin clicked her tongue. "Of course, I do it all the time," she answered in a thick Tovairin accent.

Ronja raised her eyebrows. "You speak the common language?" Two weeks crammed into that tiny ship like sardines and not once had Larkin given any indication she spoke anything but Tovairin. The Siren blushed, recalling her many awkward attempts at miming.

"Only when speaking with enemies," Larkin replied icily.

"Enemies? We're trying to save you."

"I do not see this." Larkin peeled away from the wall and prowled toward Ronja. "All I see is an ugly, scarred little *bevek* who thinks she is better than us."

"You have no idea what you're talking about," the Siren said in a low voice. Anger rumbled deep in her chest.

"My apologies, princess," the Tovairin girl sneered. She bent mockingly at the waist. "Certainly, I will leave my island to rot at the hands of Vinta while we save your *fiested* city."

Ronja closed the space between them. She had two inches on Larkin, but it felt as if they were the same height. "Call me princess one more time."

"Jonah was supposed to bring back weapons. Instead, he brought you." Larkin poked a finger into her sternum. Her white *reshkas* wound around the digit, ending in a hook at the root of her nail. "You are nothing more than a failed mission."

Ronja felt her nostrils flare. She curled her fingers into fists, willing herself to be calm. "Touch me again, I dare you."

"You think you can fight me, little girl?" Larkin laughed bitterly. "I have killed men three times your size."

"And I have been tortured, starved, imprisoned, nearly raped," Ronja said in a dangerously soft voice. "I spent nineteen years a slave to a man I hated, believing I was lower than dirt. I have killed. I have died. I have held three million minds in the palm of my hand." Larkin flinched as a reckless laugh burst from Ronja's lips. "You think you can intimidate me? Try again, bitch."

In an instant a hand was around her throat, its fingernails digging into her skin. Ronja jerked in her shockingly strong grip.

"Larkin! *Haltan!*" a sharp voice ordered.

Neither girl paid the command any mind. Ronja knocked the hand from her trachea with a scream and spun. Before either of them knew what was happening, Larkin was on the ground.

"Ronja! Enough!"

The familiar voice gave her pause. She looked around. Roark stood near the ledge with his hands raised. His elegant features were wracked with shock. Ronja relaxed her hold on Larkin.

That was a mistake.

In one fell swoop, the Tovairin girl swept her legs out from under her. Ronja cried out as she hit the ground. She scrambled to her feet, blood in her mouth and red in her vision. She spat viciously. Larkin was up, damp hair tangled and fists raised.

Then strong arms were around Ronja, dragging her away from her opponent. "Let me go!" she bellowed. Roark only tightened his grip. His familiar scent tickled her nostrils. The veil of red over her vision began to dissipate.

"Calm down," he hissed in her ear. "Calm down."

Ronja gritted her teeth, then forced out her anger with her breath. She let her knees give, allowing him to bear her weight. Across from them, Jonah and Larkin were in a similar embrace, though neither of them appeared to have relaxed much.

"*Triv*, Larkin, *verta telesk en cesterion*," Jonah ordered her. His voice was just as powerful his arms, but neither seemed to have much effect on Larkin. She shoved him off roughly, hooked her pinky finger at him, then stalked off down the tunnel. When she winked out of view, Roark released Ronja.

"What did you tell her?" she asked, looking to Jonah.

"To wait for me inside."

"What does this mean?" Roark inquired curiously, replicating the gesture Larkin had made with her pinky.

Jonah winced and hitched his pack higher onto his broad back. "Not sure I can translate it into the common language. Not sure I want to."

"Could Ronja and I have a moment, please?" Roark cut in politely.

Ronja shot him a withering glance, but kept her mouth shut.

Jonah nodded, a hint of mirth in his brown eyes. "I'll wait for you around the first corner."

"*Perlo*," Roark thanked him in Tovairin.

"*Pevra*," Jonah responded. Ronja stood with her back to Roark as their guide strode off into the tunnel and disappeared around the bend. The solitary bulb buzzed above them, battering away the darkness.

"Ronja . . . " he began.

"What do you want from me?" she demanded.

"I want you to talk to me."

She spun on her heel to face him, fuming. "I told you we do not have time for this," she snapped.

"Ro." The single syllable was stiff with frustration and empathy. She breathed deeply, the cool air scraping her throat. Roark copied her, the muscles of his shoulders relaxing slightly. "I know you're going through a lot right now, more than I can even begin to understand, but you said yourself that we need the Kev Fairla. We cannot afford to make enemies in their ranks."

"Larkin started it," Ronja muttered, nudging a bit of rock with her boot.

"More than the Kev Fairla, though, we need you. We need the Siren." Those words caused her to raise her chin. Roark reached out to cradle her cheek in his warm hand. She sank into the touch, unprecedented exhaustion rolling over her. "I'll do whatever I can to help you," he said quietly. "But I need you to try to keep it together."

"Okay," Ronja murmured, nodding against his palm. "Okay."

6: GRAVE
Charlotte

Charlotte Romancheck had never been claustrophobic. Living underground did not bother her. Creeping through storm drains did not make her skin crawl. She knew the sky was waiting for her just an elevator ride away. But now that all the exits were choked off, she was starting to feel suffocated.

"Char?" Cosmin regarded her coyly from his narrow cot.

The girl blinked rapidly to disperse her thoughts. "What?"

"You were doing it a-again," he answered, his voice breaking on the last syllable. His stutter had improved over the past weeks, but he still had a long way to go. Part of Charlotte wondered if he would ever fully recover. Neither she nor her new patient were ready to consider that yet, though.

"Doing what?" she snapped. She was in a foul mood and was not keen on being teased.

"Staring at me." Cosmin grinned, the right corner of his mouth lifting higher than the left. "I know how dreamy I am but y-you gotta control yourself."

"Shut up! I was just spacing."

"What were you th-thinking about?"

"You, finishing your exercises." She jerked her chin at the leather stress ball in his left palm. Cosmin curled his fingers around it. Since Iris and the others had disappeared, Charlotte had taken over treating the injuries he sustained at Red Bay. She was nowhere near as qualified as Iris, but she knew enough to keep him on the right path. Considering they were buried half a mile underground and had not heard from Iris and the others in over a month, she expected she was going to be in charge for some time.

At least until they ran out of air.

"This is p-pointless," Cosmin complained, not for the first time. He relaxed his grip, then tightened it again. "You know it is."

Charlotte flopped back into her shabby armchair, ignoring him. Her gaze drifted to the curtains encircling the hospital room. The hum of tense conversations filtered through the heavy fabric. There was no laughter, no singing. It was not the Belly any longer. It was a tomb. "Would you rather just sit around and wait to suffocate?"

"Or to be b-blown up?"

"That would be faster," Charlotte mused.

Cosmin chuckled humorlessly and set the ball aside. "H-have you heard anything?" he asked.

Charlotte did not need to ask what he was talking about. She shook her head, her curls whispering against her shoulders. "Nope," she said. "I asked Kala and Elliot again, they were totally useless. They've got no idea what's going on."

"Does anybody?"

The girl sighed, craning her head back to view the ceiling as if it would provide her with answers. "Doubt it. The stationary guard is everywhere. They shut down talk like that pretty quick. Honestly, I would rather just stay here."

The boy waggled his eyebrows as best he could. Charlotte

scoffed and socked him in the arm. "Oi!" he complained. "Watch it!"

"Please, could you even feel that?"

"Charlotte?"

Charlotte straightened up and looked around. Dr. Harrow had poked her head through the curtains. Her flaxen hair was woven into a messy braid. Exhaustion had collected beneath her eyes. Since the Belly had been sealed, Anthemites had started flocking to the hospital wing. Harrow sent most of them away. "Their symptoms are psychological," she had explained. "Fear does strange things to the body." Still, there *had* been several real cases of the retch, which were keeping Harrow busy enough as it was.

"Yeah?" Charlotte asked.

"Ito would like to speak with you." Harrow's blue eyes flashed to Cosmin, who was watching the exchange curiously. "Both of you."

Charlotte tossed Cosmin a confused glance. He shrugged, equally baffled. She turned back to her superior. "Um, okay."

Harrow nodded briskly and retreated. The drapes swayed lazily. Before they stilled, a tall woman swept them aside and strode into the room. She walked the way a river ran, with unbridled confidence and grace. Something was off about her, though.

"Lieutenant Lin," Cosmin greeted her warmly. "Pleasure to se-e you again." Charlotte rolled her eyes internally. The boy flirted with anything that moved. Ito did not seem bothered, thankfully. Her lips twitched with amusement.

"Cosmin," she replied politely. "Your speech has improved. I am pleased to see your progress."

The boy smiled, his greenish eyes sparking at the praise. "Could use a ne-ew nervous system, but doing all right."

"I apologize for the intrusion, but I need to speak with both of you. Privately."

"You weren't intruding," Charlotte answered, perhaps a bit too quickly. She got to her feet and offered the lieutenant her chair. "Please, sit down."

Ito obliged. Charlotte sat on the edge of the cot with a creak of rusted springs. As soon as she was settled, the lieutenant leaned toward them. Her dark irises were laced with threads of anxiety. "What I am about to tell you is top secret. It does not leave this room. Do you understand?"

The teens exchanged another uncertain glance, then nodded. Ito continued. "Two weeks ago, the commander sealed the Belly."

"Yeah, we noticed," Charlotte replied flatly. She winced at the hostility in her voice. She knew Ito wasn't responsible for their burial, but the lieutenant was the first member of the command she had come into contact with since. She was an easy target.

"I'm sure you've wondered why he made that decision," Ito pressed, unfazed by her brittle tone.

"Uh, yeah," Cosmin said with a humorless laugh. "Once or t-twice." He gestured up at the ceiling with his good hand, his eyes on Ito. "Those scrubbers are o-only going to last so long, I doubt they were built to sustain the c-compound for long in case of a cave in."

"How astute," Ito replied. She sounded genuinely impressed. Charlotte could not resist a small smile. Cosmin always seemed to impress the adults in his presence. "The situation topside was dire, but . . . " the lieutenant trailed off, working her jaw thoughtfully. "I fear we have been forced into even worse circumstances."

Charlotte and Cosmin were silent, waiting for her to carry on. Ito heaved a sigh and pinched the bridge of her nose. "What I am about to tell you is incredibly dangerous information. If the situation were any less grave I'd withhold it, but I am out of options."

"We can handle it," Charlotte said over her thundering heartbeat. "You can trust us."

"We understand more th-an you think," Cosmin added.

Ito smiled. "That is exactly why I have come to you. You are smart, not just for your age. I have been watching you both for some time now. You have the makings of great assets for the Anthem."

Charlotte narrowed her eyes to slits. Something was wrong. Ito was not one to dish out compliments without an ulterior motive. She was not cold exactly. She was calculating.

The lieutenant took a deep breath, glancing around the little room as if someone was lurking in the exposed corners.

"The curtains block more than you think, and the patients are all sleeping," Charlotte assured her. "Keep your voice low and no one will hear."

Ito nodded. "Commander Wilcox is no longer in his right mind. He has buried us in the Belly with no way out. He has informed me that he intends to let us die here rather than face what is happening aboveground."

Silence greeted the bombshell. Charlotte and Cosmin stared at the woman blankly, unblinkingly. Ito observed them with a grim expression, anxiety creeping through her stoic mask. "W-what happened out there?" Cosmin finally asked.

"The worst," Ito answered.

A memory washed over Charlotte. Ronja dragging her to the back of the bathhouse, the heavy words she had trusted her with. Understanding clicked into place in her head, causing her stomach to hit the floor. "The Music can reach us," she realized aloud. Cosmin stiffened beside her.

"I suppose I cannot be surprised that you know." Ito sighed.

She inched closer to them. "Then you know it gets worse."

"The Siren," Cosmin murmured. "Ronja."

The night Ronja and the others disappeared, music like they had never heard had exploded in the Belly. Though they had never heard her sing before, the Anthemites knew who the voice belonged to. The girl who survived The Quiet Song. The girl who escaped Red Bay. The girl who could battle The Music with her voice. Weeks later, when enraptured silence poured over the city for the first time, they knew it was her. That somehow, she had found a way into the Singers.

Slowly, steadily, Revinia began to change. It was subtle at first. Almost undetectable. Quiet acts of rebellion that would have tortured anyone in the full grasp of The Music. Graffiti appeared on walls in the outer ring. *May the Siren give us strength.* Commander Wilcox ordered agents to hunt down Ronja and the others and bring them in. Some of his most trusted soldiers had gone out into the city and returned empty-handed. *Convenient,* Charlotte remembered thinking.

Then the Belly was sealed.

"What happened out there?" Charlotte heard herself ask. She was surprised to find her voice did not shake.

"We don't know, exactly," Ito admitted. Her brown eyes slipped from their faces to the floor. "We know Ronja was able to spark some sort of rebellion. Some of our topside agents watched it happen—they said it was unlike anything they had ever seen."

"And then?" Cosmin cut in anxiously.

Ito looked up, her expression grim. "The New Music was released into the Singers."

Charlotte looked over at Cosmin, but his head was in his hands, his pale fingers twined in his dark curls. "Is it true?" he asked, his voice muffled. "What Ro said about The N-New Music?"

"Yes," Ito answered. "It can reach us without Singers, and it can obliterate emotion. Any freedom Ronja gave them is gone; the revolution is over."

The world tilted. Charlotte clutched at the white sheets beneath her as if she were about to slide to the floor. Distantly, she heard Cosmin ask about his cousin. "Ronja," he said. "What happened to her?"

"I admit I know very little," Ito said, directing her words at the boy. "But Roark did manage to get a call through to me. He and Ronja likely escaped, but Iris, Evie, and Terra are in the hands of The Conductor."

"Where are they now?" Cosmin asked.

"I wish I knew. They said they were going to get help, but . . ." The lieutenant shook her head, her artificially orange hair rustling. "I have no idea where."

"Why are you telling us this?" Charlotte spoke up. "What can we do?"

Ito leveled her gaze at her. "The revolution may be over, but there are still nearly a thousand people trapped down here, and Wilcox is going to let them die." She took a breath and brought her voice so low Charlotte could scarcely hear it. "I am going to stage a coup. I need the two of you to be my eyes and ears. I need you to listen to what the people are saying. Who believes Wilcox has lost it, who still supports him."

"Why us?" Charlotte questioned doubtfully. "Why not Kala or Elliot or . . . anyone?"

Ito smiled, a hint of nostalgia creeping into her eyes. "Terra once told me that no one expects a child to be capable of deceit."

Cosmin shifted in his seat. Charlotte glanced over at him. His eyes were red and raw. He was holding back tears, doubtlessly thinking of Ronja. Despite this, his mouth was pinched into a determined line. He gave a subtle nod. The girl turned back to her new commander and smiled.

7: THE TEMPLE OF ENTALIA

The tunnels that wove through the extinct volcano were very different than those below Revinia. They were narrow and dry with rough natural walls. Ronja could not imagine how long they must have taken to dig. Decades, maybe even centuries. They were lit with electric bulbs connected by drooping wires.

They were forced to walk single file through the catacombs. Jonah led the way confidently. Ronja trailed behind him, and Roark brought up the rear. He had been quiet since their exchange at the cliff.

"How much further?" she asked after a time.

"Not much," Jonah promised, peeking back over his shoulder. "We'll have to talk to my commander first. Then you can clean up and get some rest."

"You actually sound concerned."

Though Ronja could not see his face, she knew Jonah was rolling his eyes at the low ceiling. "I saved you from a madman, princess. I think it's pretty clear I am vested in your well-being."

The Siren opened her mouth to scold him for calling her *princess* again, but her words dried up on her tongue. She scuffed to a halt. Roark swore under his breath when he nearly slammed into her. She squinted at the walls of the catacomb. While she and Jonah bantered, they had become smooth as porcelain. Etched into the stone were threads of curling Tovairin script, not unlike the *reshkas* Jonah and Larkin bore. "What are these?" Ronja asked, tracing one of the lines with the pad of her finger.

Jonah stopped and turned to face them. "Our history," he answered. "The ancients wrote it."

Roark pushed a low whistle through his teeth. "Can you read it? Is it code?" he asked, intrigue sparking in his tone. Ronja glanced at the Anthemite sidelong, affection warming her insides. It was moments like this, when his boyish curiosity peeked through, that she remembered why she had fallen for him in the first place.

"Some," Jonah answered with a tilt of his head. "They are pretty . . . *fiest* . . . what's the word?"

"Archaic?" Ronja offered.

Jonah nodded. "Yeah." He peered over his shoulder, as if someone was calling him. "We should keep moving," he said. "We're almost to the temple."

"What do you mean, temple?" Roark asked. "I thought this was the headquarters of the Kev Fairla."

Jonah smiled. For once it was not sarcastic or vain. There was something else behind his eyes, something soft and still. It suited him more than Ronja cared to admit. "You'll see." He spun on his booted heel and marched on. The Anthemites shared a look, then followed.

For a few minutes, there was nothing but the beat of their soles against the hard ground, the hum of the electric lights above. Then, the ripple of distant conversations began to filter through the air. Undeniably human, distinctly foreign. Beyond Jonah, a column of bluish light appeared. "Hurry up, Anthemites," he called. He was swallowed by the glow.

Ronja glanced back at Roark, apprehension raising goosebumps on her skin. He was fingering the knife strapped to his belt. The Siren passed into the cold light. "Skitz me," she breathed.

The vaulted ceiling was so high she could barely see its peak. Carved stone pillars were scattered throughout the room, a petrified forest. Gray light tumbled through dozens of natural skylights, cutting through the air that was somehow heavier than that of the catacombs. Every inch of the room was black stone, not a trace of color anywhere. It was not bleak, though. It was solemn.

Hundreds of Kev Fairlans roamed the space. Some talked in small groups, but the majority were busy sparring. Most shared the same basic features as Jonah and Larkin. Smooth black hair, tanned skin, and brown eyes. A handful of people clearly not native to the island were as pale as Ronja. Others were as dark as Henry. All were tattooed with unique white *reshkas* and armed with swords and knives. There was not a gun in sight. Jonah had not been exaggerating their ammunition drought.

Two men practicing with dull blades near one of the towering pillars caught her eye. They moved the way Roark and Evie did. Faster, even. Roark knit his fingers with hers and squeezed anxiously.

"Welcome to the Temple of Entalia," Jonah said, putting his hands on his hips as he surveyed the space.

"Entalia?" Ronja asked, leaning around Roark to look at him. He radiated pride and peace. That was what it was like to be home, she supposed. To be at ease.

"The goddess of rebirth, if you believe in that sort of thing." He gestured out across the room at a massive statue directly opposite them. Ronja squinted. She could not make out its features at this distance. "We moved in a decade back. Best move we ever made. The keepers of the temple weren't happy, but they got over it when we saved their asses."

Ronja nodded mutely, feeling the gaps in her cultural understanding. Faith was not a component of Revinian society, nor was it common among Anthemites. The people of the walled city worshipped The Conductor. The revolutionaries had lost touch with their religious roots. Personally, she had never been comfortable with the idea of a supernatural being watching her every move, but here in the temple she could understand the pull of faith.

"Jonah. *Hist fen?*"

Ronja fell back into her body. Striding toward them was a short man with something of a paunch. He appeared to be in his early forties, with wire-rimmed glasses on the bridge of his round nose. While his stature was not intimidating, Ronja found herself fidgeting beneath his penetrating gaze.

"Cal," Jonah greeted him with a brief nod. He gestured at their guests. "Ronja *et* Roark. *Carlan den Anthem ev Revinia. Coste yev Easton.*"

Cal glanced back and forth between the Revinians calculatingly. They stared back. Finally, he heaved a sigh and wheeled around, cutting back through the crowds. Jonah started after him without a word. The Anthemites followed, eager not to be left behind.

Nineteen years as a mutt had prepared Ronja for waves of unwanted attention. She was accustomed to the whispers, to the stares loaded with distrust. More unnerving was the fact that she could not understand what was being said about her. Members of the Kev Fairla stopped to gape unabashedly as she and Roark trekked across the hall. She picked out a few words here and there that she had learned on the voyage.

Bevek. Foreigner. *Vestin.* Handsome.

Ronja traced the second word to a group of pretty young women eyeing Roark appreciatively. Petty jealousy surged in her gut. She let go of his hand, taking him by the elbow instead. He peered down at her, amused, but she scarcely noticed. The statue of Entalia had expanded in her view.

She stood twenty feet tall, carved from the heart of the volcano. Every inch of her was wrought with perfection. Ronja half expected her to blink, for her chest to expand with breath. She was garbed in flowing robes that cascaded to her naked feet. Her shoulders were bare, her muscular arms extended to embrace the cavern. She was clearly female, though her head was shaved. Her scalp was decorated with swirling *reshkas* a shade lighter than the rest of her obsidian body.

Entalia.

"Hurry up!"

The Siren started. Roark was at her side, his elbow still linked with hers. They lagged behind Jonah and Cal. Dozens of onlookers were watching them with a blend of curiosity and suspicion. They moved past the statue. Ronja felt the hair on the back of her neck stand on end. They passed through another entryway into a dim corridor lined with plain wooden doors.

"You okay?"

Ronja nearly jumped out of her skin. Roark watched her intently, a crease between his brows. "Fine," she assured him too quickly. He smiled, but it did not reach his eyes. Ahead of them, Cal and Jonah rounded a corner. They followed obediently, still arm in arm. Ronja jerked to a halt.

The library was nearly as massive as the entry hall. Dozens of towering stone shelves lined with countless books and scrolls ran across the room. Long polished tables stood between the canyons, littered with documents and electric lamps with evergreen shades. While it appeared as if the library had been used recently, there was not a soul in sight.

Roark hurried forward, tugging Ronja along against her will. She wanted to bathe in the scent of musty pages and cool stone. *No time*, a nagging voice at the back of her mind reprimanded her.

They crossed the library, moving into another hallway similar to the first. The further they got from the collection of books, the heavier Ronja felt. She tried to remember the last time she had read for pleasure. Maybe in the warehouse, during one of the gaps between broadcasts. Velveteen memories brushed the surface of her mind. *Roark playing with her curls as she pored over the collection of poetry Iris had lent her. The taste of the words on her tongue, of his mouth on hers.*

"Here," Jonah said. They had arrived before one of the many wooden doors with a curved iron handle. He knocked three times with a tattooed knuckle, then stepped aside. There was a loaded pause, then it opened.

Ronja screamed.

8: THE WOLF

Ronja slammed into the far wall, her eyes flown wide and her hand clapped over her mouth. Before her shout faded, Roark threw himself in front of her, pinning her to the rock.

"Pascal, *sal*," a gruff voice ordered.

Swallowing her fear, Ronja peeked out from behind her guard. A tall man in his early thirties filled the frame, his black hair cropped short, his eyes dark and sure. He was handsome, if a bit severe. He was not the reason Ronja had screamed. It was the hulking beast that stood beside him. Bristling fur, piercing yellow eyes, powerful jaws and curved fangs.

A wolf.

"*Sal!*" the man commanded, snapping his fingers at the animal. It sat begrudgingly, its brooding eyes fixed to Ronja. They seemed to drip with hunger.

Roark relaxed, dropping his arms and moving to stand beside her. She looked up at him through the haze of her terror. "What the hell is wrong?" he asked out of the corner of his mouth. She shook her head violently, choked by her phobia.

"He won't harm you."

Ronja flicked her eyes to the owner of the wolf, scrambling

to wrest her expression into something resembling poise.

He observed her neutrally. "Pascal only listens to me." The wolf pricked his ears at the sound of his name. His owner scratched the top of his head affectionately, not taking his eyes off the Anthemites.

"And you are?" Ronja managed to ask. She winced internally. Her voice trembled almost as much as her hands.

The owner of the wolf tapped a fist to his brow, then his heart, the customary Tovairin greeting. He appeared utterly indifferent to her panic. "Commander Easton," he said, introducing himself. He locked eyes with Ronja, clearly expecting her to respond in kind. When she did not, he cut his gaze to Roark.

"Roark Westervelt," he offered quickly. He returned the gesture, his knuckles thumping against the hollow of his chest. Easton nodded, returning his attention to the Siren. She struggled not to squirm or to let her eyes wander to the wolf salivating at her feet.

"Ronja," she answered.

The commander raised a thick brow. "Ronja what?"

She shook her head, her curls shivering against her cheekbones. "Just Ronja."

"Easton," Jonah spoke up. The commander rounded on the younger man. His tense mouth split into a grin. He roped Jonah into a tight embrace, slapping him on the back. The captain responded enthusiastically. They exchanged a few easy words in their native tongue, then returned to the common language. "We need to debrief," Jonah said, sobering. He glanced at Ronja, who had managed to wrestle her terror into submission. "Things are . . . complicated."

"They usually are," Easton replied grimly. He snapped at Pascal again. The wolf turned tail and retreated into the room. Ronja shuddered at the sound of his claws clicking across the stone. "Come in," the commander said, stepping aside and beckoning them with a tattooed hand.

"*Perlo*," Roark said peaceably. He started forward, leaving Ronja no choice but to join him. Jonah and Easton followed. It was only when the commander shut the door with a soft clap that she realized Cal had disappeared without a trace. Swallowing the knot in her throat, she scanned the room.

The cramped study was dominated by a roaring fireplace. The mantle was engraved with looping script and held a dozen or so trinkets. Near the hearth was a large desk and matching chair. The surface was littered with open books, maps, sheathed blades, and a polished automatic with a gilded handle. Two walls were overflowing with books. A cluster of four armchairs embroidered with the letter *A* crouched in the middle of the room. Pascal had tucked himself into a ball near the hearth.

"Sit," Easton said, more of an order than an invitation. He took his own seat in the armchair nearest the fire. Jonah shrugged off his pack, then plunked down at his right. He settled back comfortably, crossing his muscular arms and resting his head on the dark red upholstery. Roark let his own backpack fall to the ground, then sat down opposite them. The Siren was the last to take a seat. She perched on the edge of her armchair, ready to bolt.

The fire crackled merrily. Pascal twitched in his sleep. The Anthemites and the Kev Fairlans watched one another calculatingly.

Finally, Jonah broke the hush. "Easton," he said. The commander tore his eyes from Roark and Ronja, focusing on his subordinate. "The mission to Revinia failed."

Ronja braced herself, waiting for Easton to react. Wilcox was the only other commander she had come into contact with, and he was a loose cannon. Jonah appeared to be holding his breath, or maybe it was just the firelight turning his features rouge.

Eventually, Easton let out a weary sigh. He crossed one leg over the other and leaned back in his seat, his deep brown eyes on the ceiling. "It was always a long shot," he said, his voice heavy with the sort of exhaustion sleep could not fix.

"I wrote up a full report on the journey back," Jonah told him. "I have it here." He started to reach for his bag, but Easton waved him off.

"I'll read it later." He leveled his searing gaze at Roark and Ronja. The Siren lifted her chin, mustering as much dignity as she could. "Tell me, Jonah, who are these people?"

Silence swallowed the room again. The wolf was vividly present by the fireside. Ronja wondered if Easton kept him as a pet, or to intimidate guests. *Probably both.*

"They're—" Jonah started, then trailed off. He looked to Ronja, clearly hoping she would step in. She shook her head. She was tired of telling stories.

"We're members of the Revinian resistance, sir," Roark said. "We call ourselves the Anthem."

"I know the Anthem," Easton replied with a dismissive wave. "How did you meet Jonah?"

"He turned us over to a skitzing psychopath and got our friend killed."

Ronja only realized she had spoken aloud when all eyes turned to her. Jonah looked as if he had just swallowed a walnut-sized bug. Roark sighed, dragging an exhausted hand down his face. The commander just looked confused. Then, understanding passed over his features. "Ah," he said quietly, shifting his gaze to Jonah. "They were Bullon's target."

The girl narrowed her eyes at Easton. "You didn't know?"

"No one knew," Jonah cut in defensively. "Bullon contacted the Kev Fairla months before I met you, asking for an agent to spearhead a mission in Revinia in exchange for half his arsenal.

We knew it was a gamble. The fewer people who knew the details, the better."

"Did the offer of *half* an arsenal not seem a bit suspicious to you?" Roark asked in a bone-dry voice.

Jonah shrugged. "Desperate times." He cut his eyes to Easton. "Maxwell told me he was looking for a weapon that would make bullets irrelevant and that it was in the hands of a terrorist organization." He jerked his head at the Anthemites. "All I had to do was find it."

Ronja looked away, glowering at the fire. The truth was, she did not blame him for what had happened to Samson and the others, not directly, at least. If she had been in his position, she would have made the same decision. Turning in a group of strangers to save her family? It would stain her soul, but she would do it.

"This weapon, the one that would make bullets irrelevant," Easton said, calling her back to the conversation. "What is it, exactly?"

"Not what," Roark answered. Ronja passed him a warning look, which he chose to ignore. His skin was almost golden in firelight, his eyes like embers. "Who."

9: RUTHLESS
Terra

Terra sat with her back to the glass, her eyes sealed against the harsh lights. Her head throbbed dully. The pain had been with her since she first awoke in her cell weeks ago. She was unsure if it was a product of her electrocution at the clock tower or pure exhaustion.

"Terra," Mouse spoke up timidly.

"What?"

"I think Evie is . . . "

Terra was on her feet before he finished. Mouse knelt next to Evie on the opposite end of the translucent cell. She had not stirred since the Offs who took Iris stung her. Relief washed over Terra as the techi shifted against the concrete. Mouse smoothed a lock of hair out of her face in an unexpected show of tenderness.

That was a mistake.

Evie snatched his wrist like a viper. Mouse yelped, scrambling backward and fighting to free his arm.

"Good to see your reflexes are still intact," Terra said.

Evie relaxed at the sound of her voice. Her clawed grip loosened. Mouse yanked his hand back, cradling it to his chest and muttering irritably.

Ignoring him, Terra crossed the cell and crouched next to the techi. Her hooded eyes were wide and alert, but she made no move to get up.

"How do you feel?" Terra asked. It was a stupid question, but she was not really looking for an answer.

"Where is she?" Evie croaked. Terra did not reply. The techi swallowed, her throat glistening with cold sweat. Her pupils shone like black marble as tears welled in her eyes. Her lower lip quivered, straining against dread. "I can't do this without her."

"They need us alive, " Terra reminded her darkly.

"They'll put a Singer on her or . . . or expose her to The Air Song . . . "

"Listen." Terra grabbed Evie by her broad shoulders, pulling her into an upright position. Her entire body shook as fat tears rolled down her cheeks. "If they were going to put us under The New Music, they would have done it already."

Evie brought her knees to her chest and hunched forward, shuddering violently. Terra looked away. She could not afford to feel sorry for her. If they were going to make it out of this hellhole, she needed to be cold. Sharp. Ruthless.

"Pull yourself together," Terra snapped. Rather than waiting for the techi to reply, she forced her to sit up straight again. Mouse watched the scene unfold in forlorn silence, his chin on his knees and his skinny arms around his legs. "Iris is going to be fine," Terra insisted. "She's stronger than we give her credit for."

"But The New Music—"

"What did I just say? If they were going to put us under, they would have done it by now." Terra had her theories about why they were holding back, but they were just that—theories. In the end, it did not matter. As long as their minds were free, they had a chance. "They can hurt her, but they can't take her mind."

That seemed to send Evie over the edge. She began to cry recklessly, snot dripping from her nose, her breaths coming in jagged gasps.

"Evie—"

"Leave me alone, Terra," the techi begged, looking up at her. The whites of her eyes were shot with red, the skin around them puffy and raw. "We're finished, do you get that? The Belly's been found, Samson is dead, Henry is *worse* than dead, Ronja is a weapon, Trip is gone, and Iris is—"

Terra slapped her across the face. Hard. Mouse let out an indignant squawk, leaping to his feet. Both girls ignored him. Evie raised her fingers to her face slowly. The blow seemed to have knocked the panic from her. "Do *not* leave me alone here, Wick," Terra hissed. "You need Iris? Well, I need you. I need your brain. I need your skills. I need you to get *mad*. You get me?"

For a long moment, Evie left her in suspension. Mouse watched with his mouth agape. Terra waited on the edge of a razor.

Then the techi nodded. "Okay. What do we do?" she asked, using the heels of her hands to wipe away the remnants of her breakdown.

Terra leaned in, her stiff hair slipping over her shoulder. Mouse scrambled forward to put his head in the huddle. "Do you remember the Parker Street operation? What Trip did when everything went to hell?" Terra asked, her voice scarcely more than a whisper.

Evie thought for a moment, then recognition sparked in her gaze. *There*, Terra thought. She had her. The techi straightened up, raking her short hair out of her face.

"Do you think—" Evie breathed.

"I think it could work," Terra cut her off. "Only way we're going to know is if we try." She peered out at the unsettling black room beyond the glass. It seemed to watch her in return. Her instincts twitched. She did not want to find out what the purpose of the room was, but got the feeling they would know soon if they did not act fast. "We have no choice."

10: RELATIVITY

Roark did most of the talking. He must have sensed the exhaustion creeping up on Ronja. She observed Easton while he listened. His expression betrayed nothing, not a shred of doubt or trust.

It took less than an hour to relay their story. When it was finished, Ronja was left with a pit in her stomach. It felt hollow, anticlimactic even. Roark had started with a brief history of Revinia, walking Easton through the creation and imposition of The Music. Then he launched into an overview of the Anthem— their cause, their failures and successes, and their current status. He had switched gears after that, telling the commander of the night he and Ronja met.

"She almost ran me over with a subtrain," Roark admitted with a chuckle. She gave him a weak smile. Less than a year had passed since she had met Roark on the tracks, but it felt like a lifetime ago. Ronja had never been innocent, not since she was old enough to understand that as a mutt she was lower than dirt. She'd thought she had it tough when she was an outcast struggling to provide for her family.

Innocence was relative, she supposed.

Roark took Easton through Red Bay, their discovery of The New Music and her voice. Jonah listened intently as well, intermittently cracking his knuckles with his thumb. The Anthemite explained the creation of the radio station, the steady revolution that built only to collapse in a single night. "Ronja freed them, just for a moment," he finished in quiet voice. She shifted uncomfortably, unsure where to look. She settled on watching the fire shiver in its ashes. "We would have taken the city back were it not for Maxwell."

"And Jonah," Ronja muttered under her breath. Out of the corner of her eye, she saw him blanch. *Good.* She hoped he was on pins and needles.

"What exactly did this Maxwell do to . . . " Easton glanced at the Siren. "Stop her?"

"He ambushed us and put The New Music into effect," Roark repeated patiently.

Easton was silent for a while, digesting the massive amount of information he had just received. Jonah rolled a kink from his neck. Ronja picked at a loose thread on her knee.

"Do you believe she could have freed them again, if given the chance?" the commander finally asked.

Roark straightened his spine. "Yes," he said confidently. "She was able to free me when I was exposed to it. I believe she can do it again."

The commander reclined in his chair, itching the stubble that crept across his square jaw. "And you want our help to do this?"

"We just need enough men and women to take out the six mainframes and get me to the radio station," Ronja said, breaking her silence. "The weapons, the ones Maxwell promised you. When we're finished, you can have them." She felt Roark look at her out of the corner of his eye, but kept her focus on Easton.

"And who are you to offer them to me, girl?" he asked with a condescending smirk.

Ronja tensed. She locked eyes with Jonah across the way, silently begging him not to say anything. Mercifully, he kept his mouth shut.

"Say I believe you," Easton said when she failed to respond. "Why would I help you? I have my own war to fight, my own people to protect."

"Because Maxwell is coming for Tovaire, too," Roark jumped in. "He has an army of three million civilians utterly loyal to him under The New Music. He cut a deal with Vinta; they're sending a fleet of transport ships. They should be arriving at the port any day now, if they're not already there. If we do not take out The New Music, we're all skitzed."

Easton grit his teeth, his nostrils flaring. He cut his eyes to Jonah, who nodded in confirmation. The commander returned his attention to Ronja and Roark. Bitterness had seared away the last of his apathy. His lips twisted into a humorless smile. "Yes," he said with a mirthless chuckle. "That sounds like Vinta." They waited in limbo for him to say more, but he appeared to be lost in thought. Pascal twitched and snarled in his sleep. "You understand how this sounds," he finally said.

Roark started to speak, but Ronja beat him to it. "Yeah, I still have trouble believing it myself."

Easton's mouth hooked into a wry smile.

"It's true, sir," Jonah spoke up. "I was there, I saw it."

You caused half of it, she thought bitterly, but she held her tongue.

Easton heaved a sigh, and he sagged forward a fraction of an inch. He drummed his fingers on the cushioned arm of the chair. A log snapped on the fire, sending up a plume of sparks. "I need time to think," he said.

"Did you hear what Roark said?" Ronja blurted. "Maxwell has an army of three million mindless soldiers. Innocent people, *children*. Those ships will arrive any day, and if they leave port we'll miss our chance."

"If what you say is true, then we are already out of time," Easton said. "It would take a week to put together a team. The ships would leave port long before we were ready."

Ronja bit her lip. *Maybe he's right*, she thought. She knew as well as he did that the ships could have left days ago. They could be on their way to Tovaire. But something deep in her gut told her otherwise, something she had not given voice to until now. "Maxwell won't leave without me."

Roark turned to look at her, his shock searing the side of her face. She kept her eyes on Easton stubbornly.

"So sure of your importance, are you?" he asked with a sneer.

Ronja flushed. "You weren't there," she answered in a low voice. "You have no idea what he's like. He . . . " She searched for the right words amidst the bleak memories bubbling up in her psyche. "He thinks this is a game, and I am his favorite piece."

It was not arrogance or false hope. If there were no chance that the fleet remained in Revinia, she would have accepted it and switched her focus to revenge. But no. Maxwell would not begin his conquest without her. That did not mean they had time to waste. The Anthem was compromised. Their friends were wasting away in prison.

Easton, however, was not convinced. He squinted at her as if he were staring into a bright light. Before Ronja could place his expression, Jonah took advantage of the hush. "Sir," he said quietly. "There is one more thing."

The commander tore his gaze from the Siren. Jonah sucked in a steadying breath. Ronja felt as though he had stolen it from her lungs.

Please, no.

"I believe she is the daughter of Darius Alezandri."

11: RESPITE

Ronja had never been more grateful for a shower in her entire life. Partially because she was filthy from two weeks aboard a ship with limited fresh water, partially because she was desperate to get away from Jonah and Easton.

I believe she is the daughter of Darius Alezandri. She would have rather faced a unit of Offs with a butter knife than hear those words. Even worse was the spark of recognition that had flared in the eyes of the commander as he scrutinized her. What had he seen? What did he know? She was aching for answers, yet she dreaded nothing more.

Easton had asked them to leave so he could speak with Jonah in private. They gathered their things in silence while he pulled a cord that hung from the ceiling three times. A few painfully long moments later, a young woman with a round face and downcast eyes had appeared in the doorway to take them to their quarters.

"I'll send for you when I have come to a decision," Easton said as he ushered them to the exit. "Do not come looking for me." The Anthemites stepped into the hall with the Tovairin girl, then wheeled around to face him.

"Thank you, sir," Roark said formally, tapping his brow and

heart. The commander responded in kind. Ronja peeked around them and locked eyes with Jonah. Something passed between them. Acknowledgement that their strange friendship—if their volatile relationship could be called that—was about to change drastically. Then the commander had shut the door with a clap, leaving them alone with the Tovairin girl.

"He . . . " Roark started to say, but the girl just motioned for them to follow her and hurried off down the corridor. The Anthemites shared a perplexed look, then went after her.

They maintained their silence as they wound deeper into the temple. The hallways were less packed than the atrium, but they were far from empty. Half the pedestrians were dressed in thick, colorful clothing. They travelled in packs of two or three, chatting and laughing casually. The others were dressed for battle. Black leather armor, stained overcoats, blood and muck smeared across their skin. Exhaustion clung to their faces and weighed down their shoulders. The divergence between the two groups was striking. "I wonder where the front is," Roark had whispered as they passed a woman supporting a stocky male soldier. "The beach seemed so peaceful."

"Yeah, it did," Ronja replied distantly. All she could think looking at the shabby soldiers was that they were in no state to face Maxwell and the Revinians.

Eventually, the mute girl had led them to a door deep in the bowels of the compound. She chose a brass key from a ring at her hip while they waited, then sprang the lock. Without so much as a nod, she brushed past them and scampered back the way they came. "You'd think they'd be monitoring us more carefully," Ronja muttered, watching as the young woman disappeared down the hall.

The room was simple and serviceable. Most of the space was taken up by a double bed draped in thick quilts. Near the foot of the bed was a tray laden with food and drink—some familiar, some not. Several pieces of bread smothered in a delightfully tangy spread and a glass of water later, Ronja made for the door on the left hand side of the room. She nearly cried with relief when she discovered it was a bathroom complete with a tiled shower.

Now she stood beneath the scalding stream, wondering vaguely how the Kev Fairla managed to get such excellent water pressure in an ancient temple. *Who cares*, she thought. She craned her neck back, opening her mouth to taste the fresh water. With each second that passed, she felt the tension leak from her muscles, spiraling down the drain. Her fingers drifted up to her scalp, massaging her heavy curls.

"Ro?"

Ronja started, nearly slipping on the wet tiles. She caught herself, mouthed a swear, then stuck her dripping head out from behind the curtain. Roark stood in the door, fully clothed. "You're letting out the heat," she complained.

He made a noise reminiscent of a laugh, then stepped across the threshold and shut the door. He hovered near the sink, the steam curling around his body. She watched him, her drenched hair dripping onto the floor. She knew his presence was a question, not a demand. She found herself oscillating on the edge of it.

"Sorry," Roark said abruptly, massaging the back of his neck. "I should have . . . sorry." He put his hand on the doorknob. "Skitz. Sorry, I'll just . . . "

"You better not open that door again," Ronja warned him.

Roark let his fingers fall from the knob. "Yes, ma'am," he said coyly.

She rolled her eyes and ducked back into the shower. She could practically hear Roark grinning through the curtain. *No time,* a tiny voice reminded her over the drone of the water. Her heart was high in her throat. It had been leaden for so long, as if she were still anchored to the floor of that mirrored prison. She had forgotten what it felt like for her pulse to race from anything but fear.

The cloth curtain shifted as Roark approached. "Can I come in?" he asked.

Ronja hesitated. Focus. She needed to focus. But Easton had said he needed time to consider their proposition. There was little they could do in the meantime. Before she could stop herself, she peeled back the curtain.

Her breath caught in her ribs. The shards of her focus slipped down the drain. Roark had added his clothes to the pile she had made in the corner. The last time she had seen him like this was at the warehouse in Revinia. It seemed like years had passed since then. There had been so much hope. Now the future was bleak, a shade of what they once believed possible. As far as Ronja was concerned, she did not have a future beyond shutting down The New Music and killing Maxwell.

That did not make her love him any less.

Roark stepped into the shower slowly, deliberately. Ronja moved back to accommodate him, her eyes never straying from his. He had changed so much since the night they met. His eyes were the eyes of someone twice his age. The mischievous spark that once lived in them was doused. His body was littered with white scars. They were nearly luminous against his golden brown skin. He had just as many as she did, maybe more.

He lifted his hand to her face, his thumb tracing the curve of her jaw. Ronja stood still, shivering despite the heat pouring over her. It had been weeks since he had touched her this way. She had not been well enough, mentally or physically, to even think about it on the journey over. From her frailty, cold focus had claimed

Ronja, leaving little room for anything else.

But perhaps she could let herself thaw. Just for the night.

Ronja raised up on her tiptoes and kissed him. His hands drifted to her hips, pulling her toward him with gentle insistence. He parted her lips with his tongue. Their kisses grew deeper, more frantic. Ronja dragged her fingers through his hair, raked her nails down his back.

He lifted her effortlessly. She slung her arms around his neck, wrapped her legs around his torso. A low growl ripped from his chest. Roark pushed her up against the slick wall. His fingernails dug into her thighs. Her toes curled as he began to kiss down her arched neck.

"Ah!" Ronja yelped, swatting him on the arm. His teeth had nicked her collarbone.

"Sorry," he murmured in a voice that indicated he was not sorry at all. The girl rolled her eyes and kissed him hungrily, moving her hips against his. Roark took the hint. There was very little talking after that.

12: THE AMP
Evie

"Evie, wake up."

The techi opened her eyes. Terra and Mouse stood over her. Their gazes were trained on the room beyond their glass prison. Her stomach twisted. She sprang to her feet, ignoring the dizziness that ensued. Her breath snagged in her lungs. Her teeth gnashed together. "Henry," she snarled.

He stood about six feet from the glass, his hands clasped behind his back. He observed them with lusterless eyes, his head tilted slightly to the side. He wore a wireless headset complete with a curved microphone and thick pads. "Hello, Evelyn," he greeted her peaceably, his voice crackling through the intercom.

"Where is Iris?" the techi demanded.

"She will be here shortly."

"What have you done to her?"

Henry smiled, though it was closer to a smirk. Evie felt her blood run cold. "Nothing, yet. I am here to ask you a few questions."

Evie looked at Mouse and Terra. The blonde had folded her muscular arms over her chest, staring daggers at Henry. Mouse was shifting from foot to foot, as if he were about to break into a sprint. The techi turned back to their interrogator. "What do you want?"

"We have the Belly surrounded," he began. "The Conductor would prefer your comrades be taken alive."

"How generous," Terra seethed.

"Explosives are out of the question," Henry continued. "We know there is a back door somewhere, some sort of emergency exit." He made eye contact with each of them in turn. Evie swallowed dryly when his empty gaze landed on her. "One of you is going to tell us where it is."

Evie licked her lips, her thoughts whirring like gears. If the elevator was a viable option, they would have used it by now. There were six emergency exits scattered throughout the Belly, each sealed by mountainous walls of rubble. The only way they could be brought down was with powerful explosives buried deep within the stone. Why had they not blown them yet?

Unless . . .

Unless they used the explosives to blow the elevator and cave in the sewers to protect themselves from The New Music.

"The exit, Wick," Henry promoted. "Where is it?"

"You know where it is," Evie snapped, copying Terra and crossing her arms. Beyond the translucent wall, she saw Henry stiffen. She squinted out at him in the loaded silence. Something itched her about his last words. Then it hit her like a ton of bricks. "Unless you don't remember," she said slowly. "Unless The New Music skitzed up your brain."

"You will tell us—" he started.

"The New Music scrambled your memory." Evie stalked toward the glass. "How much do you remember? Do you remember us? Your family? Charlotte? Ronja?" Strange lightness settled over her, the slightest relief from an impossible burden.

Somehow, it was easier to stomach Henry working for the enemy knowing he did not really remember them.

"You will tell us where the exit is," he snapped, his voice rebounding off the curved walls of the black room.

"We're not telling you shit," Evie growled, the sheen of relief dissolving.

The boy smiled, a wickedness not native to him uncoiling in his eyes. "We'll see." He turned on his heel and strode back to the door, rapping it twice with a knuckle. It opened at once and he stepped aside. Two Offs stood in the frame, one male, one female. Between them was a wilted figure with flaming red hair.

"Iris!" Evie screamed.

Mouse clapped his hands over his mouth to cover a gasp. Terra remained stoic, but her fingers curled into fists at her thighs.

"Iris!" Evie repeated. "Are you okay?"

"She cannot hear you," Henry reminded her over the intercom. He looked down at Iris, tilting his head to the side in mock consideration. "Can you, Ms. Harte?"

The surgeon raised her head, her hazel eyes round as full moons. Evie exhaled with relief. She did not appear to be injured. The Offs shoved her forward unceremoniously. She landed on her hands and knees without a sound. Pride swelled in Evie when she sprang to her feet and spun to face her guards.

"Do you know why you are here, Ms. Harte?" Henry inquired. He paused while Iris responded, his hands still clasped behind his back. "Very good," he said after a moment. "You are certainly more intelligent than your friends."

Iris peeked back at them over her shoulder. A bolt of terror shot through Evie as they locked eyes. There was too much there, too much fear and too much love. Iris turned back around. She took a challenging step toward Henry, clearly shouting at him.

"Yes, very good," he replied. He snapped his fingers and the

Offs retreated, leaving the door open in their wake. Henry refocused on Iris, slipping his hands into the pockets of his crisp white slacks. The surgeon was breathing hard; even across the room, Evie could see the rapid rise and fall of her shoulders. "Do you know what this place is, Ms. Harte? We call it The Amp. The late Victor Westervelt II designed it—we discovered the plans in his office after his untimely death. It is designed to maximize the effects of The New Music."

Panic seized Evie. She slammed her fist into the thick window. "Henry!" she bellowed, her voice cracking. "Ronja will never work with Maxwell if she finds out you took her mind!"

"Who said anything about taking her mind?" Henry asked smoothly.

For a beat, Evie stared dumbly at the shade of her friend. Then realization snapped into place. Her knees nearly buckled. "No," she whispered, but no sound came out.

"I'll return in fifteen minutes," Henry said briskly, starting toward the door. "I am sure by then you'll have reconsidered." Without another word he passed through the exit and slammed the door behind him.

Silence reigned.

Slowly, Iris turned to face them. She looked even smaller than usual, her short curls sticking out at all angles, her hazel eyes too large for her bloodless face. For a long moment, no one moved. Then Iris flew at the window, pressing her palms to it desperately. Her terrified breaths fogged on the glass. Evie aligned her hands with hers. The inch between them was haunting. It would have been easier if it were a mile.

"You're okay, you're okay, you're okay," Evie whispered. Iris held her gaze unsteadily. There was no room for tears in her eyes, they were filled to the brim with panic. "You're okay, you're okay, you're o—"

Iris jerked back from the glass as if stung. She stumbled, looking around wildly for something she could not see. Her hands flew to her ears. Her mouth opened in a soundless scream.

"NO!" Evie wailed. She rammed her shoulder into the glass, ignoring the pain that exploded under her skin.

Iris crashed to her knees and folded forward, covering her head as if to protect it from a blast.

"NO!" Evie shoved Terra and Mouse out of the way and slammed her bare heel into the barrier. The shock radiated from her foot to her hip. She barely felt it. She leapt back and delivered another powerful sidekick to the wall. Iris had gone limp on the floor. Her hands slid from her ears, revealing ribbons of blood. She slumped to the side like a rag doll. Her eyes rolled back as convulsions wracked her body.

Evie lunged at the wall again, pounding bruises into her knuckles and knees. Then she was on the floor, a strong arm locked around her neck. "ENOUGH, WICK!" Terra roared.

The techi ignored her, writhing and sobbing. She could not see. Her whole body throbbed with agony. Her hands were hot and slick. *Blood*, she realized dimly. Mouse sat on her legs, pinning her.

"Evie," Terra said again, her mouth pressed to her ear. "Enough."

The fight drained from Evie. Mouse scooted off her legs and knelt beside her head. Slowly, Terra relaxed her choke hold. "Iris . . . " Evie murmured, her eyelids fluttering.

No one said a word. There was nothing to say. Instead, shockingly tender hands cradled her head, lifting it from the hard concrete. Terra laid her head on her thighs, gently turning her face inward to shield her from the horrors beyond the glass.

13: OLD WOUNDS

The air was heavy with sweat and pleasure. Ronja and Roark lay side by side on the bed, the sheets tangled between their legs. Their hair had dried a while ago, but their pillows were still cool and damp. "What about this one?" she asked, tracing the raised white scar that curled around his hip bone. Roark raised his head to see what she was referring to, then flopped back down with a chuckle.

"Training accident with Terra, though I always wondered if it was really an accident."

Ronja smiled. They had been playing this game for the better part of an hour, telling the stories behind their scars. It should have been more difficult than it was. It was not cathartic, not exactly. It was a distraction. Ronja let her hand drift across his abdomen to a knot of scar tissue the size of a small coin. "What about this?"

"Ah, ah, ah," Roark chastised her. "My turn."

Ronja rolled her eyes. Her annoyance faded when his fingers found the thin scar beneath her left breast. "How did you get this?"

She winced. "I was ten, maybe eleven. Some kid gave it to me during our lunch break, not sure I remember how."

"I wish I could have been there. I wish I had known you a long time ago."

Warmth blossomed in Ronja. She inched closer to him, hooking her leg around his. He smiled absently, and the pads of his fingers drifted over to the scar directly above her heart. It was no longer swollen, and most of the color had faded. With its ragged edges it looked like a blazing star. "I meant to ask," Roark spoke up after a time. "When you saw the wolf . . . "

He trailed off as Ronja blushed scarlet. She buried her face in the pillow with a groan. "Leave me alone," she mumbled.

"Never."

Ronja turned her head to the side, glaring at Roark with one eye. "Okay, so maybe I get a little freaked out around dogs."

"A little," he repeated dryly.

She huffed.

"Oi." He put his hand on her naked shoulder, rocking it back and forth gently. "I'm not here to judge you. I have plenty things I'm afraid of for no good reason."

Ronja sat up quickly, lights popping in her vision. She twisted to look at Roark, who still lay on his side. "No reason?" she hissed. The boy remained still, his lips parted in shock. "No reason? Can you really not think of a single reason I might not like dogs?"

"I—"

"Where do you think the word *mutt* comes from, Roark?"

"Ro—"

"Because mutts look like dogs," she cut him off brutally. "They act like them. They pant, they drool. The ones like Layla can attack at any moment. People used to bark at me when I walked past them because their Singers told them to, and I know it wasn't their fault but—"

Roark sat up and grabbed her hand. "I know, love," he

murmured, squeezing her fingers. "I understand."

Ronja pursed her lips, biting back a scathing comment. "Sorry," she said, forcing the word out through her teeth. The bitterness she had tried to swallow was creeping back up her throat. She took a deep, shuddering breath. "I'm sorry."

"No, I should have guessed." His brow knit with concern and he gave her hand a quick squeeze. His warm breath played on her face as he tucked a curl over her remaining ear. "You went through hell. If I could take it away, I would."

"No." Ronja shook her head with a bit too much ferocity, flinging the carefully placed curl of hair out of place. "It's not your fault. These days I guess I'm just . . ." *Angry. Terrified. Bloodthirsty.* "On edge."

"We all are," he reminded her. "You're not alone."

"I—I know."

They fell silent, tension growing between them like moss on a stone.

"Ronja?" Roark tried again, her name a tentative question. Her throat tightened. She knew where this was going. "We should talk about your fath . . . about the king."

"Jonah said he wasn't sure," she replied in a deceptively even tone.

"The Conductor saw the resemblance" Roark reminded her. His voice was achingly tender. It would have been easier if he had yelled at her. "He called you by name."

"He was skitzed," Ronja shot back through clenched teeth.

"But Easton—"

"Hasn't said *anything*, Roark," she snapped. "We know *nothing*, and until we do I'd appreciate it if you would skitz off." More silence, even heavier than the first. Ronja felt her insides curdle with shame. Roark looked as if she had slapped him.

"We should sleep," he said curtly. He flopped down onto his

pillow and rolled over, tugging the quilts up around his shoulders. Ronja watched him for a long time, drinking in the steady rhythm of his body. She could not see his eyes from this angle, but she knew they were open. Full of hurt.

She sighed, then reached over and flicked off the lamp on her nightstand. Blackness engulfed them, tickling the hairs on the back of her neck. She lay down blind and pulled the covers up to her nose, tucking into a ball.

She was still cold.

14: THE VISITOR
Roark

Roark slept fitfully, weaving in and out of uncertain dreams. He gave up around five a.m. and sat up, flipping on the lamp at his bedside. Ronja was sleeping like the dead, so he did not fear waking her. He could see her eyes roving beneath her nearly translucent lids. Her curls were bunched around her face, her lips parted as her steady breaths came and went. Roark leaned over and tugged the quilt up higher around her shoulders.

This close, he could still see the marks Maxwell's torture had left around her. They were healing well; in the low light, they were scarcely visible. The scars left on her mind were far more enduring. He did not know exactly what had been done to her over the course of their imprisonment. Whatever it was, it clung to her, stubborn as a shadow. It was as if everything that made her *her* had been scrambled, leaving her scattered and unstable.

No amount of affection would bring Ronja back to him. He knew that. She needed closure, justice. It was hypocritical of him to try to soothe her rage when the same fire burned in him. Still, he tried. She twitched in her sleep, her nose wrinkling. The sight knocked a smile onto Roark's face. It disappeared as quickly as it had come.

The Siren. The girl with a voice like thunder. His heart. His home. He did not know where her powers came from, if they were supernatural or a simple matter of clashing frequencies. All he knew was that they were rooted in emotion. He was not even sure if her voice would work if she kept choking down her feelings.

Soft knocking broke Roark from his thoughts. He rose quickly, glancing over at Ronja. She was still fast asleep. Pulling on his pants, he strode over to the door and unlocked it. Cracking it warily he peered out into the hallway.

A stranger stood before him. He was of average height with silver-brushed hair, a square jaw, and white skin. He was dressed casually, a worn leather bag slung over his shoulder. "Can I help you?" Roark asked, keeping his voice low.

"Ah—yes," the man said, tripping over his answer. "I am here to take you on a tour of the temple. Roark Westervelt III, I presume?"

Roark narrowed his eyes as the strange accent pricked his eardrums. There was a hint of Tovairin there, and something else. Something familiar. He opened the door a bit wider, his nerves humming anxiously. "Tour?"

"Yes." The older man offered a wavering smile. His skin shimmered dully as the muscles of his face moved. Sweat. "I also have some fresh clothes for you." He dug into the bag at his side. Roark tightened his grip on the doorknob, then relaxed when he withdrew a bundle of garments.

"Thank you," he said, opening the door all the way to accept the offering. "Is this tour required? My partner could use the sleep."

"Your partner?" the stranger asked. He leaned to the side a bit, trying to get a look over his shoulder.

Roark stepped in front of him pointedly. "Yes, my partner."

Realizing his error, the man took a generous step back. "No matter," he said briskly, adjusting the strap of his leather bag. "Commander Easton requested your tours be conducted separately. She can sleep as much as she needs."

"Of course," Roark muttered. It was a common tactic, splitting prisoners up to interview them separately. The idea was to see if their stories lined up. Generally, there was a cell involved and not a walking tour, but the result was the same. He would have preferred Easton dispensed with the pleasantries and cut to the chase. "How generous of him."

The man smiled knowingly. "Change if you like, I'll wait."

Roark shut the door without comment. He cast his eyes to Ronja, listening to the music of her breath. If he woke her, she would insist on accompanying him. He would not put it past her to punch the man aiming to divide them. The last thing they needed was another scuffle.

Making up his mind with a groan, he peeled off his pants and dressed in the Tovairin clothes: relaxed black leggings, a thick woolen sweater, soft undershirt, and fresh socks and underwear. Tugging on his boots, he took one last look at Ronja. Leaving her alone felt like a mistake. Staying would mean disobeying an order from Commander Easton. Neither option ensured her safety. He slipped out into the hallway, closing the door behind him.

"Good choice," the man commended him.

"Do you have a name?" Roark asked.

"Darren," he replied, saluting him in the customary format.

"All right. Lead the way, Darren."

They started off down the corridor in silence, their footfalls rebounding off the curved walls. The temple was all but deserted at this early hour, though they passed the occasional Kev Fairlan. Some were dressed in black leather armor, others in relaxed clothing similar to his own. They gawked openly as the two men passed. They were not just looking at him, Roark realized, but at Darren.

"What do you do around here?" Roark asked as they moved past a battle-ready woman with a penetrating stare.

"I am an advisor of sorts to Commander Easton," Darren answered, keeping his eyes straight ahead. They were an odd blend of green and grey, made brighter by the electric lights threaded through the catacombs.

"Of sorts?"

"I help him run this place. He spends quite a bit of time at the front, you know." They reached a fork in the path. Darren jerked his thumb to the right. Roark followed him into another hallway identical to the last. It seemed to roll on for miles. There was not a soul in sight.

"Where are we going?" Roark asked, prickling with suspicion.

Darren glanced over at him, amusement tugging at the corner of his mouth. "You ask too many questions."

"Forgive me, I thought tours were supposed to be educational, unless this is more than a tour."

"Talkative *and* astute."

"I do what I can," Roark replied in a flat voice.

"I thought you might be interested to see the hub of our operation," Darren said.

"What gave you that idea?"

"Intuition." When Roark did not reply, the older man asked a question of his own. "How did you find your journey?"

"Fine, given the circumstances."

"The circumstances?"

The Anthemite cut his sharp eyes to Darren. "I would expect an advisor to the commander to be better informed of our situation. Were you not debriefed?"

Darren cleared his throat. "Here," he said, gesturing at a

narrow staircase off the hall. Roark did as he was told, mounting the steps two at a time. The older man struggled to keep pace with him. The passage was not well lit. Still, squinting into the dimness, he could see an iron door ahead. By the time they reached it, Darren was breathing hard and trying desperately to hide it. Roark observed him as he rummaged through his bag, presumably hunting for a key. He appeared to be in decent shape, but his lungs rattled like a freight train.

"Not as young as I once was," he wheezed. "Ah, here we are." Darren pulled a brass key from his satchel and tossed it to the Anthemite, who caught it single-handedly. "Go on."

Roark complied. The lock stuck for a moment, then gave with a screech. He pushed the door open slowly, his instincts on high alert. Warm light and the hum of machinery spilled over him. He relaxed slightly. They had arrived at what appeared to be a control room, free of guards and interrogators. Various pieces of tech Evie could have identified whirred away hypnotically, and a large window took up most of the far wall. He could not see beyond it from his low vantage point.

"After you," Darren said.

Roark stepped over the threshold cautiously. His guide trailed him, shutting the door. He did not lock it.

"Have a look," Darren implored him, clearly indicating the window.

Roark approached slowly, unsure of what to expect and keenly aware of the eyes glued to the back of his head. His eyebrows lifted as he arrived at the window. "Impressive."

It was. Beyond the thick glass was a massive, multi-story hangar packed with scores of vehicles—everything from autos and motorbikes to armored tanks. There were even a few moderately large aeroplanes. Kev Fairlans the size of ants hurried between the transports. Sparks burst from power tools as mechanics tweaked the metal beasts. Twin doors at least three stories high stood at the far end of the hangar, ready to unleash wrath upon the Vintian invaders.

"Jonah told us you were struggling to make ends meet," Roark commented without turning back to Darren. "This seems like a pretty high end operation."

"Half those tanks are out of commission," Darren admitted, sidling up to stand beside him. "We're down to nineteen fighter planes. The Vintians have hundreds. The only place we dominate them is on the water."

Roark nodded, still scanning the hangar. "This is all very interesting, but I'm wondering when you're going to tell me why I'm really here, your majesty."

For a long moment, the conversation stalled. The machines chugged away around them, straining to fill the hush. "What gave me away?" he finally asked quietly.

"Everything." Roark turned back around and slipped his hands into the pockets of his new sweater, offering the monarch a pitying smile. "But mostly, I never told Easton I was the third of my name."

"Rookie mistake," he muttered. He sighed, letting his bag slip from his shoulder to the floor with a solid *thunk.*

"Is it true?" Roark asked. "Are you her father?"

Darius Alezandri nodded, his expression unreadable. "I believe so." He held up a finger and reached into the deep pocket of his pants, withdrawing a worn, yellowed photograph. He held it out for Roark to see. The paper shivered in his grasp. "Is this her mother?"

Roark felt his stomach vault. He pursed his lips and took the faded picture in hand. It felt strangely heavy pinched between his thumb and forefinger. In the photograph, a younger version of the man who stood before him had swept a young woman off her feet. She was plain but charming with wild dark curls and a smattering of freckles across her nose and cheekbones. The last time he had seen Layla, she was yellow-eyed and snarling like an animal. A mutt.

Here, she looked like the girl he loved.

"Layla," Roark found himself saying quietly.

"The love of my life," Darius said. He took the photograph back quickly, as if afraid Roark might rip it up. "Is it true she named her Ronja?"

Roark looked up at the exiled king, studying the plains of his face. "Yes," he conceded. "Ronja Fey Zipse."

"Zipse?" Darius asked, his brows knitting. "Are you sure?"

"Yeah, she changed it," Roark answered carefully. He was not sure how much Darius knew about what had happened to Layla after his departure from Revinia. Whatever the case, he felt it was not his place to relay the story. "You never came back for her, for either of them," he said. Anger he knew did not belong to him simmered beneath his skin.

"The Kev Fairla forced me to leave. They were trying to protect me, but I begged them to let me stay." Darius reached up to scratch his temple, looking guilty despite his excuse. "If I had known Layla was pregnant, I would have returned no matter what it took."

Understanding dawned on Roark, melting his secondhand rage. "You didn't know."

"No." The king shook his gray head. "I did not."

"Why did you bring me here? I'm not the person you should be having this conversation with."

"Cowardice, I suppose." Darius smiled wanly, looking over his shoulder at the hangar. Roark followed his gaze. Half a dozen soldiers marched single file toward a hulking tank belching black fumes. Ahead of them, one of the mammoth doors was rolling into the side of the mountain, ushering in gray sunlight. "I am not a father, Mr. Westervelt. I know nothing of my daughter. I swear, I will go before her and beg for her forgiveness, for a chance to know her. But first, will you tell me about her?"

Roark dragged his fingers through his hair, forcing out a tense breath. "Ronja is . . . " He paused, unsure where to begin. "Ronja is strong. The strongest person I've ever known. She's loyal, fiercely protective, funny, bullheaded. Beautiful."

"You love her."

Roark nodded, looking Darius straight in the eye. "I do. And I'll protect her with my life."

"You seem like a good man, Mr. Westervelt. I'll admit I was wary when I heard your name."

"I am not my father, or my grandfather." Roark drew himself up to his full height. He had half an inch on Darius, which felt important in the moment. "I have spent my life trying to undo what they did to Revinia."

"The Anthem is still active, then?"

Roark froze. "You—you know about the Anthem?"

"Know about it?" Darius chuckled. "How do you think I met Layla?"

15: SERVE

Ronja awoke from a nightmare she could not remember. Her muscles were coiled, her skin coated with stale sweat. When she was under the influence of her Singer she had trained herself to block out dreams of any sort. They ran the risk of triggering The Quiet Song. She sometimes wished she could still force them away. That was the price of freedom, she supposed. She was free to feel anything. The trouble was, she usually felt everything.

The Siren sat up slowly, yawning and stretching. Her arm flopped over to the place Roark should have been. Her hand cut through air, landing in the depression his body had left. She looked over, her brow puckering. *Where are you?* She disentangled herself from the blankets and planted her feet on the stone floor. Dizzy, she made her way to the bathroom and flicked on the light.

No Roark. She itched her nose anxiously. He would not have gone to any official meetings without her. He was off sulking somewhere, then. The thought set her on edge. She shoved the shower curtain out of the way roughly and cranked the knob all the way to the right. Icy water shot out of the shower head. Ronja cursed, leaping away from the spray.

After a few tentative tests with her hand, she climbed back into the shower. She was not usually one to bathe every day, but she still felt grimy from the voyage. For a few minutes, she stood beneath the hot stream, allowing it to raise color in her skin. It did not soothe her as it had the night before. Rather, the heat stoked her paranoia. She snatched up the soap and began to scrub her body viciously. As soon as she was finished she shut off the water, hopped out of the stall, and grabbed the damp towel she had used the night before. Wrapping it around her torso, she stepped back into the bedroom.

"Skitz," she muttered when she caught sight of her pile of dirty clothes at the foot of the bed. The second she put them back on she would reek, no matter how hard she scrubbed her skin. Ronja weighed her limited options, hugging herself as a little puddle of bathwater pooled at her feet. A tentative knock at the door made her jump, clutching the towel higher around her breasts. "Who is it?" she called, her voice cracking.

"Elise," came a soft reply, thick with a Tovairin accent. Ronja raised her eyebrows at the unfamiliar name. As if registering her confusion, the visitor elaborated. "I have for you clothes."

Ronja could not help it. She smiled. Holding up her towel with one hand, she padded over to the door and pulled it open. A pretty girl with a round face stood in the frame. Ronja quickly identified her as the girl who had led them to their room the night before. Today, she wore a warm brown shift that fell to her knees and black winter stockings. In her arms was a bundle of fresh clothes.

"Thanks," Ronja said gratefully, pinning her towel to her chest with her forearm and reaching out for the garments. Elise handed them over, then turned to leave. "Wait," the Anthemite yelped. The girl stiffened, peeking over her shoulder with eyes flown wide. "Uhhh . . . "

Ronja did not know why she had stopped Elise from leaving. She was not in the mood to socialize, particularly with a stranger. Hugging her clothes to her chest with one arm, she stuck out her free hand. "Ronja," she introduced herself. "*Perlo.*"

Elise stared at the offered hand blankly. Ronja kicked herself internally. Tovairins did not shake hands. She was about to exchange one greeting for another when Elise gripped her fingers lightly.

"*Pevra,*" she said in a whispery voice. She retracted her hand at once, as if the touch had shocked her. Ronja let her arm drop.

"I . . . " Her stomach growled as if on cue. "*Kann,*" Ronja blurted the Tovairin word for food. She laid her hand flat on her stomach. "Hungry."

"Yes," Elise said, brightening up. Ronja had started to wonder if she was capable of smiling. "Hungry," she repeated, rolling the word around on her tongue.

"Great," Ronja said with a relieved sigh. She opened the door wider and scooted aside. "Come in, just give me a minute to get dressed."

Elise paled. She shook her head fervently, her black hair rippling. "*Nis,*" she muttered, casting her eyes to the floor.

"I'm not going to hurt you," Ronja assured her. Elise shifted from foot to foot, tucking a strand of hair over her ear. The Siren shrugged. "Suit yourself." She shut the door, letting her towel crumple at her feet. Stepping over the sopping cloth, she carried her new clothes to the bed to examine them.

They were simple and well made. Thick brown leggings with a drawstring at the waist. A knit navy sweater with soft fur around the collar. Clean woolen socks, underwear, and a cotton undershirt. Ronja felt a surge of longing for the leather coat Evie had given her after their return from Red Bay. Her chest tightened.

Evie. Brave, impulsive, smart as a whip with a right hook that could dent steel. Somehow, Ronja had started to take her for granted. Iris, too. Now, they were . . .

Ronja snapped the thought in two. Food. She needed food. Then she would find Roark and they would force Easton to make up his damn mind. Sparking with sudden resolve, she dressed quickly. Part of her feared Elise would evaporate if she left her alone for too long. She tugged the sweater over her head. It was a bit loose, but then maybe it was supposed to be. The leggings fit her perfectly and the undergarments and socks were surprisingly soft. She found her boots at the end of the bed, laced them tight, and hurried back to the door.

Thankfully, Elise was still waiting for her outside, chewing her lip. "Thanks," Ronja said as she shut the door. The Tovairin girl nodded, then started down the hall. The Anthemite followed, her footfalls bouncing down the corridor. No one else was around. For that, Ronja was grateful. She was not in the mood to be gawked at like a circus animal. "So, what do you do around here?" she asked Elise.

The girl did not reply, nor did she turn around. Her long black hair swayed against the small of her back.

Fine, Ronja thought gruffly. She was not usually one for small talk, anyway.

"Serve."

Ronja blinked. "What?"

"Serve," Elise repeated without turning around. "I serve."

"Elise, *triv el ent la*?" a stern voice called.

Elise scraped to a halt, her muscles bunching with fear. She wheeled around, her eyes flown wide and her tanned skin bleached. Ronja stiffened as warning bells pealed in her head. She spun to greet the owner of the voice.

A young man with night-dark skin and short dreadlocks was

striding toward them confidently. White *reshkas* crawled up the side of his neck, branching all the way to his right temple. He scraped to a halt, his deep set eyes darting back and forth between them suspiciously. "*Hist fen?*" he asked, clearly speaking to Elise.

"Ronja," she answered in a tiny voice. She angled her face toward the floor and twisted the fabric of her dress.

"Go," the man ordered, jerking his thumb over his shoulder. Elise hurried away without so much as a glance at Ronja. The Siren watched her go with narrowed eyes. The entire exchange had left her feeling unsettled.

"You must be the Anthemite."

Ronja looked at the man, her pulse stumbling. "Who are you?" He did not appear particularly threatening, yet Elise had trembled before him as if he were ten feet tall. *Just like she did with Easton*, she realized faintly.

"My name is Paxton," he answered, pressing a polite fist to his forehead and chest. "Personal assistant to Commander Easton."

"Ronja," she replied shortly. She jerked her chin in the direction Elise had taken off. "What did you say to her?"

Paxton cocked his head, considering her. "Is that really your business?" Ronja did not have a good answer for that. The man smiled tightly. "Elise was due to report to her *grav* twenty minutes ago, and she was not cleared to approach you."

"*Grav?*"

"The closest word you have would be *boss*."

"Right." Ronja gave Paxton another quick scan. He was clean cut, strong, a bit on the short side. He appeared to be about her age, maybe a few years older. She cleared her throat. "Can I help you?"

"Commander Easton is deliberating your request," Paxton answered, adopting a formal tone. "He sent me to show you around."

"I'm not a bloody tourist," Ronja seethed. "I need you to take me to the commander, now."

Paxton shut her down. "The commander is not receiving guests at the moment." His tone was even, but his eyes were sharp as flint. "He has requested you and your partner be shown around so that you might better understand our way of life."

Ronja raised an eyebrow at him, her thoughts thrumming. His accent was a blend of Tovairin and something else she did not recognize. His grasp of the common language was as good or better than Easton's. "My partner," she said. "Where is he?"

"On his own tour," Paxton answered. "You'll see him soon."

Ronja did not reply at once, chewing on the new information. Her brain threatened to spin out with panic, imagining Roark being tortured for information, or worse, dead on that black sand beach. *Jonah would never let that happen*, she reminded herself. *But why the tours? What the hell was Easton playing at?*

There was only one way to find out. "Fine," she said, surrendering. "Give me the grand tour. Maybe you can answer some of my questions."

Paxton smiled, but it did not reach his eyes. "Perhaps."

16: THE BURNING ONES

Paxton led Ronja through the meandering corridors of the temple. He was easier to keep up with than Roark and Jonah, but still they moved at steady clip. It was impossible to tell which direction they were headed—all the halls looked the same—but she got the sense they were moving toward the edge of the compound. The air was growing steadily colder, the tunnels busier. She did not see any soldiers today, mostly just Kev Fairlans in civilian clothes similar to her own. They whispered to one another in their native tongue as she passed.

"They're just cautious around newcomers," Paxton explained. Ronja glanced at him sidelong. He must have sensed her twinge of discomfort. He was perceptive, maybe too perceptive. "They're not saying anything unsavory."

The Siren shrugged. "Whatever it is, I promise I've heard worse."

Paxton tilted his head to the side, clearly expecting her to elaborate. When she did not, he changed the subject. "The Temple of Entalia has been here for generations," he said. "The main room you entered through is carved from the volcano, Entalia."

Ronja raised her eyebrows. "The volcano is named after the goddess?"

"No." Paxton shook his head, his dreadlocks flopping against his temples. "The ancients believed the goddess *was* the volcano."

"Huh." Ronja paused, chewing her lip. "What do you believe?"

Her guide smiled vaguely, but did not answer. It seemed she was not the only one prone to skirting around personal questions.

"Why set up your headquarters in a volcano?" she asked, curiosity bleeding through her agitation. "Is that not a little . . . "

"Dangerous?" Paxton passed her a wry smile. "No. Entalia has been extinct for thousands of years. I am not sure when the last eruption was, you would have to ask Cas. He's the keeper of the temple."

Ronja nodded. "Yeah, we met last night."

Paxton chuckled under his breath. "He likes to greet newcomers, wants to make sure they're not here to steal the treasure."

"Treasure?" she repeated dubiously. "Jonah said the Kev Fairla was broke."

Paxton grinned, revealing a small gap between his front teeth. "Just an old legend, but it occasionally draws treasure seekers crazy enough to walk through a war zone."

They rounded a sharp corner that dumped into a narrow hallway. It was considerably dimmer than the one they had come from and was entirely vacant. Ronja tensed. She struggled to keep her anxiety off her face, but felt as though her guide could smell it on her skin. "The beach we arrived at seemed pretty quiet," she said in an attempt to distract him. "Not how I pictured a war zone."

"Most of the fighting is on the other side of the island, or on the water," Paxton explained. "The Vintians took the main port, Yeille, a few months back. They're basing out of there."

Ronja hummed thoughtfully, intrigued despite herself.

"Why did you choose this as your base?"

"Difficult to bomb, easy to get lost in these tunnels. We set bonfires in the crater every now and then. As far as the Vintians know, Entalia is ready to blow."

Ronja could not help but smile at that, thinking that Terra would be impressed with their tactics. "Smart."

"That was all Easton," Paxton said, his voice surprisingly tender. "He has a knack for that sort of thing. Part of what makes him a great leader."

Ahead of them, a door opened, spilling cold light and raised voices. Ronja stopped, her muscles coiling. A middle-aged man with thinning hair and narrow shoulders stepped into the corridor, his eyes on a stack of papers. He was dressed in civilian clothes, but had an official air about him that made her think he might be some sort of general.

"Silas," Paxton called. Silas looked up, surprised. He started to smile, but faltered when he caught sight of Ronja.

"*Hist fen?*" he asked, directing the question at Paxton as he approached them.

"Ronja," the Siren answered before he could. She was getting tired of others introducing her. Remembering the Tovairin custom, she tapped her fist to her forehead and chest. "Nice to meet you."

"Silas," he introduced himself, copying her greeting. He looked vaguely impressed. "You are the Revinian."

"Yeah."

Silas smiled, his honey-brown eyes illuminating with intrigue. "I would talk to you, sometime. Revinia is . . . " He trailed off, rifling through his knowledge of the common language. "Strange."

No shit. "I'll only be here for a few days," Ronja replied, feigning regret.

Out of the corner of her eye, she saw Paxton pass her an inquisitive glance. She ignored him pointedly. "We have to go, Silas," he said. "*Rel'eev,* Entalia."

"*Rel'eev,*" Silas replied with a disappointed sigh. He saluted Ronja again, then stepped around them and continued on down the hall.

"Come on," Paxton said, starting forward.

"What does that mean? *Rel'eev?*" Ronja asked as she fell into step beside him.

Paxton chewed on the question for a moment before responding. "There is no exact translation. The closest I can equate it to is *may the goddess Entalia be with you.* You can use it to refer to any god, though."

Ronja found herself bobbing her head. "We have something like that in the Anthem. May your song guide you home."

"May your song guide you home." Paxton tested the phrase on his tongue. "What does it mean?"

Ronja paused, weighing her reply. "I guess it means something different to everyone." Before he could ask her for more details, she changed the subject. "So, Entalia. Who is she, exactly? Jonah said she was the goddess of rebirth. What does that mean?"

"Depends who you ask." Paxton scraped to a stop before one of the doors. She followed suit, eyeing it dubiously. It was considerably larger than the others lining the hall, its frame engraved with whirling Tovairin script. "There are many gods, if you follow Contravora. Entalia is the wife of Morde, the god of death."

"Death and rebirth," Ronja muttered. "Do all gods have temples?"

"They used to," Paxton answered grimly. He pressed his palm to the face of the unremarkable door. "Most were destroyed during The Great War, the rest when Vinta attacked."

"I'm sorry," she said quickly. Uncertain as she was about the Kev Fairla, she was not blind to their plight. They faced the destruction of their culture and the loss of their autonomy. If there was anything she could understand, it was that. "That's horrible."

Paxton nodded. He dropped his hand to the wrought-iron knob, drumming his fingers on it. "I grew up here. My father was a devout follower of the Contravoran faith. My mother was more open-minded. They left Sydon before I was born, so I have never known another home."

"My partner Roark, his mother was from Sydon."

"I thought I saw that," Paxton said, a genuine smile curling his full lips. "I'd guess she was from the northern territories."

Ronja shrugged. Roark rarely spoke of his family. She understood why. His father was a psychopath, his sister a martyr, and his mother . . . his mother was a ghost in more ways than one. All Ronja knew about her was that she was Sydonian and that she had died when he was a child.

"This is my favorite place in the temple," Paxton said, drawing her out of her thoughts. He twisted the knob and pushed the door open. Heat spilled over them. "I think you might like it, too."

Ronja's jaw hit the floor. Before her was an inferno. Twin rivers of lava cut straight through the black stone floor. The aisle between them was six feet wide. At the far end of the room was a shrine with engraved pillars and curved stone steps. At its core was a massive bowl of flame. The air itself shivered with heat, giving the whole space the feel of a mirage.

"This is the Contrav, the burning place."

Ronja looked at Paxton, struggling to find her voice. She swallowed, smoke scraping her throat. "What is this?" Her instincts were screaming at her to run. Thoughts of elaborate interrogation tactics rattled around in her head. She took a step back.

"No, no, no," Paxton assured her quickly, fluttering his hands to soothe her. "I should have explained. The Contrav is part of our faith."

"Oh, great."

"Contravoran means *the burning ones*," he explained. "The Contrav, *the burning place*. You have nothing to be afraid of. Look." He stepped into the heat-choked room, walking backward down the aisle.

Ronja stayed rooted on the spot. If the Kev Fairla was planning on torturing her, this was not how they would do it. It was convoluted and risky. The interrogator could easily end up in the lava himself. Paxton did not really have the look of a torturer, either. *Neither did Roark*, she reminded herself, thinking back to their violent first encounter.

"No one in this temple will harm you, myself included," Paxton assured her from halfway down the aisle.

Pushing aside her better judgement, Ronja stepped across the threshold, leaving the door open behind her. The man turned and continued toward the shrine. She trailed him at a distance. The canals of magma hissed and simmered at her feet. They seemed to spill closer with each step she took. She sped her pace.

Up ahead, Paxton had already mounted the wide steps to the altar. He stood beside the flaming bowl, watching the fire as if it were speaking to him. Ronja tapped up the short flight of steps, pausing just before she hit the top. The basin was perched on a shockingly narrow dais. One nudge and it would surely crash to the ground.

"Here."

Ronja started. Paxton regarded her expectantly, his hand

outstretched. Pinched between his fingers was a blank slip of paper. She took it cautiously, as if it might bite her. "Uh, what is this?"

"Paper," he replied unhelpfully.

"Thanks." She snuck a peek over her shoulder. Beyond the flames, the door was still wide open. It was twenty paces away, give or take. Panic spiked in her gut. What the hell was she thinking, coming in here alone? Roark was going to kill her if Paxton did not do it first.

"Take this."

Ronja turned back to him. He now brandished a sleek fountain pen. She accepted it gingerly. "Now what?"

"Now you write your deepest fear down and throw it in the fire. The ancients wrote them in blood, but that seemed unnecessary."

"Yeah," she agreed lamely. "So why would I do that?"

Paxton shot her a vaguely condescending smile "So you can let it go." He stepped around her and retreated down the steps.

Ronja spun around, heart in her throat. "Oi! Where the hell are you going?"

"I'll be outside," he called. "The door will be unlocked, come out when you're done."

"But—"

Paxton breezed through the door and shut it with a snap. Ronja stood rigid before the shrine, listening, expecting to hear the thud of a deadbolt or the click of a lock. Neither came. *Stupid skitzing pitcher.* She imagined Evie punching her on the bicep, Iris shaking her head, Roark slapping his hand to his forehead. *Have you learned nothing*?

Focus. Ronja took a shuddering breath and began to analyze her surroundings. There were no other exits in sight. No cameras, no speakers or visible microphones. No assailants lurking in the shadows. "What are you playing at?" she muttered. What could the Kev Fairla possibly have to gain from her burning her fears in private? She looked down. Anxiety had crumpled the slip of paper into a ball. *Fine.*

She plunked down on the top step and smoothed the paper over her thigh.

What am I afraid of?

The Music. The obvious choice leapt to the front of her mind. But no, not anymore. It was no longer an invisible, insurmountable enemy. She could see it, she could beat it, if only she could access it.

Death, then. She had already conquered it twice. When it claimed her for a third time, it would just be taking what was owed.

The Conductor . . . was rotting in a shallow grave, if Maxwell had bothered to bury him at all. Maybe he was still rotting at the top of the tower.

Maxwell. Ronja weighed his memory. His deranged grin and explosive rage. His searing genius and grotesque imagination. She let her eyelids drift shut, centering herself. The very thought of the madman made her shiver, but it was not with terror. It was rage. The only fear she had regarding that monster was not getting the pleasure of killing him with her bare hands.

If not her enemy, than what was she most afraid of?

She feared for her friends trapped beneath the palace. Maxwell would keep them alive as long as she was still breathing. She was almost certain he would not put them under The New Music, either. What good was bait that could not feel fear?

Ronja kept digging.

Losing Roark. That was a thought that kept her up at night. She knew she could survive without him, but surviving did not mean living. It sounded right to say losing him was her deepest fear, but there was something else cowering beneath it. An unexamined core so poisonous she had refused to look it in the eye until now.

Ronja scratched out a single word, then crumpled the paper and rose. She lobbed the ball at the bowl of flames like a brick at a window. With a hiss and a crackle, it was gone. She waited, her nerves singing. Nothing happened.

Ronja huffed, rolling her eyes, then spun on her heel and jogged down the steps. Her anxiety burgeoned as she approached the exit. Maybe it was locked after all. Bracing herself, she twisted the warm knob. The door opened at once. Fresh air and light spilled over her. Paxton leaned up against the opposite wall, his hands in his pockets. "So?" he asked.

"What are you playing at?" Ronja demanded, shutting the door with a crack. "Why did you leave me in there?"

"You could have followed me out." He took his left hand from his pocket to examine his nails, which were extremely well kept. "You made the choice to stay."

"For the last time, I am not a skitzing tourist."

"You still chose to stay."

"I am here to stop—"

Paxton raised a palm. "I am aware of your purpose here."

Ronja folded her arms across her chest, drawing on her brewing anger. "I want to see Easton. Now."

"The commander is occupied with other matters."

"Fine," she said, throwing up her hands. "Then take me to Roark and show me where I can get some food."

Paxton laughed, catching her off guard. "I see what they mean."

Ronja flushed. "What are you talking about?"

"Your eyes, your nose . . . " He reached up a hand, then thought better of it and put it back in his pocket. The Siren glowered at him, daring him to come closer. "Even your . . . " He stumbled over his words, chewing his lower lip contemplatively. "The stars on your face."

Ronja touched her cheek, her brow wrinkling. "What?"

"The marks."

"Freckles?"

Paxton dipped his chin. "Right, freckles."

"What about them?"

"Your father has them, too."

Ronja went rigid. A high pitched ringing built in her ear, so loud she wondered if Paxton could hear it. She took a step toward him, her lip curling. "My father is dead," she ground out. "Which is none of your business anyway. Now either take me to Roark, take me to Easton, or put me in a bloody cell."

17: CRESCENDO
Ito

Ito wound the cord of the headphones around her index finger, basking in the haze of the somber piano solo. The record was unnamed. She had discovered it years ago in the basement of a safe house in the outer ring. She had always believed music was meant to be shared, but she had never told anyone about this particular album. There was something sacred in the knowledge that she was the only person in the city who knew every note, every pause, every crescendo.

"Ito."

The lieutenant started. She swiped her headphones from her ears, letting them ring her neck. "Charlotte," she greeted the girl hastily. "I didn't hear you come in."

"I know, I said your name three times." Charlotte stood a couple of feet from the desk, not even trying to hide her smirk. Her coarse curls were pulled into a knot at the base of her skull. She wore a loose black dress and an evergreen sweater with a missing button. "I was just reporting back to you."

Ito gestured at the chair opposite hers. Charlotte obliged. She crossed one leg over the other, the picture of poise. The lieutenant felt her heartstrings tighten. She would never know just how much like her mother she was.

"Lieutenant? Are you all right?"

Ito blinked. "Yes, I apologize." Music still crept through her headphones. She bent down and shut off the record player under her desk. The black disk coasted to a halt. Lifting her headphones from her neck, she set them aside and returned to Charlotte. "What do you have for me?"

"You're a lot closer to command than you think."

Relief wrapped around Ito, squeezing a smile onto her face. It was immediately followed by a burst of shame. Wilcox was one of her oldest friends and comrades. They had been inseparable and idealistic in their youth. So much had changed since then. She did not recognize the person he had become. "Go on," she encouraged Charlotte.

"People are pissed, scared. Most of them think Wilcox is . . . " She tapped her temple and made a clicking noise with her tongue. "Skitzed."

"Unfortunately, I believe they are correct."

Charlotte nodded seriously. "I heard Vincent Bell talking to Clarke Hartford about the emergency exits."

Ito cocked an eyebrow. Both men were members of the council, which had not convened since their commander trapped them in the Belly. Hartford was sharp as a tack with a heart of gold. Bell was a bit of a wild card, but one hell of an agent. "What did they say?"

"Bell thinks they can dig through the rubble at the back of their bathhouse," Charlotte said. "He reckons it would take a couple weeks." Ito felt her expression harden. The girl tilted her head to the side. "Is that bad?"

"In theory, no. But if people start fleeing without a plan, they're as good as dead."

Charlotte nodded, a crease forming between her brows. "They were going to get to it soon. Do you want me to keep following them?"

"Yes, keep me informed."

The girl bobbed her head again. "There's more. You're not the only one who's worried about Wilcox. Cosmin overheard Kala and her crew debating a coup."

Ito could not resist a smile. "I should have guessed. Roark rubbed off on them."

"Yeah, maybe," Charlotte replied, her voice abruptly cold. "Anyway, the main thing is, people want answers. They want to know why they've been buried alive and why being stuck here is better than taking their chances topside. Everyone knows something bad happened, but no one knows what."

"What have they guessed?"

"They're not idiots." Charlotte reclined in her chair, folding her arms thoughtfully. "They know it was something to do with The Music. That doesn't mean they're willing to die without answers."

Ito steepled her fingers, her thoughts whirring. None of this was unprecedented, she reminded herself. It was not even as bad as it could be. No one was panicking. Not yet, at least. "Stay on Bell and Hartford," she ordered Charlotte. "You've done well, Romancheck."

"Thanks." The girl climbed to her feet, glowing with pride. "I'll report back tonight."

"Where is Cosmin?" Ito inquired.

"Wheeling around somewhere on the north end of the station, last time I checked. He's getting pretty fast in his chair."

"His nerve damage, is it permanent?"

Charlotte sighed, her aura dimming. "Wish I could tell you. Iris would know." She cracked a dour smile. "But if the scrubbers give out, what does it matter?"

Ito made noise of agreement. She laid her palms flat on the surface of her desk. Charlotte was right. They could spy on the council members all they wanted, but it would not bring them any closer to freedom. "Bring me Kala Pent, Elliot Mason, and Sawer Gailes."

"Sawyer? That crazy girl you picked up at Red Bay?"

"Yes."

"What do you need her for?"

"Just do it, Romancheck."

"Fine, fine. On it." Charlotte saluted wryly and started toward the exit, her dress swaying around her knees. "I'll bring them back as soon as possible."

"Charlotte—"

Ito never finished her sentence. A high pitched scream sliced through her words. She shot to her feet, snatching up the revolver she kept hidden under the lip of her desk. Charlotte had gone rigid, her eyes round as saucers. "Stay here," Ito ordered as she rushed past her. Before she reached the exit, a surprisingly strong hand shot out and snatched her forearm. She looked around. Charlotte regarded her intensely, fear and focus wrestling in her gaze.

"That was Georgie."

18: THE TRIÉ

Ronja was relieved to step back into the bustling central corridors. Her skin was still coated in sweat from the blistering Contrav. Paxton tried heroically to strike up a fresh conversation with her, but she had mastered the art of avoiding small talk. Eventually, he gave up and they continued on in sullen silence. She busied herself observing the people around her.

Despite living in the middle of a war zone, the Kev Fairlans were a lively bunch. Even the soldiers dressed for battle chatted amongst themselves nonchalantly. Ronja had learned a lot about humanity since being freed from her Singer. Humans possessed the strange and remarkable ability to pull normalcy from the most desperate situations. The Anthemites were the same way. They drew art and beauty from desolation.

That was where the similarities between the two rebellions ended. Anthemites dressed in vibrant colors, pierced their ears, and wore their hair in a wide variety of styles. The Kev Fairlans wore thick dark garments and furs. The women wove their hair into elegant braids. The men either wore theirs in knots like Jonah or cut it short like Easton. Everyone was tattooed with unique white *reshkas*.

Ronja stuck out like a sore thumb: pale and freckled with a head full of curly hair that scarcely brushed her jaw. The Kev Fairlans had not lost interest in her overnight. If anything their whispers had intensified. Once again she found herself wishing she had a better grasp of their language and social cues. Then she would know whether to smile or scowl. She settled on lifting her chin and marching on with all the grace she could muster.

"This way," Paxton said, jerking his thumb to the right. Ronja followed him around a corner, turning sideways to avoid an oncoming knot of Tovairin boys about her age. Their eyes stuck to her like brambles. She ignored them, unsure if they were leering or simply curious. When she looked up, it did not matter.

"Whoa."

"Welcome to the *trié*," Paxton said. "I think you would call it a mess hall."

Ronja nodded mutely. Just when she thought the temple was out of surprises, it had stolen her breath again. The *trié* was massive, easily as large as the entry hall or the library. The walls were painted with breathtaking murals. Towering mountains, charging armies, cityscapes littered with domed rooftops, and rolling ocean waves. Stalactites dripped from the lofty ceiling. Beneath them were three long tables big enough to seat hundreds. The air was thick with the delicious aroma of sizzling meat and an unfamiliar spice. Her mouth watered. *Focus*, her subconscious prodded her. "Where is Roark? You said he would be here."

Paxton shot her a withering glance. "Last I heard he was touring the temple. He should be here by now."

"Should be?"

The Kev Fairlan sighed, lifting his eyes to the ceiling. "Have you always been this impatient?"

"Yes."

"Ronja!"

The Siren spun on the familiar voice. Her heart jolted. Roark strode toward them with his trademark confidence, dressed in fresh clothes not unlike her own. "Where have you been?" she snapped as he arrived.

Roark frowned. "Do I need to get your permission before I go out?"

Ronja put her hands on her hips, drawing herself up to her full height. "When we're in a volcano full of armed strangers, yeah, that would be nice."

The boy heaved a sigh. It was then she noticed the violet shadows pressed to his eyelids, the tightness at the corner of his mouth. Her anger fizzled like a match in the rain. She pulled him into a tight embrace, burying her face in his chest. He drew her ever closer. "Sorry," she mumbled, her words muffled by his sweater.

"Me too," he said into her hair.

Ronja pulled back, clasping him by the forearms. "Where were you?"

"I was—"

Paxton coughed. Ronja flushed. She had all but forgotten his existence. She released Roark to glower at him, but she was more embarrassed than annoyed. "I assume this is your partner," he said, unruffled.

"What gave it away?"

"Roark Westervelt," Roark cut in, saluting him in the typical Tovairin fashion.

"Paxton," he answered, mirroring the gesture. "Advisor to Commander Easton. I was just showing Ronja around the temple. You had a tour as well, right?"

"Yes. It was . . . enlightening."

Ronja eyed him sidelong, wondering at the subtle hitch in his tone. He reached out to take her hand, his eyes still on Paxton.

If the Kev Fairlan noticed the silent exchange, he did not let on. "Will you be all right without me?" he asked, directing the question at Ronja.

"I'll manage." Pressure around her fingers. She cleared her throat. "Thank you for, uh . . . " *Wasting my time and scaring the shit out of me.* "Everything."

"Of course. If you have trouble getting back to your quarters, just ask. Most of us speak the common language."

"*Perlo,*" Roark said politely.

Paxton nodded, his gaze bouncing back and forth between them. "*Pevra.* I'll be seeing you soon." With that, he spun fluidly and started back across the vast room. Ronja and Roark watched him go for a moment, then turned to face each other.

"Why didn't you tell me you were leaving?" Ronja asked.

"Sorry," he muttered as a blush crept up his neck. Genuine regret bloomed in his eyes. Still, she cocked an incredulous brow at him. "I *am*, but they showed up around five and you slept through it. They told me not to wake you."

"Where did they take you?"

"Various spots around the temple, the hangar where they keep their autos and aeroplanes. I think they were trying to show off."

Ronja snorted. "I like your trip better."

"Why? Where did Paxton take you?"

"Later," she said, waving him off. She was not in the mood to discuss her bizarre experience in the Contrav. "Did you learn anything useful?"

Roark rocked his head from side to side. "Their soldiers are highly trained. Swords, hand to hand combat, you name it. Guns are pretty scarce, and I didn't see any stingers." He shrugged. "We knew all of that. Honestly, I think these tours were more about them studying us than us studying them."

"My thoughts exactly."

Roark smiled, slinging an arm over her thin shoulders. "You as hungry as I am, Siren?"

"More," she answered. "No more sneaking off, okay?"

"I promise."

19: COLLISION

Roark and Ronja tracked the mouthwatering aroma of sizzling meat to a serving station at the far corner of the *trié*. Six women in plain clothes stood behind the table, ladling steaming mush into bowls and stacking meat and dried fruit onto plates. Hungry patrons formed a queue at the far end of the table. They ambled over to join the line, speaking in hushed tones.

"Let me get this straight," Roark said. "This guy takes you to a room of fire—*alone*—and you just followed him in?"

Ronja herself blush. "What was I supposed to do? Deck him and run?"

"Possibly . . ."

Someone tapped her on the shoulder. Ronja looked around. The man was in his late twenties with black hair and soot dark eyes. He wore a thick leather coat lined with fur and a broadsword strapped to his back. Fogged goggles ringed his neck, and his cheeks were ruddy with cold. He smiled genially. "Sorry," he apologized in a lilting Tovairin accent. "You are the Revinians, yes?"

"Yeah," Ronja replied with a backward glance at Roark. He moved closer to her, his shoulder brushing hers.

"Kai," the man said, laying a gloved hand on his chest. "You are called . . ."

"Roark."

"Ronja."

He nodded at each of them in turn. Clearly, he was less formal than Easton and Paxton. "Why have you come here?" Kai asked. It was a loaded question, but his tone was not particularly accusatory.

"Uh . . . " Ronja cast her gaze sidelong to Roark, who gave a slight dip of his chin. "We're here to speak to Easton about the war." It was not a lie, not exactly. It was just a different fight than the one Kai was engaged in.

He folded his burly arms, his brow crumpling. "You seek an alliance?"

"It's complicated." Roark offered a charming smile. "But we're here to help."

"This is what matters," Kai said, his easy grin returning. He jerked his chin over their heads. Ronja checked over her shoulder to see the line had moved. They scooted forward. "How did you come here?"

"Jonah and Larkin brought us," Roark answered.

Kai made a clicking noise with his tongue, something like envy rising in his eyes. "You are lucky to sail with them. It is a difficult journey."

Ronja stifled a grimace while her partner agreed politely. The line moved again, depositing them at the edge of the serving table where metal plates and bowls were stacked like cairns. Roark picked up three bowls and passed them out. Kai thanked him graciously. "You are rebels, part of the Anthem, yes?"

"We are," Roark replied.

"What do you do for this rebellion?"

"We're soldiers," Ronja answered simply.

"Ah, same as me," Kai exclaimed.

The line inched up, dropping them off before the first server. Ronja turned to offer them her bowl. "Oh, Elise," Ronja greeted the girl, a surprised smile flickering across her face. "How are you?"

The girl did not answer, keeping her eyes downcast as she took the dish and began to ladle oatmeal into it.

"Elise," Kai growled, sidling up to stand beside Ronja. "She asked you a question."

"Oh, no worries," Ronja said hastily.

"No," Kai barked. "She must learn respect."

Elise glanced back and forth between the two of them as steam curled from the ladle she held. She looked like a rabbit caught between a wolf and a snare.

"You're fine," Ronja told her firmly. She reached out for her partially filled bowl. "*Perlo.*"

"*Melai trist, pestre,*" Kai snapped.

Elise flinched, losing her grip on the dish. Ronja yelped as hot goo splattered across her front. She swore, wiping the mess off her new sweater. Silence flooded the *trié*, thick as oil. For the briefest moment, the two girls locked eyes, understanding growing between them. Kai drew himself up, violet rage creeping across his face. He cranked his arm back and backhanded Elise across the face. The sound echoed through the *trié* like a gunshot. The world swayed as Kai smirked, satisfied. Ronja did not think. She lunged and shoved him to the side. He stumbled, catching himself on the edge of the table. Righting himself, he rounded on the Siren, snarling.

"This is just a misunderstanding," Roark interjected loudly. Ronja scanned the room. Several Kev Fairlans had risen from their seats, their hands on their weapons.

"I will discipline the *pestre* as I wish," Kai replied tersely.

"*Pestre,*" Ronja repeated. She knew that word. It was the

same thing Jonah had called Evie when they first clashed back in Revinia. It meant whore. Specifically, Arexian whore. "Elise is Arexian." She looked around for the girl, but she was gone. The other servers had drawn into a tight knot at the far end of the table.

Kai rolled his eyes at the stalactites. "If you paid attention, you would see the difference between a Tovairin and an Arexian."

Ronja flushed, "I apologize for my ignorance," she said levelly. "But Elise did nothing wrong. It was an accident."

"Was it an accident when her people slaughtered mine by the thousands?"

"My friend back home is Arexian," she countered boldly. "She said the same thing about you." Whispers rustled through the *trié*. Roark drew closer to Ronja, his breath tickling the back of her neck.

"Arexians are liars," Kai spat. "You would do well to stay away from them, Anthemite."

"You would do well to stay away from Elise," Ronja shot back.

Kai took a menacing step toward her. With the grace of a dancer, Roark spun her behind his back. "Hey, we all need to settle down," he said, raising both hands in surrender. His tone was even, but Ronja caught the edge buried within.

Kai smiled, sending a chill down her spine. "I don't think so."

"*Triv*, Kai."

All three of them looked around. He was a bit shorter than Roark, with salt and pepper hair. Stubble shaded his jaw, and faint freckles dappled his light skin. The lines on his handsome face placed him in his early fifties.

"I was—" Kai began.

The older man jerked his chin at the arched entrance to their left. "Go," he said.

Kai shot Ronja a loathing glare, then stalked away, muttering under his breath. Some of the tension leaked from the room. Conversation reignited around them. Still, the man lingered before the Anthemites.

"Uh, can we help you?" Ronja asked.

The stranger arched a gray brow, the corner of his mouth quirking upward. "Odd question coming from someone who narrowly avoided a fight with a soldier three times her size."

Ronja frowned as she attempted to place his accent. There was a hint of Tovairin there as well as something else. Something familiar.

"We had it sorted," she replied tersely. Roark nudged her in the ribs with his elbow. "I mean, thanks."

The man chuckled. "You're quite welcome." He crossed his arms loosely. "Kai is a particularly vicious young man. I think you will find most members of the Kev Fairla are more moderate."

"Moderate is still complicit," Ronja said, mirroring his stance. "How many slaves are there?"

"Fifty, give or take a few." Muted shame rolled across his face. "On the whole island, many more. Arexis holds many Tovairin slaves as well."

Ronja swallowed dryly, dropping her eyes to her boots as a heavy weight descended. Somehow, she imagined that the rest of the world would be better without the influence of The Music. But this was just as bad as life behind the wall. Maybe worse, because people were making the conscious choice to enslave one another. Sickening claustrophobia wrapped around her. There was nowhere to go, nowhere that was not infected with injustice and suffering.

When she finally lifted her gaze, the man was watching her with unabashed curiosity.

"Can we help you with something?" she repeated.

He scratched the back of his head. It might have been her

imagination, but Ronja could have sworn he was blushing. "Yes, actually. I was wondering if I might have a word with you."

Hope ignited in her chest. "Did Easton send you?"

He shook his head. "No, actually. He asked me not to come."

"Ro," Roark said quietly.

She ignored him, fixated on the stranger. Sweat beaded on her forehead. Her pulse made her bones tremble. "What do you want?" Her voice sounded strangely distant, as if she were hearing it through a long tube. "If this is another skitzing tour, I swear . . . "

"Ro," Roark hissed urgently.

"What?" she snapped. Her pulse faltered. He was staring at her with pleading full moon eyes. He looked as if he had just seen a ghost.

"I never thought this day would come," the man muttered seemingly to himself.

Ronja turned back to the stranger. His expression was glazed, distant. "You have her hair, her nose." His hand drifted up as if to caress her cheek. She flinched away. He recoiled, too. "Is it true?" he asked.

"Is what true?"

"Ronja," he said softly. "My name is Darius. I believe I am your father."

20: BELLY OF THE BEAST
Terra

They came to collect Iris when her shirt and hair were soaked with blood. Two Offs grabbed her and hauled her from the room without so much as a glance at the other prisoners. Terra held Evie until they were gone, until all that remained of Iris were the red ribbons left by her dragging heels. Moments later, Henry strode into The Amp. He still wore his wireless headset. "Evie," Terra muttered, holding eye contact with him. Evie did not stir, so she gave her shoulder a rough shake. "Get up. Henry is here."

The techi sat up immediately, her eyes brimming with almost animalistic rage. *Good,* Terra thought grimly. They were going to need that. The girls climbed to their feet. Mouse, who had secluded himself in the far corner of the cell, darted over to stand beside them. He wiped his nose with the back of his wrist, sniffling discreetly.

"Iris will live," Henry said, his monotone sliding through the intercom. "Though, I have never seen anyone take more than three sessions in The Amp."

"YOU SICK BASTARD!" Evie bellowed, jamming a useless

finger at him. "IRIS LOVED YOU!" Her body was wracked with chills. Terra could feel them coming off her skin. "Do you really not remember?" she asked, her voice breaking on the last syllable.

"I remember enough to know that I am better off without you," Henry answered flatly. "I was weak, sick with emotion."

"No, Henry," Evie said. She shook her head. "You were the strongest person I knew."

"I was not sent here to reminisce." Henry slipped his hands into the pockets of his starched slacks, considering them. "Now, are you ready to tell us how to get into the Belly?"

"Yes," Terra answered.

"What?" Evie and Mouse shouted in unison. Even Henry looked vaguely surprised.

"But I will only speak to Maxwell." Terra kept her eyes glued to the boy beyond the glass, praying that Evie would recall their plan through her grief. Thankfully, the techi said nothing, though she could feel the weight of Evie's disbelieving gaze.

"Not possible," Henry said at once. "The Conductor has far more important things to focus on than a few insurgents."

"Does he?" Terra inquired with mock politeness. "Because last I checked, he wanted to take the Anthem alive. Eventually, they're going to run out of food or air." She lifted one corner of her mouth. "Unless you want to take that chance, but I doubt your boss is in a particularly forgiving mood."

Henry did not respond at once. She could see the cogs of his diluted brain spinning through his eyes. Terra held her breath, clinging to her wits by her fingernails. Evie still stared at her intensely.

Then Henry twitched. He blinked once, twice, and nodded. "Someone will come to collect you shortly. Wait on the floor with your hands behind your head." With that, he swept from the room, slamming the door behind him.

If Terra did not know better, she would have said he was angry.

Evie grabbed her by the forearm, wheeling her around to face her. "What the hell are you doing?" she demanded under her breath. "You think they're going to just let us go if we play nice? Are you really ready to give up almost a thousand people, our friends?"

Terra shrugged, exaggerating the movement so the camera would pick it up. "Maybe." She leaned a bit closer to Evie, pinning her with her gaze. "What would Roark do?"

"He would . . . " The techi cut herself off. Understanding clicked into place on her tearstained face. Terra reached up to itch her remaining ear, praying she would get the message. "He would want us to save ourselves," Evie finished.

Terra nodded, relieved she was not alone in her plot.

"What the hell are you two talking about?" Mouse squawked indignantly, moving to stand before them with his hands on his hips. "There's no way in hell Roark would ever—" Terra slammed her bare heel into his toes. The trader swore profusely, hopping up and down on his good leg and cradling his injured foot. "What the hell was that for?" he shouted.

"Cockroach," Terra answered.

"You're nuts," Mouse sputtered. "Clinically insane." He dropped his foot, wincing when it made contact with the concrete.

"So they tell me." Terra shot Evie a meaningful look, frustrated that the boy had missed her rather overt signal. That's what you got when you mingled with civilians.

Violent banging on the cell door shot chills down Terra's spine. Gathering her composure, she sank to her knees and locked her fingers behind her head. She heard Evie and Mouse do the same. The door opened with the screech of rusted hinges. "You," a gruff male voice intoned. "On your feet."

Terra opened her eyes, sliding into a deep, meditative focus. She rose slowly. Booted footsteps tapped toward her, then gloved hands grabbed her arms, forcing them behind her. She held perfectly still as the Off slapped a pair of thick metal cuffs to her wrists. He dragged her around to face him. He was young, about her age with tanned skin and wild reddish-brown hair. His youthful dishevelment clashed with his pristine black uniform. "Walk," he intoned, gesturing at the door.

"You got it," she replied, starting toward the exit. She felt Evie and Mouse watching her from their knees as she passed, but did not spare them a look. The Off was right on her heels, his breath tickling the back of her neck.

"Wait," he ordered her as they stepped into the corridor. Terra did as she was told. He slammed the cell door with a shuddering clang. She watched as he picked through the collection of keys at his belt loop, eventually settling on a large iron one. He jammed it into the lock and twisted. Terra swallowed on a dry mouth. She had felt less alone in her isolation cell.

She had never needed anyone before, she reminded herself. It was no different now.

"Follow me," the Off said, beckoning with a leather-clad hand. She gave him a quick scan in their fresh surroundings. He was something of a looker, were it not for his hooked nose and utter lack of empathy. It was impossible to determine his rank—all the Offs wore the same badges with three vertical bars. His Singer shone bright in the gaslight. It looked almost new.

Interesting.

"Move, scum," he snapped, pushing her forward. She stumbled, off balance without her hands to steady her.

"Keep your pants on," she muttered.

"What was that?"

"Nothing." They walked down the deserted corridor in

silence. The gas lamps bathed everything in an eerie orange glow. They passed thirteen sets of doors before they reached an intersection and turned right down another empty hall. It was as quiet as a tomb. "Where is everyone?" Terra asked.

The Off ignored her, staring dead ahead. Terra rolled her eyes and forged on. Thirteen doors later, they hit another cross and turned left. She tucked the pattern away in the back of her mind. They took two more lefts, a right, and another left before arriving at a door labelled XVI. "Get back," the guard commanded. Rather than waiting for her to cooperate, he grabbed her by the arm and yanked her behind him.

"Easy," she grumbled. Her bicep throbbed where his vice-like fingers gripped it. Using his free hand, the Off rapped on the face of the door three times. Silence. Then it sprang open, quick as a shot. Terra gritted her teeth, forcing down the bile rising in her throat.

"Terra, darling," Maxwell purred. He grinned, his mouth stretching too wide across his pale face. "How lovely to see you again."

21: REVOLVER
Charlotte

Charlotte ran, her bare feet slapping against the stone floor. Ito was ten steps ahead, a symphony of power and grace. Her dyed orange hair rippled behind her like a banner. Anthemites darted in and out of their path, shouting and calling for loved ones. They were not running in any particular direction, but had scattered like ants from a boot. Another sharp scream punctured the babel.

Georgie. She was sure of it.

Her stomach clenched. Ronja had left Cosmin and Georgie in her care. If anything happened to either of them, she would never forgive herself. Charlotte gritted her teeth and poured on more speed. She had already lost her mother, father, and brother. She was not going to lose anyone else.

Ito rounded a canvas tent, cutting into the Vein. Charlotte was hot on her heels. When the lieutenant slammed to a halt in the middle of the wide pathway, Charlotte choked on a gasp, pinwheeling to avoid smashing into her. She looked around desperately. The Vein was nearly deserted. Most of the Anthemites had fled to the far reaches of the compound. Only a handful of stationary guard members and three council members hovered near the edge of the path, eyes wide and jaws loose. She did not blame them.

Commander Wilcox stood in the middle of the Vein. He was almost unrecognizable. Days of scruff shaded his jaw. His gray hair was stiff with grease. His feet were bare, his shirt stained with suspicious brown splotches—*the sap*. In one hand, he held a glinting revolver. With his free arm, he crushed a small child with mousy brown hair to his chest.

Georgie.

Charlotte started forward, her mouth twisted into a snarl worthy of a wolf. Before she could take another step, Ito grabbed her by the arm and dragged her back. "Tristen," the lieutenant called, her voice soaring to fill the cavernous station. "Put the gun down."

The commander jerked, his eyes snapping to Ito as if he had just noticed her. He gripped Georgie tighter, pressing the mouth of the gun to her temple. She whimpered, squirming helplessly. Her dress was torn, her upper lip split. She had tried to fight him off. A thousand horrific scenarios ripped through Charlotte's mind, each worse than the last.

"Commander," Ito barked. "Let her go."

"Or what?" Wilcox spat, his eyes flashing like honed steel. "You'll kill me? Take my command?"

Ito stiffened. The cluster of guards and councilors stared at her, shock and confusion etched into their faces. Charlotte cut back to Georgie. She had squeezed her eyes shut. Tears spilled down her round cheeks. Charlotte could not remember the last time she had seen her cry. Even as a toddler, Georgie was unusually stoic. Only Ronja could get her to laugh. On the rare occasion that their schedules aligned, the Zipse children, Henry, and Charlotte gathered at the Romancheck house. Henry and

Ronja would toss Georgie between them like a sack of flour. That really got her laughing. It was a sound as sweet as honey, rare in the bleak world of Revinia.

Ronja. She should be here. But she left them. Just like Henry.

"Georgie!"

Charlotte spun. Cosmin was speeding toward them down the Vein, spinning the wheels of his chair as fast as he could. His round glasses were askew, his dark hair dripping. He screeched to a halt next to Charlotte and Ito. He was panting, the arteries in his neck throbbing. "WHAT THE HELL ARE YOU DOING?" he shouted. "LET MY SISTER GO!"

"Cos!" Georgie shrieked, her eyes flying open. She began to struggle again, wriggling against the thick arm that restrained her. "Cos, help me!"

Helplessness engulfed Cosmin, Charlotte saw it wash over him. His gloved hands trembled at the crests of his wheels. She laid her hand on his shoulder.

"Tristen," Ito implored in a gentler tone, raising her hands soothingly. Her gun had disappeared, Charlotte noticed with a lurch. "Tell me what is going on."

"No one understands!" Wilcox shouted, fear warping his voice into something monstrous. "You think you can take my command? You think you can kill me?"

Ito took another tiny step forward. "Tristen . . . "

Georgie let out a strangled cry as the commander jammed the revolver under her chin, forcing her head back. Cosmin began to shake beneath Charlotte's hand. She held on tighter, her fingernails digging into his skin to anchor him. "Take another step, and I'll blow her brains out."

"Your grievance is with me, my friend," Ito said levelly. "Let the girl go, and we'll talk about this."

Wilcox laughed, a sound like an out of tune violin. "The time for talking has passed. I know what you're up to. I know you had those two brats spying for you. This one told me." He glared down at Georgie, who dissolved into hysterical sobs.

"He made me tell!" she wailed. "He made me!"

Charlotte sucked in a deep breath through her nose and blew it out through her mouth. Of course, Cosmin had told Georgie they were spying for Ito. "It's okay, Georgie, it's okay," her brother said, his voice cracking like ice. "You're gonna be okay."

Ito dropped to her knees, locking her willowy fingers behind her head. Charlotte gasped. Cosmin went silent, watching her like a hawk. "Tristen," the lieutenant said quietly. "Let Georgie go, and I'll surrender."

"I doubt that very much, lieutenant," Wilcox snarled, spittle flying from his lips. "But you *will* do as I say. You would never risk the family of your precious Siren."

A shadow passed over Ito's neutral expression. "I would never risk the life of a child, no matter who they were."

"Yet you would open up the Belly, expose us all to The New Music?"

Fearful muttering swelled around them. Charlotte glanced around, her heart in her throat. The small gathering of Anthemites members had tripled in size. Curiosity had overwhelmed fear, as it often did. She recognized Elliot and Kala in the expanding throng. They focused on Ito intently. She still wasn't sure what the lieutenant had asked of them in the meeting, but she could guess. Kala had drawn a serrated blade; Elliot palmed a throwing knife.

"They deserve to know the truth," Ito said, raising her voice to reach the onlookers. "They deserve the chance to fight for their lives instead of waiting here to die." Murmurs of agreement rippled through the Belly. Charlotte found herself nodding along with them.

"ENOUGH!" Wilcox roared. It was a wonder his voice did not shake dust from the ceiling. Georgie had gone still in his grasp, her face sapped of color. "Enough! Swear your loyalty to me. All of you!" He aimed his revolver out over the throng, triggering screams of terror. "Anthemites, swear your loyalty to me, or the girl dies. Swear—"

The commander never finished. Someone shot out of the crowd, slamming into his side and bowling him over like a stack of books. The revolver flew from his grasp, sailing through the air in a lazy arc and clattering against the floor. Charlotte lunged after it, but Cosmin was closer. He threw himself from his wheelchair, scrambling after the weapon, his weak leg dragging behind him. He snatched the gun up with his good hand, clicking on the safety and curling it to his chest.

"Cos!" Georgie bawled. Charlotte rounded on the call just in time to see the girl fly at her brother and crash to her knees before him, sobbing. The boy discarded the gun and pulled her into a tight embrace, rocking her back and forth.

"Enough, Sawyer!" Ito shouted.

Charlotte tore her eyes from the reunion. Commander Wilcox was flat on his back, his arms raised to shield himself from the skinny girl mauling him with clawed fingers. Sawyer. The girl Ronja and the others had hauled back from Red Bay. Clearly, no one had ever taught her to fight, but her lack of form did not deter her. Wilcox's forearms were crosshatched with hemorrhaging cuts. He could not seem to get the ninety pound demon off him.

"Sawyer!" Ito cried again. "Stop!"

The girl froze, one hand drawn back to rake across Wilcox's exposed arms. "Really?" she complained, climbing off the stunned commander and padding over to Ito on bare soles. "I could have done him in."

Ito did not respond. Wilcox was climbing to his feet slowly, arduously. He spit out a wad of blood, then raised his eyes to them. "Guards," the lieutenant called out. "Arrest the commander. He is not in a fit state to lead."

For a moment, all was still. The station itself seemed to hold its breath. Then two of the guards on the outskirts of the scene started toward Wilcox. One of them drew a pair of handcuffs from the pocket of his jacket. "Guards!" the commander yelled. "I order you to stop!" They faltered, looking first at each other, then at Ito.

That was the last mistake they ever made.

In a flash Wilcox reached behind him and pulled another gun from the waistband of his pants and fired. The shot was nearly drowned out by screams of terror. The bullet went straight through the first guard's eye, spraying blood everywhere. Charlotte blinked, frozen as the warm fluid splattered across her face. He dropped the second guard without hesitation.

"TRISTEN!" Ito screamed over the uproar. Her hands were raised high above her head, her pistol nowhere in sight. Wilcox trained his weapon on her brow, trembling visibly. "TRISTEN, PLEASE!"

Distant ringing flooded Charlotte's ears. Her eyes dropped to the floor. There, only a half-step away, was the gun Cosmin had discarded.

"YOU'RE GOING TO KILL US ALL, YOU BITCH!" Wilcox bawled, still aiming at Ito. "YOU'RE GOING TO—"

Charlotte did not hear the rest. Her body worked of its own accord, leaving her consciousness in the dust. She bent down, wrapping her fingers around the revolver. It was heavier than she remembered, its belly full of bullets. Her thumb laid the safety to rest. Her gaze and arm lifted, aiming at Wilcox. She drank in his bloodshot eyes, his shivering arm, the unhinged rage soaking his mind and body.

And she pulled the trigger.

22: SKEWERED

"This is ridiculous," Ronja scoffed glaring at the bathroom mirror. "I have nothing to say to that man. We should be tracking down Easton and getting him to make up his damn mind. "

"We will, first thing tomorrow." Roark soothed her. He was perched on the edge of their bed, hunched forward with his elbows on his knees. "The Commander is still considering, and we have no idea where Jonah is. Besides, you just picked a fight with a Kev Fairlan solider. Might not be the best time to have a heart-to-heart with Easton."

"He deserved it," Ronja grumbled, scowling at the fresh memory.

"Undoubtedly," he agreed with a solemn nod. "And I love you all the more for it. But it was risky and not likely to help us win our case."

Ronja sighed and turned back to her reflection, considering. She dragged her fingers through her curls. It was a relief to have a full head of hair again. She had always liked her hair, even if it was difficult to care for. Her green-grey eyes seemed brighter against her deep blue sweater, and she had never minded her freckles. Her nose was a bit long and she could do without the fading wounds around her jaw . . .

She cut the thought short, disgusted. They were in the middle of a war, and here she was primping for dinner. Dinner with a man who claimed to be her father.

The conversation in the *trié* had taken less than five minutes. The stranger had swooped in to break up the mounting tension between her and Kai. Then, as if commenting on the weather, he had revealed himself to be her father.

Was it even possible?

Growing up, Ronja had thought little of her absent father. She was told he had died in an accident at a factory. The only other shred of information she had about him was the photograph her mother had squirreled away in their attic. In it, a man in a long coat held Layla in his arms. In the deepest parts of the night, when Ronja would sneak a peek at it, she generally focused on her mother. It was the only proof she had that Layla had once been human. Young. Vibrant. Pretty, even

Her father—or the man she assumed to be her father—rarely drew her gaze. His face was a smudge of gray. He must have moved the second the shutter clicked. Ronja's focus had always been on survival. Surviving The Music. Surviving her mother. Surviving her mutt brand and the cruel streets of the outer ring. She had never had the time or ability to dwell on the hole her father had left in her life.

"Maybe you can convince him to tell Easton to speed things up," Roark mused, tugging her back to the present. He didn't seem to have noticed her trip to the past. He flopped back onto the bed, his arms stretched out at his sides, his eyes fixed to the ceiling. "Jonah said he helps fund their operation, so he must have some influence."

"Are you trying to bribe me?" Ronja asked dryly.

Roark smiled, but did not reply. She returned to the looking glass again. *He's right,* she thought reluctantly. Darius likely had an in-road with Easton. They needed to take advantage of every possible asset if they were going to gain his support in time.

Soft knocking at the door made the Siren go stiff. Roark got up at once, striding over and prying it open without hesitation.

"Elise," Ronja said, her eyes popping. She hurried across the room, coming to a halt next to her partner. "Are you all right?"

Elise lifted her gaze. Ronja felt her throat constrict. An angry bluish bruise crept across her cheekbone. "Come," the girl said in a hoarse voice. "Dinner." She turned her back on them and started down the hall.

Neither of them moved. "I thought it would be better," Ronja said in a small voice, not looking at Roark. "Without The Music."

"My father never needed a Singer to abuse me." He slipped his strong arm around her shoulders. She reached up to hold his forearm, running her thumb over one of his many white burns as if she could smooth it away. "The Music never told him to torture you, or kill Sigrun."

"Then what are we fighting for?" Ronja asked quietly, looking up at him through foggy eyes. "If this is as good as it gets, what are we fighting for?"

Roark gave a ghost of a smile. "The right to choose."

"Dinner."

The Anthemites looked up. Elise lingered in the middle of the hallway three doors down, fingering her worn sleeve anxiously.

"Go," Roark said, giving Ronja a gentle push. "Good luck."

She leaned in and gave him a brief kiss on the cheek. "I'll need it." His gaze heavy on her back, she took off after Elise.

It took fifteen minutes to cross the temple to the apartment Darius called home. Elise maintained her silence the whole way, keeping her eyes locked ahead to avoid engaging Ronja. The halls of the compound were less crowded than they had been earlier, but the whispers that followed Ronja were twice as thick. Curiosity had been replaced with animosity, which she understood in theory.

But every time she looked at Elise, she heard the ring of Kai's hand connecting with her cheek. Ronja lifted her chin and walked on.

"Here."

She crashed back into her body as Elise motioned to a doorway to their right. Lost in her thoughts, she had not noticed that this particular corridor was entirely deserted.

"Are you coming in?" she asked, anxiety welling inside her.

"No. *Trié.*"

"You're going to work at the *trié*." Ronja rounded out the sentence. Nausea rolled over her as she wondered how often Elise was beaten. She sighed, then raised her fist to her brow to salute her.

"No!" Elise whispered harshly, catching her wrist. "No."

"Why?" Ronja asked, bewildered.

"No!" she snapped again.

The Anthemite raised her eyebrows, taken aback by her sudden ferocity.

Elise shook her head, her heavy hair swishing back and forth. "Tovairin," she said, tapping her hand to her brow and chest. "Arexian." She checked around the hall, then crossed her fingers and pressed them to her heart. Before Ronja could react, she wheeled around and careened away.

For a split second, the Siren held still. Then she crossed her fingers and placed them over her heart. *May your song guide you home*, she thought as Elise winked out of view.

Ronja cut her eyes to the side. The door watched her

reproachfully. She straightened her sweater and tucked her curls over her ear. Before she could lose her nerve, she grasped the doorknob. She froze, her knuckles whitening around the metal. She steadied her breathing, squared her shoulders, and opened the door.

The room was small and intimate with a roaring stone fireplace. A polished wooden dining table stood at its center. Two silver platters sealed with reflective domes sat on opposite sides of the table. Proud crystal goblets filled with wine waited beside them. In the far right corner, a bookshelf sagged beneath the weight of several dozen books. An armchair upholstered in dark red cloth and embroidered with a golden letter *A* squatted beside the case.

Alezandri.

"You came."

Ronja nearly jumped out of her skin. In the low light, she had failed to notice Darius enter through the open doorway opposite her. He was dressed in a fresh button-down and a deep green sweater. His gray hair was slicked back in a manner that did not suit him, and silver rings glinted from his fingers. His expression was stuck in limbo between anticipation and fear.

She could identify with the latter.

"Uh . . . " Every word Ronja had ever known fled her brain.

"Come in," Darius said quickly, beckoning with a jeweled hand.

"Right." She stepped over the threshold and shut the door. The hair on the back of her neck stood on end. How far was the table from the door? How many seconds would it take to flee if this man was not who he claimed to be? Skitzing hell, she should have brought Roark with her; he had offered at least three times.

"Please, sit."

Ronja glanced up. Darius stood by the table, watching her

with quiet fascination. Her hands twitched at her sides. She moved to put them in her pockets, realized she did not have pockets, and clasped them before her. "Thanks," she managed to say. She started toward the seat nearest the door, but he beat her to it. He pulled the chair out and gestured for her to sit. Ronja opened her mouth. Looked at him. Looked at the chair. Then sat. Darius pushed her in smoothly and rounded the table.

"When Easton told me about you, I didn't believe him," he admitted, plucking his folded napkin from the table and spreading it in his lap. Ronja copied him hastily. "But now that I see you . . . " He shook his head, a marveling smile unfolding on his lips. "You have to be. You look just like Layla."

A punch in the gut would have been more welcome. Ronja cleared her throat. "Right."

"I see some of me in there, too," Darius went on. "I had more freckles in my younger days. You have my eyes, too." His smile widened, revealing a shallow dimple in his cheek. "You definitely got your beauty from your mother."

Ronja flushed. The memory of Layla rose in her mind like a specter, jaundiced and snarling, defiled by the mutt blood roaring through her veins.

"How did you come here?" he inquired. He lifted the silver dome from his plate and set it aside. Ronja swallowed a gasp. Steam curled from a pristine slab of fish. Cooked vegetables of yellow, orange, and green mixed with brown rice were heaped two inches high, and three pieces of fresh bread leaned against each other like toppled dominos.

"Is this all right?" Darius asked, his voice teeming with anxiety. "Do you not like fish? I can assure you, Tovairins know their way around a swordfish. Best in the world, or so they say."

"N-no." Ronja cleared her throat, wondering what the hell a swordfish was. "I mean, yes, I like fish. Fish is great."

"Oh, good." Darius picked up his utensils and set about cutting the white meat into smaller pieces. "Please," he said, gesturing at her covered platter with his fork. "Eat. You must be hungry. I doubt you got the chance to eat breakfast this morning after your . . . altercation with Kai."

His tone was not accusatory, but Ronja found herself blushing all the same. "Roark brought me lunch," she explained, lifting the dome from her plate and setting it aside with a muted clang. She had been provided the same meal as her host. Aromatic steam pricked her nostrils, making her stomach complain noisily. She hoped Darius did not hear it.

"How did you come to Tovaire?" he asked again.

"A boat," Ronja replied lamely. Darius took a bite, his eyebrows lifting a fraction of an inch. She looked down at her plate as her nerves gripped her insides. "I mean, Jonah and Larkin brought us from Revinia. By ship."

"I see." Darius paused, his fork posed to skewer a square of fish. Ronja swallowed, wiping her clammy palms on her napkin. The man sighed, his elbows sagging to the table. "I'm not very good at this, am I?"

Ronja shrugged offhandedly. She picked up her fork and used it to dice her fish into smaller pieces. It was as soft as butter. "How am I supposed to know?" she asked, careful to keep her eyes on her food.

"Good question." Darius coughed, or maybe it was a forced chuckle. "I have about as much experience being a father as you have having one."

Ronja tightened her grip on her fork. "A father," she repeated tensely, raising her eyes to meet his. "You're a stranger. How do I even know you're telling the truth?"

Darius stared at her blankly, his lips parted. If she did not know better, she would say he looked wounded. "Did . . . did your mother never tell you about me?"

Ronja let out a cold laugh. The bitterness that had long festered in her chest was bubbling up into her mouth. "No, she never mentioned you." Darius wilted. Ronja looked down at her plate. She stabbed a steamed carrot and put it in her mouth, swallowing it whole. It slid down her throat like a hot pebble. "If she had been well, she probably would have said something," she conceded begrudgingly.

"Well?" Darius asked, straightening up. "What do you mean? Is Layla all right?"

Dread enveloped Ronja. She set her utensils down gingerly. A log snapped on the fire behind her. She could feel the man watching her intently, but could not stomach the sight of him.

"We both have stories to tell," he finally said. "We have years to catch up on. Lifetimes."

Again, Ronja did not respond. The colors of her plate blurred before her, smearing like wet paint.

"I would very much like to know about you," Darius said quietly. "And if you want, I can tell you my story."

Ronja picked up her fork and knife mechanically, still not looking at him. She impaled a piece of fish and stuck it in her mouth. She chewed slowly, allowing the flavor to sink in. She swallowed, then raised her eyes to Darius. "You first."

23: LAYLA

I was born five years before the implementation of The Music, when Revinia was still a monarchy." Darius raised his crystal glass to his lips and took a sip, observing Ronja over the rim. "I was the second son of King Perseus IV. My older brother, Perseus V, was first in line for the throne. He died of the retch when I was three."

He paused, waiting for Ronja to offer her condolences. She remained mute, sticking another piece of fish in her mouth. It dissolved on her tongue.

"When I was five, Atticus Bullon rose to power, claiming Revinia as his own. I assume you know of him."

"Yeah," Ronja confirmed. The name still gave her chills, though she knew he was nothing but ashes. "I know him."

"I would have hoped your mother would have taught you *some* of the royal history," Darius muttered. "Never mind that. When Bullon declared himself The Conductor—ridiculous name if you ask me—he sent his men after our family. All of us, not just the king."

Darius paused again, his eyes falling to his wine. Ronja scarfed down some more rice to distract herself from the phrase *our family.*

"My father had friends in Tovaire," he went on. "Allies to the crown. One of them was the commander of the Kev Fairla at the time, Kostya. My father knew he was going to die. The enemy was at the palace steps. They had set the grounds on fire, a ring around the entire estate. My father decided to surrender to save the rest of us."

"He sounds brave," Ronja said. She took a swig of her wine to avoid eye contact. It was dry and heavy and would go straight to her head, if she were not careful.

"He was," Darius agreed solemnly. "Before he turned himself in, he crowned me King of Revinia." He smiled distantly, the corners of his greenish eyes crinkling. "One of the guards put the crown on my head and it slipped down to my nose."

Ronja raised an eyebrow. "How old were you?"

"Seven." He grinned cheekily, flashing two rows of marble teeth. "What did you do when you were seven?"

Ronja set down her glass with more force than was necessary. The dark red liquid sloshed back and forth, a few droplets leaping over the rim. "I took care of my cousins and mother."

"Ah." Darius frowned. "Layla, what happened to her?"

She shook her head. "Go on."

He sighed, then picked up where he left off. "As soon as I was crowned, my father sent me with his most trusted guard, Levi, to flee the palace. Levi was Tovairin by descent, he knew the way across the sea. Father drafted a letter to Commander Kostya explaining the situation, loaded up a trunk with enough gold to last a lifetime, and sent us into the storm drains below the palace."

Ronja flicked a breadcrumb off the table.

"How we made it to the docks, I'll never know. But we got there. When we arrived at the ship, we found it too was full of riches." He shook his head in bittersweet awe. "He must have been planning it for months."

Darius leaned back in his chair, folding his arms with a sigh. "So we set off for Tovaire. I remember standing at the bow of the ship, watching my home disappear. The palace was on fire, and the sky was almost bright, the flames were so high. That was the last time I saw Revinia for twenty years."

Ronja maintained her silence, scrutinizing Darius with guarded eyes. She had always had a knack for weeding out liars. There were no alarm bells blaring in her head. He was telling the truth, or at least what he believed to be the truth. "Why did you go back to Revinia?" she inquired.

"Curiosity. Rebellion. I grew up with the Kev Fairla. They taught me to fight, to bargain, to be a man. But I was never one of them. Never received any *reshkas*. Commander Kostya was a man of his word. He kept me alive and comfortable. In return, my fortune helped fund their wars."

"Why not just kill you and take the money?" Ronja asked bluntly. "Seems like a lot less trouble."

"The Kev Fairla are not in the business of murdering children," Darius said, a faint edge entering his tone.

"No, just enslaving innocents."

"Arexis did the same," he pointed out. "As did Revinia."

Ronja narrowed her eyes at him, her meal forgotten. "That makes it better?"

"No." Darius gave a slow shake of his head. "Not in the slightest."

Ronja dipped a piece of bread in the sweet sauce that drenched the vegetables.

"Commander Kostya provided me a comfortable life. Mentorship, friendship, purpose, safety," the man went on. "In my younger days I even helped them defend the island at the end of the Coal Wars. But Tovaire was never home. As I grew older, I yearned to return to my homeland, my birthright."

Ronja snorted in disbelief. "Why would you willingly go to that hellhole?"

"When I was a child, it was a wonder of the world." His expression glazed over with nostalgia. "Untouched by The Great War, a beacon of artistic expression and innovation. Equality prevailed, peace reigned. It was a wonderful place to grow up."

"For a prince, maybe."

"I'll admit it had its dark sides," Darius allowed with a grave nod. "Some had it easier than others, though the slums did not exist when I was a child. Nor did the wall. People came and went as they pleased, though in all honesty it was one of the safest places to live on the planet, so few chose to leave."

Ronja rubbed the bridge of her nose. It was difficult to imagine Revinia without its behemoth black wall. It was even harder to picture it as some sort of glowing metropolis. Darius continued his tale before the image could solidify in her mind.

"When I was twenty-six, I stole a ship and sailed back to the Arexian border. Looking back, I was lucky I chose not to dock at port. I dropped anchor in an inlet nearby. Red Bay, I think they called it."

Ronja, who had been taking a sip of her drink, choked.

"Are you all right?" Darius exclaimed over her hacking coughs.

She waved him off, using her sleeve to wipe the wine from her chin. "Go on," she wheezed, blinking back hot tears.

Darius gave her a strange look, then pressed on. "It was a three-day walk to the city limits. I'll never forget seeing that wall for the first time—it was like seeing death. But in the end, I think it just made me more hot-headed. It felt like a challenge."

Ronja put her hands in her lap, clenching her napkin until her fingers ached.

"I hopped on the back of a farming truck and hid under a tarp," Darius said, oblivious to her sizzling temper. "Luck must have been on my side—they missed me at the checkpoint. Once we cleared the wall, I jumped out into what I soon learned were the slums. It was horrifying." He shook his head. "I had seen war, living and fighting with the Kev Fairla, but this was a different level of suffering. How people survived in such desolation, I'll never know."

"The Singers help," Ronja answered flatly.

"Which I realized as soon as I hit the ground," Darius agreed with a nod. "The Music was barely a whisper when I was a child. No one thought it would happen, no one thought The Conductor would rise to power. He was a madman on the fringes of the parliament. But once I saw the Singers, I knew what they were." He looked her straight in the eye and smiled. "I am thankful you grew up away from all that."

Ronja barked a laugh, then swallowed it. The king was not laughing. In fact, he was utterly solemn. "Wait," she said slowly. "You're serious?"

"Well . . . " Darius cleared this throat. "I suppose you were affected on some level, but I hoped growing up in the Anthem with your mother would shield you from the worst."

Ronja felt her blood still in her veins. Her heart seized. Her lungs crystallized. She opened her mouth, grasping at words that no longer held meaning.

"Ronja," Darius said from far away. "Are you all right?"

"The . . . Anthem?"

"Yes, the Anthem," Darius repeated, sounding somewhat bewildered. He reached across the table to take her hand. "Are you ill, darling?"

Ronja shot to her feet, knocking her chair flat on its back and sending her fork clattering to the floor. Shadows swelled in her vision. She began to back toward the exit. Darius followed, his hands stretched before him as if to embrace her.

"Don't touch me!" she spat as her spine struck the door. "What the hell do you think you're playing at?"

"Ronja, darling—"

"Don't call me darling!"

"Ronja," Darius corrected himself, coming to a stop a good three feet from her. His hands were still raised. Not to embrace her, she realized, but to guard himself. "This is just a misunderstanding. I knew your mother was a member of the Anthem, I thought that after I was taken back to Tovaire, she would have stayed. I suppose with the money I left—"

"WHAT THE HELL ARE YOU TALKING ABOUT? WE ALMOST STARVED EVERY WINTER! DON'T YOU GET THAT?"

"No," Darius said pleadingly. "Please, tell me."

"YOU'RE A BLOODY LIAR!" Ronja jabbed a trembling finger at him. "My mother was a mutt, do you hear me? She was sick and twisted and she made my life hell! I lived with a mutt Singer for nineteen years!" She yanked back her hair to reveal her white scar, all that remained of her ear. Sick satisfaction ripped through her when Darius gasped audibly. "She died! Right in front of me! Victor Westervelt murdered her!"

Darius tripped backward, gripping the edge of the table for support. "*Entalia, geresh vies,*" he murmured. "I had no idea. I thought the Anthem would protect—"

"SHUT UP!" Ronja shrieked. "My mother was never part of the Anthem! Someone would have told me! Someone . . . " Her thoughts dissolved her words.

Only the most dangerous criminals were turned into mutts. Their minds were stripped, their bodies defiled, their families outfitted with powerful Singers to keep them in check. Eventually, their unnatural genetic material would unravel, killing them slowly. Petty criminals were beaten or imprisoned. Murderers were executed.

Traitors to The Conductor were turned into mutts.

Ronja felt her knees go weak. Her field of vision shrank to a pinhead. Distantly, she heard Darius calling her name. *How? How had she not seen it before?* Maybe she had always known. Somehow, Layla had always been defiant. To her last breath she fought her Singer. It made her wicked, abusive. Rage was all that could bleed through The Music. But she should have been a vegetable, a mindless slave to The Conductor with a decaying body.

Unless she had a preexisting tolerance. Unless her mind was so strong, her emotions so potent, that nothing could kill them completely. Unless she was an Anthemite.

Ronja.

"Stay away from me!" she cried, lashing out blindly.

Ronja, let me help you.

"You abandoned her," Ronja rasped. She was not sure if her eyes were open or closed. Everything was black and blue, like bruises over her corneas. "She was pregnant with me, you abandoned us." Her eyes felt hot, her face damp and sticky. "You let her become a mutt. You took my mother from me."

The world came screaming back into focus. Ronja found herself on her knees next to the door. Darius crouched before her, concern plastered across his face. She reached up and grasped the cool doorknob, pulling herself to her feet. "Never speak to me again," she said softly. "Do you understand?"

Darius did not reply, his head bowing beneath the weight of her words. His daughter turned around and wrenched open the door, storming away and leaving it wide open. She wanted him to see her go. She wanted him to know she did not look back.

24: PEACE, PROTECTION, PERFECTION
Terra

The Off secured Terra to a metal folding chair opposite Maxwell, who was seated in an ostentatious armchair upholstered in black silk. Once her ankles and wrists were chained, the guard bowed low to him and stepped out into the corridor. He locked it with a jarring clang.

Silence rang out, buffered only by the faint tick of the clock above the door. Terra checked it discreetly. 2:53. In the morning or the evening, she had no idea. She was starting to lose track of time. *Focus*, she commanded herself. She took stock of the room. It was surprisingly small, bordering on cramped, with an oak desk and matching chair like a small throne. The walls were undecorated, but a lush patterned rug blanketed the stone floor.

Then there was Maxwell.

He observed Terra with his chin in his hand, his lips twisted into a smile like curling smoke. He had cleaned up since their last encounter in the clock tower. His black hair had been cut short, exposing his severe bone structure. His watery blue eyes glittered with interest as he drank her in. His altered Singer perched proudly on his right ear. He wore a tailored suit with a high collar and silver clasps. His emblem—the three red pillars—glared at Terra from his lapel.

"Why the lines?" she asked.

Maxwell beamed. He straightened up, touching the button fondly. "I am pleased you noticed," he purred. His voice was oddly disjointed, as if it did not belong to him. "My father's sigil represented the three rings of the city. I always found that rather silly, as he left out the slums."

"How thoughtful of you to consider the needy."

Maxwell adjusted his jacket, stretching his pale neck with a luxuriating groan. Terra tucked her fingers into fists. The desire to rip out his exposed jugular was overwhelming. "I consider each and every citizen in this city, Ms. Vahl. Every citizen in this world, for that matter. The pillars represent the foundation of my new order: peace, protection, and perfection."

"I used to see that all over the place," Terra commented. She settled back into her chair with a mocking smile, her chains clinking softly. "Stealing from daddy, are we?"

The Conductor smiled, but his eyes tightened. "My father was a coward. Even before his body went, he was hiding behind The Music, using it to keep the great people of Revinia devoted to him."

"As opposed to what you're doing."

"He did not deserve their reverence. I intend to." Before Terra could whip up a response, he moved on. "Despite his innumerable shortcomings, my father was an excellent speechwriter and a master of propaganda. Peace, protection, perfection. Why build from scratch when a perfectly good foundation already exists?"

"I assume that philosophy also applies to The New Music," she drawled. Satisfaction erupted in her chest when Maxwell did not answer immediately. He sat back, crossing one leg over the other. The silver buckles of his leather boot glinted in the firelight. "You have information for me," he finally said in a flat tone.

"I do," Terra confirmed. "But it comes at a price."

"How predictable," Maxwell scoffed, rolling his eyes. "Let me guess, you want me to let Ms. Alezandri and the rest of your friends go free."

Confusion pricked Terra. She struggled to keep it off her face. *Alezandri?* "Yes, that would be preferable."

Cold laughter tumbled from Maxwell's lips. He waggled his finger admonishingly. "Come now, Ms. Vahl, did you really think that was going to work?"

"That depends." Terra flexed her fingers, examining her dirt crusted nails. "How badly do you want to get to the Anthem?"

"I could expose you to The New Music at any time," he reminded her. "There would be no more lies."

Terra clucked her tongue, chastising. "And risk the amnesia? How good is the truth when we can't remember it? No. I don't think you will." Maxwell's jaw bulged, his nostrils flared. Terra grinned wickedly, her suspicions confirmed. "So there *is* a glitch."

"Growing pains," The Conductor said with a dismissive flick of his wrist. But it was too late. The damage had been done, and he damn well knew it. For the briefest of moments, Terra had the high ground. "Certain members of my staff have suffered mild, selective amnesia. This will soon be amended."

"How soon is soon?" Terra asked with an innocent tilt of her head. "In time for your best warriors to suffocate in the Belly?"

Maxwell got to his feet swiftly, striding across the room to stand above her. Terra held eye contact with him in the wash of his shadow. "Not bad, Ms. Vahl," he murmured, reaching out to trace the sharp curve of her jaw with his forefinger. Her upper lip curled, but she did not flinch away. "You must know that I cannot free your friends, especially my little bird."

"I said it would be preferable," Terra reminded him. "Not that I expected it." Maxwell pulled his hand back, catching her chin with the edge of his nail. She had caught him off guard. "Do you remember when we spoke on the airship leaving Red Bay?"

"Vividly," he replied in a voice like velvet.

"You said you thought I was being groomed for command. You were right." Finally, Terra tore her eyes from his, glowering at her knees. She could feel his gaze resting atop her head. He was hanging on her every word. "But everything changed that day. I risked everything to rescue those stupid *pitchers* and lost. I was stripped of my status, humiliated." She raised her eyes to him slowly, deliberately. "The Anthem betrayed me. Wilcox can rot for all I care."

"Yet you care for your comrades," Maxwell interjected smoothly.

Terra gave a nod. The more truth she could work into her story, the more likely he was to buy it. "Yeah, I suppose I do. Which is why I am willing to make another deal with you."

Maxwell slipped his hands into his pockets, observing her hungrily. "I'm listening."

"Keep my friends alive and free of all forms of The Music, and I'll show you the back entrance into the Belly."

"Do you think me a fool?" The Conductor hissed. Terra raised her eyebrows. "You cannot expect me to believe you would leave your friends behind."

"I would if it saved their lives. Speaking of, I'll need proof that Ronja, Roark, and Iris are still breathing."

"The Siren and Mr. Westervelt are occupied with other matters. Ms. Harte is recovering from her interrogation."

"You're going to need to give me more than that."

Maxwell narrowed his eyes a fraction of an inch. "I am a man of my word."

"I know my value, Mr. Bullon," Terra said, leaning toward him challengingly. "You can bet none of them will deliver the way I will. They would rather die than give up the Anthem. I'm not so sentimental. Show me my friends, keep them alive, and I'll get you into the Belly."

"And after that?"

Terra twisted her chapped lips into a smile. "You'll never see me again."

Maxwell laughed, a sound like a plate shattering against the floor. "You are ruthless, Ms. Vahl. Is there no way I can convince you to fight for me?"

"I fight for myself," she answered flatly. "But my offer stands."

"Truth from the lips of a deceiver," Maxwell murmured. "You have yourself a deal, little fighter." He stepped toward her again, leaning in so that their noses almost brushed. His breath was cold, stained with mint. "If you make me regret this, you and your friends will die slowly, do you understand?"

Terra showed her teeth, something between a growl and a smirk. "I would expect nothing less."

25: BREAKING
Roark

Roark did not ask what had happened when Ronja stormed into their room after a mere 40 minutes. She was glowing with agony, a barrier against the softest touch. She refused to make eye contact with him, keeping her face tilted toward the floor to hide the fact that she had been crying. She shut herself in the bathroom and turned on the shower. Roark sat on the edge of the bed, listening to the murmur of the stream. Waiting.

Ten minutes limped by, then twenty. Steam crawled through the gap between the door and the floor. Thirty minutes. Roark got to his feet.

"Ronja," he called, tapping a knuckle against the wood.

"Go away, Roark."

"Come on, love. Let me in." The shower continued to run stubbornly. He was just about to raise his hand again when it ceased. The rustle of the shower curtain and the sound of bare feet on the tiles pricked his ears. He stepped back just as Ronja peeled open the door. She had wrapped herself in a towel, hugging it to her chest like a life preserver. Her sopping curls fell to her jaw, the skin around her eyes red and raw.

"Ronja," he began softly.

"Stop." She cut him off, lifting her exhausted gaze to meet his. His heart seized. What he would give to kiss the pain from her. "Just hold me."

He took her in his arms in less time than it took her to request it. He used one hand to cradle the back of her head, the other to pull her chest to his. Lukewarm water began to soak into his clothes. "I'm here," he whispered, laying his cheek on her crown. "I will never leave you."

Ronja gripped the back of his sweater as if to wring the words from him. "I can't lose anyone else, Roark," she whispered. Her voice shuddered like the strings of a violin. Her green gray eyes flooded with fresh tears. "But I will. We will. Layla. Henry. Samson. They're all gone. The Belly is compromised. For all we know, Evie and the others are dead."

"No," Roark countered sharply. He released her waist and took her by the shoulders instead. "They're alive."

"He was only keeping them alive to keep me in line, and I ran." She raised her hands to clutch her skull. Her towel slipped to her feet. Her pale skin glistened, her scars like beacons.

"Ronja," Roark said softly. She did not answer, her eyes staring past him into oblivion. His hands moved to cup her face, drawing her attention back to him. "Ronja, you are the Siren. You freed Revinia with one song. You can do it again. We'll get them out, everyone, even Henry."

"The New Music is so much stronger than the original. Roark . . . " She paused, swallowing hard. "I can see it," she breathed.

Roark stared at her for a long moment. She shivered, pulsing with life and impossibility in his hands. "You beat it before, when my father used it on me."

"What if my voice stops working? What if—what if Maxwell

broke me?"

Roark felt his throat tighten, temporarily restricting his words. "Maxwell could never break you. No one can."

She shook her head, flinging droplets of water across the room. The whites of her eyes were threaded with red. "He—he kept me in that cell for so long. Too long. I hate him so much it hurts. Everything was so loud, so bright. I never slept, I just passed out. I couldn't scream, I could barely eat. He—he took everything from me and I broke, Roark. I was going to do it, I was going to sing for him."

Ronja dissolved into heaving sobs, her hot tears spilling over his fingers. Roark saw her through a rose sheen. He was going to kill Maxwell, slowly. Painfully.

"He broke your body, Ronja," he finally managed to say. She squeezed her eyes shut against his words, shaking her head again. "Your mind, your soul, they belong to you. No one can take them from you. Ronja Zipse, you have always been and will always be the Siren."

He pressed his brow to hers fiercely. "I love you. You are worth more to me than all of Revinia, more than the stars and the air we breathe. I want to take you away from all this. I want to find some quiet corner of the world and grow old with you. But I know we would never forgive ourselves if we turned our back on the Anthem."

Ronja did not respond, but her sobs dissipated to sniffles. Her breath was hot in his face, but he did not pull away. "You're the Siren," Roark said. "We need you. I need you."

"Alezandri," she mumbled.

"What?"

Ronja took a trembling breath and pulled back to look at him. Her eyes were bloodshot, exhausted, but steady. "My name is Ronja Alezandri."

Roark nodded slowly, letting his hands slip from her damp cheeks. "I know."

"You know?"

"Darius found me when we first arrived. When I told you I was touring the temple, I was talking to him," Roark admitted, looking sheepish.

"You lied to me?" she hissed, curling away from him as if stung.

"He begged me not to tell you. He wanted to get to know you on his own terms, and I thought it was best not to interfere."

Roark held his breath as her mouth opened and shut several times, her expression blank. Then she scoffed. "Of course he did," she muttered. "Bloody liar."

"What happened in there?"

"I'm tired, Roark," Ronja said, shaking her head. "And I want nothing to do with that royal asshole."

Royal. The thought was still such a shock. It made him sway on the spot. He had not even known Revinia was a monarchy before The Conductor seized power. Yet here she stood. The last princess of Revinia—a rebel, a mutt, a victim, a weapon—and a girl. The girl he loved. His vision blurred, then snapped back into sharp focus when he noticed she was shivering.

"Here," he said, darting around her to grab her clothes from the bathroom floor. "Time to get dressed." Despite her protests, he helped her into her woolen sweater. He tried to do the same with her leggings, but she snatched them away and put them on herself, grumbling about being coddled.

"I can get my socks," she said, plopping down on the edge of the bed. He knelt before her, taking her ankle in hand. She rolled her eyes. "Is this because I told you I'm a princess?"

"No," Roark replied levelly, sliding a sock onto her left foot. "This is because I love you." She flushed as he tugged the other sock on and got to his feet. Her stomach growled audibly. She placed her hand on it as if to quiet it. Clearly, she and Darius had not gotten around to finishing their dinner. "I'm going to go get us some food, unless you want me to stay."

"No, you can go," Ronja said, waving him off. Fatigue washed over her face. "I think I'll lie down for a while."

"Good." He nodded approvingly. "Good. I'll be right back— you better stay here."

"Like you did this morning?" she shot back with a halfhearted smirk.

Roark winked and started toward the door. He feigned nonchalance, but in truth he was loathe to leave her.

"Roark?"

He froze with his hand on the knob, looking back at her over his shoulder. "Yeah?"

Ronja smiled, just a slight curve of her pink mouth. "Thank you."

"Always."

26: AFTERSHOCK
Ito

Silence echoed through the Belly in the wake of the gunshot. Stillness claimed the Anthemites gathered around the burst of violence. All that moved was the blood running from the eye socket of the fallen commander. Her oldest friend. Dead. Metal rang against stone, breaking Ito from her stupor. Charlotte was backing away from the body, her hands clapped over her mouth. Tears leaked down her face as she stared at the smoking gun.

Charlotte had killed Wilcox.

"Get her!" a male voice bellowed.

Chaos erupted. Screams rushed to fill the silence. Ito launched herself at Charlotte, but was immediately buffeted back by the mob.

"Ito!" the girl wailed, her voice arching over the babel. "Help!"

Instinct seized the lieutenant. She whipped out her gun, aimed at the ceiling, and fired three times. The screams crescendoed, then ceased. All eyes turned to her.

"Let me through!" Ito shouted, her weapon still aloft. "Now!" The crowd parted like a zipper. In the middle of the aisle was Charlotte, restrained by two young men. Ito recognized them immediately as James Mason and his friend Mark Shepard. The girl was silent in their grip, paralyzed with shock and fear.

Ito lowered her aim and started forward. Mark shuffled back, attempting to use Charlotte as a shield. James held his ground, his mouth contorted into his usual snarl.

"Release her," Ito ordered, halting several paces from them. "Or I'll shoot."

"You didn't have the guts to kill Wilcox." James sneered. "What makes you—"

Ito aimed at the ceiling and pulled the trigger. James swore, but it was drowned out by the shot. He too moved to stand behind Charlotte, which was rather ineffectual given that he was twice her size.

"Let her go," Ito commanded again, her tone even and patient. "Or the next one goes between your eyes."

James blanched. He looked to his friend uncertainly. Mark locked eyes with him, then released Charlotte and scuttled back into the crowd.

"Skitz you, Ito," the older Mason brother growled. He let go of Charlotte and shoved her forward by the back of her head. She stumbled. Ito sprang forward to catch her with her free hand.

"You're all right," she murmured, hooking Charlotte to her side. The girl did not react, her face angled toward the floor. Ito straightened up, still holding tightly. "Kala, Sawyer, Elliot," she called out.

Uncertain shuffling, nervous rumblings. Then Kala appeared between two onlookers. She shouldered past them, forcing her way into the clearing. Her blade was sheathed at her hip, but her light brown hand rested on it apprehensively. "Well done, Ito," she hissed sardonically.

The lieutenant chose not to respond as Elliot and Sawyer squeezed into the clearing. The girl sported a split lip, which she wore like a badge of honor.

"Elliot, Kala, take Charlotte to my quarters," Ito said, ushering her toward them. "Keep her safe. Understand?" The two Anthemites nodded, their fingers tightening around their respective weapons as the implications of her words sank in.

"We'll protect her," Kala assured her confidently.

Ito gave a curt nod. Elliot curled Charlotte to his side, coaxing her forward with soft words of encouragement. Her face was blank, sapped of life. She took one step, then two, then stumbled into a tedious pace. Kala walked ahead of them, parting the crowds with nothing but her searing gaze.

"What about me?" Sawyer inquired as they were swallowed by the throng.

"Find Cosmin and Georgie," Ito said, her eyes flicking over the skittish Anthemites. Wilcox's body was still vividly present. The encroaching pool of blood would soon reach her boots. "Take them to my quarters."

"But . . . "

"Now, Gailes."

Sawyer huffed, then trudged off to find them, muttering under her breath.

Ito took a deep breath, then raised her weapon over her head for a third time. Gasps flew up and were immediately replaced by sighs of relief when her thumb clicked on the safety. She stashed the gun in her waistband, leaving her coat open so they could see.

"Anthemites," she addressed them. "Your commander is dead." Silence. Ito waded through it. "It's true. I was planning a coup, but I never meant to kill him. I am not interested in power. I am interested in our survival." She paused, her words sticking in her mouth like cotton. Saying them aloud was a risk, but she knew it was one she had to take. "Wilcox buried us down here for a reason. He swore me to secrecy, but you deserve to know the truth."

"What is the truth?"

Ito rounded on the familiar voice. Delilah stood at the edge of the clearing with her hand on her younger brother Alfie's shoulder. The little blond boy gazed up at his sister with reverence she would never see.

"The truth," the lieutenant answered, "is that a new form of The Music has been released, far more powerful than its predecessor. It does not just dilute emotion, it obliterates it." Anxious murmuring struck up. Ito wet her lips. It was now or never. "And what's worse, The New Music can reach us without Singers."

If terror had a sound, it was the uproar that followed. Ito braced herself. She felt like a rabbit surrounded by wolves. Her gun was useless against hysteria. All she had was her voice, but it was no match for the cacophony. Panic wrapped around her. "Everyone, please!" she tried to shout, but her throat was dry and tight. "Please, stay—"

"Oi."

Ito whipped around. "Sawyer," she snapped, taking the girl aside. "I told you to find Cosmin and Georgie."

The girl rolled her coffee-colored eyes at the ceiling. "Relax. I got them to your office. They're with Kala and Elliot. I thought you might need a little help."

"You need to get out of here, now. There's nothing you can do."

Sawyer grinned, revealing crooked teeth. She glanced down pointedly. Ito followed her line of sight. Her breath evaporated. "Where did you get that?" she demanded. "How did you . . . ?"

"Just take it."

Ito smiled, her tense mouth aching at the motion. She grasped the handle of the megaphone like the hilt of a sword.

"Thanks, I owe you."

"No. I owe you, for Red Bay." She waved a lily-white hand dismissively.

The lieutenant used her free hand to clap Sawyer on her boney shoulder. The girl looked up, her pupils dilating. "I'll get you out of here, too," Ito promised. "Anthemite."

"Uh," Sawyer fumbled with her words, her face flushed. "I . . . "

But Ito was already turning around. Chaos reigned. Somewhere in the writhing crowd, a child was crying. Friends and family shouted at one another, seeking answers no one had. Ito flicked the switch on the megaphone. Static cracked in her hand. She raised it to her mouth.

"ANTHEMITES!" Feedback screeched, followed by a wave of devastating silence. Ito tried not to sway as hundreds of shocked faces turned toward her. She tightened her grip on the handle of the megaphone. It vibrated in her fingers. "I know you're afraid." She laid a hand on her chest. "I am, too. Wilcox was afraid, and he let his fear control him. We cannot let our fear control us."

"What are we supposed to do?" someone yelled.

Ito scanned the crowd, searching in vain for the owner of the voice. "That is not my decision to make," she answered. "We have to decide together. Our lives, our minds, all hold the same value. We have two options. We can stay down here and waste away, or we can find a way out of this grave and fight for our freedom." Ito paused again, allowing the feedback to steal the charged silence. "I cannot guarantee we will survive, but I can guarantee that if we stay here, we *will* die."

Ito opened her mouth to continue, then closed it. There was nothing else to say. All her cards were on the table. She let the megaphone fall as silence momentarily reigned in the Belly.

"Who wants to die in this hole?"

Ito wheeled around, her heart in her throat. Sawyer stood at the lip of the clearing with the other Anthemites, a cocky grin illuminating her youthful face.

"Not me."

"Me either." Delilah resolved. Her milky eyes were trained on the ceiling, a crease between her brows. "If I'm going to die, I want to taste the air first."

"I'm with her," Alfie piped up. The blind girl smiled, slipping her arm around him and drawing him to her side.

"I say we go."

"Me too!"

" . . . sister on the surface . . . "

"Skitz The Conductor!"

" . . . need to see the sky . . . "

Pride swelled in Ito, heating her skin and pumping air into her lungs. Then her eyes found Wilcox. The dull twang of mourning vibrated through her. It felt wrong to celebrate with the body of her friend at her feet, especially when she had all but put him there. But it was hard not to, with hope rippling through the Belly for the first time in weeks.

27: ROAR

Ronja felt the roar in her dreams. It rumbled along her bones, rattling her teeth in her skull. She was the string of a violin quivering beneath a bow. *Get up!* Sharp pain across her cheekbone freed her from sleep. She sat up like a shot, her palm flying to her face.

"Did you just slap me?"

"Get up, princess."

"Jonah?"

He stood over her bed, dressed for battle with blood and dirt crusted on his face. His broadswords were strapped to his back and a small automatic to his muscular thigh. Fear and focus danced in his hooded eyes. He offered her a gloved hand, which she accepted, bewildered.

"Get dressed," he said grimly, yanking her to her feet. "We're under attack."

"By who?" she asked, hurrying over to pull on her boots.

"Vintians."

"They found the temple?" Her left boot caught her heel. She swore, then stomped on it twice to force it on.

"No, the town about a mile out. They're bombing it. We're

helping them evacuate."

"Where's Roark?" she demanded, snatching her fur cloak from the hook on the wall and wrapping it around her shoulders. Jonah shook his head. "I thought he was with you."

Ronja whipped around to check the clock on the nightstand. Barely twenty minutes had passed since he left to get them dinner; she must have dozed off.

"He'll be safe here," Jonah assured her.

"What do you need from me?"

"Half our army is fighting at the port of Yeille." Jonah unbuckled a wicked looking knife from his hip and tossed it to her, straps and all. "We need every able-bodied person to help us get the civilians to safety."

Ronja nodded, her thoughts buzzing as another mechanical roar shook dust from the ceiling. She looked up, swallowing the stone in her throat. *If I die, who will free Revinia?* She pushed the thought aside. How could she ask the Kev Fairlans to risk their lives for her if she were not willing to do the same? Moving with newfound resolve, she wrapped the leather strap around her hips and tightened it to the last notch, securing the blade at her side. It was easily as long as her forearm.

"Put these on." Ronja looked up just in time to catch the pair of leather gloves Jonah had tossed at her. She pinned them to her chest, then slipped them on. They were fingerless, capping off just above her knuckles. "And these." He handed her a pair of round goggles, which she accepted with pinched brows. "You'll thank me later. Come on."

They hurried into the hallway, which was swarming with light and sound. Soldiers armed to the teeth sprinted past them without so much as a look, shouting at one another in Tovairin. Another distant roar flooded the temple. "What is that?" Ronja shouted, clamping her gloved hand over her ear.

"Bombers," Jonah yelled over his shoulder. They rounded several corners, then descended a black stone stairwell. The deeper they went, the colder it became. Still, by the time they reached the bottom, Ronja was sweating beneath her furs. Jonah did not pause for a breath when he hit the ground, so she was forced to drink in her new surroundings on the move.

The size of the hangar put the *trié* hall to shame. It was multiple stories high and so far across she could not see the other side. Aeroplanes, trucks puffing exhaust, and even a handful of armored tanks littered the vast space. Kev Fairlans raced between them, boots thudding and weapons clanking. Silver light spilled across them as a behemoth door slid into the mountain, revealing a dark sky and even darker ocean.

Jonah grabbed Ronja again, dragging her across the concrete. She let it happen, still awestruck. He led her between two idling autos, making a beeline for a huge truck with at least half a dozen wheels as high as her shoulder. The front cabin was twice the size of a normal auto, the trailer as long as a subtrain car. The front door banged open. Ronja stiffened as Larkin stuck her head out, but the girl paid her no mind. She said something to Jonah in rapid-fire Tovairin. He nodded briskly, releasing Ronja and climbing up into the compartment. She moved to follow when a hand gripped her shoulder.

She would know that touch anywhere.

"Roark!" she exclaimed, spinning around to take him by the forearms. He was dressed in his borrowed coat and had snagged a pair of goggles. He touched her cheek briefly with a gloved hand.

"You okay?" he asked over the rumble of engines and voices.

Ronja bobbed her head in affirmation, her eyes darting to the yawning hangar door, then back to him. Resolve sparked between them. Without wasting another second, they hurried to the truck and clambered up into the main cabin, sliding across the cracked leather bench. Larkin was driving, her knuckles white around the wheel. Jonah sat to her right, loading a meager handful of bullets into his gun. Roark slammed the door behind them. Ronja choked on a scream as Larkin stomped on the gas, throwing her head back. In less time than it took her to right herself, they were outside.

Larkin made a hard left, the grooved tires spitting up black sand. Ronja leaned forward, bracing her hand on Roark's thigh. Her stomach dropped. The sky was swarming with blue and black fighter planes flying in formation like birds fleeing south for the winter. Only they were not running away. They were attacking.

The sky was swallowed abruptly, taking Ronja by surprise. Larkin flipped on the headlights, illuminating a massive tunnel with stalactites dripping from the ceiling. "We're parking five hundred meters from the edge of town," Jonah told them, raising his voice to speak over the engine. "We've been assigned to one block. We'll gather as many civilians as we can and lead them back to the truck." He looked to the Anthemites pointedly. "Stick with me and Larkin. If you see anyone in a blue and black uniform, kill 'em."

Ronja nodded wordlessly, her hand flying to the hilt of her blade. The truth about the wars between Vinta, Tovaire, and Arexia were vastly more complex than she would ever be able to understand, but if the Vintians were murdering innocent civilians, she knew where she stood.

"Here." Ronja pressed herself back as Jonah handed Roark a knife. The Anthemite took it in hand confidently, sliding it from its sheath to examine it. "Best I can do for now."

"What about guns?" Roark asked. "Stingers?" His dark eyes darted to the automatic at Jonah's thigh.

"This is mine," Jonah said sharply, giving the gun a loving pat. "No stingers, but we do have these." He dipped into his breast pocket again and produced a handful of small black pegs the size of thimbles. "*Zethas*. Paxton invented them. They're like comms, but they also block sound over a certain decibel. Gets pretty loud in the field."

Ronja pinched one of the *zethas* between her thumb and forefinger, examining it with narrowed eyes. Red light winked from the tip.

"How do they work?" she asked, closing one eye to get a better look at the little device.

"Beats the hell out of me. The man's a genius though." Jonah said, twisting his own *zethas* and stuffing them into his ears. Her eyes flashed to Roark, only to find he was already looking at her, a pair of the tiny devices nestled in his palm. *They block out sounds above a certain decibel.* Possibilities swelled between them. Ronja felt as if she were going to lift off her seat. *Could they be adapted?*

Ronja slipped the *zetha* into her ear. Nothing changed. Either it was not working or the clank of the auto engine was not loud enough to crest the threshold.

"Are we expecting any Vintians on the ground?" Roark asked, popping his own *zethas* into his ears.

Jonah shook his head. "Not yet. The bombing runs are just wrapping up."

"But they'll swarm the place soon enough." Larkin chimed in grimly.

Ronja glanced at her, surprised she had spoken the common language without insulting her. She kept her eyes on the road, her strong jaw clenched. A dangerous vein pulsed at the center of her brow. Like Jonah, she was dressed in leather armor, her heavy black hair braided away from her face.

"Yeah," Jonah agreed. "They will. The Vintians will take the survivors as slaves within hours. We cannot let that happen."

Roark took Ronja by the hand, practically crushing her fingers. Larkin switched gears expertly. The engine screamed as they barreled forward.

"Follow my lead, stay close." Jonah repeated, shouting above the whine of the engine. "We're leading as many survivors as we can back to the truck. Most will be in cellars beneath their homes."

Ronja directed a glance at Roark. Determination shaded his handsome features.

"We can fit sixty in the back, seventy if we squeeze," Jonah went on. He flicked the safety off on his gun, examining it in the semidarkness. "We're in and out, fifteen minutes. I'll keep you on target over comms."

The Anthemites nodded. Ahead of them, light and heat blossomed. They hurtled toward it. Larkin bent forward, hunching over the wheel. Ronja sucked in a deep breath. The world slowed around her, creeping by like a lazy current. They exploded into the war zone..

28: HELLFIRE

The fires stained the landscape orange and red. Distant craggy peaks looked on in horror as the town was engulfed in flame.

Even as it burned, Ronja could see its beauty. High domed roofs, wide cobbled streets studded with cast iron street lamps, ancient pine trees between the houses. And high above them, relentless aeroplanes dropping their payloads.

The truck lurched to a halt in a thick cluster of pines. Ronja threw her palms out to keep from flying into the dashboard.

"Move!" Jonah shouted as Larkin and Roark threw open their doors. Ronja started as the voice burst through her *zetha*, as if his mouth were pressed to her ear. Steeling herself, she jumped down from the compartment and landed on the moss-padded ground with a muffled thump.

The air was hot and foul, choked with smoke and distant screams. Blinking back the sting, Ronja snapped her goggles over her eyes. Roark did the same, then yanked his scarf out from around his neck and ripped the material with ease. He handed one half to her, tying the other around his nose and mouth. She copied him with shaking hands.

Jonah and Larkin flew out from around the other side of the

auto, goggles down and cloths obscuring half their faces. "Follow me!" Jonah called through the *zetha*. Ronja and Roark shot after them at once, their footsteps syncing. They had scarcely taken ten steps before a scalding flash of light lanced through the air. The rush of heat that followed sent Ronja pinwheeling backward. Roark caught her before she could hit the ground.

"You okay?" he demanded.

Ronja did not respond. Her thoughts swarmed. *A bomb. That was a bomb.* There was no doubt in her mind, but she had not heard it. The *zetha* had blocked it out.

"*Yessan!*" Jonah ordered in her ear.

Ronja scrambled to her feet, taking Roark by the hand and sprinting after their allies. The closer they got to the town, the more choked the air became. Her entire body felt heavy, cumbersome. She unlaced her beautiful cloak and tossed it aside. Ahead of them, Jonah and Larkin were only steps from the edge of the town, heading for an opening between two blazing buildings. Screams of fear and agony broke through the shield of her *zetha*. Ronja poured on more speed, Roark hot on her heels. They shot down the alleyway, skidding to a stop when they reached the Kev Fairlans at the intersection of the main road.

"Roark, you're with me," Jonah said, his voice echoing slightly as she heard it through her *zetha*. "Princess, you're with Larkin."

"No!" Roark snapped. "We're not separating!"

"This is my turf, *bevek!*" Jonah barked. "You're not in charge here, you're—"

"Shut it, both of you!" Ronja broke in, whipping her own weapon out and locking eyes with Larkin. "We've got our priorities straight." Something reminiscent of respect swept across the Tovairin girl's face. It disappeared as quickly as it had come. Larkin spun on her heel and beckoned Ronja to follow.

The Siren looked up at Roark, mirroring the muted panic shuddering in his gaze. "May your song guide you home," she said. Giving his hand a final squeeze, she took off after Larkin. Blistering air slammed into her as she burst onto the main road. Chaos. Smoke. Bodies strewn across the cobblestones. Men, women, and children, their eyes open and their bodies mangled.

War.

"Ronja!" Larkin screamed into her *zetha*, already twenty paces down the road. "*Yessan!*"

Ronja pumped her legs harder, her borrowed knife flashing in the inferno. She caught up with the Tovairin girl in seconds, wheezing through her cloth mask.

"You take right side, I take left!" Larkin directed, gesturing with her gloved hands.

"On it!"

They separated, hurrying toward their targets. The first home Ronja arrived at looked like a charred, cracked egg. The roof had been blown off completely along with most of the second floor. Glass littered the sidewalk below, splintering under her boots as she ran around the back of the house. Just as Jonah had said, a metal cellar door jutted from the ground just behind the obliterated home. She banged on it with her fist.

"I am with the Kev Fairla!" Ronja called, praying someone inside spoke the common language. There was no response. She glanced at the hellfire sky. She could not see any war planes from this angle, but that did not mean they were gone. "Please!" She pounded on the door again. "Open up! *Yist fen Kev Fairla!*"

Her pronunciation was horrendous, but she was fairly sure that meant something along the lines of *I am with the Kev Fairla*.

Still, there was no reply. How many seconds had passed since she and Larkin split? Fifty? Sixty? She stomped on the door with her heel, pain rippling through her muscles. "PLEASE! OPEN

UP! I—" A thought struck her with the force of a steamer. Ronja crouched down, bringing her lips close to the crack in the iron door. "*Rel'eev Entalia.*"

Ronja barely had time to jerk back before the door banged open. A middle-aged man carrying a toddler wrapped in a stained blanket appeared, locking eyes with her as he ascended the short flight of steps. Ronja helped him up, then stuck her hand down to assist the next survivor. He was about Cosmin's age, with unsettlingly calm eyes and a shock of dark hair.

"Do you speak the common language?" she asked, rounding on the man she assumed was the father. He nodded, but did not reply. "Is anyone else down there?" He shook his head, rocking his youngest soothingly. "Make for the alley directly across from us," she told him, pointing to illustrate her words. "Our auto is parked in the trees fifty meters out."

The air shivered. Ronja craned her neck back, her nerves knotting. The black and blue war planes were back, silent as wraiths through her *zetha*. "Go!" she hollered, shoving the father toward the street. "Now!"

The family did not need to be told twice. Ronja rocketed toward the next house, which was engulfed in hungry flames.

The next fourteen minutes were a blur. Time skipped like a record through the shroud of her absolute focus. Jonah punctuated it with updates on their time.

Once, a bomb detonated one street over, sending Ronja flying into a trash bin. Now her ribs ached with each breath, making it even more difficult to breathe through the smoke. It felt like seconds and hours had passed by the time she reached the house at the end of the block.

Ronja found the cellar at once. It opened as soon as *Rel'eev Entalia* left her lips, spilling a family of seven—a mother, father, and a gaggle of children ranging from teenagers to infants.

"Follow me!" she cried as she launched into a sprint. They were ten paces behind her, struggling to corral their frightened children, but they were going to make it.

Hope and rattled euphoria surged in Ronja. She had done it. She had cleared her last family. Twenty three lives in total, most of them children. They were going to make it. They were—

White light cracked in her vision and she knew no more.

29: TIMESTAMP
Terra

Terra sat cross-legged on the thin mattress, her eyes closed and her senses unfurled. They had transferred her to a new cell hours ago. Compared to her last residence, it was luxurious. It was equipped with a high, barred window, a narrow cot, and a functioning toilet and sink.

The first thing she had done after the Off locked her up was strip and wash herself with frigid tap water. Sweat and grit sloughed off her in layers, splashing to the concrete and trickling down the drain. The soft part of her longed for a bar of soap and a razor, but this was no place for wants beyond the next breath.

Despite her exhaustion, Terra had not been keen to sleep. Meditation, she found, was a close second. Cicada had taught her the art as child. She used to get restless spying for him in tight spaces. Quieting her mind allowed her to spend hours tucked away in air vents and broom cupboards, gathering information more valuable than gemstones.

Her eyes flickered beneath her sealed lids. Her adopted father had scarcely crossed her mind since their capture. Had he fled the city? If not, was Maxwell still allowing him to live without a Singer as he had promised?

Metallic screeching ripped her from her contemplation. Terra got to her feet, ready for anything. But it was just the slot in the cell door sliding open. Her eyebrows lifted when a plate laden with generous helpings of meat, vegetables, and fresh bread was pushed inside. A tin cup of water followed. No utensils, of course.

Terra started forward, but stopped when something else was slipped through the portal. She scrutinized it from afar as the panel shut. It was a large manila envelope marked with Maxwell's red emblem. The Anthemite padded over cautiously. After a moment of hesitation, she tucked the envelope under her arm and collected her meal, stuffing the roll in her mouth. It was heavenly. Returning to her cot, she set the rest of her food aside, munching on the bread as she tore the package open. She dumped the contents into her lap unceremoniously.

Before her were three photographs, black and white prints labeled with dates and times. Terra examined the first, wiping crumbs from her lips with the back of her hand and reaching for the cup of water. The photograph showed a hospital room with tiled floors and featureless walls. A cot not unlike her own stood beside a dangling IV bag. Hooked to it was a slender girl who appeared to be asleep, her short hair plastered to her brow. Iris.

Terra's eyes flicked to the time stamp. 15:31- 9:18:40. She took a swig of her water, her pulse thudding in her ears. They had been imprisoned for over a month.

The Anthemite set the first photograph aside, bracing herself for the second. This one depicted a young man with dark hair sitting in the corner of a concrete cell, his head thrown back against the wall. Roark, brooding as ever—but alive and without a Singer. *The New Music could be playing over speakers*, she reminded herself. But no, he did not have that look about him. Her eyes darted to the timestamp. 15:33 — 9:18:40.

Setting aside the photograph of Roark, she picked up the third. Her jaw tightened. *Skitz.* At first glance, there appeared to be multiple girls strewn across the floor of a vast room. Then she realized the walls were paneled with mirrors, reflecting a single girl curled into the fetal position. Ronja. There was no mistaking her. Wild curly hair, moon-white skin checkered with bruises. 15:35 — 9:18:40.

Terra's brow crumpled. She stood, downing the last of her drink and kneeling before her cot. She spread the prints before her. Each was taken exactly two minutes apart. Oddly specific. Why had Maxwell given her photographs? Why not just take her to see them in person? He delighted in tormenting them in that way.

Terra clamped down on the thought, but it was too late. She was back on the marble floor of the clock tower, face down with leaden limbs. Her mind was untethered, floating somewhere far above the horrors around her. It was the gunshot that brought her back. Somehow she knew it was him before she opened her eyes. She forced herself to look anyway. No one noticed her stirring in the chaos.

Samson. Dead. His blue eyes glassy and staring straight at her. She had not loved him, but she thought one day she could have. Terra got to her feet again, still scowling down at the snapshots. Maxwell would have reveled in taking her to see her friends as they suffered. So why the photographs? They could be faked; so could timestamps. They were hardly concrete evidence. Dread welled in her chest.

Were they dead?

The thought withered almost as soon as it sprouted. Maxwell wanted them alive, just as he wanted the rest of the Anthem alive. If Iris were dead, they would likely have used her body to torment Evie. If they had killed Roark, there was no way in hell Ronja would cooperate. Most importantly, if the Siren were dead, The Conductor would have already begun his conquest without her.

Terra stiffened. Her field of vision narrowed to a pinhead.

Why had Maxwell not left on his bloodthirsty mission to conquer untold nations? It couldn't just be that he was waiting to get his hands on the Anthemites. He had no real need for them. He had a civilian army of millions willing to sacrifice their lives for him. Hopped up on the voice of the Siren, their own desires wiped clean, they would be unstoppable. No matter how much capturing the rebel enclave would bolster his fragile ego, it didn't make sense for Maxwell to delay his entire operation.

Three weeks until the Vintian ships arrive, Cicada had said. Roughly five weeks had passed since that fateful day, so what was the hold up?

Electric hope surged in Terra, heating the tips of her fingers and toes. Before she could choke it back, a smile burst onto her lips. She reached out and grabbed a slice of what looked like chicken with her fingers, savoring the taste. The photographs, the delay, Maxwell's fixation on the Anthem, his willingness to trust her. Together, they could mean only one thing.

Somehow, the Siren had escaped.

30: CRY NO MORE

The world was reborn in white. Diffuse pain followed, spreading from her core to her limbs. Sound came next, distant cries, pounding footsteps. Only the howling of the warplanes was muted by her *zetha*. Ronja sat up with a noise between a groan and a cough. Tiny pieces of rubble tumbled down her body. She blinked slowly, as if her lids were coated in honey. Her vision crept back. Smoke. Debris. Fire.

"No," she croaked. Her words were muffled by her makeshift mask, which had miraculously remained in place. She yanked it out of the way and ripped off her goggles. They were cracked and dangerously close to shattering. Moving with the grace of a newborn fawn, Ronja struggled to her hands and knees. "No!"

Less than ten steps away were the remains of the house that had been blown to pieces. It was nothing more than a smoldering mound of brick and foundation and wood, five feet high in the middle of the backstreet. And beneath it, the family she had been leading to safety.

Ronja staggered to her feet, limping over to the smoking pile of rubble. She began to push aside the splintered remains of the wooden frame, bits of drywall, pieces of concrete. Hope pierced her chest when a youthful hand appeared, but when she grasped its fingers they were limp as worms. She swayed where she stood. Hot tears swallowed her vision. She blinked them away, looking up. The sky was still painted orange, but there were no bombers in sight.

"*Li-liest . . .*"

Ronja stiffened. That voice. The voice of a child, startlingly close. "Where are you?" she called, not caring if her voice echoed, if the Vintians were already stalking the streets in search of slaves.

"*Liest . . .*"

Ronja clambered over the debris, ignoring the stone that cut at her exposed fingers. "Hang on!" she called. She coughed and sputtered as a piece of smoldering wood snapped, belching a plume of smoke. "Just hang on!" She scrambled down the rubble and landed on her knees. Shoving her tangled curls out of her face, she looked around desperately. A strangled cry ripped from her throat.

Before her was one of the middle children, a boy with tousled hair and a pink birthmark on his cheek. He was on his back on the road, arms splayed, torso pinned by a jagged slab of concrete. Blood pooled beneath him, flowing through the mortar canals between the bricks.

Ronja crawled to him as fast as her aching body would let her. She leaned over him, holding his face in her hands. "You're gonna be okay, you're gonna . . . " She trailed off as he spit up a wad of dark blood, which sprayed across her face. "Stay still!" she ordered. He did not appear to hear her, sobbing and hacking under the concrete. Ronja stood, hooked her fingers under the slab, and heaved.

Nothing happened. She wiped her hands on her pants, then lifted again. Flakes of stone crumbled from the hunk of rubble. Ronja let out a scream of frustration as her boots slipped on the blood running from his broken body.

"*Liest . . .*"

Ronja froze, staring down at the child. His shivering brown eyes were trained on her. Blood ran from his lips to his chin, soaking the fabric of his handmade sweater. Slowly, she released the slab and sank to her knees. He raised a slick red hand, trembling with exertion. Ronja grasped it, scooting closer to him.

What could she say?

What did one say to a child bleeding out in the middle of a war zone?

He coughed again, spewing more blood. His eyes flickered shut, but she could still see them roving beneath his lids. He had minutes, maybe seconds. Before she knew what she was doing, Ronja wet her lips and began to sing.

Be still, my friend
Tomorrow is so far,
Far around, the bend
Cast your troubles off the shore . . .

Her voice was raw with smoke and heat, but it did not matter. Before her, the physical manifestation of her voice bloomed. It had changed since the first time she saw it at Red Bay. It used to be black, studded with distant pockets of color. Now, it was nearly translucent, luminous and ever shifting. It wrapped around the boy like ribbons and bows.

Unlace your boots and cry no more
Because today, my friend
I promise you are on the mend

As the verse came to a close, his frantic breaths slowed to

easy sighs, then dissipated altogether. His grip loosened on her hand. His arm became heavy. Ronja laid it down gently. Her tears splashed onto his face, diluting the blood and grime there.

"Alezandri."

Ronja spun, still crouching low, and whipped out her knife. She let it fall at once. "Larkin," she said hoarsely. "I tried to save him."

The Kev Fairlan girl stood at the mouth of an aisle between two broken homes. Her tawny face was black with soot, her braids frayed and dusted with debris. A trail of dried blood was crusted on her temple. "I know," she said. "Get up."

Ronja did as she was told, using the slab as a crutch. Her knees and hands were drenched with red, which was quickly turning brown. "Jonah and Roark—" she started to ask.

"Headed for the auto."

Ronja cut her eyes to the boy at her feet. Despite the carnage, a faint smile clung to his stained lips.

"Alezandri, *yessan*."

Moving mechanically, she started after Larkin, who was already running toward their exit point. Across the deserted street, past the demolished houses. Nothing moved but their sprinting bodies and the smoke curling from the homes turned graves. Through the alley, past the edge of town. Up ahead, Ronja could see their auto waiting among the pines.

"*Yessan!*" Larkin shouted again. Ronja pumped her legs harder, her injured ribs screaming at her to stop. By the time they reached the auto, her vision was black and blue. She stumbled to a graceless stop as the cabin door popped open. Distantly, she heard Larkin yelling in Tovairin. Then strong arms hoisted her into the compartment like a sack of flour.

"Go!"

A door slamming. An engine rumbling. Tires screeching. A

soft touch against her cheek. Ronja sucked down a lungful of oxygen. Her vision snapped into sharp focus. She was back in the truck, heading toward the jagged heights of Entalia. Jonah was behind the wheel, shrouded in soot and sporting a fresh gash on his exposed forearm. Larkin was on the opposite side of the cabin, staring out the windshield with a vacant expression. Ronja and Roark were sandwiched in the middle.

Roark. He was speaking to her in hushed tones. He was pale beneath the filth on his face, but appeared to be unharmed.

"Roark . . . are you okay?" Ronja rasped.

"Fine, love, fine," he murmured. He curled her toward him, holding her tight against his chest. She could feel his heart thundering through his heavy jacket. The cloth did not smell like him. It smelled like smoke and death. "What happened?"

"I lost them, I lost the last family," she breathed.

"You saved dozens, Ronja," Roark reminded her, smoothing her stiff curls with his gloved hand. "They're in the back, they're going to live because of you."

"I ran ahead," she whispered. "I left them behind. I—"

"*Kel resi infini, kel pien levest.*"

Ronja jerked away from her partner, twisting to stare at Larkin. She was still gazing out the windshield. Exhaustion clung to her as thick as the grit caked on her skin and armor.

"What does that mean?" Roark inquired, his tone guarded.

Larkin cast her eyes to him, then to Ronja. There was no malice there, only resolve. "Let the dead sleep, let the living dream." Silence fell, broken only by the guttural hum of the engine. They were not pursued as they raced back to the base. Ronja let her lids drift shut when they passed into the tunnel, her head on Roark's shoulder. As sleep claimed her, she imagined she was back in Revinia, comfortably numb beneath her Singer, still driving a subtrain headed nowhere.

31: BEDSIDE MANNER
Iris

Waking up felt like dying. Every fiber of Iris's being was twisted, knotted, and frayed. Her head was the worst, aching and pulsing like a relentless drum. She raised her hand to touch it. Sharp pain pricked her wrist. She forced her eyes open. The world blared white, then gray, then drew into focus.

She was in a bare bones hospital room with white walls. They had placed her on a small cot with bleached sheets and a thin pillow. The sting at her wrist was an IV. Iris followed the clear tubing with her eyes, landing on a bag of fluid dangling above her. Saline. They were keeping her alive to torture her again. The irony was not lost on her, but she did not have the energy to crack a smile.

"You're awake."

Iris jerked beneath her crisp sheets, sitting up on her elbows. Terror crawled into her throat. "Henry," she rasped. The boy sat directly opposite her cot, legs crossed and arms folded. His Singer glinted from the crest of his ear, and the red badge on his chest stared her down. "What are you doing here?"

"I was sent to observe you," he replied tonelessly.

Iris felt her hopes wither; a small part of her had hoped some fragment of his former self had drawn him to her room. "How long was I out?"

"Seventeen hours and nineteen minutes."

"Where is my family?"

Henry cocked his head to the side. "Family?"

"Yes, family." Iris winced as she maneuvered herself into a fully upright position. "Evie and the others are my family. You were part of that family, too. You still are."

"No, I am a faithful servant of The Conductor."

Iris opened her mouth to rebut him, but a question came out instead. "What happened to you, that day at Red Bay? We heard the shot over the radio. We thought you were dead." *Maybe the stars are alive after all.* His last words still crept up on her when she was on the edge of sleep. Part of her wished they *were* his last words. Henry—the Henry she knew—would rather have died saving his family than live as a shell.

"The details of my survival are unimportant," Henry told her.

"You don't remember," Iris murmured. He did not answer, but his dark eyes flickered subtly. That confirmed Evie's theory, then. Extended exposure to The New Music caused partial amnesia. "Do you remember me?"

"I remember your trade, mutilating abiding citizens, cutting them off from The Music."

"I set them free," Iris snapped, surprising herself with the power of her voice. "You know that."

"No, you burdened them with emotion." Henry uncrossed his limbs and leaned forward in his chair.

Iris glowered at him, refusing to shrink herself. "Even Maxwell sees the value in emotion."

"The Conductor understands that honed rage can be a valuable tool in small doses."

"What do you feel right now, Henry?" Iris asked quietly, pinning him with her gaze.

Henry drew himself up in his seat. "I am free of emotion by the hand of The New Music."

"What about when you killed Samson? What did you feel then?"

Henry got to his feet swiftly, advancing on her until he loomed at the edge of her bed. She raised her chin, feigning defiance as she scanned his features. There was *something* there, in the tightness around his mouth, at the corners of his eyes. Or maybe it was just her scrambled brain playing a cruel joke on her. Henry had the capacity to feel rage when triggered by the Siren's voice—was it possible to draw it out without her intervention?

"I am honored to serve The Conductor," he said in a dangerously soft voice. "The traitor dug his own grave by joining the rebels."

"No, you don't get to run from the blame. You murdered him." Iris swallowed the burgeoning lump in her throat. What would happen, if she pushed him too far? "He was your blood brother. He taught you to read, to fight, to play the drums with your hands."

"Enough," Henry said through his teeth. He clutched the bedrail and bent toward her, his knuckles whitening. "I do not have to listen to you, scum."

"Then shut me up," Iris dared him, opening her arms wide, ignoring the way her IV tugged at her skin. "Go on, do it. Kill me. I can't stop you."

"The Conductor wants you alive."

"To torture me." The surgeon shook her head with a reckless laugh. "Another round of The Lost Song will kill me." It was not a bluff. Henry had said she could tolerate three rounds in The Amp, but she knew her body. She knew The Music. She was one note away from system failure. It should have scared her. Not long ago, it would have. But she did not fear death anymore. She only feared leaving Evie alone in this horrible place. "If you think torturing me is going to get the others to give up the Anthem, you're wrong."

"You are mistaken," Henry replied smoothly. "Your comrade has already made a deal. She will lead us into the Belly within a day."

Iris felt the blood drain from her face. Her lips split, but no sound came out. No. It was not possible. They were trained to guard their home with their lives. Even Evie would never crack, she was almost sure of it. Something didn't add up. "Terra," Iris muttered under her breath. "Terra did this." Dozens of different scenarios cycled through her head. Betrayal. Self-preservation. Treachery. Or—a ruse, a plan.

Henry did not answer. Instead, he spun toward the exit. It was then Iris noticed that he was trembling. "Sleep," he said in a perfectly level voice. "You will need it." Before she could reply, he opened the metal door and slammed it behind him, leaving her alone with her scattered thoughts.

32: DISCARDED
Henry

He stood at the center of his bedroom, his fists clenched at his sides, his eyes trained on the floor. The New Music shivered against him, a palpable entity running over his skin, his clothes. It was as unpredictable as a skittish stray. One moment, it was high and feather light. The next, it would threaten to crush him.

He would let it, if The Conductor determined it best.

What did you feel? the girl had asked. He recognized her from his past life. Iris Harte, the surgeon hell-bent on separating people from their Singers. From the very thing that prevented them from descending into chaos.

Evil, The New Music hissed without words.

What did evil look like, he wondered vaguely. Did it have a face, a name? What did it matter?

A knock at the door. Henry turned on his heel and opened it at once, standing at attention. He relaxed slightly when he saw it was only Thomas. Like Henry, he had been a lost rebel before The Conductor found them. He had not been a member of the Anthem, but of a small group of anarchists that had cropped up in the middle ring after the Siren started spewing her blasphemy.

"The Exalted Conductor requests your presence in ten minutes," Thomas informed him.

"Thank you."

Thomas saluted him, then retreated down the stone hallway, his reddish hair glowing in the gaslight. Henry shut the door, turning back to face his pristine cot. His room was bare and clean. The Conductor was incredibly generous to allow him and the other upper level Officers to stay in the palace basement.

What did The Conductor want with him at this hour? The New Music pinched him and he shook his head. Questions were counterproductive. He grabbed his stiff jacket from the hook and put it on with a snap. He did up the clasps slowly, painstakingly. His fingers hovered over the red badge at his chest. It felt oddly warm beneath his fingertips. He flicked off the lights and stepped into the hall, shutting the door behind him. The lock on his door had been disabled.

It did not matter. He had nothing to hide.

Henry made his way to the far end of the palace basement, walking with his hands behind his back. It was the middle of the night, so he encountered few Offs along the way. Those he did intercept paused to salute him. He nodded back politely, but did not stop. The Conductor did not like to be kept waiting.

By the time he reached the elevator, Henry had only two minutes to spare. He fidgeted impatiently as the rickety gate rolled open, revealing the aged wooden interior of the elevator. Stepping inside, he punched the button labeled "5." The elevator sealed itself and began its shuddering ascent.

What did you feel when you killed Samson? The voice of the rebel pricked him through the protective shield of The New Music. It was like a buzzing gnat he could not shake. The way she had looked at him, her eyes luminous and wet, her face crusted with her own dried blood.

His stomach heaved. He must have eaten something rotten.

The elevator ground to a halt and opened with a polite peal of chimes. A shining reception hall sprawled before Henry, cold and fine. Towering windows with crystal panes looked out over the palace grounds. Between them, black and red banners hung proudly. The hall was empty, save for a servant girl in a black shift polishing a vase halfway down.

Henry started forward, his boots tapping against the polished marble. His gaze swept to the side. The winter moons were bloated in the midnight sky. The palace grounds were pitch black, save for the blazing searchlights that swung back and forth above the gates a hundred yards out. Beyond the walls, Revinia shone like a beacon. It expanded as far as the eye could see, an inferno of electricity and brass. The great clock tower loomed large in his view, less than a mile away.

What did you—?

"Henry."

"Sir." Henry snapped to attention. Somehow he had failed to notice The Conductor step out of his chambers and into the hall. "You sent for me."

"Right on time, as usual." The Conductor smiled widely. His teeth were as bright as the marble beneath them. He wore a black silk robe. His feet were bare and pale. He nodded toward the metropolis, moving up to stand beside Henry. "Beautiful, isn't it?"

"Yes, sir."

"Tell me what you see, Mr. Romancheck," The Conductor said, clapping an enthusiastic hand to his shoulder. He gave Henry a little shake, gesturing at the view.

"The palace grounds, the clock tower, the—"

"Peace, Henry." The Conductor dug his fingers into his shoulder. In the past, it might have hurt him, but he had been freed from the burden of pain. "You're looking at peace that I proctored."

"Yes, sir."

"Shut it." Henry tripped forward as he was whacked on the back of the head. Confusion sparked in him, but was instantly doused by The New Music. "Ah, you do not feel pain, do you boy?"

"No, sir."

The Conductor rolled his eyes with a huff, then paced forward to stand before the window. Henry remained rooted to the spot. He had not been invited to stand beside him. "What do you think of the girl, Terra?"

"Sir?"

The Conductor sighed, silhouetted against the light of the moons. "What memories do you have of her?"

Henry wracked his brains, torn between not wanting to disappoint his leader and the frantic hum of The New Music in his ear, telling him not to poke at the disjointed memories. "She— she was strong. Cruel. But dedicated. Sir."

"She's a born commander, that one." The Conductor chuckled to himself, slipping his hands into the pockets of his robe. Still, he did not turn around. "Do you think I am a fool?" he asked softly.

"S-sir?"

"DO YOU THINK I AM A FOOL?" Rather than waiting for Henry to answer, he stalked over to a nearby table and snatched up a decorative vase. He hurled it toward the elevator with a savage cry. It shattered against the marble. Someone screamed. Henry rounded on the sound to find the servant girl staring at them with wide eyes. "COME HERE, GIRL!" The Conductor shouted, spit flying from his lips.

The girl shuffled toward him slowly. She was short and thin with milky skin. As she drew closer, Henry saw she was covered in angry purple bruises centered around her neck and wrists. In the end, they were not what secured his gaze. It was her naked right ear. She did not have a Singer.

"You look surprised, Mr. Romancheck," The Conductor said, grabbing the girl by her battered wrist and yanking her to his side. She was stiff as a board, her gray eyes on the floor.

"She . . . she has no Singer."

"No, indeed." He tucked a strand of limp blond hair over her bare ear. She shivered at the touch, biting her lip until it bleached white. "The New Music has saved this city. Soon it will save the world. But forgive me, Henry, when I tell you that you lot have become—well—boring."

"Sir?"

"Valorie here spent her entire life without a Singer, living off scraps in the slums with her brother." The Conductor gave Valorie a rough shake. Henry felt his stomach tighten again. He wracked his brains, trying to remember what he had eaten that day.

"Her brother gave me too much trouble—I stuck a Singer on him weeks ago. But I kept this one as she is. She does keep things interesting."

Henry did not respond. He could not seem to take his eyes off the girl.

"I have never been betrayed, Henry," The Conductor continued. "Because I cannot be betrayed. If you so much as consider aiding the enemy, The New Music will destroy you. I will destroy you."

"I would never betray you, sir," Henry answered vehemently, bringing his gaze back to The Conductor.

"Even if it were Iris in my grasp? Or perhaps, Ronja?"

The New Music surged in Henry's head, battering the walls of his skull. His vision went white. He blinked rapidly. "I would never betray you, sir," he repeated.

"My little bird will return soon. She has flown far away."

There was a wistfulness in The Conductor's voice that did not match his exterior. "I want to ensure that there will be no problems when she returns. She must be punished, of course, before my conquest can begin properly."

"Of course, sir."

The air was oddly thin.

What did you feel?

"Excellent," The Conductor said with a grin. "Tomorrow, you will take Terra into the city to confirm her claim. Watch her carefully, and report back to me."

Henry raised his hand to salute his commander. "Yes, sir."

"The New Music hears you, Henry." The Conductor took Valorie by the waist, drawing a whimper from her bruised mouth. She closed her eyes, shutting out the world. "I hear you." Without another word, he swept past Henry, dragging the girl with him.

The boy remained in the hall long after the door slammed.

33: THE AURA

The last thing Ronja wanted to do was eat, but both her body and Roark insisted. She gulped down a steaming bowl of soup, barely tasting it, then chased it with two slices of bread and a glass of water. "Happy?" she asked, setting her empty cup on the table.

Roark smiled, but did not reply. They sat across from each other at one of the *trié's* long tables, which had been pushed to the far end of the great room. The other side was packed with refugees from the town. Kev Fairlans were handing out blankets, bottles of water, and bowls of the same reddish soup Ronja had choked down. In the southeast corner, a medical station had been set up to treat minor burns and wounds. Those with lacerations, broken bones, and missing limbs were taken to the infirmary. The drone of conversation was enough to drown out their horrific screams, but they still echoed through her brain.

When they arrived back in the hangar, the mood had been frantic and grim. Jonah opened the back of the truck and the townspeople flooded out. Some cried, some clutched at their loved ones, others were silent. They were gray-faced and exhausted, so quiet they could bleed into thin air. Ronja and

Roark quickly discovered that the rebels had a well-oiled system when it came to processing hundreds of frightened civilians. The Anthemites tried to assist them, but mostly ended up getting in the way. Defeated, they had retreated to the far end of the *trié*.

"How are you feeling?" Roark asked.

Ronja reached up to brush her temple with her fingertips. It still ached distantly, but it was nothing compared to the constant barrage of pain The Music had once inflicted. "Fine."

"How many do you think there are?" Roark asked, looking out over the throngs of listless Tovairins.

"Two hundred, three?" she guessed. Whatever the number, there should have been seven more. They fell silent for a time, hypnotized by the shifting crowds. Ronja stiffened when she spotted Kai walking with purpose across the room. He approached an elderly woman in a deep blue headscarf and threw his arms around her, holding her while she wept. Ronja turned away, her skin prickling.

"Strange," Roark murmured, following her line of sight to the heartfelt exchange. There was a question ringing in the word, one he did not need to voice. The same one was on her mind. How could someone demonstrate such cruelty, then turn around and act with such warmth?

"I guess no one is all one thing," Ronja finally concluded.

Roark chuckled. "Well said."

Faint warmth washed over Ronja, tugging a smile onto her mouth. Her face fell when a thought struck her. She leaned toward him across the table. "Roark, the *zethas*."

The boy dug into his pocket and produced the two little black orbs Jonah had given him, weighing them in his open palm. "Do you think . . . ?"

"Yeah," Ronja said with a nod. She took one of the *zethas* from his hand, pinching it between her thumb and forefinger.

"Jonah said Paxton invented them. I think Evie would like him. Mouse, too."

"Yeah," Roark agreed. "Yeah, they would." He closed his fingers around the solitary *zetha*, his brow furrowed. "We're not talking about the bigger problem we have here."

Ronja snorted, rolling her eyes at the stalactites far above them. "You're going to have to be more specific."

"The Kev Fairlans are fighting their own battles, and by the looks of it they're outgunned. Badly. There is no way in hell they're going to leave this place defenseless."

"But if Maxwell starts his insane mission, they're doomed."

Roark sighed, sagging visibly. He was covered in filth from the rescue operation, but somehow still managed to look startlingly handsome. It made Ronja want to kick him in the shins.

"We know that," he said. "They do not."

Ronja wracked her brains, rolling the *zethas* between her fingers. "Maybe . . . "

Her thoughts evaporated. Goosebumps flared all over her body. Across the room, haunting music was rising from the crowd, a lone string instrument among the rebels and refugees. She stared, hypnotized as her synesthesia kicked in, threading silver and green through the air. Her heart expanded. She had almost forgotten the ecstatic beauty of real music. It was the creeping fingers of The New Music that stalked her dreams. Ronja dropped her eyes to Roark. "I wish you could see the music." she said, glancing up at the twisting bands of light and sound. "It's beautiful."

Roark shook his head, a rueful smile tugging at the corners of his mouth. "With you in the room, everything pales, Siren."

Ronja rolled her eyes but felt her chest swell, battering away the hopelessness ensnaring them. She might have lifted from the floor had movement to her right not caught her eye. Her insides turned cold as time scraped to a halt. In the space between the crowds and the tables stood a man, his face tilted toward the ceiling. She followed his line of sight to the bands of green and silver hovering above the *trié*.

Before Roark could stop her, she leapt to her feet and started toward him. He did not see her coming until she was practically on top of him.

"Ronja!" Darius exclaimed, backpedaling away from her. "I had no idea you were going on the rescue operation."

Darius was dressed in the uniformed armor of the Kev Fairla. The rings on his fingers had been exchanged for thick work gloves and his gray hair was matted with sweat and dirt. She took him in through narrowed eyes. "What were you looking at, just now?" she demanded, keenly aware that the pulsing colors were growing brighter as the song progressed.

His surprise was smoothed over by quiet understanding. "Easton told me they call you the Siren," he finally said, his voice barely audible over the mournful strings. "I thought it was just a coincidence. The Anthemites always were fond of their mythological codenames."

"Coincidence?" Her heart was like a jackhammer in her ribs. It nearly drowned out the song. "What are you talking about? What did you see?"

"The same thing you're seeing right now," he said. "The Aura." Ronja felt the world tilt. Darius, the *trié*, the colors, all bled from existence. "Your mother would have told you about it, had she been able."

Her vision clicked back into focus at the mention of Layla. "What is it?" she whispered.

"Your birthright." Darius lifted his stubble-shadowed chin to look at the Aura, reverence and nostalgia flickering in his gaze along with the reflection of the colors. "Revinia was so much more than just an aesthetic capital. It was the birthplace of song, long before our family came to rule it."

"Birthplace of song. What does that mean?" Ronja pressed him frantically.

"It means you are far more powerful than you know, Ronja Alezandri," Darius said, turning to her. His gaze pinned her in place, making her feel like a bug under a magnifying glass. "Most of the lore has been lost to time and The Conductor's warpath. What we do know is that forces beyond our fathoming came together to lace the city—and then our bloodline—with music."

"That—that's impossible," Ronja stuttered, stepping away from him. "What, are you saying this is *magic*?" No, it was ridiculous. She and the other Anthemites had joked about it in the past, but it was just that, a joke. It was just frequencies clashing, or synesthesia, or some leftover neurological scarring from The Music, or . . .

"I am saying it is beyond our understanding."

"Roark said it was synesthesia," Ronja shot back, a twinge of desperation in her voice.

Darius studied her. Orchestral music swirled around them, its physical manifestation riding the air currents like birds. Then he turned his eyes to the ribbons of light. Slowly, he raised a gloved hand toward them. His eyelids flickered shut as concentration rolled over him. For a heartbeat, nothing happened.

Then Ronja felt the world kick beneath her feet.

One of the silver threads peeled away from the mass, slithering toward his outstretched hand. It snaked around his forearm and pooled in his hand. Its edges were blurred, like the boundaries of a dream. Ronja reached out slowly, her gritty fingers trembling in the pulsing glow. She flinched when her hand passed through it sending warmth coursing along her bones. "It's real," she whispered. "I can feel it."

"With time, you can learn to control it, if you wish," Darius said, examining the gracile light with a faint smile. "Music is more than just beauty, Ronja. It is life." The song drew to a close, the last mournful notes reverberating through the hall. Bittersweet applause followed. The crowd dispersed as sobriety was reinstated, parting to reveal a young man sitting on an upturned crate playing what looked like an elongated cello. He was covered in dirt, dressed in a newsboy cap and baggy shirt. He grinned broadly as rebels and refugees alike clapped him on the shoulder and tousled his hair. She looked back at Darius just in time to see the glistening thread evaporate from his hand like fog in sunlight.

"I thought I was insane," Ronja finally said, her eyes glued to his now empty palm.

"Not insane," Darius replied with a knowing chuckle. "Gifted."

"What can you do?" *Can you do the things I can do? Can you kill The New Music?*

"Our gifts vary. My brother was a healer. He could stitch skin together with song, make a stomachache disappear with a lullaby. Me, I could sing the truth out of people. All of us can see and touch the Aura, make it solid."

"I freed Roark from The New Music by singing," Ronja said, switching her gaze to Darius's face. He appeared calm, if weary. Utterly different from the man she had encountered at dinner. "I freed Revinia, too at least, until Bullon cut off my broadcast. Did—did anyone in our family ever do anything like that?"

The shadow of a memory passed over his weathered face. "Even if they could have, they never got the chance. The Conductor wiped them out."

"Which is why he came for the whole family, not just the king," Ronja realized with a chill. "And why he was so afraid when he recognized me."

Darius nodded patiently as she continued to sift through her tangled thoughts.

It was insane, preposterous. Yet it made more sense than any other theory she had come up with since she first saw The New Music writhing in the air at Red Bay. Ronja bit her lip. Not six hours ago, she had stormed out after railing at Darius and ordering him never to speak to her again. She cleared her throat, her face heating. "I—"

"I believe I owe you an apology, Ronja," he broke in. The Siren stared up at him, her mouth hanging open dumbly. He scratched the back of his head, something she had come to associate with Roark. "I was terrified to meet you, and I made an ass of myself. I wanted to impress you, but I believe I only succeeded in showing you the worst parts of me." He gave a tiny, hopeful smile. "Can we start over?"

He held his hand out for her to take, the same one that had moments ago been wrapped in the ethereal light of the Aura. Ronja twisted around, suddenly remembering Roark. He was watching them from the table, a bemused smile on his face. Their eyes met, and he gave a subtle nod. *Go.* She turned back to Darius. "Can you teach me how to control my voice, how to become more powerful?"

"Yes."

Ronja grasped his hand firmly. "Then we have a deal."

34: BLOODLINES

Darius begged Ronja to get some rest before they began their first lesson, but she insisted they start immediately. When the king refused, she beckoned Roark to back her up.

"Once she makes up her mind, there is no changing it," he told Darius with a brief chuckle. "Just go with it."

"Fine," Darius conceded with a sigh. His tone was aggravated, but beneath it she could sense he was just as eager as she was. "I'll wait for you by the south exit, Ronja," he said, backing away from the couple. "Take your time." He locked eyes with Roark, nodded formally, then started off across the *trié*.

Ronja rounded on the Anthemite, nearly vibrating with excitement.

"So are you going to tell me what happened, or do I have to guess?" he asked, his eyebrows high on his forehead.

"He can see the colors, Roark," she whispered, the words tumbling out of her mouth like stones down a hill. "He can see them. He's just like me."

Roark tilted his head at her, surprised. "He has synesthesia?"

"No." She shook her head, a shocked grin exploding onto her mouth. "No, we were wrong, this is not synesthesia. This is

something else." Ronja had stopped herself before she said the
word on the tip of her tongue, but he seemed to understand.
"Darius is going to teach me how to use my voice—I mean, really
use it." She grabbed him by the hand, gazing up at him with
watering eyes. "Do you want to come?"

Roark smiled, affection blooming on his face. "No, love. I
believe this is a family matter." He leaned down and kissed her on
the brow. "I'll find Jonah and see if I can do anything to help.
Maybe they can find a place for me."

"Good, good."

Roark snorted, rolling his eyes good-naturedly. "Go," he said,
jerking his head in the direction Darius had moved off in. "Find
your voice, Siren."

Ronja bobbed her head, buzzing with adrenaline. "Okay. I'll
find you later. I love you."

He winked at her coyly. "I know."

She spun on her heel and rushed after Darius, darting
between somber Kev Fairlans. The king was waiting for her near
the southern exit, just as he had indicated. He smiled as she came
up on him, his greenish eyes luminous against his dark clothes.

"Hi," Ronja greeted him, awkwardness slamming into her
like a rogue subtrain.

"Hello, again," he said, looking away from her. Evidently, she
was not the only one feeling awkward. "Come on," Darius said,
starting down the busy corridor. "We're going to the library."

"The library?" she asked, jogging to catch up to him. "Why?"

"Space and privacy," he answered. "No one will be there
tonight, not with the influx of refugees."

Ronja felt her enthusiasm wane. She had been so fixated on
the prospect of better understanding her abilities, she had almost
forgotten the horrors of the day. The image of the boy crushed by
the concrete wormed back into her brain. Shame wrapped around

her, bowing her head.

"You have nothing to feel guilty about," Darius said, reading her thoughts. "How many people did you save today?"

"Not enough."

The king surprised her by barking a dark laugh. "It never is."

Ronja passed him an inquisitive look as they made their way through the packed halls. Today, no one was eyeing her. They were too focused on the crisis at hand, not to mention she was probably unrecognizable under the layers of soot. "You're different," she commented. "What changed between now and dinner?"

"As I said, I was behaving like an ass," Darius said with a visible wince. "I thought I could impress you with—"

"Those stupid rings?"

Darius blushed. "My father gave me those."

Ronja smirked up at him. His face fell, and for a moment she thought she had gone too far. Then he spoke. "You look so much like Layla when you do that."

Now it was her turn to frown. They rounded a bend in silence. To her surprise, they had already arrived at the impressive entrance to the library.

"Shortcut," Darius explained as they crossed the threshold.

"Right," Ronja murmured. She craned her neck back to view the lofty stone stacks, the weight of her troubles slipping away. It was even more beautiful than she remembered.

"You like to read?" Darius asked, watching her.

"Yeah." She spun in place slowly, drinking in the full effect of the room. The green shaded lamps bathed everything in an unexpectedly warm light. Just as Darius had predicted, there was not a soul in sight. "I had to drop out of school to work when I was fourteen, but I kept reading." Ronja chuckled mirthlessly as she came to a stop, motioning at the thousands of volumes. "I bet these books have fewer redactions than the ones in Revinia, though."

"I see," Darius murmured. She leveled her gaze at him, trying to place the hitch in his tone. Before she could, he clapped his hands together smartly. "Shall we?"

"Yeah," she said, straightening up. "Uh, what are we doing, exactly?"

The king crossed to the nearest polished wooden table, scooting aside a stack of books to perch on the edge. He looked rather out of place with his leather armor and stiff gray hair. "Now, tell me what happens when you hear real music."

Ronja considered for a moment. No one had ever asked her the question point-blank. "I see colors, but they're more than that," she explained. "They move, almost like they're alive, and they're different with every song."

"Indeed," Darius said with a subtle nod. He leaned toward her, lacing his gloved fingers loosely. "Each song is like a fingerprint. No two are exactly alike."

"Do we see the same thing, when we look at a song?" Ronja asked. The question jolted her insides. The entire situation felt like a drug-induced dream.

"Yes. The Auras exist without us; they do not come from us. The first mistake would be to believe that they did. Now." Darius raised a finger, as if to illustrate his point. "What happens when you sing?"

"Uh." Ronja itched the bridge of her nose, fidgeting under the weight of the question. "I used to see a black cloud with flecks of color in it, but now I see this bright white thing." She flushed as Darius stared openly at her, abruptly certain that she was crazy after all. "Is—is that normal for us?" She winced. The word *us* had leapt from her tongue before she could swallow it.

If Darius noticed her tumult, he chose to overlook it.

"That is actually fairly common," he told her. "For personal Auras to evolve with time, that is. Mine was bright red when I was young, but as I aged it became more of a copper."

"But what are they?" Ronja pressed him.

Darius sighed, old disappointment radiating from him. "Like I said, most of the lore was lost. My father was never much of a historian. He packed my ship with plenty of gold when he sent me away, but I imagine most of the books burned when the palace did."

Ronja felt her heart sink. She had been hoping for some sort of text that might help her puzzle out her supposed inheritance.

"What I can tell you is that the Auras are the physical manifestations of songs, and that they are, in a sense, alive."

"What do you mean, alive?" she asked. Chills crept up her spine, born of both fear and fascination.

"Not in the sense that you and I are alive," Darius assured her. "They're not sentient, but they do live and die. They are born when a song begins and fade when it ends." Ronja nodded, though she found the concept rather unnerving. "You can bend any Aura from any song to your will, but your voice is your most powerful tool. With me so far?"

"I think so."

"Tell me about your voice," he prompted. "What can you do, exactly, and how did you come to discover it?"

Ronja chewed the inside of her cheek, letting her eyes wander throughout the vast room. "That is a bit of a long story," she answered. "I feel like I've told it a million times."

"You've been through a lot."

He did not phrase it as a question, but the Siren found herself nodding anyway, gradually allowing her gaze to drift back to him. "More than I can take."

"Sit down," Darius said, scooting over on the edge of the

table. "Will you tell me about it, one last time?"

For a long moment, Ronja stood rooted on the spot. She knew the question ran deeper than just understanding the mechanics of her voice. It was an invitation to open up to a man who should have known everything about her. He should have been there to protect her, to hold her, to watch her grow.

"When you left Revinia," she said, keeping her voice low so it did not shake. "You really didn't know Layla was pregnant?"

"I had no idea," Darius assured her gently. "Even without you in the picture, I would have given anything to stay with her. Kostya dragged me away, quite literally."

"Will you tell me about her, sometime?" Ronja asked. There must have been some dust in the air, because her eyes were watering. "Layla, I mean."

"Anything and everything you want to know."

"Okay." Ronja sucked in a steadying breath, then sat down next to her father. They both smelled like war and looked like hell, but somehow it did not matter. "It started when I met Roark on the subtrain tracks . . . "

35: SENTIMENT

Terra

"Put these on."

The Off with the reddish hair tossed a coarse black prison uniform at her feet. Canvas slippers followed, landing on the hard floor with two successive slaps. Terra eyed the outfit distastefully, then looked up at her warden. "No thanks."

"You won't survive the cold in your current attire," he replied, eyeing her filthy tank top and ripped pants.

"Your concern is touching," Terra said dryly. "But I'll pass."

"Concern is corruption. This is a command."

The Anthemite raised her brows, genuinely surprised. "Oh, a new one. You fascists really dig alliteration."

The Off drew the stinger at his hip, snapping it to life with a twist of the handle. Violent electricity crackled at its tip, close enough to sear her skin. She lifted her hands in surrender. "Fine. Turn around." The guard did not. *Worth a shot*, she thought dully.

Sighing, she tugged her reeking shirt over her head and tossed it aside. She felt the Off watching her as she took off her pants, then bent down to retrieve the uniform. She snuck a glance at his face. There was no desire there, not even a flicker of arousal.

The shirt and pants were a couple of sizes too large, but the shoes fit like a glove. When Terra had finished adjusting her sagging garments, the Off tossed a pair of heavy manacles at her. She caught them to her chest with a whoosh of breath. "Put those on."

"I get it," she muttered as she clamped the cold cuffs around her already bruised wrists.

The Off sheathed his stinger and took her by the arm. He yanked her from the cell, her handcuffs rattling as she stumbled. "Easy, I can walk on my own," Terra complained.

He ignored her staunchly, dragging her along down the hallway.

"Do you have a name?"

"Thomas."

"You took me to meet Maxwell."

Thomas looked down at her with empty gray eyes. "I am aware of this."

"Why have you been assigned to babysit me, Thomas?" Terra inquired as he tugged her around a sharp bend. They passed a pair of guards, one male, one female, clomping along like robots with their hands on their hulking machine guns. They did not even steal a glance at the prisoner. "Is this really what you want to be doing with your Saturday?"

"The Conductor has tasked me to guard you, in case you try to double-cross us, and it is Wednesday."

"Huh," Terra said vaguely. She scanned his body discreetly. He was fit, but not particularly muscular, and she was at least an inch taller than him. She had certainly fought more formidable opponents in the past. Hell, even Ronja had been able to give her a black eye despite her utter lack of technique. Still, between her cuffs and his dead nerves, taking him down would not be easy.

"Here," Thomas intoned. Terra looked up. They had come to

the end of the corridor, which was marked by a large iron door with a heavy deadbolt. The Off released her and slid it back with a grunt of effort. Cold air rushed in as he opened the door, stirring her blonde hair. She breathed in deeply, savoring the sharp taste.

Thomas took her by the arm again, leading her through the exit into a stairwell. It was clearly a new addition to the prison, made of concrete rather than stone. The Off mounted the steps, still dragging her along behind him like a rag doll. "Let me go, it'll be faster," Terra suggested.

He did not respond at first. Then he released her and continued to climb. She smirked at the little victory, marching after him obediently.

They traversed five flights of steps in total. By the time Terra crested the landing, she was panting. Being trapped in a tiny cell for weeks on end did not allow for much cardio. Thomas went to open the door at the back of the landing, his breathing perfectly even. Fresh air washed over them, sharp and cold as a blade. "Go," he commanded, holding open the door for her.

"How quaint," Terra said, stepping through. She stood at the edge of an aeroplane hangar buzzing with military activity. Dozens of red and black fighter jets stood in long rows. Large autos with hulking trailers were parked in a line opposite them. Men and women in grease-spotted jumpsuits rushed around like drones. Despite their lack of expression, it was clear they were overworked. Their eyelids were bruised, their spines curved forward. The hanger doors were wide open, allowing winter light to spill in. Outside was a runway sandwiched between mounds of snow turned brown slush. Beyond that, roughly a mile away, was Revinia. It surrounded them, a gray beast choking on its own smog.

Even from far away it seemed too still.

"Thomas," a familiar voice called. Terra rounded on it, dread filling her stomach. Henry stood beside a sleek obsidian auto, dressed for the cold in a long woolen coat and leather gloves. He was undeniably handsome, even with his void eyes and the crimson badge on his lapel.

"Sir," Thomas addressed him with a sharp salute.

"You'll be driving today," Henry told him, adjusting one of his gloves. "Get the engine running."

"Sir." The Off stepped around Terra and popped the front door, slipping in behind the wheel. She watched carefully as he selected a small silver key from the ring at his hip and plugged it into the ignition. The engine revved smoothly.

Henry opened the back door. "Get in," he ordered Terra.

"You people are so bossy," she muttered as she climbed inside. The interior of the auto was upholstered with slick, dark brown leather. Terra scooted across the backseat, the engine rumbling beneath her. Henry followed swiftly, slamming the door behind him. He settled in, then looked to her expectantly. She checked over her shoulder, as if someone were pressed up against the tinted window. "What?"

"Where are we going?" Henry snapped.

Terra considered him with her head cocked to the side. *Interesting.*

"Vahl."

"Hmmm?"

"Where are we going?" he repeated slowly, as if she were a bit dense.

Panic shot through Terra. She had not expected to get this far. *Think, you idiot, think.* "719 Winthrop Avenue between 52nd and 53rd." *What the hell am I doing?*

Henry locked eyes with Thomas in the rearview mirror. The young Off dipped his head in assent. The engine growled, and they began to roll forward. They coasted past the rows of planes and trucks, the workers scurrying through the aisles like hungry rats. Terra winced as they passed into the muted sunlight, but forced herself to keep her eyes open. Her lips twitched into a pale smile, her assumption confirmed. They were on the palace grounds.

The palace was situated near the core, just south of the clock tower. The magnificent building was huge, five stories high and looked to be a quarter mile long at ground level. White as ocean surf, the palace boasted gold-plated double doors at its front. The structure was enveloped by a high white wall with at least dozen guard towers. From what she had seen, the basement was far more vast than the palace itself. Perhaps it even dumped out beyond the wall.

"Huh," Terra said, squinting out at the behemoth estate. "Not as impressive as I thought it would be." Henry did not react, staring at the back of the front seat. She turned toward him with a loaded sigh. "So," she opened. "Tell me, what *do* you remember about your life before all this?"

"I remember enough."

"Want to elaborate? We have a long drive ahead of us, and it'll be a lot more interesting if one of us is talking." Somewhere in the back of her mind, Terra registered the irony of the situation. Not long ago, she and Samson had sat in a similar position while he pestered her about her past. Back then, she had not been keen to open up. Now she was the one digging for information. Her intentions, though, were not as pure as his had been.

Henry only answered after a lengthy pause. "Silence," he said, his fingers caressing his Singer absentmindedly. "I remember silence." For a split second, Terra thought he was going to say more. The moment passed.

"Can I ask you something?" she prodded him again. Henry did not respond, which she took as an invitation. "You were pissed when I insulted Maxwell in The Amp. Want to tell me how that is possible with The New Music in your ear?"

"I was not angry," Henry shot back without missing a beat. "I was protecting the honor of The Conductor."

"Mmhmm, interesting." Terra tapped her fingers to her chin in mock consideration. "What, are you his knight in shining armor, or something?"

"No."

"You sure?"

"If you continue to speak to me this way, I will gag you."

"Not really into that, but thanks." Terra chuckled to herself as Henry shifted away from her, crossing one leg over the other and looking out the window. She scooted toward him and leaned in, puncturing his personal space. "One more question. What do you remember about Ronja?"

"The Siren," he corrected her automatically.

"She was Ronja to you."

"She's a traitor, and now she belongs to The Conductor."

"Well, if you'll recall, she was also your best friend," Terra said. "She was a subtrain driver, I think. Roark whacked off her Singer. You lot went to Red Bay on a bloody suicide mission to get her cousins back. Stupid as hell. Brave, though."

Terra kicked herself internally, knowing Ronja would never let her forget it if she heard about what she was going to say next. "Yeah, you know, Ronja was brave, hardheaded, reckless, emotional—and she loved you. She still does. I know for a fact that she would rather see you dead than a slave to The Conductor."

Faster than she could track, Henry jerked around and snatched her by the throat. He slammed her head into the window and drove his knee into her stomach to pinning her. Terra grinned through the sharp pain in her head, her eyes shifting across the twisted plains of his face. "You sure you're not angry?" she wheezed.

"Keep quiet or I'll cut out your tongue," he replied, the words hot against the skin of her face. "The Henry you knew is long gone. Keep trying to draw him out, and you'll face the consequences."

"Funny," Terra hissed, straining to speak around the thick hand compressing her windpipe. "You didn't hit me nearly as hard as you could have."

Henry recoiled slowly, withdrawing his restraining hand. Terra sucked in a breath, her lungs expanding gratefully. The boy sank back into his seat, straightening his suit. Terra massaged her throat tenderly. Her head throbbed with the rhythm of her pulse.

"I remember you."

Terra looked at Henry sidelong. He was staring at the back of the front seat, all traces of emotion wiped clean from his face. "I remember you betrayed the Siren. I remember you are not to be trusted." He met her gaze levelly. "Which is why I do not believe a single word you say."

36: LUMINOUS

By the time Ronja was finished talking, the weathered silver watch Darius wore read 12:31. She assumed it was after midday, but she would have believed either. Time had bled out of existence while she told her story. The king listened attentively the whole time, only cutting in to ask the occasional question. When Ronja finally settled into silence, he watched her for a long time. She in turn kept her eyes on her knees, feeling his eyes drilling into the side of her face.

She had spared almost no detail, only glossing over a few private moments with Roark that she figured he would rather not hear about. The rest of her story she documented with glaring precision. Her life with Layla under a mutt Singer. Her introduction to the Anthem, the violent removal of her Singer. Cosmin, Georgie, and Layla's kidnapping. The discovery of The New Music and her voice at Red Bay. Layla's death. Henry's demise. The creation of the radio station, of the Siren. How her voice worked to counteract The Music. Lastly, the fall of Revinia, of Samson, and her weeks in the mirrored cell.

The silence in the library grew heavier. Ronja felt her stomach begin to work itself into knots. "That was a lot," she said with a wince. "Sorry, I—"

"Thank you for telling me," Darius said over her. She peered over at him, surprised. He regarded her with oddly bright eyes, the tip of his nose blushing red. "To say I am sorry would never be enough."

Ronja shook her head slowly. "I'm not sorry." Darius raised his eyebrows at her, clearly questioning her sanity. "I mean," she amended. "Yeah, I could have done without the torture and murder. But the people I have loved, even the ones I have lost, they've made it all worthwhile." She straightened her spine, nearly bringing herself to eye level with him. "That's why I have to go back, to save them and to make Maxwell pay for what he has done."

Darius sighed, a melancholy smile dusting his lips. "You have so much of Layla in you. She was always putting herself in danger to protect others. I swear she enjoyed it. It drove me mad."

Ronja could not help but smile back at him. "It's so strange to imagine her as human, as a rebel." Her face crumpled. "Why did no one tell me? Ito must have known, or Wilcox."

"Roark told me that she had her last name changed to Zipse. I assume that happened after—"

"She became a mutt," the girl finished quietly. She bobbed her head in affirmation, more to herself than to Darius. "She did that to protect me. Actually, she did a lot to protect me. She begged a woman to delay the conversion procedure until after I was born and to alter her last name on the records so that no one could find us. That way I could be born safe, and human." Ronja bit the inside of her cheek to distract from the sudden ache in her chest. "She gave up everything to give me a shot at a decent life, even her name."

"I can promise you, she wouldn't have regretted it for a moment," Darius said. He laid a strong hand on her shoulder. She did not look at him, nor did she pull away. "Her real name was Layla Maradici."

"Maradici," Ronja repeated. Her names rolled around in her head like boulders. Ronja Zipse. Ronja Alezandri. Ronja Maradici. The Siren. She was not sure where one name ended and the other began.

"Tell me again about what your voice does," Darius said, breaking her from her contemplation.

"Um." She blinked rapidly, dissolving her thoughts. Some of the lights in the hallway beyond the library had been switched off, but the lamps still blazed bright around them. "It counteracts The Music, all forms of it as far as we know."

"It has to go deeper than that," Darius muttered, massaging his chin. When he noticed Ronja watching him with a cocked brow, he elaborated. "The Music is a human invention—an abomination, if you will. Our gifts are natural, stretching back thousands of years, long before that kind of technology was even a whisper."

"I can see The Music too," Ronja reminded him. "It looks different than real music, like white snakes." She grimaced, imagining the threads slithering through the air, worming into the ears and minds of helpless listeners.

"Maybe your gift is not just nullifying The Music," he mused. "Maybe your gift is about enhancing emotion, giving people the freedom to feel what they need to feel regardless of interference by Singers."

"Just like real music," Ronja murmured. She slid down from the table they had been perched on. Her legs groaned with relief. Putting her hands on her hips, she began to pace back and forth before Darius, her eyes trained on the floor, but not really seeing it. "When we were running the radio station, it took weeks for us to affect any major changes. We thought it was because the signal wasn't strong enough, but maybe the signal wasn't the problem."

The gears of her brain whirled in dizzying circles as she carved a path in the stone. Darius looked on silently, his fingers pressed to his mouth in contemplation. "Maybe it wasn't the strength of the signal that made the difference at the tower. Maybe I was just getting stronger."

"Maybe it was both."

Ronja tossed him a glance. "Maybe. That was the night my Aura evolved—it turned white." *Like The New Music*, a distant part of her whispered. She stamped it out like a cigarette.

"And the Revinians immediately rose up at your call," Darius filled in, joining her on his feet.

"After all that time." Ronja snapped her fingers as she came to halt before him, then let her arms fall to her sides. "If I could get stronger, if I could hone my voice, I could free them from The New Music, no problem." Her voice sparked with bravado and reckless hope. "I could make it last this time, make them immune to it."

Darius shook his head. "I am not sure about that, but maybe there is no need to make them immune."

"What?"

The exiled king folded his arms, grinning like a child waking up to a load of presents on his birthday. "Those mainframes you were talking about before, I know where they are."

Ronja felt her knees buckle. The skin of her face went numb as she struggled to breathe.

Darius continued. "Right before I was taken back to Tovaire, Layla ran a mission to steal some documents from a government office. She gave them to me for safekeeping." Aching sadness welled in his face. "One of those papers had a list of six locations on it. One of them was the clock tower, I'll bet you anything they're—"

"The mainframes," Ronja breathed. She swayed on the spot, partially from shock, partially from the exhaustion that was steadily gaining on her. "Skitzing hell, we've been looking for them for so long, and you had them this whole time." Darius jumped as a breathless laugh exploded from her lips. "Wait until I tell Roark."

"If we destroy these mainframes, Revinia goes free?" he asked. "That would be easy, we could just bomb them from the air."

"Not quite. If we just destroy them, the shock could kill everyone in the city. But if I could sing first, I could help them separate naturally, then we could blow the mainframes." Ronja sobered as reality settled around them like heavy snow. "But to do any of that, we would need the Kev Fairla to cooperate."

"Let me talk to Easton," Darius said, determination knitting his brows. "The problem is, you've asked him for the wrong thing. You don't need his army, you need an elite task force. If we want this to work, we need stealth on our side."

"We?" Ronja inquired, her heart in her throat.

"We," Darius answered firmly. "Did you really think I was going to let you do this alone?"

"I have Roark."

"Ronja, I have been absent from your life for eighteen years."

"Nineteen," she corrected him.

"Nineteen years," he amended. "Now that I have you here, I am not letting you out of my sight. I know there is no stopping you from returning to Revinia, you have too much of your mother in you." Darius paused. "And me."

Ronja studied him for a long moment. Her heart was threatening to beat straight out of her chest. "I don't know what to say," she finally admitted.

"You don't have to say anything. I know I am never going to

be your father in the sense that I'll teach you to read or brush your hair or take you to school, but I can help you take back your city."

Ronja blinked. "My city? You're the king, not me."

"I have been struck from history. Not even the Anthem knows my name. You're the one they will look to when the reckoning comes. The Siren." He smiled, creasing his stubbled cheeks. "I know I have no right to be, but I am so proud of you."

Ronja opened her mouth. Closed it. She was not sure where to look or what to do with her hands. Strange warmth ballooned at her core, heating her from her fingers to her toes. "Th-thank you," she said hoarsely.

"I'll talk to Easton first thing tomorrow morning," Darius said, getting back to business. When she opened her mouth to protest, he raised a hand to shush her. "I know I said we could start work on your voice tonight, but it is late. We both need sleep."

"Fine," she huffed, but as she spoke a yawn betrayed her. The king chuckled at her. Ronja glared at him pointedly. "Tomorrow morning, early?"

"Tomorrow," he promised with a somber dip of his chin. "Goodnight, Ronja."

"Wait," she yelped. The word had leapt from her tongue before she could bite it back. Darius, who had already started toward the exit, peered back at her perplexedly. She swallowed, tucking a wayward curl behind her ear. "Before you go, could we sing?"

For an endless moment, Darius stood utterly still. Ronja held her breath, mortification clawing at her insides. Then he spun to face her completely. "It would be my honor, Siren."

Ronja stood up straighter as relief washed over her, making her feel strangely lightheaded. "Do you know *Little Wars*?"

Surprise knocked a grin onto Darius's weathered face. "By

Adna Banks, of course."

"Is, or was, it popular?"

"Not exactly, but your mother loved it."

"Oh," Ronja said weakly.

There was another pause, which neither of them knew how to fill. Ronja found herself looking at the floor. She had sung for an entire city every day for two weeks without flinching. Why she struggled to find her voice now, in front of one man, she could not say. But it was not just any man, she realized distantly. It was her father.

"On three?" Darius proposed.

Ronja nodded, her curls bouncing.

He righted his spine, taking in a deep breath. He cracked his neck, then held up three fingers. Ronja swallowed again, struggling fruitlessly to coat her dry throat with spit. "One, two . . . " Darius dropped his last finger, and they began to sing.

First day you saw me I was
Way down low with my hands
In my pockets and nowhere to go

Their voices blended like acrylics on a pallet, blooming to fill the deserted library. Ronja watched in awe as her Aura billowed from her lips, pure white and luminous. It was difficult to concentrate on the lyrics as it swirled above her, elegant as a dancer. Darius's swam up to join hers. It was a deep rust cloud with feathered edges. It reminded her of the scar over her heart, if it glowed like a sunrise before a storm.

You were standing on my neck
Just to reach so high, sifting for those
Diamonds in the sky

Across from her, Darius was beaming through the lyrics. They locked eyes across the living fog. As Ronja watched, he reached up a hand and hooked a finger at his Aura. It glided toward him, curling itself into a tail and wrapping around his body. His skin blushed pink in the reddish glow.

Blood in my veins and you say it's cold
But if you cut my skin it will come out gold

Ronja lifted her hand toward her gleaming Aura, acting on instinct alone. She knew she was still singing, but she could no longer hear herself. It went deeper than that. She *was* the song, and it was singing *her* into existence. The Siren crooked her finger at the warm white ribbons.

It struck her in the chest with the force of a bullet, sending her flying back into the table. Her back cracked against the wood and she crumpled to the ground with a whoosh of breath. Books and scrolls thumped down around her like debris.

"Ronja!" Darius shouted, darting over to her and kneeling before her. "Ronja, are you all right?"

"Y-yes," she answered. Her entire body pulsed with dull pain, putting the bruises she had received in the bomb blast to shame.

"Auras are more difficult to control than they appear, and yours is particularly powerful. I should have warned you."

Ronja looked up at Darius through swimming eyes. He was paler than the light that had bowled her over. He was keeping his distance, too. Minutes ago he had not hesitated to clap her on the shoulder, like a father might. *Am I dangerous?* Keening filled her brain, like a tea kettle whistling from the stovetop.

"You'll learn to control it. It comes with time."

Ronja climbed to her feet laboriously, barely hearing him

over the noise in her brain. "I have to go," she said mechanically. "I have to go."

"Ronja—"

"Goodnight, Darius."

"Wait—"

But the Siren had already bolted, racing across the library on the wings of her terror.

PART TWO: THE RECKONING

37: CONFESSIONS

Ronja thought about going back to her room. Sleep sounded like a blessing. But when she arrived at their door, she could not bring herself to open it. Her body still vibrated with power and her skin was hot to the touch. She felt as if she were going to explode, sending shards of bone flying. Despite the absurdity, it felt like a realistic possibility at this point. Rather than put Roark in danger, she turned and roamed the empty halls of the temple, lost in the forest of her thoughts.

It might have been minutes or hours later that she found herself outside another door. Heat radiated through its cracks. *What am I doing here?* Ronja opened the door cautiously, peeking inside like a thief. The inferno bloomed before her, shrinking her pupils. The Contrav was deserted in the middle of the night, but the flames burned just as bright as before. She stepped inside and left the door open behind her.

Ronja approached the altar slowly, carving a path down the center aisle between the rivers of stewing lava. Dark memories stirred within her, some fresh, some old. Equally potent. They raised goosebumps on her skin though she increasingly felt as if she were going to melt. She mounted the steps, her eyes locked to the bowl of flame. Looping around the dais, she ran her fingers across the faultless walls of the basin. It was surprisingly cool to the touch. She took her hand back, keenly aware that the slightest push could send it crashing to the ground.

Ronja allowed her vision to drift. As her racing mind slowed, the keening that had haunted her since the library faded. She breathed in deeply. Her hand slipped beneath the collar of her grimy sweater, searching for the raised scar over her heart. She would never forget the searing pain of the stinger she had slammed into her own chest. It was nothing compared to the force that had knocked her off her feet when she reached for her Aura.

It felt was as if life itself had shot through her, unbearably bright and impossible to contain.

Ronja cleared her throat. She stared at the basin as if waiting for it to speak. "I've never done this before." The flames regarded her uncaringly. "This is probably stupid. I don't even believe in gods."

If Entalia was out there, she was not much of a talker. Ronja wetted her cracked lips. "The thing is, I am afraid, and I don't know how not to be." She clasped her hands before her to quell the shaking. The heat festering beneath her skin overpowered that of the flames. "I am afraid we won't be able to convince Easton to help us. I am afraid my friends and family are dead. I am afraid of not being able to stop The New Music."

Sparks popped in the belly of the bowl. For a fraction of a second, Ronja ceased to breathe. Then the flames receded, falling back into their usual dance. "I am afraid of losing Roark," she went on. "I need him, but I think I am most afraid of—"

The word snagged on her tongue. It had been easier to write it down, to throw it in the fire and turn it to ash. Ronja closed her eyes, tucked her fingers into fists. Her nails bit into her palms.

"Me. Of what I can do, what I have done. Of my voice and the things that I want. I want to kill Maxwell. I dream about it, and it feels good. I feel powerful. I want him—no, I need him to pay, and I am afraid."

Ronja fell silent. Her breaths came quick and heavy. Her chest still ached where her Aura had struck her. Roark had once told her that she was more than a weapon. Maybe that was true, in another life. But not here, not in this reality. She was the Siren, and she was coming for The Conductor with or without an army.

The ghost of a smile was just unfolding on her face when blunt pain exploded at the back of her skull.

38: GHOST TOWN
Terra

Passing through the wrought-iron gates of the palace grounds was surreal. Terra had braced herself for anything when they entered the streets of Revinia. When the word *war* popped into her head, she saw bloodshed, bombed-out houses, bodies stacked on sidewalks. But Revinia was not a war zone. It was a ghost town. The streets were empty, the autos parked in neat lines on the roadsides, their hoods and roofs capped with snow three feet high. The street lamps were lit, but not a single pedestrian walked in their pleasant orange glow. The windows of the mansions crammed into the core were shuttered.

"Where is everyone?" Terra asked Henry, her forehead pressed to the tinted auto window. Her breath fogged the frigid glass. She wiped away the veil with her sleeve.

"That is none of your concern," he answered in a clipped tone. He sat with one leg crossed over the other, a manila file open in his lap.

"What is that?" she inquired, craning her neck to see.

Henry snapped the folder shut, tossing her a dirty look. "I may not remember much about our past," he said. "But I do remember you used to be a lot quieter."

Terra gave an offhand shrug. "People change. You did."

The ex-Anthemite grunted, then cracked the file again, angling it away from her. Terra smirked down at her manacled hands. She was a prisoner, chained and without a plan in the middle of a soulless city. But she carried with her two threads of intel. If Cicada had taught her anything, it was that knowledge was sharper than any knife.

They passed through the streets of the opulent core without seeing a single person. A gentle snow began to fall from the awning of gray clouds. It all looked so peaceful. Nature had a sick sense of humor. Terra watched as the mansions turned into the modest row houses characteristic of the middle ring. Unwanted memories came loping back. Her strange childhood. Playing in the streets with the other children on the rare days she was given free time.

Samson, greeting her the day she arrived at the Belly with Ito. *You're gonna like it here, I promise*, he had said with that hundred-watt grin. She remembered glaring at him as if he had just insulted her mother, shouldering past him as Ito took her to her new quarters.

The auto jolted to a stop, nearly sending Terra flying into the front seat. It was difficult to keep her balance with her hands bound.

"We're here," Thomas informed them from the front. He glanced back at them in the rearview mirror. His flat gray eyes mirrored the sky.

"Thank you, Thomas," Henry intoned. He reached into his coat pocket and pulled out his leather gloves, pulling them on with two precise jerks. "Stay here. Radio if there are any problems."

"There are a lot of shady characters around here," Terra warned him, gesturing out at the dark homes and empty sidewalks.

Both of them ignored her. Henry opened the auto door and stepped onto the snowy street. "Hurry up," he snapped.

"Yeah, yeah," Terra mumbled as she slid across the leather. It was something of a challenge to get out of the auto with her hands locked together, but somehow she managed to do it without slipping in the muddy snow. The wind whipped her hair, cutting straight through her prison uniform. Her shoes, at least, seemed to be holding up for the moment.

Henry reached around her and shut the door with an echoing thud. "Why are we here?" he asked suspiciously, glancing around at the uniform white homes through the drifting snow.

Terra jerked her chin at the house behind him. He followed the motion, scanning for signs of an ambush. The building looked like all the others, colorless and narrow with large windows and plants shrouded in white. The sidewalk was buried, as were the steps leading up to the front door. It appeared to be abandoned, just like the rest of them. "This is one of our safe houses," she explained. "There is a hatch in the floor that leads to the sewers. It'll take us straight to the Belly."

"Try anything and—"

"You'll cut my tongue out. I get it, tough guy." Ignoring the dread creeping up on her, Terra started toward the house, wading through the drifts. The damp cold bit at her ankles. So much for her shoes working out. "I have to get the key," she told Henry, veering off what she assumed was the sidewalk and into the brushes. "Should be around here somewhere."

Henry did not respond, following her like a specter as she trudged over to the side of the house where a bundle of white capped bushes crouched. Terra brushed two layers of snow off the plants with her forearm. The foundation of the house was revealed, smooth as an eggshell. Terra reached out with raw hands, running the pads of her fingers over the stone. Henry hovered nearby, his shadow encroaching on her view. "Get back," she said over her shoulder. "I need to see."

Surprisingly, he did as she requested. Terra refocused on her task. Her pulse climbed with each second that ticked by. Would it still be here, after all these years? The callused pad of her finger scraped against an imperfection in the wall. *There.* She pressed down hard with her palm, which was difficult with her handcuffs. The hidden compartment popped open with a hiss.

Skitz yes. Terra reached into the little drawer and pinched the key between her fingers triumphantly. She rounded on Henry, dangling his prize before him. He snatched it up and marched back to the hidden sidewalk, then up the shrouded steps. Terra tailed him, brushing snow from her front.

When they reached the porch, he stood aside and handed the key back to her. "Open it, slowly."

"Of course." Terra stretched her neck, relishing the crack of her stiff vertebrae. *Here goes.* She stepped forward and inserted the key into the lock fluidly. She turned it left, then right. Then left again.

"Hurry up," Henry growled at her shoulder.

"Sorry, it always gets jammed."

Left. Right. Then, a single full twist. The tumblers clicked like her spine snapping into alignment. Terra shoved the door open. The wind caught it, smashing it against the wall. She squinted down the familiar hallway. Nothing had changed since she last saw it. She was not sure if she found that comforting or unsettling. Before she could decide, Henry shoved her aside.

"Watch it," she complained as he drew his gun and switched off the safety, holding it up before him with military precision. He had been a good agent before he left the Belly. Apparently, those instincts remained.

"You first," Henry commanded, motioning into the dim hall with his automatic.

Terra did as she was told, stepping across the threshold cautiously. Warm air engulfed her. Her lips twisted into a secret smile.

He's here.

"Go," Henry ordered, nudging her between the shoulder blades with the muzzle of his gun. Terra hurried inside, the floorboards creaking beneath her drenched soles. Her warden tailed her cautiously, his dull brown eyes darting around as he took in the wall hangings, the books stacked on the decorative table against the wall. "These should be burned," he said.

"This way," Terra replied, crooking a finger at him. She started off confidently and heard him follow. The doors lining the narrow corridor were shut, hiding the rooms brimming with illegal artifacts and manuscripts. "Just down here," she called when they reached the split staircases at the end of the hallway. One led to the second floor, the other to the basement.

Henry jerked his chin at the descending stairs, his automatic still up. Terra obliged, starting down at a steady clip. He went after her in his heavy boots. Cool underground air crept up toward them. Sweat beaded on her brow despite the chill. There was every chance this would end with a bullet in her brain. If Maxwell found out she had deceived him, she doubted her status as bait would protect her for much longer.

The shadow of the staircase above them swallowed Terra. Her throat constricted as they approached the door at the basin of the stairwell. A million frantic thoughts, a million ways her hastily stitched plan could go wrong, flew up in her face. Her feet graced the last step. Her hand stretched out, closed around the doorknob. She shut her eyes. The knob was ripped from her hand as the door was yanked open from the other side.

"DOWN!"

Terra dropped like a stone, tucking her chin to her chest. Violent electricity crackled above her. Henry roared, dropping his gun. It bounced off the last step and landed with a crack on the concrete. Silence, then a sickening *thump* as the boy crumpled to the stairs.

Terra raised her head. She grinned, her first real smile in over a month. "Father," she greeted the man holding the extendable stinger.

Cicada mirrored her smile. "Terra, glad you could join us."

39: HOWL

Ronja crashed to the floor, rolling to avoid the bowl of flames. Skull throbbing, she shot to her feet and threw her guard up.

Before she could defend herself, a hand closed around her throat, lifting her off the ground. She struggled to see her attacker through her failing vision. All she caught was the proud gleam of silver from the right side of his head.

Pitch.

Ronja cranked her leg back and slammed her shin into his groin with an animalistic scream. Nothing, not even a flinch or a grunt. Shadows swelled in her eyes. She kicked again, harder this time. The sounds of their struggle, the heat of the Contrav receded. The pain began to bleed away. Then he released her.

Ronja folded to her knees, coughing and gasping. Her senses slammed back into her. She scrambled to her feet backing up to crouch behind the altar, her breath rattling painfully in her throat. Peering out, she scrutinized her assailant. He was garbed in baggy Tovairin clothes. His blond hair was cropped short, his blue eyes deep set and vacant as boarded windows. Just as she had thought, a silver Singer clung to his ear.

If The New Music flowed through his veins, nothing short of

death would stop him. *Unless* . . .

"How did you find me?" Ronja snarled. It came out as more of a rasp.

"The Conductor compels you to return to Revinia immediately," the Off replied in a monotone. His eyes did not quite meet hers, as if he were not seeing her clearly.

"The Conductor is dead."

"The Conductor compels you to return—"

Ronja laughed bitterly. "Maxwell." She coughed again, shaking her head at his vanity. "Figures."

"The Conductor will not tolerate your absence any longer," he said as if she had not spoken. "If you do not return, your comrades will pay for your recklessness."

Ronja felt her eyes widen. "They're alive," she breathed.

"They will remain so as long as you return—"

"Shut it," Ronja barked. To her surprise, the Off fell silent, observing her from the edge of the altar. *He can't kill me*, she realized with a jolt. *They need me alive.* "What happens if I don't come with you?"

The man blinked twice, as if he had misheard her. "This is not an option. I am authorized to use whatever force necessary to bring you home."

"My home," Ronja answered, inching subtly to the right, "is not with Maxwell."

Before the Off could respond, she sprang and slammed her palms into the basin of flames. It groaned as it tilted on its dais. She lunged as it fell, darting past it down the steps. A deafening crash rang out, stone hitting stone. Her foot struck the bottom step and she was yanked back by her hair. She cried out, struggling against the unyielding grip.

"The Conductor—" The man pulled up short, as if someone had slapped a hand over his mouth. Ronja looked around wildly, squinting through the sharp pain at her scalp. Her heart ground to a halt.

Standing between the seething canals, fur raised and teeth barred, was the wolf. Pascal. Ronja squirmed in the grasp of her attacker, attempting both to free herself and to twist away from the animal. The Off drew her closer, taking a step back. The wolf snarled, saliva dripping from its powerful jaws.

"Call off your animal," the Off ordered in her ear. There was no fear in his voice, of course, but there was *something* there. The understanding that the beast could tear him limb from limb. That no amount of numbing could help him escape its jaws.

"He's not mine," Ronja choked out. Pascal growled again, long and low as rolling thunder. He began to prowl forward, the firelight dancing on his silver coat. The Off began to retreat up the flight of steps, picking his way through the remains of the basin and dragging the Siren with him.

"Stop."

Ronja raised her head and felt her attacker do the same. Easton filled the doorway, a pistol clasped firmly in his hands. He wore nothing but a loose pair of pants, displaying the breathtaking white *reshkas* snaking across his chest. His hooded eyes flicked from Ronja to the man who held her hostage.

"Easton!" she shouted. "Shoot him!"

The commander ignored her. "Let her go," he said, his voice perfectly level. "This can end without further violence."

"Violence is valor," the Off replied. "If it means the Siren returns to Revinia with me."

Easton glanced at Ronja, a cloud of uncertainty passing over his face. "I am going to count to five," he said, his gaze switching back to the Off. "If you have not released her by then, I'm an excellent shot." Pascal growled to underscore the ultimatum. "One."

Ronja squirmed, fighting the iron grasp.

"Two."

Pascal barked, a guttural sound that shot chills down her spine.

"Three."

Easton curled his finger around the trigger, aiming between the Off's eyes.

"Four."

Ronja squeezed her eyes shut.

"Five."

The Off shoved Ronja aside. She landed on her shoulder, hissing in pain as she rolled down the stairs along with clumps of rubble. She scrambled to her feet, clutching her arm as the Off flew down the staircase. Pascal shot up to meet him his jaws locking around the Off's calf until it spurted blood.

Still, the Off kept moving.

"Shoot him!" Ronja bellowed at Easton, who was watching the scene unfold with a blank expression. Movement behind the commander. Relief flooded her when she saw it was Jonah, Paxton, and Larkin. All three of them were armed and clad in pajamas. Even across the room, she could see their eyes pop as they drank in the stranger who continued to struggle toward them with a wolf clamped around his leg.

"You have to kill him!" Ronja shouted. "Jonah, you know you have to kill him!" The captain locked eyes with her, wavering in the door frame.

"In the name of The Exalted Conductor, Maxwell Sebastian Bullon, you will surrender the Siren to me," the Off said over the muffled snarling of the wolf. He stumbled as a tendon in his leg split, but continued to limp forward. "Cooperate and you and your people may be spared."

Easton aimed low and fired. The bullet struck the Off in the knee. He crashed to the floor unceremoniously. Pascal yelped, releasing his calf. His silver muzzle stained red. The Off began to crawl forward, trailing blood. "In the name of The Exalted Conductor, Maxwell Sebastian Bullon . . . "

"Easton! Shoot!" Ronja begged. She sprinted down the steps and leapt onto the Off's back. She pinned his head as he struggled to throw her off. "Jonah, get over here and help me, you pitcher!"

"In the name of The Exalted Conductor . . . "

They don't get it. She squeezed her eyes shut, shutting out the chanting of the Off beneath her. She could still feel the words vibrating in his chest. She drew a deep breath through her nose, full of smoke and the tang of blood and exhaled a song.

> *When the day shakes*
> *Beneath the hands of night*

The Off stilled beneath her. She could feel the Kev Fairlans watching her across the Contrav and wondered what she looked like. *They must think I'm insane.* She forced the thought from her mind, focusing on the lyrics.

> *When your page is ripped*
> *From the Book of Life*

Her white Aura began to bloom. The light of the fires stained it pink and orange. She wanted to flinch away from it, but she refused. She would not be afraid. Not anymore. *Go to him*, she urged her Aura to action. *Free him.*

"Ronja!"

The Siren lifted her head in time to see Darius stumble into the Contrav, still wearing his filthy armor. She opened her mouth to shout at him, but her hold on the Off shattered. He bucked beneath her, throwing her off with a grunt of effort. She went flying, hitting the floor and skidding to a stop inches from the lava's edge. "Easton! Shoot him!" she screamed.

"In the name of The Exalted—"

The shot reverberated through the Contrav, dragging a deafening silence in its wake.

Ronja clambered to her hands and knees. Her neck and shoulder throbbed, her knees were drenched with blood. When a whine pricked her ear, she looked around. Pascal sat on his haunches a few feet way. Their gazes locked. There was more in his eyes than there had been in the eyes of the Off. Slowly, she lifted her hand from the floor, offering him her palm. He hesitated for a moment, then approached to nuzzle her hand with his leathery nose. It was shockingly warm and soft.

"Here."

Ronja raised her head. Darius stood over her, his pale hand stuck out for her to take. She recoiled internally, remembering the fear in his eyes as he crouched before her in the library. Despite herself she grabbed his hand and allowed him to pull her to her feet.

"I—" he began.

"Thank you." Ronja ignored his attempt to explain and turned to face the others.

Easton, Jonah, Paxton, and Larkin gathered around the body of the fallen Off. Pascal loped over to sit beside the commander, licking at the blood on his muzzle. Ronja dropped her eyes to the Revinian.

It was a clean shot. Dead center between the eyes. Evie would have been impressed. His eyes were open, as cloudy as they had been while he was breathing. His Singer glinted maliciously in the orange light. Easton squatted before the body on the balls of his feet, his gun loose in his fingers. Pascal snuffled at the body, more curious than anything. "How the hell did he get in?" the commander asked in a low voice.

"He must have snuck in with the refugees," Jonah surmised. Ronja looked Jonah up and down. His hair was loose at his shoulders and his pants rumpled, as if he had pulled them off the floor. He held one of his dual blades in a tattooed hand. Larkin carried the other bare-legged. Ronja could not help but notice her shirt was much too large for her.

"We'll double the guards at every entrance and screen the refugees," Paxton said firmly. "Gather everyone in the *trié*, make sure everyone's accounted for." He placed a gentle hand on the commander's shoulder. Easton did not respond vocally, but reached up to take it. Faint surprise rippled through Ronja, which was quickly doused when Jonah spoke.

"Easton," he said, squatting down next to his superior. "This is exactly what I was trying to tell you. These people with Singers are unstoppable."

"Unless you're Ronja, apparently." Easton lifted his nearly black eyes to the Siren, who stood her ground. "When you sang to him, he stopped. Only an Alezandri could do that."

She nodded. "I think I could have freed him, if my concentration hadn't been broken." She had not intended it as a jab at Darius, but she saw him shift awkwardly in her peripheral vision.

"I saw his face when you sang. His expression changed completely, like he was waking up." Jonah confirmed.

"Very impressive," Paxton chimed in, gazing at Ronja with newfound respect. He turned to Larkin, who was fingering the hilt of her borrowed sword, her expression brooding. "Larkin, *vin se ka?*"

"I do not know what I saw," she said, flipping her jet black hair over her shoulder.

Jonah and Ronja rolled their eyes in synchronization. The Kev Fairlan girl passed them both withering looks, which they pretended not to see. "These men," Easton went on, getting to his feet with quiet grace. "How many of them are there?"

"Not just men," Ronja corrected him. "Women and children, too. Three million, at least."

"None of them feel pain?"

Ronja gave another somber shake of her head.

"How many can fight?" Paxton asked.

"Does it matter?" Easton crossed his muscular arms, gazing down at the lifeless body of the Off. "You say this Maxwell is planning to invade us?"

"Not just Tovaire," Jonah cut in. "Any nation he thinks he can get his hands on, except maybe Vinta. Like I said in my report, they have something of an alliance. It might prove deadly to us." He spat at the Off, missing by an inch and hitting the stone.

"Three million people like this and we don't stand a chance. Unless . . . " Easton's eyes fell on Ronja. "You can free them."

"I think I can, but it's complicated. See that thing on his ear?" Ronja crouched down to point out the silver device. "That's a Singer. It acts like a receiver for The Music. In the past, the Anthem were protected since we don't have Singers. But now, The New Music can reach anyone in the city. It broadcasts over the air. We would need a way to block the signal." Ronja rounded on Paxton. "I was thinking about the *zethas*, how many do you have?"

"A few dozen, but they're just prototypes." He reached up to itch his brow, eyeing her pensively. "You think the *zethas* might help?"

"You tell me," Ronja replied.

"It's possible. I don't have much to go on but, if I could isolate the signal from his Singer, I should be able to come up with something."

"Assuming the *zethas* would protect us, do you have a plan beyond that?" Easton inquired.

"We do." Ronja stiffened as Darius spoke up.

Easton looked to Paxton, who gave a subtle nod. He turned back to Ronja and Darius. "All right then. What do you need?"

40: BLUEPRINTS AND DOMINOS

How the hell did you all show up at the Contrav at the same time?" Ronja asked.

Jonah snorted, cracking the knuckle of his index finger with his thumb. "Apparently Pascal started growling and woke up Easton and Paxton. Easton radioed me. Larkin overheard. Like dominos."

"Convenient." She adjusted the bag of crushed ice Jonah had given her for her bruised shoulder. "I had no idea you and Larkin were together."

They sat across from each other at his kitchen table. His apartment was surprisingly well kept. It was just one room, two counting the bathroom, but spacious and furnished. The sheets of his double bed were rumpled and several pillows were on the floor. The other Kev Fairlans had run off on various errands. Ronja wanted to join them, but Darius insisted she needed rest. "Take care of her," he had said, passing Jonah a sharp look.

"Why do people keep forgetting I was the one who sprang her from prison?" Jonah had replied under his breath.

At first, Ronja had been loath to be left behind. Now, she found she was relieved to talk about something other than ancient magic and war. "We've been together off and on for a few years," Jonah now replied. "It works for us."

"How do you stand her?"

"Mmm . . . well, she is a hell of a lot nicer to me than she is to you." He rolled his eyes in mock ecstasy. The Siren snorted, switching her ice pack to the lump at the back of her head. Jonah had performed a rudimentary concussion test on her, making sure she could follow his finger with her eyes and that she knew where she was. It appeared she was lucky, but it still hurt.

Jonah leaned back in his chair, which groaned beneath the added pressure. "Well princess, you do keep things interesting, I'll give you that. I think that is the first time we've had a Revinian bounty hunter on the premises."

"I do what I can," Ronja replied with a dark laugh.

"Maybe you do have a concussion."

"Huh?"

"I called you *princess*. That usually makes your head spin."

"Yeah, well, we have better things to worry about," she muttered, her face flushing in the lamplight. "Like how did that Off track us across the ocean and how did he get in?"

Jonah ran a tattooed hand down his face. He looked as tired as she felt. "Wish I could tell you," he said. He reclined further in his chair, closing his eyes and letting his head tip back. The wood gave another pitiful moan as its front legs lifted from the rug. "We haven't had a breach in years. Most people are turned off by the smoking volcano."

"Fake smoking volcano," Ronja corrected him.

He held up a finger, his eyes still closed. "Real volcano, fake smoke."

"True."

Jonah heaved a sigh and righted himself. "I have no idea how he followed us, and now he's too dead to tell us."

"I was getting through to him until Darius distracted me," Ronja said, a hint of resentment shading her tone.

"Daddy issues, huh?"

"Leave it alone," she mumbled, her fingers tightening around the bag of ice.

"What does that mean?"

"It means I am not in the mood to talk about it, skitzer."

He lifted his hands in surrender. "Yep, definitely a royal."

Ronja opened her mouth to retort, but the energy fled her bones. "Yeah," she said quietly. "I guess so."

"Darius is actually a good guy—go easy on him," Jonah suggested.

"Yeah, I know."

"Then why are you—"

"Jonah," Ronja snapped, shooting him a deathly glare. "Leave it alone."

Loud knocking saved her from having to explain further. Jonah got up and crossed to the door. He checked through the peephole, flipped the lock, and pulled it open. "Larkin," he greeted her. "*Kel est va?*"

The Kev Fairlan girl shouldered past the boy twice her size and swept into the apartment. Shooting the Anthemite a dirty look, she collapsed onto the green couch in the far corner. She said something to Jonah in Tovairin, her lids shut and her strong arms slung over the back of the couch. The boy rolled his eyes, then translated for Ronja. "She was helping Paxton dispose of the body."

The Siren nodded. "Good."

Jonah took a seat next to Larkin, leaving Ronja alone at the dining table. They began to converse softly in their native tongue. Ronja gave up trying to pick out familiar words after a few sentences. When another knock came at the door, she popped to her feet. "Got it," she said, already halfway there. She rose up on her tiptoes to check the peephole. The warped image of Easton greeted her, nose hooked and left eye bulging. She opened the door, standing aside.

The commander had donned a jacket and boots, his gun and radio now holstered at his sides. He hovered in the frame for a moment, his eyes falling to her neck. It was only then Ronja realized she was probably sporting a wreath of bruises. "I'll send for Elise," he said, pulling out the radio at his hip. "She can take a look at those."

"No, thank you," Ronja replied coldly.

Easton gave her a perplexed look, then holstered the communicator. "As you wish," he said, stepping past her and striding to the center of the room. Ronja started to shut the door behind him but a scarred tawny arm shot through to block her.

"Roark!" she exclaimed. He rushed forward and enveloped her in a bone-crushing embrace.

"Roark," she wheezed, patting him on the back.

"Ouch. Let me go." He pulled back, holding her by the shoulders. His black hair was mussed with sleep, his dark eyes flickering fearfully. He reached up with tender fingers to touch the marks on her neck, then pulled them back.

"I should have been there," he whispered. "I am so sorry, Ronja."

She shook her head. "You thought I was with Darius. There was no way you could have known."

He pulled her into his chest again. She surrendered, allowing him to rock her gently back and forth.

"Excuse me."

Ronja and Roark pulled apart. Paxton stood in the hallway, waiting to enter. The Anthemites scooted aside, muttering apologies. He crossed to Easton swiftly. They greeted each other with a quick squeeze of the hand, then began to speak in rapid Tovairin. Three sharp knocks. The Siren released Roark and checked the peephole again. *Skitz.*

Sucking in a steadying breath, Ronja opened the door on Darius. He had scrubbed his face and hands of grime since their last encounter, but he still wore his leather armor. A weathered bag was slung over his shoulder. He offered her a tentative smile, which she attempted to return. "Sorry I'm late," he said. "It took me awhile to find the right documents."

"Lock the door," Easton replied neutrally. Darius stepped over the threshold and shut the door, twisting the lock briskly. Once it engaged, the atmosphere shifted. "Paxton has doubled the guards at every entrance to the temple," the commander began, making eye contact with each of them in turn. "I have a team interviewing the refugees as we speak."

"Do you know how he got in?" Ronja asked.

Paxton spoke up. "We assume he slipped in with the crowds, but we can't prove that. We haven't found a ship or a plane. His clothes were Tovairin, which means he either took someone hostage or killed them."

"Offs rarely take prisoners," Roark said darkly. "If Maxwell is still chasing Ronja, he likely has not left on his conquest yet. If we act fast, we can stop them before they leave port."

Easton nodded in agreement, surprising both Anthemites. "I spoke with Darius. He believes a small team will suffice." Silence gripped the room. Ronja snuck a peek at her father, who was rummaging through the bag at his side.

"What is our mission, exactly?" Jonah inquired from the sofa.

"Our number one priority is getting Ronja to the clock tower and plugging her into the radio," Roark responded at once. "Just like before."

"Priority number two is the mainframes," Darius cut in,

whipping out a tightly bound scroll.

Roark glanced over at him, his eyebrows raised. Ronja bit her lip. She had not had the chance to tell him about the documents.

"I have the blueprints and addresses here."

"How the hell did you get those?" Roark demanded.

Darius gave a rueful smile, the corners of his eyes creasing. "When one falls for an Anthemite, they tend to get mixed up with the Anthem."

Roark glanced down at Ronja, as if to gauge her reaction. She kept her expression passive, pretending to stare at the documents. "The Anthem has been looking for those papers for years," he said, returning his attention to Darius. "How did you get your hands on them?"

"Layla gave them to me for safekeeping. Unfortunately, that was the day my Kev Fairlan guards came to collect me." He offered the scroll to Roark as if he were offering the hilt of a sword. "These belong to you."

Roark took them tentatively, his eyes glazed. He popped the seal with his thumb and unrolled them. Ronja raised up on her tiptoes to peer over his shoulder. The pages were yellow, but the ink was still legible. Black and white skeletons of the mainframe were scrawled across the pages. Each page was labeled with a handwritten address in the top left hand corner. The writing was distinctly feminine, clean and curling.

Clock Tower
592 1st St.
91 32nd St.
835 45th St.
9 57th St.
878 67th St.

"What does it say?" Paxton asked. He and the other Tovairins had been watching the exchange curiously until now, but were apparently growing impatient.

"It means we have a shot," Roark said, passing the documents off to Commander Easton. He scanned them quickly, then gave them to his partner.

"We have to blow all six mainframes at once," Ronja explained as Paxton pored over the blueprints. "And it has to be done *after* I sing. If we destroy them before the Revinians are free, the shock could kill all of them."

"Understood," Easton said with a sharp dip of his chin. "We'll need six teams of six, each armed with enough explosives to take out a tank."

Ronja felt the blood leave her face. She knew she should be grateful that the Kev Fairla were working with them at all, but the prospect of charging into Revinia with thirty-six soldiers seemed like a suicide mission. But then so did the majority of their missions. "One team will need to come with me to the radio station at the clock tower," she said, her gaze sweeping over the room.

"I will accompany you there," Easton said. He looked to Jonah and Larkin, who were side by side on the couch, their thighs pressed together. "They will also be joining us."

"I'll be there, too," Paxton added.

Easton rounded on him, his teeth slamming together. "No."

"But—"

"We'll discuss this later," the commander growled.

Paxton narrowed his eyes to slits, his nostrils flaring. Ronja was surprised that steam wasn't pouring from his ears.

"We will make a preemptive strike against this Conductor," Easton said in a louder voice, speaking to the gathering as a whole. "Those ships will never leave the harbor."

Ronja blinked. "Just like that?"

Easton arched a brow at her. "Would you prefer to spend another few days deliberating?"

"No!"

The commander heaved a sigh, reaching up to massage his forehead with his thumb and forefinger. Paxton, despite his simmering anger, slipped a hand onto his shoulder. "I just saw a man walk thirty steps with a wolf on his leg and a bullet in his knee without flinching," Easton said. "I saw the Singer, I saw the way he reacted when you sang." He looked up at Ronja, who twitched under the spotlight of his gaze. "I would be a fool to ignore you."

"Thank you, sir. *Perlo*." Ronja tapped her fist to her brow, then her chest. Roark copied her hastily.

"*Pevra*," Easton answered.

"When do we leave?"

"Tomorrow evening." Ronja started to protest, but the commander spoke over her. "We need time to gather a team, to prepare weapons and food."

"The journey is what, two weeks by boat?" she inquired, looking to Jonah for confirmation. He nodded once, his arm around Larkin, who was scowling at the far wall.

Easton smiled, the first genuine smile she had ever seen him wear. "Who said anything about sailing?"

41: ALLY
Terra

Terra stood beneath the scalding stream, her head thrown back and her eyes closed. She had never been one to linger in the shower, but after five weeks in prison, she figured she deserved a break. If the Offs busted down the door while she was bathing, at least she would die clean.

After washing her hair three times and scrubbing her skin raw, Terra shut off the shower and hopped onto the bath mat. She peered around the pristine bathroom, focusing on the tall mirrors and fluffy towels. It was strange to be back in her childhood home. Though *home* was perhaps not the right word to describe it. *Residence* had a better ring to it.

Terra waded through the lifting steam to the porcelain sink. She used her forearm to wipe the fog from the looking glass. She grimaced. Her cheeks were sunken, her eyes bruised with exhaustion. The side of her head that she usually kept buzzed had grown an inch and stuck out at all angles. Her hand dropped to the drawer automatically, pulling it open to reveal various toiletries, including an electric razor.

When Terra plugged in the razor and took it to her scalp, she immediately felt better. She took her time, making sure every hair was precisely the same length, following the line of her part like a roadmap. Blond clippings sprinkled down around her, pooling in the sink. Cicada would be livid, but she could not find it in her to care.

When she was finished, Terra used a damp towel to clean the excess hair from her neck and shoulders. She checked her reflection again. Better. Wrapping herself in one of the thick white towels hanging on the wall and leaving the razor plugged in, Terra padded from the bathroom into the second floor hallway. Her feet carried her to her old bedroom naturally.

It was dark inside, the drapes tied shut and the lights sleeping in their sockets. She flicked the switch. The room was just as she had left it. Purple walls, the color she had picked when she was a child, militant bed, comfortable chairs for reading. Cicada had always insisted she read thick nonfiction books. She had preferred the fairy tales, not that she would ever admit it.

Terra spied fresh clothes folded on the bed and crossed to them. Thick black pants with leather patches sewn to the knees. Long-sleeved black shirt and leather jacket with plenty of pockets. Clean underwear. Black, of course. How Cicada had managed to guess her sizes, she had no idea. She was not entirely sure she wanted to know.

She let her towel fall and began to dress methodically. With each item of clothing she slipped on, she felt more herself. The pants were tight but moveable, the shirt warm but breathable. The jacket she could not have chosen better herself. It hugged her waist and zipped to her chin to protect her from the cold. Now all she needed was . . .

"Damn, Cicada," Terra muttered, begrudgingly impressed to find a pair of laced boots and wool socks waiting near the door. She crossed to them and slipped her feet in. Of course, they fit perfectly. The Anthemite turned to the vanity to greet her reflection. Still exhausted, still underfed, still haunted, but not defeated.

"Ruthless," she reminded herself. With one last glance at her reflection, Terra exited into the hallway. She strode to the polished wooden staircase that led to the main floor, pausing at the landing. The faint lilt of tense conversation brushed her ear. She tapped down the steps, her booted feet whispering against the wood. She came to a halt again at the bottom of the stairs, turning her head so she could hear.

" . . . only a matter of time before they find us," an unfamiliar male voice was saying.

"I told you," Cicada replied. "Maxwell trusts me, and he has no idea of our connection. He would never expect her to be here."

"You're right."

The voices cut off as Terra stepped into the study. It was just as she remembered it. The walls were lined with hundreds of contraband books, all with cracked spines. An elegant desk littered with precious artifacts from around the world crouched before a high window with drawn drapes, and a cluster of four green armchairs sat before a roaring fire. Two of the chairs were occupied.

One of the occupants was Cicada. He was dressed in a sleek pinstripe suit, a glass of brandy in his hand. He smiled at her, slow and calculating. Terra nodded at him, then flicked her attention to the other man. He was about her age, with messy brown hair and a long nose. His right ear was not burdened with a Singer. He stood up swiftly and advanced on her.

Terra darted backward, dropping into a fighting stance. He scuffed to a stop, lifting his hands in surrender. "Sorry," he said. His voice had a genuine ring to it that made her want to trust him. Of course, she did not. He cleared his throat. "I just . . . have you . . .

you're friends with Mouse, right?"

"Why?" she asked cautiously.

"Have you seen him?" He took another step forward, chomping at the bit for answers. "Please tell me, is he all right?"

Understanding clicked in. Terra dropped out of her stance, facing the stranger with her arms at her sides. "You're Theo," she said quietly. "You're with Mouse."

Theo nodded eagerly, his hair flopping like the ears of an excitable puppy. "Yeah, I am. Is he all right? Is he—" His voice broke. He pressed a hand to his mouth, his dark blue eyes flooding.

"Mouse is alive," Terra assured him. "I saw him yesterday."

"Is he—"

"Still free."

Theo exhaled the weight of the world. "Thank the gods," he murmured, retreating to his stuffed chair and collapsing into it.

Cicada rolled his eyes discreetly. "Terra," he said in his usual drawl, gesturing for her to sit at his right. "You must be exhausted."

"Thanks for the clothes," she replied, taking the only other available seat next to Theo.

If Cicada was bothered by this, he did not show it. He set his glass down on the coffee table between them, then motioned at the bottle.

"No thanks," she said. "I need food."

"In a moment. First, I would appreciate it if you would tell me exactly why you are here."

Terra felt her lip curl. *Bastard.* "I could ask you the same question," she said through her teeth. "Why the hell haven't you run?"

"Maxwell is indebted to me," Cicada said, as easily as if they were discussing the weather. "I brought him the ships, he allows me to live in peace, free of The New Music. He keeps me very comfortable."

"Last time I was here you almost seemed remorseful," Terra spat with a disgusted shake of her head. "I should have known you were a bloody traitor until the end."

"Traitor?" Cicada raised a trimmed gray brow. "I work for no one but myself. I have betrayed no one."

Terra smiled tightly. "Whatever helps you sleep at night."

Her adoptive father sighed, sitting back in his armchair to get a better look at her. "The last time you were here, I told you to run," he reminded her. "Why didn't you?"

"I have this thing called a soul."

"I gave you an out," Cicada went on, his voice prickling with irritation. "You should have taken it. Now here you are at my door again, with two Offs in tow. Sooner or later, they're going to come looking for you."

"What happened to the Offs?" Terra asked. "What did you do with them?"

"They're passed out tied up in the basement," he replied.

"How did you get Thomas inside without anyone noticing?" Terra asked, impressed despite herself.

Cicada smirked. "Easy enough when most citizens aren't permitted outside."

Terra nodded, vowing to ask why the hell everyone was housebound later. "What about the auto and the radio?"

"I smashed the radio, drove the auto thirteen blocks west," Theo answered.

Terra grunted, impressed. If she ever saw Mouse again, she would have to tell him she approved of his boyfriend.

"Why are you here, Terra?" Cicada demanded again, snapping her out of her thoughts.

"Believe me, I wouldn't be here if I'd had another choice," she answered icily. "Maxwell took me and several other

Anthemites hostage, friends of mine."

"I know," Cicada said with a curt nod.

Of course, you do. "I convinced him to let me lead him to a secret entrance to the Belly. He sent me with Henry, the one you stung, and Thomas, the one from the auto, as guards."

"So you decided to pretend this mysterious entrance was in my basement," the trader finished, resting his elbows on the cushioned arms of his chair and regarding her coldly. "I am terribly grateful."

"Piss off," Terra muttered.

Cicada blew out a tense breath through his nose, reaching up to massage his temple. He used to say that she was a headache. She sincerely hoped he meant literally. "Well, you're here now," he finally said. "I can get you out of the city, but it'll take a few days. What happened to your boyfriend?"

Terra swallowed. "His name was Samson, he was not my boyfriend, and he was murdered."

"I am sorry to hear that," Cicada said flatly, retrieving his glass from the table. He swished the amber liquid around, observing it through the crystal facets of the cup. "If you two had just listened to me . . . " He clucked his tongue admonishingly.

Terra lunged and knocked the glass from his hand. It flew in a lazy arc and shattered on the hardwood. Theo barked a curse. Alcohol sprayed at their feet, hissing when it hit the flames on the hearth. "Say that again," she said quietly. "And I will cut your ear off like you did mine."

Cicada, whose hand was still curled around a nonexistent glass, smiled luxuriantly. "You have learned well, child." Terra spun on her heel and marched to the door. "Where are you going?"

"To find a bloody ally," she shouted over her shoulder.

42: WINTER AND EARTH
Roark

Roark lay on his side on the mattress, curled around Ronja as she slept deeply. Her thick curls tickled his face, her heartbeat strong and resolute against his skin. It was half past four in the morning. Their meeting with Easton and the others had wrapped up around two. They had finalized their plans, selected the members of each strike team, pored over the schematics of the mainframes like holy texts.

It was all so simple. Anticlimactic, even. For as long as Roark could remember, the Anthem had searched for the locations of the mainframes that controlled The Music, and now The New Music. Of all the places they could have been, the documents were stashed on an island across the ocean, preserved by the unsuspecting exiled king of Revinia.

Ronja twitched in her sleep. Her lips parted, then closed without a sound. Roark brushed a lock from her brow. Her skin seemed to glow in the lamplight. With each passing day the cuts that stretched across her jaw grew fainter. Soon they would disappear altogether. Roark would never forget the sight of the raw, infected gashes left behind by the bit Maxwell had forced her to wear. He fought the urge to trace one of the white lines with his thumb, as if he could wipe her pain away.

Nothing is simple, his sister Sigrun had once said while they were staying at one of their spacious apartments in the core. It was a golden afternoon in late autumn, only a month before she would smuggle Roark out of the city to meet Parker, the Anthemite she had fallen in love with. Only a month before their father would murder her. She had been so vibrant, overflowing with life and wisdom. Luminous. *Simple just means you don't have all the facts.*

Ronja moved against him, a quiet moan escaping her mouth. Roark began to stroke her hair with the lightest touch, his eyes fixed to her troubled face. He did not know exactly what had happened between her and Darius, but he knew it had something to do with her voice and that it had shaken her to the core. When Easton showed up at his door to tell him that she had been attacked in the Contrav, he nearly passed out. It was only after Paxton assured him she was all right, that he wondered why she had been there in the first place. Then again, they called it the burning place where people went to release their fears.

Or tried to . . .

Sighing, Roark inched closer to Ronja, tucking his arm around the soft skin of her waist. He buried his face in her mess of curls, drinking in her scent. Winter and earth. Snow and soil. He pulled her closer still, cherishing the way their bodies fit together.

Their plan of attack had come together in a matter of hours. It was about as solid as it could be given the circumstances. So many things could go wrong which was exactly why Roark had been sitting on a plan of his own since they left Revinia. If all else failed, he would take Ronja and run—as far and fast as he could. They would use one of his father's yachts. He hoped desperately that the bribe he'd paid to his contact at the harbor had worked, and that the ship was ready and waiting. They would sail to Sydon. He had never set foot in his ancestral homeland. It was something he had dreamed about for as long as he could remember. His mother used to speak of Sydon as if it were paradise. Golden cities, vast deserts, tropical flowers of every color, salt water as clear as glass.

The hazy images took root in his heart, enhanced by the prospect of sharing a life with Ronja. They could live in peace, get a small cottage by the sea. Free from The Music. Free of Maxwell and his legions. Free from the burdens of what they had seen, of what they had done. Shame snuffed out his musings. He was many things, but not a coward. He would face an army with a bread knife to protect the family he had created for himself. Still, Ronja had changed things.

It was not that she was weak, or couldn't handle herself. She was the strongest person he had ever met, stubborn as a mule and resilient as a desert flower. She held on her lips powers he could scarcely fathom, abilities he could not begin to explain. But she was not immune to bullets. Roark had survived the deaths of his mother and sister. He had endured the loss of Samson and Henry, two men he considered brothers. Each loss left a gaping hole in chest. Some of the wounds had started to scab over, but they would never stop aching. Not completely. In the end, though, he could handle it.

Ronja was different.

She was stitched into the fabric of his being. If she were ripped away, those threads would tear him to shreds. If that made him a coward, so be it. Roark studied the planes of her face. Every freckle, every fading scar, every inch of pain and hope.

He realized abruptly that she would never run. She would never leave anyone behind. It was not in her nature. She would walk through a hurricane to save the ones she loved. She was creation and destruction. He was nothing more than the hand that protected her. He could not stop her. He could not steal her away. But he could fight for her until his last breath.

43: TO BE HUMAN

Ronja woke with a start, jerking against the warm body pressed to her back. Residual panic from a nightmare she could not remember squeezed her throat, tearing a cry from her.

"Shhh," Roark hushed her, his sleep-stale breath tickling her ear. "Everything's all right, you're safe."

Her muscles unwound, her breathing slowed. She tried to think of something clever to say to gloss over her vulnerability, but all she managed was a noncommittal noise of thanks. "What time is it?" she asked groggily.

"Around nine," Roark answered. Ronja started to sit up, but he wrapped his arm around her and buried his face in her neck, careful to avoid the angry bruises left behind by the Off. When she had checked them in the mirror last night, they were light blue and purple. "Easton left a note. We're not due at the armory until noon. Elise will come to take us there."

Ronja bristled, the battered face of the Arexian girl swimming before her eyes. "Funny how they claim to fight for freedom when they're keeping slaves," she muttered.

Roark hummed in agreement. "People have a way of justifying their actions, no matter how heinous."

"I bet Maxwell thinks his actions are justified," she replied, staring daggers at the stone wall opposite her. "This is different though," she went on, speaking more to herself than to him. "Maxwell is a psychopath. These are just people. They paint murals and build temples and fight to protect innocent people. They're—"

"Human," Roark finished for her gently. "They're human and they're complicated." He began to run a soft hand up and down the curve of her shoulder rhythmically, as if to lull her back to sleep. "Nothing is simple. Simple just means we do not have all the facts."

Ronja heaved a sigh. She didn't have a good answer for that. Instead, she stilled his hand by reaching around and lacing her fingers with his. She tucked deeper into the curve of his body and closed her eyes. Warmth blossomed between them. She so wished they could stay in bed for the rest of the day. She vowed that if they made it out of this mess alive, she would do just that.

"Ronja . . . "

"Hmmm?"

"Why do you want to save Revinia?"

Ronja opened her eyes, frowning. "What do you mean?" she asked carefully, loosening her grip on his hand. "I want to stop that monster and save our friends, our family. Should I be focusing on something else?"

"No, but why do you want to save the city?"

Ronja wracked her brains. She was not entirely sure what he was getting at. "Maxwell deserves to be taken down for what he did to Samson and Henry," she said. The words sounded rehearsed, as if she were reading them off a notecard. She felt Roark nod, the movement tugging on her curls gently.

"You want revenge," he summarized. "Of course, you do. But why do you want to save Revinia?"

"What are you getting at?"

"Just think about it." Roark gave her waist an encouraging squeeze. "Please."

Ronja huffed. Her brow puckered and her lips pursed. The more she thought about his question, the more it itched her. No one had ever asked her *why* before. The truth was she owed nothing to the people of Revinia. They had abused her and her family for nearly two decades, treating them like garbage. It was not their fault, but the result was the same. Why was she so hell-bent on saving them? "Because," she answered slowly. "They deserve the chance to make the choice between good and evil, or to stand somewhere in between. They deserve the chance to live."

"To be human," Roark said. "They deserve the chance to be human. We can give them that chance."

"But what if I choose something besides good?" Ronja asked, hating the way her voice cracked on the last word. "What if I dream about killing Maxwell with my bare hands, and I like it?"

"What would you say if I told you the same thing? Or that I was relieved when my father was killed?" The girl did not answer. Roark continued. "War changes us, love. You and I have done awful things. Awful things have been done to us." His fingers drifted up to brush the branching scar over her heart. "Maxwell said that your heart was too good for war," he said. "He was right."

"No—"

"But the Siren," he continued, speaking over her, "walks in the gray. The Siren was born in war. The Siren can put an end to The New Music and take down a madman. The Siren is who you need to be right now." Roark propped himself up on his elbow, peering down at her with eyes that were at once tender and resolved. Ronja looked up at him mutely. "Let Ronja sleep," he said, pressing his palm to her cheek. "She will be waiting when the war is done."

"Promise?" she whispered.

"Promise."

"There and back?"

"There and back."

Ronja nodded, her hair whispering against her pillow. Roark lay back down beside her. She closed her eyes to the world. The flames of the Contrav danced on the backs of her lids. One by one, she tucked away the gentle shards of her soul. Minutes or hours snuck by, curling around her as she snapped her armor into place.

When she opened her eyes, there was nothing but hope, rage, and her voice.

44: THE ARMORY

When a knock came at their door less than an hour later, Ronja rushed to open it, expecting to find Elise. Her hopes were dashed when she was greeted by an old man with white hair she had never seen before. He raised his fist to his forehead and chest in greeting. "My name is Jae," he introduced himself formally. "Good morning."

"Where is Elise?" Ronja asked without preamble. Roark appeared at her shoulder, smiling at Jae politely.

"Elise is occupied with other matters," Jae answered smoothly. "I am here to take you to the armory."

"Thanks," Ronja said, burying her disappointment. She cut her eyes to Roark. He gave a slight nod. "We're ready."

Jae led them through the twisting halls of the temple. He was unusually quick on his feet for his age. Even Roark struggled to keep up with him. The corridors were twice as crowded as usual. Several times Ronja nearly smashed into a Kev Fairlan who appeared to be lost in thought. The atmosphere was somber, the air swampy with mourning. No one so much as glanced at the Anthemites as they passed.

"*Sae!*"

Ronja whipped around, her heart in her mouth. Two women bearing a stretcher were hurtling down the hall, their faces stained with dried blood. The man they carried between them was howling in agony. The Siren slammed up against the wall, allowing them to pass. She craned her neck to see the wounded man and immediately regretted it. His bare chest was a mess of blood and seared flesh, a battleground in itself.

"*Sae!*" one of the emergency responders shouted again, clearing a clot of Kev Fairlans further down.

Ronja peeled away from the wall, watching them until they disappeared around a sharp bend. "What happened?" she asked. "Was there another attack?"

"No," Jae replied, his voice tight with pain. "They're coming from Yeille. One of the bases was bombed, I think."

"Oh."

"Come," Jae coaxed them along briskly. "We're not far." He was not lying. They only had to walk for another couple of minutes before the song of metal slamming against metal permeated the air. It sounded like a steamer roaring down the tracks, hurtling straight at them. Ronja found it both unnerving and exhilarating. Jae rounded a tight corner, motioning for the Anthemites to follow.

"Whoa," Ronja breathed. Roark nodded mutely in her peripheral vision.

The entire room was drenched in the orange glow of open kilns. Dozens of Kev Fairlans darted between them. Some hammered at freshly-wrought blades, still glowing white hot. All of them wore goggles, thick leather gloves, and aprons to match. The air was heavy with smoke, steam, and determination. Ronja wondered if the blacksmiths were always so focused, or if the recent loss of the town was driving them.

"Through there," Jae said, pointing a wrinkled finger straight through the shop. Ronja squinted through the sheen of smoke. She could just make out an unremarkable door in the far wall. "Good luck."

"*Perlo*," Roark replied, tapping his fist to his forehead and heart. Ronja was too absorbed with the mechanics of the workshop for niceties.

"We're grateful for your help with the evacuation." Those words pulled her attention back to Jae. The old man smiled, saluting them with fervor. *"Rel'eev, Entalia."*

Before either of them could respond, Jae spun on his heel and strode off down the corridor, moving with the grace of a man half his age. Ronja and Roark shared a look, then ducked into the shop. They had to walk single file to avoid the blistering ovens and workstations. Ronja led the way, sweat rapidly beading on her skin.

As they wove deeper into the shop, a table full of bullets standing like headstones caught her eye. Two boys were in the process of coating them in a clear, sticky liquid with paint brushes. *Poison*, her gut told her. She pressed on eagerly, Roark on her heels. They arrived at the door Jae had indicated. Ronja raised her hand to knock, but before she could, it was yanked open. Standing before them was an old man, easily ten years senior to Jae. His colorless hair was chopped short, and he was covered in white *reshkas*. On his long nose were a pair of thick glasses. They magnified his eyes to twice the average size. He smiled, deepening the lines on his face. "You must be the Revinians," he said.

"Your accent," Ronja said, her brows shooting up. "You're Arutian." It was similar to the Revinian accent, but broader and heavier.

"I was raised on the coast, yes," he replied with a fond dip of his head. He stuck out his hand, which was dry and wrinkled as a paper bag. "My name is Quinton," he said, shaking hands first with Ronja, then Roark. "I'll be providing you with your armor." He stepped aside, beckoning them to enter. They obliged, scanning the strange room with wide eyes.

It was half the size of the shop outside and twice as cluttered. The walls were lined with every sort of weapon imaginable. Swords, knives, staffs, guns, rifles, even an ax that looked as if it weighed as much as Iris. *Evie would love this*, Ronja thought with a pang. In the center of the space was a rough wooden table littered with sketches, gnawed pencils, rolled up documents, scissors, thread, and half-empty coffee cups. There was no other furniture, but piles of leather and metal armor surrounded the table, pushed up against the walls unceremoniously.

"Pardon the mess," Quinton apologized, picking up a cup and sniffing its contents. He made a face and set it down. "Last time I cleaned up, my hair was still black."

"No problem," Roark said hastily.

"So." Quinton leaned against the table, his weathered palms pressed flat against the surface. "Tell me about my beautiful Arutia."

Ronja passed Roark a bewildered glance. He gave a helpless shrug. "Uh," she said, clearing her throat. "We're actually Revinian."

"Right," Quinton said with a bright smile. "Beautiful city, I used to drive in to visit the casino, Adagio. Do you know it?"

"Sir," Roark broke in gently. "Revinia and Arutia have been separated for decades."

"Of course, but—"

"Revinia was taken over by a madman, closed off from the rest of the world," Ronja said. "We're trying to take him down." When she put it like that, it all sounded so simple. *Nothing is simple*, Roark had said. He was damned right.

Quinton was silent for a long moment. The muted symphony of the shop beyond the door filled the hush. His lower lip quivered as his failing eyes searched for a trace of a lie on their faces. "Revinia was a beacon," he said softly. "The last time I was there, I was a young man. It was a free city, an oasis in a world at war." He pushed off from his work table, looking back and forth between them. "Do you believe you can restore it?"

Ronja recognized the hope scrawled across his aging face. Doubt began to rear within her but she shut it down, like slapping a lid on a jar. She was not Ronja, not today. Today she was the Siren. "Yes," she told him. "I do."

"Then you'll need armor," Quinton said with an affirming nod. "You," he said, jabbing a finger at her. "Come with me."

45: THE SOLDIER AND THE SIREN
Roark

Roark leaned against the table with his elbows on the rough wood as he waited for Ronja and Quinton to return. They had disappeared into a side room twenty minutes ago, and he had not heard from them since. He would have been anxious were he not certain Ronja could knock the old man on his ass.

The Anthemite yawned, his eyes watering. The low light and the smoky air were making him sleepy. A rattling to his right drew his gaze. He straightened up and turned to face the back door. It opened slowly, the rust-caked hinges creaking. Quinton strode through, wiping his hands on the front of his apron. He smiled, satisfaction radiating through his yellow teeth, and stood aside.

Roark nearly fell back onto the table.

The creature before him was not a girl, not an Anthemite, not even an artist. It was the Siren.

She was dressed in black from head to toe. Her fitted boots crested her knees. Twin blades were strapped to her back, lighter and sleeker than the ones Jonah used. A subtly curved breast plate of black leather protected her chest, partially hidden beneath an old fashioned cloak. Her eyes, earth and steel, glinted wickedly.

Then Ronja peeked through the mask, a sheepish smile twisting her full lips. "See anything you like?"

Knowing no words could do her justice, Roark closed the space between them, grabbed the sides of her face, and kissed her. For a brief moment she was still; then she reciprocated enthusiastically.

Quinton cleared his throat. They ignored him, sinking deeper into the embrace. The craftsman gave a phlegmy cough, and they broke apart, eyes and cheeks burning.

"You, boy: you're next."

Roark nodded, still staring at the Siren, still lost in her power and grace. She smirked up at him. "Get going," she muttered. "Be ready, he likes to talk."

"Come," Quinton said, spinning on his heel and marching back into the side room. "We have our work cut out for us."

Roark grunted irritably, kissed Ronja once more on the lips, then followed him inside.

"Shut the door behind you," the old man called.

The Anthemite did as he was told, taking in his new surroundings with vague interest. It was about the size of the other workspace, filled with glaring electric lamps and full-length mirrors. Haphazard piles of armor were stacked along the walls, leaving little space for anything else. The center of the room, however, was clear. Sitting at its core was a small upturned crate. "Stand there," Quinton ordered, his back to Roark as he rummaged through a pile of mismatched boots.

"The box?"

"Yes, boy, the box."

Roark did as he was told. Between the bright lights and the pedestal he stood on, he felt uncomfortably exposed. He caught sight of his reflection in the long mirror across from him. Though his friends used to tease him for his vanity, Roark spent very little time in front of mirrors these days. He looked older. The last shreds of youth had left his cheeks. Stubble crawled across his sharp jaw. His eyes were quiet, steady. He looked like a soldier.

"Take off your sweater," Quinton ordered breezily, sweeping over to him with a tape measure in hand. Roark yanked his knit sweater over his head and tossed it aside. Beneath it, he wore a loose white shirt with the sleeves rolled up. The tailor set about measuring him at once. He took down the length and width of his torso, the length of his arms, the circumference of his biceps. He eyed the white discoid scars on the boy's forearms, but did not ask. Roark was certain he had seen worse.

"How long have you been with her?" the craftsman asked as he crouched to measure the distance from his hip to his knee.

"Uh," Roark stumbled, careful not to look down at Quinton as he blushed. "Not long. We only met a few months ago, but it feels like longer."

Quinton bobbed his head in understanding. "Love and war warp time," he said as he wrapped the measuring tape around Roark's thigh. "I bet the two of you have been through more in a few months than most couples go through in a lifetime."

Roark chuckled despite himself. "I actually said the same thing, once."

Quinton straightened up with a dour smile. He tossed the tape over his shoulder, then strode over to what appeared to be a stack of breastplates. They all looked relatively similar, the only significant variance being their size. His fingers fluttered over the pile for a moment; then he shoved the top three aside to access a dark plate not unlike the one he had given Ronja.

He approached Roark again, grasping it with both hands. "Hold out your arms."

The Anthemite did as he was instructed, and the craftsman began strapping it to his chest. It was lighter than he had expected it to be. Anthemites rarely wore armor. Then again, they had never engaged in absolute warfare before.

"Your girlfriend doesn't talk much," Quinton commented as he tightened one of the straps.

"She does with the people she trusts."

"Fair enough," Quinton said with another bob of his head. He stepped back to examine the fit. Roark watched him in turn, curious. "That should do it," he finally said. "You're easy to fit."

"Uh, thanks."

"Those boots should be fine," he went on, gesturing at the lace ups the Kev Fairla had given him. "Hold on, I need to do some digging."

Roark waited like an awkward statue as Quinton pawed through a haphazard hoard of arm guards, tossing them aside without care. "Do you make all of this stuff?" he asked as the man chucked aside what looked like a kneepad.

"Yes," Quinton called over his shoulder. "You're wondering why I treat it so roughly. My philosophy is if it can't survive me, it shouldn't be on the battlefield."

"Makes sense," Roark said.

"Here we are." Quinton snatched something out of the pile with a clatter of metal and leather. He got to his feet and faced Roark. "Try these on," he ordered, lobbing a pair of matching armguards at him.

By some miracle, he managed to catch them to his chest. While Quinton rummaged around for another piece of armor, Roark slipped the tough leather guards over the scars that dappled his forearms. Like the chest plate, they fit him perfectly.

"Can I give you some advice?" Quinton asked, his hunched back still to the Anthemite.

Roark shrugged. "Yeah, sure."

Quinton turned, a pair of tough knee pads in hand. "You'll

lose parts of yourself in war," he said, tossing the armor at him. Roark caught both without looking, his eyes fixed to the older man. "But whatever you do, do not lose her."

"I would rather lose my head."

"Good," Quinton said. "You'll have something to hold onto."

46: BARGAINING
Evie

Evie had always like the dark. It was comfortable, safe. But it had been hours since she had seen a lick of light, and it was starting to get to her.

Only minutes after Terra was whisked away by Maxwell, a pair of Offs had come to collect her and Mouse. Neither of them put up a fight as they were carted back to their individual cells. They did not even try to say goodbye. Mouse was likely silent due to fear; Evie, pure exhaustion. The lights were already off when they shoved her back into her room and locked the door. She was not exactly sure what they were trying to accomplish by keeping her in the dark— clearly they had better methods of torture than solar deprivation.

Evie knew she should be planning an escape. She knew she should be doing something, anything. But every time she tried, she found herself curled into a ball on the cold floor, images of Iris seared to the backs of her lids. Even sleep eluded her.

That was why, when the lock on her cell door clanged, it was almost a relief. Almost. The door screeched open. Evie gasped as scalding light poured over her like hot oil. She squeezed her eyes shut, blocking them with her forearm. Two sets of heavy footsteps approached. Then gloved hands wrapped around her arms, yanking her up. She let them lead her from the cell. There was nothing else to do.

Stumbling, shivering, she was dragged through the halls of the prison. The Offs—two young men not much older than she was—did not speak, nor did they slow down when she tripped. Eventually, they came to a stop and released her arms. She was only free for a split second before a hand grabbed her by the back of her neck and shoved her forward. Evie fell with a cry, landing on her hands and knees.

She struggled to her feet, still blind, as a door slammed shut behind her.

"Ms. Wick," a familiar voice greeted her.

"Maxwell," Evie growled. Grasping at the last threads of her strength, she forced her eyes open. Her pupils contracted painfully. She blinked and the room came into focus. Faint surprise pricked her. She was not in a torture chamber or prison, but an office. A modest desk sat against the far wall; a fire crackled merrily in the corner; and two chairs sat at the center of the room. One was short and made of metal, the other an overstuffed armchair upholstered in velvet.

That, of course, was where Maxwell sat. He had cleaned up since she last saw him, his black hair trimmed and patchy beard shaven. He wore a navy suit and shined leather boots. Not exactly the costume of a maniacal tyrant. "Please," he said, gesturing at the hard chair as if it were a throne. "Make yourself comfortable."

Evie stared at him, trembling visibly. She scraped the bottom of the barrel, hunting for a shred of adrenaline. She had him alone. He was not a fighter. She had killed men with her hands before, she could do it again. She could end it now. "I see," Maxwell murmured, his eyes roving over her as if she were an abstract painting he was trying to work out. "You want to kill me."

"What did you expect?" Evie spat.

The Conductor laughed a bit too hard, cracking his composed persona. "Yes, yes, I suppose that makes sense. I did torture your lover."

Something like a growl ripped from her chest and her vision was shrouded in a rosy veil.

Maxwell clucked his tongue admonishingly. "My father was terribly prejudiced toward your kind. Ridiculous if you ask me. I have no problem with homosexuality."

"No, you have a problem with love in general."

"Love is weakness, Ms. Wick. Attachments only weigh you down." He spread his arms wide, his spindly fingers uncommonly pale in the firelight. "I have freed myself from all attachments, and look where it has gotten me."

"To a mediocre office in a leaky basement?" It might have been a trick of the light, but Evie thought she saw his eyes flash. "What do you want, Maxwell?"

"I want to make a deal with you," he said, leaning back in his armchair and crossing one leg over the other.

"A deal," she repeated blankly.

"Yes, a deal." Maxwell grinned broadly, revealing too many of his marble white teeth. The techi fought a shudder. "You see, there has been a slight hiccup in my plan. Your friend Terra has been rather naughty."

Evie gave a tight smile. "Shocking."

"I believed she was intelligent enough to take the deal I offered her, but it appears she has fled."

Somehow, the techi managed to keep her neutral expression. Her thoughts rioted, her heartrate ratcheted up. Terra had done it. "Fled?"

"It appears so," Maxwell answered solemnly. "She was more

than happy to abandon you and your friends in order to save her own skin."

"Typical," Evie muttered. Her pulse was so loud in her ears, she wondered if he could hear it. Maybe his altered Singer gave him enhanced hearing. These days, anything was possible. "What do you want from me?"

"I want you to tell me where Ms. Vahl might have gone," Maxwell said, spreading his hands peaceably. "If you do, I can make your life and the lives of Mr. Constantine and Ms. Harte far more comfortable."

Evie cocked her head the side. "What about Roark and Ronja?"

"Of course, of course," Maxwell corrected himself hurriedly. "The Siren and Mr. Westervelt would also be provided with greater comforts."

Evie weighed his words, scrutinizing his face. It was too strange to be handsome and too handsome to be ugly. There was something off about the way he was talking, even more than usual. It was not the words themselves, but the intonation. "What do you mean *comfortable*?" she asked, folding her arms and leaning back in her seat. "Do you mean The New Music?"

"Of course not," Maxwell said smoothly. "I cannot let you go, of course, not after Terra walked out the door."

"You mean after you let her walk out the door."

Irritation flashed like oncoming headlights in his blue eyes. "Careful, Ms. Wick," he warned her quietly. "I can retract this deal at any time."

"I can tell you where she might be," Evie said. "But like you said, she left us behind. Not like she told us where she was going."

"Naturally."

"She would have wanted to get out of the city as fast as possible," Evie went on, her brain working in time with her mouth.

"But she had no supplies, no weapons. She would have needed those."

Maxwell inclined his head, watching her intently.

"There is a safe house," Evie said. "A cottage outside the city, halfway between the wall and Red Bay. I can draw you a map. If she was trying to escape, she would have stopped there first."

"A cottage," Maxwell tested the theory on his tongue.

Evie nodded in confirmation. "That's where I would have gone." It was not a lie. If she were trying to flee Revinia, alone and unarmed, she would make a stop at the little cabin. There was a cache of weapons under the floorboards, dried goods in the cabinets, even a hatch where one could hide from invaders.

"I will send a team of agents to this cottage," Maxwell said. "But understand, if do not find Terra, or evidence that she has been there—"

"The deal is off, I get it."

"No, Ms. Wick," Maxwell corrected her, his eyes glittering with black mirth. "No. If you are lying to me, the consequences will be far more severe." He looked down to examine his fingernails. "So you understand how serious I am, know that I am speaking of Ms. Harte's life."

Evie sprang to her feet. "You . . . you . . . no," she sputtered. "Ronja . . . "

"You have benefitted from the deal I struck with the Siren for far too long, Ms. Wick," Maxwell snapped. He climbed to his feet swiftly, then reached out to brush a knuckle across her cheekbone. She flinched, but did not move to knock his hand away. "I am a man of my word as long as it suits my interests, but I will not allow my vision to unravel as a result of sentimentality. If need be, I will find other ways to bend the Siren to my will." Maxwell jerked back from her as if shocked, shaking his head.

Evie watched in horror as he crossed to the door and rapped

on it with a solitary knuckle. It opened at once, revealing the two Offs that had dragged her to the office in the first place. They grabbed her by the arms, leading her from the room. The Conductor called as the door closed. "Not to worry. I am quite sure you are an honest girl."

47: SEVERED
Terra

Terra stood at the bottom of the basement stairs, her throat tight and her skin prickling. In her slick hands she held a bulky recorder. It had taken her nearly an hour to dig it out of the storage closet and sneak into the humming wire-stitched surveillance room to get what she needed.

"Need some help?"

Terra rounded on the voice, hiding the recorder behind her. Theo was silhouetted at the top of the steps, his arms at his sides and his head cocked askance. "No," she said shortly. "Thanks."

"If you're going to interrogate an Off, it might be useful to have someone who worked with them for years on your team."

Skitz. She had forgotten that Theo had been a contractor for the Anthem. They had never interacted before—there had been no reason for them to. She only knew about him now because of Mouse, who talked about his boyfriend as much as he talked about their imminent deaths, which was constantly. "Fine," she said, turning back to the door and flipping the lock. "But no killing the big one."

"Might I ask why?" Theo inquired as he started down the steps to join her.

"He's a friend."

"Friend?"

"He *was* a friend," Terra corrected herself. Theo arrived at her shoulder. He was considerably taller than she with a kind face and intense blue eyes. She could see why Mouse liked him. "Why the hell are you here, anyway?" she asked, taking her hand from the doorknob.

"Cicada is a friend of sorts," he explained with a wince. "Nearly everyone in the underworld knows each other. That's how I met Mouse." His eyes misted over. He blinked several times to clear them. "When everything went to hell, I knew Cicada would find some way to weasel out of it. He owed me a favor, and I figured if anyone had any information on Mouse, it would be him." He shrugged. "Plus, I know the Off's patterns. I can help him fly under the radar."

"Of course. He would never do anything that didn't benefit him."

Theo offered a thin smile. "Indeed."

"Right," she said, snapping back into focus. "The big one is Henry, he lives. The other one is Thomas. What happens, happens with him."

The boy pushed a low whistle through his teeth. "Damn, you're cold."

"Hope so."

Not keen to waste another second, Terra twisted the knob and kicked the door open. It banged against the wall, revealing the cellar. Cold and damp with stone walls and leaking pipes, it was the perfect setup for an interrogation. Henry sat in the middle of the room lashed to one of the dining table chairs. He raised his head as she and Theo entered, his expression blank. She glanced over at Thomas, who was slumped in a chair of his own nearby. He appeared to be unconscious, the ropes around his middle the only things holding him up.

"Glad you're awake," Terra said, turning her attention back to Henry. "My father has his stingers made special. They have a bit of a kick."

"Vahl," Henry spoke up in his monotone. "Torture is futile. You know we do not feel pain." The Anthemite did not reply, pacing toward him with the recorder tucked behind her back. She heard Theo close and lock the door, his eyes burning curious holes in the back of her head. "Sooner or later, they'll find you, and you'll pay. Maxwell may want you alive, but he knows how to make you wish you were dead."

Terra scraped to a halt a safe distance from him. His dark skin glistened in the light of the naked bulb dangling above. His mind might have been void, but his body certainly registered the potential danger. "Who said anything about torturing you?" She held the recorder out for him to see. "Not long ago, Ronja recorded herself singing into one of these. She used it as a diversion to escape the Belly. Those recordings are long gone, of course, but it gave me an idea."

She tossed the black box into the air and caught it in the same hand, not taking her eyes off her prisoner. "Cicada was always obsessed with monitoring The Music and recording its anomalies. He has been tapped into the signal for as long as I can remember." Her lips curled into a sly smile. "So I figured he must have caught the Siren's broadcast at the clock tower." The blood drained from Henry's face, his pupils shrinking to needlepoints. Terra was not sure if it was genuine fear bleeding through The New Music or pure instinct.

Either way, she had his attention.

It had not been difficult to locate the exact moment the Siren had tapped into the radio station among Cicada's recordings. All she had to do was sort through the hanging files in the surveillance room. When she spotted the overstuffed folder marked with a red tab, she knew she had her ammunition, her antidote.

Now she stood before Henry, the loaded weapon in the palm of her hand. "If you think you can break me, you're wrong," he warned her. "I am loyal to The Conductor—nothing can change that."

Terra began to prowl toward him like a stalking cat. "Your name is Henry James Romancheck," she began, pacing around his chair. "You are the son of Peter and Beatrix Romancheck, brother to Charlotte Romancheck. You are nineteen years old, soon to be twenty." She rocked her head from side to side considerably. "I think."

The Anthemite paused when she wrapped around to the front of his chair, staring down at Henry. Her knuckles were white around the silent recorder.

"I know all this," he said. "You are wasting your time. Whatever this is, it will not work."

"Your name is Henry Romancheck," Terra repeated, lingering in front of him this time. "You were born into the Anthem and grew up in the Belly, surrounded by music and revolution." The words were far too sentimental for her taste, but desperate times called for desperate measures. "Your first crush was on Kala Pent. We were kids. She barely gave you the time of day."

Henry remained silent, his dispassionate eyes still latched to hers. Terra could feel Theo's confusion radiating, but she paid him no mind. "Your name is Henry Romancheck. Your parents were murdered by Offs when you were a child—"

"They were traitors, they deserved to die," he cut in

mechanically.

Terra began to circle him again, swallowing her frustration. "When your parents died, you moved away from the Belly with Charlotte to protect her," she continued, slinking around the chair to view him again. "That was where you met Ronja."

Henry did not respond this time, nor did he look at her. The recording device seemed to pulse with life in her hand. *Not yet.* "You loved her. I doubt you had the guts to tell her, but you did. You almost died to protect her."

"I . . . "

"You sacrificed yourself to protect us," she raised her voice to cut him off. "All of us. Roark, Iris, Evie, Ronja, and me. Your last words were to Ronja. You said *maybe the stars are alive after all.* That meant something to her. What did it mean to you, Henry?"

Henry blinked. *Now.* Terra clicked the button on the face of the recording device. There was a pause filled with static. Then the voice of the Siren graced the room. It filled the space from floor to ceiling, forcing back the suffocating walls. It was startling, electrifying, exquisite. Terra hated to admit it, but it made her feel light as air.

"Stop this!" Henry bellowed. He squeezed his eyes shut, whipping his head back and forth as if to shake off a snake.

"You killed Samson, Henry," Terra shouted over the lyrics.

When your knees crash into the ground
And your desperate lips won't make a sound . . .

"You killed your friend. He was a good man and I . . . " Terra trailed off before she could lie. "I think I could have loved him. Maybe, after the war ended. Just like you loved Ronja."

"Stop," Henry begged in a raspy voice, letting his head loll backward against the chair. The arteries in his throat were straining, pulsing. "Please."

Terra looked over her shoulder at Theo, who was watching the exchange with his jaw hanging loose. She jerked back around when Henry hissed in pain. His entire body vibrated with agony, his teeth chattering in his skull. "Tell me about Ronja, Henry," Terra ordered, advancing on him until they were a breath apart. She could see every pore in his tortured face, every raw capillary in the whites of his eyes. "Tell me why you loved her."

Sing my friend
Into the dark . . .

"TELL ME!"

"I DON'T KNOW!" he screamed, spraying hot spittle in her face. Terra backed off, studying him intently. He could not seem to focus on her. His breaths came in short pants. Terra smiled bitterly. There it was, the most basic human emotion. It was rolling off him in waves. Fear.

Sing my friend
There and back . . .

Before the song could draw to a close, Terra drew the knife at her hip with a ringing hiss. The blade was razor sharp and sterile; she had cleaned it thoroughly with alcohol. "This will hurt," she warned him under her breath. "Theo!"

The boy rushed to her side, looking down at the writhing prisoner with wide eyes. Whatever he had been expecting, it was not this.

"Hold his head steady," she commanded sharply. "Do not let him move, do you understand me?"

Theo nodded, grasping Henry by the head. One hand cupped his strong jaw, the other pressed into his crown. Terra sucked in a deep breath. "Sorry," she said, looking down at Henry. He did not seem to hear her. She took his right ear and Singer and pulled them taut. The metal parasite was warm to the touch, almost as if it were alive. "If this works, you owe me," she muttered.

Terra raised her blade, then sliced through the wire and cartilage in one swift motion. The ear and Singer fell, hitting the floor with a sickening splat and the ring of metal. The song had ended. There was nothing but toneless static in its place. Blood spurted from the gaping wound in Henry's head, soaking into his creased suit. Theo released the prisoner, his pale hands slick with red. Terra stepped back hurriedly, her knife still clasped in her own bloody fingers. She was as still as a glass lake as she watched Henry, waiting for a sign. His open eyes were dull, his mouth a flat line.

Shit. Shit. Shit.

Then Henry blinked. "Terra?" he croaked, his bloodshot eyes focusing on her face. Before she could respond, he slumped forward in his chair, still hemorrhaging heavily.

"We need to get him untied," Terra said. "Now."

48: FALLING AWAY

It took them an hour to finish up at the armory. It would have gone faster were Quinton not such a talker. After they finally said their goodbyes, the Anthemites retreated to their quarters.

"Now what?" Ronja asked, tossing her sheathed weapons onto the bed. "We have hours to kill."

"Well," Roark said, leaning up against the closed door. "We could get some food. Sleep. Spar. Go over the plan for the fiftieth time."

"All good options," Ronja said, bobbing her head in agreement. Silence built a bridge between them. They regarded each other in steady awe. Roark looked as if he were made to wear armor, she thought. If the Siren was born in war, so was he. "Tonight might be our last night," she said quietly.

Roark did not deny it as she had expected him to. Instead, he approached her slowly, his eyes never straying from hers. Her pulse climbed with each step he took, peaking when he was a breath from her. "No matter what happens," he murmured, the words caressing the skin of her face. "I am glad I met you, Ronja Alezandri."

Ronja raised up on her tiptoes to kiss him. He pressed a

finger to her lips, stilling her. His hands drifted to the tie that held her cloak in place, unlacing it in a single motion. It crumpled to the floor as he began to unbuckle her armor. With each piece that was removed, heat swelled in her body. Once he had removed the last piece, she bent down to take off her boots. She straightened up, standing before him in nothing but her sheer undershirt. When he moved to embrace her, she tapped her finger to his lips. "My turn."

She took a tiny step forward, leaving a charged inch between them, and began to remove his armor. First his breastplate, then his shoulder and armguards. She sank to her knees slowly, unbuckling the tough leather pads that protected his knees. Roark shivered as Ronja got to her feet, tracing her fingers up his thighs and under his shirt, lifting it over his head.

"Wait," he breathed as his shirt slipped to the floor. Ronja looked up at him in askance. "Let me look at you, just for a moment." She watched him watch her, marveling at the way his pupils dilated as he drank her in. She had never imagined that anyone could look at her that way. It was not simply desire, it was awe. It was aching affection.

"Roark . . . " She spoke his name as if it were a prayer.

Her voice broke him from his stupor. He crushed his mouth to hers, lifting her from the floor. Ronja wrapped her arms around his neck as his fingers dug into her thighs. Roark pushed her back onto the bed. Rather than following her, he dropped to his knees and pulled her to the edge of the mattress by her hips. She trembled as he began to kiss along the insides of her thighs, nudging them apart. A gasp tore from her chest. She dug her fingers into his hair, her back arching.

Minutes or hours might have passed while she twisted beneath him. When he finally rose to his feet, she was shivering and sweating, caught between pleasure and exhaustion. "Look at me, love," Roark said gently, leaning over her and tethering her with his gaze. "Do you want to keep going?"

Ronja pulled him down toward her as an answer, kissing him like the world would cave in beneath them. When he settled between her legs, he let out a low growl. They sank into a steady rhythm, bodies and heartbeats twined. Everything fell away. Their pain and their history. Their guilt and their fear. When they finally finished, they lay side by side, their limbs heavy with sweat and delicious exhaustion.

"We could just keep doing that for the next few hours," Roark suggested.

Ronja made a noise of agreement, burying her face in the warm space between his neck and shoulder. "If we make it out of this," she said, closing her eyes. "We're going to spend a whole week like this."

"I appreciate the vote of confidence, but I do need the occasional break."

"No," Ronja said with a laugh. "Together. Peaceful. Happy."

"You say a week, I say a lifetime." He pressed his lips to her warm brow.

She smiled, her eyes closed. "Deal."

The rest of the day crept by with the speed of an earthworm. They ate up some of the time showering, then devoured a huge meal in the *trié*. Most of the seats were taken up by refugees from the town. The adults paid them little mind, but the young children crowded around Ronja, fascinated by her heavily freckled skin. She allowed them to touch her hands and cheeks while Roark looked on, eating his soup with a gloating smirk.

Once their food settled and the Tovairin children had been convinced that Ronja was not suffering from pox, the Anthemites ambled down to the main hall where dozens of Kev Fairlans were sparring. They picked an unoccupied corner of the vast room and spent the next hour sparring. Roark beat Ronja every time with frustrating ease, but by the time they were through she was confident she remembered how to flip someone over her shoulder and throw a punch without breaking her knuckles.

Eventually they found their way back to their room, settling in until evening rolled around. When a sharp knock finally graced their door, they both vaulted for it like caged animals.

"Paxton," Ronja greeted their caller breathlessly. "What time are we leaving?"

The Sydonian was dressed in full armor, his dreadlocks tied back with a length of cord. Clearly, he had won the argument with Easton and would be accompanying them to Revinia. "We're meeting in the main hall near the statue of Entalia in an hour," he told them formally, his eyes flicking back and forth between them. "Do you know how to find it?"

"Yeah," Ronja answered, mentally walking herself through the temple. "Yeah, we're good."

"Good," Paxton said, preparing to leave with a nod. "I was going to send Elise to take you, but—"

"Wait," Ronja yelped, causing both men to jump half a foot. "Actually, I think we might get lost. Please, send Elise."

The Sydonian gave her a bewildered look, then blinked rapidly. "Of course," he said. "I'll send for her." He started to back away again. "I'll see you both shortly."

"Wait," Ronja said again, reaching out as if to pull him back. Paxton arched a brow at her, irritation sparking in his eyes. "Could you ask her to bring some black paint, or charcoal?"

"I'll see to it."

Once Paxton was gone, the Anthemites set about packing their bags and donning their armor again. The former was the easier task. They had few belongings between the two of them, barely enough to fill one knapsack. Some food, a canteen of water, the *zethas*, the knives Jonah had given them, and several other useful items they had picked up on the voyage over. An old fashioned spyglass, a pocket knife with multiple tools, and a length of rope.

The armor was a different story. It took thirty minutes and a great deal of swearing to snap the leather plates back in to place. Ronja was still certain they were doing something wrong. The cap on her shoulder was uncomfortably tight, and Roark complained of a pinching sensation beneath his breastplate.

"We should have kept it on," she muttered as she hunted for the problem.

Roark finally waved her off. "Leave it. I'll ask Jonah."

Ronja smiled. "He'll give you hell."

"Hell I can handle," he replied. His eyes swept up and down her body. He gave a disbelieving shake of his head. "You look magnificent," he said softly.

Before she could roll her eyes, another knock came at their door. Ronja hurried over to open it. Her heart seized when Elise filled her gaze. This time, her face was not angled toward the ground. Her gaze was as steady as the moons over the sea. The bruise across her cheek was turning yellow, but Ronja knew it would not be her last. The Arexian girl reached into the pocket of her dress and produced a small tin. "Good luck," she said softly.

Rather than taking it, Ronja pulled her into a fierce hug. Elise was still for a moment, then wrapped her arms around the other girl and held fast. "Good luck," Ronja replied. "May your song guide you home."

"*Tigal frie lire avat,*" Elise answered.

They pulled apart. Neither knew what the other had said, but somehow the sayings transcended words. Elise took Ronja by the wrist, turned her palm to the ceiling, and placed the tin in her hand. She crossed her fingers over her heart. The Siren mirrored her. With a polite nod at Roark, Elise turned and strode back down the hall with her head high.

Ronja watched her go until she faded from view. Her fingers closed around the cool tin. She did not notice she was shaking until Roark laid a gentle hand on the small of her back.

"I wish . . . " she started to say, but she trailed off. There was nothing she could say that he did not already know. That the world was a mess, with or without The Music. That Elise might very well spend the rest of her life a slave, and there was little they could do about it. That even if they conquered The Conductor tonight, Revinia was still a broken nation. "Come on," Ronja said. "I'll do your war paint."

She sat Roark on the edge of the mattress and stood before him, popping the tin open with her thumb and examining the contents curiously. It was true charcoal, not paint, but it would have to do. She dipped her index finger into the powder and brought it to his face.

"You've never done this before," Roark commented as she drew the first streak down the center of his brow.

"Yes I have," she muttered, focusing on the second line across his cheek.

"No, I meant to someone else," he went on quickly. "Giving someone their war paint, it means a lot."

"Evie did mine, once," Ronja replied, thinking back to that night with a flicker of nostalgia. "Close your eyes." Roark complied. She dipped her finger into the soot again, then began to draw a thick line from his eyebrow to his cheekbone, straight over the tender skin of his lid. "It was right before my first jam. I think it was green and blue to match that dress you brought me."

"We use bright colors for celebration," he told her as she started to work on his other eye. "Black for war. White for weddings and funerals."

"I never knew that," Ronja murmured. She blew on his face gently, making his nose twitch. The sight brought a tiny smile to her face. "Open your eyes."

Roark did as she asked. The Siren swallowed the knot in her throat. He was fierce and beautiful, body and soul. His eyes, brown shot with gold, were luminous against the black paint. "How do I look?" he asked coyly.

"Like a raccoon," she lied, dipping back into the tin. "Hold still." Ronja finished his war paint hurriedly, keenly aware of the time slipping between their fingers. When she was finished, she wiped the excess charcoal on her pants and passed the container to Roark. "Do mine," she said, pushing her hair out of her face and closing her eyes.

"I am honored you trust me, Ms. Alezandri. Now," Roark said, his breath brushing against her skin with devastating gentleness. "Stay very still." He worked faster than she did. She felt him tracing lines across her cheeks and brow, even one through the center of her lips. His touch was heaven, even in the looming presence of war. "Done," he said, satisfaction ringing in his tone.

Ronja opened her eyes. Roark grinned down at her. The expression did not match his ferocious paint. She nodded her thanks and slid off the bed, striding over to the bathroom and flicking on the light. Her jaw dropped. The strokes of black sprawled across her face were not mere lines. They flared at the edges, just like the feathers of a raven.

Or a Siren.

Ronja turned to face Roark, only to find he was already gazing at her, pride flaring in his dark eyes. "Thank you," she said softly.

"Thank you," he countered. "For being my home."

"Thank you for the same."

"Come on, Siren," Roark said, holding his gloved hand out

for her to take. "We have work to do."

49: RALLY

Roark and Ronja were the last to arrive at the main hall. Easton and Paxton stood beneath the towering statue of Entalia, equally impressive in their leather armor. The wolf Pascal stood beside them, his intelligent yellow eyes roving across the vast space. Nearby, Jonah and Larkin were arguing, hands and mouths flying. Both of them had braided their hair back in a similar fashion and were armed to the teeth. All around them, several dozen soldiers talked amongst themselves.

"Ronja, Roark," Easton called when he spotted them approaching. He beckoned from across the floor. They sped their pace, weaving through the knot of soldiers who whispered as they passed. "Is this why you are late?" he asked, gesturing at their war paint.

"You have your rituals, we have ours," Roark responded in a clipped tone.

At the mention of rituals, Ronja felt the pull of Entalia. She craned her neck to view her looming stone face. The eyes of the goddess seemed to look in every direction at once, including straight at her. She gulped, fighting the urge to apologize for breaking her bowl.

"Fair enough," Easton said with a nod. "Before we leave, I need to speak to my people. I would appreciate if you would remain silent." The Anthemites agreed at once. "Thank you. Step aside."

Paxton motioned for them to stand beside him, giving Easton the floor. Ronja watched him curiously as they fell into place beside the Sydonian. Compared to Wilcox, who was chronically a breath from exploding, Easton was the picture of poise. He took a deep breath, then spoke in a voice that commanded attention. "Kev Fairla." Moving as a unit, the soldiers snapped to attention. "I will speak in the common language today to honor our guests," he said, his voice ringing through the temple.

No one said a word, though several pairs of eyes flicked to the Anthemites. "You have been chosen for a mission of the highest priority," Easton went on. "You were chosen for your courage, skill, and heart. I will not lie to you. This mission is dangerous, and different from anything we have faced before. The fate of our island—and perhaps our world—hinges on its success."

Easton gestured at Ronja, who stiffened. "Our top priority is protecting Ronja."

The Siren clung to her composure as every eye turned to her and did not waver. There was confusion there, apprehension, curiosity. Thankfully, she did not see much animosity, except from Larkin. She locked eyes with Jonah, who stood near the front with his arms at his sides. He gave her a subtle nod, which she returned.

"We are going to the walled city of Revinia," Easton said, reclaiming their focus. "There, a madman who calls himself The Conductor has brainwashed his people into fighting for his unjust cause. Men, women, and children. He intends to claim our minds as well and bring the rest of the world to its knees."

Silence. Ronja scanned the expressions of the Kev Fairlans,

hunting for a shred of disbelief. She saw none, only trust and determination. They put their faith in Easton, and she knew it was not blind. It was earned. That, she supposed, was what it meant to be a leader. "This man, The Conductor, harbors a weapon no one should possess. A synthetic form of music that can bend minds to its will. He has armed thousands of soldiers and placed the whole of his people under the control of this technology. He intends to send legions of his army to our shores and others. I have seen what these soldiers can do," Easton hesitated, drawing in a steadying breath. "Last night, one of them found his way into our temple and desecrated the Contrav."

Horrified whispers struck up like snares. Ronja winced internally, wondering if they would still be willing to help if they knew who really broke the bowl.

"They do not feel pain, they do not listen to reason under the influence of the weapon. You will need to use deadly force if you encounter them."

Ronja felt her mouth go dry; the knives strapped to her back were suddenly impossibly heavy. So many innocents were caught in the grasp of The New Music. If they died, they would die without ever experiencing freedom.

Easton held up a single *zetha* between his thumb and forefinger. "Paxton has modified our *zethas* after dissecting a device found on the Revinian insurgent. The *zethas* will now block the unique signal of the weapon instead of high decibels. You must wear them at all times. If you are exposed to this weapon, your mind will fall. The weapon's signal emanates from multiple broadcasting hubs within the walled city. Thanks to King Alezandri, we now know the location of each hub."

"There are six of them in total. Each of your teams has been assigned one of the hubs. Your task is to destroy that hub on my command and get out as fast as possible. We will fly over the city and drop in. Paxton, Jonah, Larkin, and I will be with the Anthemites on a dual mission. Ronja holds within her an antidote to the weapon born of her bloodline, one that can break the hold the Conductor has on his people. If she cannot prepare the Revinians with this antidote before the hubs are destroyed, the majority of them will perish. Our team will get Ronja where she needs to be, then we can all blow the targets and get out."

Ronja fidgeted in the charged silence, staring at her feet.

"You should know, Ronja is the daughter of Darius Alezandri and heir to the Revinian throne."

She snapped her head up, her eyes wide and her mouth hanging open dumbly. Easton was pointing at her with a calloused finger, his attention still on his soldiers. "For years, King Alezandri has funded our defense against Vinta and aided us in our struggle. We are indebted to both him and his family."

Rumblings of surprise and agreement rippled through the sprawling room. Ronja glanced at Roark sidelong. They nodded at each other silently agreeing that it was best the Kev Fairlans knew who she was.

"Kev Fairlans," Easton said, raising his voice to a shout. "Will you fight for your country?"

"*Ai!*" came the rallying cry.

"Will you fight to repay the Alezandri line?"

"*Ai!*"

"Will you fight for your freedom?"

"*Ai!*"

"Will you fight for Entalia, the goddess of rebirth?" Easton yelled.

Ronja found herself looking up at the statue as the resounding *ai* echoed. Entalia stood with her arms spread wide, her bald head tilted toward the lofty ceiling. Ronja felt her hand twitch at her thigh, longing to reach out and touch the stone. But it felt wrong to disturb her peace.

Easton raised his fist to his head and his heart. The Kev Fairlans responded in kind, a series of vibrant *thumps* resounding through the chamber. "Move out!" he ordered.

The soldiers spun as a unit and began to jog toward the exit. Only Jonah remained behind. He hurried up to the Anthemites, grinning far too broadly for the situation at hand.

"That went well," he said slyly.

"Thank you, Jonah," Ronja replied, passing him a genuine smile. "You've given us a chance."

He laid his tattooed hand on his chest, feigning a gasp of shock. "Did you just thank me, princess?"

Ronja shoved him back roughly. But her spark of humor faded seconds later, when a familiar voice pricked her ear: "Sorry, I got held up looking for the map."

The Siren turned around slowly, her spine creaking like clockwork. Darius strode toward them dressed in his freshly-cleaned armor and a worn coat that fell to his ankles. With a jolt, Ronja recognized it as the coat he had worn in the photograph with her mother. Twin pistols were sheathed at his sides, and a bag slung over his shoulder. He smiled at her tentatively as he arrived before them. "I told you, I am not letting you out of my sight."

Ronja tried to speak through her constricting throat. She searched his face for a wink of the fear he had looked at her with the previous night, when her Aura had smashed into her like a wrecking ball. She found nothing, only hope and determination. A slow smile spread across her mouth. "Good to see you," she said.

"We're late," he said, beckoning as he hurried after the disappearing Kev Fairlans. "No time to waste, Siren."

Ronja snorted. Still grinning stupidly, she started after him. Footsteps struck up behind her—Roark and the others falling in.

She felt the eyes of Entalia watching her all the way across the temple, searing away her paralyzing fear.

Entalia give me strength, she found herself thinking. *Guide me home.*

50: STITCHES
Terra

I said hold him steady," Terra snapped at Theo for the third time in five minutes.

"I am trying," he said, his slick red hands clasped around Henry's lolling head. "You really did a number on him."

Terra grunted, her hazel eyes never straying from the needle and thread as she closed the wound she had left in his head. She had never been particularly good at stitching up wounds. Slicing people open was more her forte. If Henry survived, his scar would not be clean.

She cut her eyes to his face, which was still, save for the sweat beading on his brow. Terra could feel his pulse thudding beneath her fingers, strong and steady. It did little to comfort her. Her entire plan had been a gamble from start to finish. It was entirely possible that the stress had fried his brains, or that the recording was not as powerful as Ronja herself. *What if he never wakes up?* She shoved the thought away.

"That should do it," Terra said, tying off the final sloppy stitch. She set the needle aside, trading it for a pair of kitchen scissors to snip off the end of the thin wire.

"You did good," Theo said, craning his neck to view her handiwork.

"It looks like shit."

"Yeah, it does."

Terra snorted. It felt like years since she had laughed. Theo smiled, perhaps sensing this. They had set Henry up in a chair at the dining room table. Blood, gauze, alcohol, and medical supplies littered the kitchen. Cicada was going to have a fit.

"Get me a rag," Terra ordered. Theo nodded, crossing the kitchen to the set of drawers beneath the countertop. "Second one down," she called when he did not return immediately. Moments later, Theo appeared at her shoulder, holding out a white cloth. "Thanks," she said, taking the cloth without looking at him.

"Sure." Theo sank back into his chair at the table, watching as she uncorked a half-empty bottle of vodka and poured it onto the cloth. "I forgot how much people bleed after this."

Terra began to dab at Henry's stitched wound. "Have you seen a lot of Singers cut off?"

"Some," Theo answered vaguely. He did not elaborate, and she did not push him. Some things were better left unsaid. "So what was that, exactly? That recording you played."

"Long story." She continued to sponge at the puckered stiches, her cloth turning red. "Short version is, her voice can free people from The Music—old and new. I would have just cut off his Singer, but—"

"That would have killed him."

"Right." Terra felt a blip of affection for Theo. He was no-nonsense, the polar opposite of Mouse. She liked that. "I meant to ask, where the hell is everyone?"

"You mean—?"

"Everyone," she confirmed. Henry twitched as she scraped

away a trail of dried blood crusted under his jaw. "The Revinians."

"The city is pretty much shut down," Theo said, crossing his arms and leaning up against the counter. "All the businesses are closed. Only the hospitals and Off stations are functioning. Off patrols come through every hour or so. Not sure what they're up to, exactly. Not like anyone can disobey The New Music."

"What about food?"

"The Conductor controls the rations now."

She rolled her eyes as she scrubbed at a splotch of blood on Henry's exposed collar bone. "Of course he does."

"From what I can tell, people are only allowed to leave their houses for training and to collect their rations. They do it a block at a time."

Terra arched a brow at Theo, who grimaced in distaste. "Honestly, it's creepy as hell. Offs show up with these big assault rifles and wait in the middle of the street. Then all the doors to the houses open up and they just march out." He shuddered at the memory. "They move as a unit. I have never seen anything like it."

"What do they do?"

"Target practice, mostly. Cleaning and assembling weapons. Basic hand-to-hand combat."

Terra frowned, pausing in her task to look up at Theo. "What are they shooting at?"

Theo gulped, the lump in his throat bobbing. "Mutts."

The Anthemite, who had been reaching for the bottle of liquor on the table, nearly knocked it over. "Pitching hell," she muttered. She snatched the bottle by its long neck. Rather than dumping it onto the soiled cloth, she took a generous swing. The liquid seared her throat. Unfortunately, it did nothing to burn away her memories.

Her mother had died to keep Ronja from being turned into

a mutt. Layla was already in labor when she was captured and taken to Red Bay. She had begged Terra's mother to allow her to give birth to her daughter before being warped into a mutt, so that she would have a chance to be human, even if it was under the crushing hand of The Music. Her mother had allowed it, even going so far as to help them relocate to the outer ring under a false name.

She had paid the ultimate price for it.

"I heard what you said, about that guy, Samson."

Terra set the vodka down with a hollow thunk and refocused on her task. Henry had not moved an inch. "Yeah," she said in a voice that was a shred too calm. She felt Theo watching her with pity she did not want.

"I lost my first love to an Off. His name was Benjamin. We worked on the black market together. He was the reason I started working with the Anthem, actually."

"Sorry," Terra muttered, still avoiding his blue gaze. She snatched up a roll of gauze and began to wrap it around Henry's head.

"It was a long time ago," Theo replied with a weighty sigh. "It gets easier."

Terra did not respond, focusing acutely on her task. When she ran out of gauze, she grabbed another roll from the table and continued to swaddle the wound. Once that was done, she taped up the end and got to her feet. If she squinted, Henry almost looked like he was sleeping. "Help me carry him upstairs."

It took them a good ten minutes to maneuver Henry out of the kitchen, down the hall, and up the staircase. He was over six feet tall and weighed twice what Terra did. Two breaks and half a dozen curse words later, they managed to get him to the spare room and lay him out on the navy bedspread.

"Well, at least the bedding will hide the stains," Theo said as they peered down at Henry. His chest rose and fell steadily, his full lips parted slightly. He did not appear to be feverish, nor did he seem to be anywhere close to waking up. Terra turned her back on him and marched from the room. Theo followed her half a moment later.

"Where are you going?" he asked as they made for the staircase.

"To find Cicada. We need to have a chat."

"Can I ask what about?"

"No."

Theo fell silent as they traipsed down the stairs, one after the other.

Terra sighed. "Thanks for helping, Theo," she said as they reached the first floor. "You did good."

The man smiled, his blue eyes glinting with mirth. "You aren't fond of people, are you?"

"No."

Theo chuckled under his breath, then jerked his chin down toward the front of the house. "I think Cicada is in his study. I'll clean up the kitchen."

Terra nodded her thanks and started down the familiar corridor. She approached the polished door on the balls of her feet, though she was not entirely sure why she was sneaking. She raised her fist to knock. Took it away.

"Come in," Cicada called. *Cocky bastard.* The Anthemite twisted the cool knob and entered the office with her head high.

Cicada sat at his desk, his booted feet up on a stack of documents. He had removed his suit coat, which now hung over the back of his chair. His sleeves were rolled, and sweat stained his underarms. He was poring over what appeared to be a letter. "Terra," he greeted her without looking up. "Are you finished using my kitchen as a hospital?"

"For now."

He glanced at her over the edge of the paper, a faint smirk twisting his lips. "How is the boy?"

"He'll live," she answered honestly. "No idea about his brain, though. Could be mush by now."

Cicada laughed coolly. He set the paper down with a flourish and swept his feet off the table. "What can I do for you?"

"You can start by telling me what has been going on since I was taken," Terra said, approaching his desk. She shook her freshly-clean hair over her shoulder, a challenge flashing in her eyes. He stared up at her with a lazy smile. "I know you have ears everywhere."

"I used to," he corrected her, raising a manicured finger. "I am mostly crippled, these days. I never go out. Someone comes to bring me groceries and . . . company once a week."

"You're Maxwell's pet," Terra inferred, disgust welling in her again. "You're even slimier than I expected."

"I have just saved your life," he reminded her, a sharp edge entering his tone. "Not to mention, you still owe me a debt, dear Terra."

"I've paid my debt in full by not gutting you right now."

Cicada got to his feet slowly, never taking his eyes off her hardened face. "I have never claimed to be anything but what I am, Terra," he said. "You're no better. When was the last time you did something for someone that did not benefit you personally?"

"I risked everything to try to free this city," she snapped. "You're a coward, and I am ashamed to have called you a father."

Cicada was silent for a long moment. Terra found she was panting, as if she had just sprinted a mile.

Finally, he blinked. "You can stay here for the night—then I want you gone. Take Theo with you. He's starting to wear on me."

"No," she snapped, slamming her palms into his desk. Cicada

flinched as the inkpot rattled. "You are *not* shutting me out, you skitzer. Tell me what you know. Have you heard from the Anthem?"

"Radio silence," he muttered, looking anywhere but her thunderous face. "No signals coming in or going out from anywhere. This whole place is a ghost town."

Terra made a noise of irritation at the back of her throat, scanning the room with sharp eyes. Dusty books. Trinkets from his travels before the walls went up. Glittering bottles of alcohol, most of them half empty.

Then the bulky machine sitting on a low shelf near the fire hooked her gaze. Her stomach clenched. "Does your transmitter still work?"

Out of the corner of her eye, she saw Cicada throw her a loathing glance. "Of course it does."

"I need to use it."

"Absolutely not, you'll bring The Conductor to our doorstep."

"But it has a built-in scrambler, right? So it shouldn't be a problem."

Cicada flushed, his lips flapping uselessly. That was answer enough. Terra started toward the transmitter, her steps heavy with purpose. "No." The man had finally found his voice and was hurrying out from behind his desk. "I will not—"

Terra cranked back her arm and socked him in the nose.

A howl tore from his throat as blood burst forth, staining his pressed white shirt. "You little—!"

"Shut up."

While her mentor let out a string of curses and rummaged through his desk for something to staunch the bleeding, Terra knelt before the transmitter. She flicked the metal switch on the side of the machine. It hummed to life, its screen lighting up orange. She dusted off the thick headphones that sat beside the transmitter and crowned herself with them. Cicada's grunts of pain were muffled. She checked on him over her shoulder. He was perched on the edge of his desk, a handkerchief pressed to his hemorrhaging nose, staring at her the way one might look at a rat found in a cupboard.

She saluted him with two fingers, then returned to the transmitter. She clicked on the scrambler with the push of a button, then began to fiddle with the knob that controlled the frequency. Static rippled. "Come on, old boy," Terra muttered, cranking the dial to the proper channel. "Come on," she muttered. "Come on."

" . . . th . . . "

Terra stiffened. She cranked the volume all the way up, pressing the headphones closer to her remaining ear. "This is Medusa," she said into the microphone. "I repeat, this is Medusa. Does anyone copy?"

" . . . is . . . "

Shaking, Terra fussed with the dial, coaxing the signal closer. " . . . is Harpy. Medusa, do you copy?"

Terra shot to her feet, the cord connecting her to the transmitter swinging wildly. "Harpy," she shouted, bringing the built-in microphone closer to her lips. "Skitz, you're alive, where are you?"

"We're trapped in the Belly," Ito said, desperation not native to her coloring her tone. "Sphinx is dead. We're running out of time. The scrubbers won't hold for much longer."

Terra shook her head, digesting the barrage of information. "What about the emergency exits?"

"Negative. The elevator is out, too."

Terra swore colorfully. She glanced back at Cicada again. He was watching her with begrudging interest, his nose still gushing. Her thoughts threatened to spin out. She sucked in a calming breath, settling into the role of a solider. "There has to be another way out," she muttered.

"Even if we got out, The New Music would get us," Ito said, her hopelessness palpable over the line. "We're out of options."

Terra bit her lip. She didn't want to give her false hope, which was worse than no hope at all. There was every chance Henry was fried, and no guarantee that he would know where the mainframes were if he woke up. Then a thought struck Terra, nearly bowling her over.

"Wait," she said. "What about the hatch, the one under Roark's tent? It was sealed with concrete, right?" Ito was silent on the other end of the line, static rustling as she considered. "The tunnels lead out past the wall. You could crack it open with a pick ax."

"And go where?" Ito asked carefully.

"Out, away."

"They would spot a thousand people spilling out of the city."

"Not if they're distracted," Terra said grimly.

"What are you talking about?"

"Bullon has a fleet of transport ships from Vinta waiting in port. He's planning a conquest," the Anthemite explained, swinging around to look Cicada dead in the eye. His nose appeared to have stopped bleeding, though he still pinched it with his ruined handkerchief. He narrowed his eyes at her, a warning. Terra smiled wickedly. "I'm going to burn them. Burn the ships." Before Ito had the chance to respond, a distant thud followed by a scream permeated her headphones.

Henry was awake.

51: REL'EEV, ENTALIA

The hanger was nearly empty when they arrived, both of people and vehicles. The mammoth doors were open, revealing the charcoal beach and darkening sky. Ronja felt her stomach twist at the sight of the thick fog. She had never been in an aeroplane before, but could not imagine the conditions were good for flying. The Westervelt Industries airship they had escaped Red Bay in was more like a floating oasis, full of luxurious furniture and stained glass. The craft they were bound for was a different bird entirely.

The black aeroplane waited for them at the far end of the hangar, looming over the smaller fighter jets and decommissioned tanks. Its wings were as long as a subtrain engine, its twin propellers sharp enough to cut through bone. Ronja grimaced, willing herself not to think about it. She had not considered herself to be afraid of flying, but maybe it was not the flying that was getting her.

"Why the hell do we have to jump out of the damn thing?" Ronja asked weakly as they approached the plane. "Can we not just find somewhere to land?"

"In the city?" Jonah asked dryly. "Sure, we could give it a shot.

Maybe the explosion would take out one of the mainframes by accident, who knows." Ronja shot him a dangerous look. He only laughed in response.

"The only runway is on the palace grounds," Roark reminded her gently. "Which seems like a bad idea."

Ronja grunted, glowering at the metal beast ahead of them. "No worse than jumping out of the goddamn aeroplane."

They arrived at the base of the retractable stairs that spilled from the plane. Paxton stood at the top, scribbling something on a notepad. A memory slammed into Ronja. Henry, taking notes in his black book before their mission to Red Bay, silhouetted by the comfortable fire. He had always been the organized one, even when they were children. It bordered on obsession. She wondered if he had maintained that trait under The New Music.

She wondered if she would see him tonight.

They mounted the stairs one at a time, Jonah taking the lead. Darius followed him, his eyes on an old document clenched in his gloved fingers. When he nearly missed the second step, he stuffed the paper into his pocket and continued with his eyes on his feet. Roark trailed him and Ronja brought up the rear. She kept her eyes on Roark's leather clad back as they ascended. Frigid wind rolled in off the sea, stirring her curls. She paused for a brief moment when she crested the stairs, looking out at the scene.

There was something hauntingly beautiful about the shores of Tovaire, something that made her feel more like a memory than a person.

"Ronja," Roark called softly.

She glanced over at him. He was halfway inside the plane, reaching past Paxton to offer her his hand. Ronja took one last look at the crashing, bruised waves.

Re'leev, Entalia, they whispered.

Ronja took Roark's offered hand and stepped into the plane,

leaving the aching shoreline behind. Red light washed over her. She blinked rapidly as her vision adjusted. Paxton pressed a button on the curved metal wall. The staircase began to roll back into the plane with a wheezing groan; then the door slammed shut with a hiss. Ronja drank in the aeroplane.

It was larger than she had expected with long cushioned benches pressed up against windowless walls. Safety belts dangled from the ceiling like cobwebs. Most of the Kev Fairlan soldiers had already clipped themselves in and were conversing in their native tongue. In the center of the aisle was a huge pile of what appeared to be black backpacks. *Parachutes*, Ronja realized with an internal groan.

"Ronja, Roark," Jonah called, waving at them from the back corner of the plane. He sat with Darius and Larkin toward the end of one of the benches. The Anthemites started toward them, squeezing between the luggage and the knees of the soldiers. "We're in for a long flight," Jonah said, scooting away from Darius to pin Larkin against the wall. She shoved him off roughly, muttering what sounded like a slur.

"How long?" Ronja asked, taking a seat next to Darius. Roark sat down on her right.

"Shorter than our trip here," Jonah said with a low laugh. When she raised her eyebrows at him, he rolled his eyes. "Five hours, give or take thirty minutes. Hope you can sleep sitting up."

Ronja scoffed. She could sleep anywhere, but her nerves were fizzing with adrenaline. Sleep was the furthest thing from her mind. "When are we leaving?" she asked, reaching up for the complicated harness above her and yanking it down. It did not budge, its buckles clinking softly.

"Any minute," Jonah answered.

Ronja nodded, still fighting the safety harness. Roark was already belted in place. Across from her, two Kev Fairlan soldiers were watching her, grinning. Before she could even blush, a weathered hand intercepted hers. "Let me," Darius said with a quiet smile.

"Uh, okay."

Ronja let her hands fall to her lap as he pulled down on the harness gently. It released at once. "Excuse me." Darius leaned across her and clipped the metal buckle into place. The straps tightened automatically across her chest as he sat back in his seat. She saw Roark watching the exchange with a faint smile out of the corner of her eye, but she could not bring herself to meet his eyes.

"Thanks," she mumbled, picking at a loose thread on the belt.

"Of course," Darius replied.

"Attention!"

Ronja looked up, grateful for the diversion.

Paxton and Easton stood toward the front of the plane, facing the strike team. "We'll be leaving in two minutes," the commander said. "Flight time is approximately five hours, so try to get some rest. We'll inform you of your drop zones as we approach." He gestured at the pile of parachutes at the center of the aisle. "You are all aware of your targets, correct?"

A collective *yes* flickered through the aeroplane.

"This is the last time I'll address you as a group until we arrive," Easton said, looking out over them all with steady eyes. Everyone sat up a little straighter. "Watch each other's backs, work fast, and get to the extraction points marked on your map by 0500." The commander smiled. "I'll see you all at daybreak. *Rel'eev, Entalia.*"

"*Rel'eev, Entalia,*" came the response.

"*Rel'eev, Entalia,*" Ronja murmured.

The engines rumbled to life beneath them. Paxton and Easton took two individual seats near the front of the plane. The

Siren looked over at Roark, hoping her anxiety did not bleed through her war paint. It must have, because he took her hand and brought it to his mouth. With a jerk they began to roll forward, quickly gathering speed.

Rel'eev, Entalia. Maybe the stars are alive after all. Freedom is a state of mind. May your song guide you home . . . The mantras chased one another in circles in her brain, growing louder and louder until she felt them lift off the ground. Ronja closed her eyes, leaning her head back against the wall of the plane.

They were on their way back—to hell.

52: REBIRTH
Ito

Ito set the radio down on her desk with a soft click, staring at it with blind eyes. When it had crackled with life, its light flashing red, she'd thought she was dreaming. Then the voice had sliced through the static. *This is Medusa, does anyone copy?*

"What are we gonna do, boss?"

Ito looked up. She had forgotten the presence of the young Anthemites entirely. Kala and Sawyer stood before her desk, watching her expectantly. Behind them, Elliot sat next to Charlotte on the edge of her bed. The girl was still a shell, shivering beneath the knit throw the boy had wrapped her in. Cosmin sat in his wheelchair, Georgie asleep on his lap. He stroked her hair while she snored softly.

Beyond the insulated walls of her tent, nearly a thousand Anthemites were waiting for her to come up with some sort of plan.

"You all heard what Terra said," Ito said, meeting each of their gazes individually. "What do you think?"

"We can probably break the concrete over the hatch," Kala spoke up immediately, tossing her shiny black hair over her shoulder. "It'll take a couple hours, but I bet it can be done."

"Yeah, but then we have to get nine hundred people to go down a hole into the sewers and walk single file for three miles into the bloody wilderness," Sawyer said, crossing her skinny arms. "That'll be a treat."

"It'll take a hell of a lot of organization, but I imagine it can be done," Elliot said in his gentle lilt. His eyes flicked to Cosmin. "I can carry you on my back, Cos."

"Thanks," the boy muttered, looking down at his sister with flushed cheeks. Ito felt her heart tighten.

"Do you think Terra can do it?" Kala asked.

Ito weighed the question. Their exchange over the radio was the longest conversation they had shared since Ito demoted her following the Red Bay incident. Ito had known their relationship would never be the same, that she had lost the trust of her prodigy. But she had never stopped believing that when it came down to it, Terra would do what needed to be done to protect the Anthem.

"Yes," she answered with a slow dip of her chin. "Absolutely."

"Then we have an exit to crack," Kala said, clapping her golden brown hands together smartly. "I'll try to find a pickax or something."

"Take Sawyer with you," Ito ordered. "No one goes anywhere alone, understand?"

Both girls nodded, then ducked out of the tent without another word. The rumble of anxious throngs filtered in through the thick flap that served as a door.

"Elliot," Ito said, getting to her feet. "Stay with the children."

"Commander," Elliot replied, saluting her formally.

A shiver ripped through Ito at the title. She hoped it did not register on her face. Grabbing the megaphone off her desk, she followed Sawyer and Kala outside. She was immediately engulfed by a tidal wave of apprehension. Hundreds of Anthemites milled around the Vein and clustered around cook fires. The air was tense enough to snap in half. Ito took a deep breath, her fingers tightening around the handle of the megaphone, then started forward.

The crowds parted as she approached, the gaps filling with whispers. She tried not to pay them any mind, but caught the words *commander* and *dead* more than once. When she finally reached what seemed like the middle of the throng, she stopped. It was utterly silent, as quiet as it had ever been in the Belly. She almost did not need the megaphone, but she raised it to her lips anyway.

"Anthemites," Ito began, her magnified voice ringing out across the station. "Thank you for your patience. I know you're afraid, and I know you want answers." She paused for a moment, allowing the rumbles of agreement to dissipate. "We may have discovered a way out of the Belly, and out of the city itself. Please hold your questions until I am finished."

Ito wet her dry lips, her eyes scanning the hundreds of faces turned toward her. Though they were clearly itching to celebrate, to pelt her with questions, they held their tongues. "There is a hatch in the floor of Roark Westervelt's tent. It was sealed over with concrete, but we should be able to crack it open and escape into the storm drain beneath it."

"And go where?" a male voice cried out from somewhere in the mob.

"One of the drainage pipes lets out beyond the wall," Ito replied to the group at large. "It will be a long walk, single file in the dark. If we make it out of the city, we'll be facing a new kind of danger. The wilderness. It's a ten day walk to the nearest Arutian city, Paravar." *And the chances of them letting in a nearly a thousand Revinian refugees are slim to none.* "It will be a difficult journey, and I cannot guarantee that all of us will make it."

She paused here, letting her words sink in. No one spoke, not even to mutter something to their neighbor. "But," Ito said, twisting her tone into something resembling confidence. "We will be safe from The New Music below ground, and the men undoubtedly watching our movements will be otherwise occupied."

"What do you mean?"

"How can you know that?"

"Tell us!"

Ito raised her hand high, hushing the flapping mouths. "One of our own has escaped the clutches of The Conductor. As a diversion, she and our allies are going to burn a fleet of Vintian ships intended to transport thousands of the Conductor's soldiers to other nations." Ito hesitated for a moment. "Her name is Terra Vahl, and we are indebted to her."

Uncertain whispers struck up around her. Ito waited for them to die off before returning to her speech.

"What's more, Terra suspects that the Siren—Ronja—is alive and free. As long as she breathes, The Conductor has something to fear." Ito smiled, her hooded eyes glinting like a blade in sunlight. "We are the last seed of humanity within these walls, and we will carry on. We will preserve the legacy of those who came before us. We will keep the rebellion alive."

The station erupted with a roar of assent, powerful enough to shake dust from the arching ceiling. Ito shivered as hope and fear swelled inside her, threatening to turn her bones to dust. Somewhere in the chaos and the noise, a drumbeat struck up, the first she had heard in over a month. The cheers turned to song, the song to dance.

And in that moment, the Anthem was reborn.

53: BROKEN RECORD

Ronja flexed her jaw, attempting to pop her ear. The pressure released with a high pitched squeak. She sighed in relief, reclining against the metal hull. Warm breath dusted her cheek. She glanced over at Roark, who had fallen asleep about an hour ago, along with the majority of the soldiers. Beyond him, Larkin and Jonah conversed in hushed tones.

Roark shifted in his harness, but did not wake. He looked troubled in the red glow of the cabin, his brow creased beneath his war paint. She was just glad he was getting *some* rest. They were certainly going to need it.

"Not a fan of flying?"

Ronja glanced at Darius sidelong. He too had fallen asleep some time ago, but now sat straight, rubbing his eyes.

"Not a fan of jumping out of planes," she corrected him.

"Have you done it before?"

Ronja passed him a disparaging look. "Yeah, between working two jobs and taking care of two kids and my mother, I made sure to fit in some time for sky diving."

Darius winced. "Sorry, that was—"

"Forget it." She waved him off. "Have you jumped?"

"Twice," the king said with a nod. "I quite enjoyed it, though I was in far better health at the time."

"Better health?"

"I just meant . . . age takes its toll," he replied a shred too quickly.

"Right."

Silence grew between them. Ronja itched the bridge of her nose unconsciously.

"We should talk about what happened with your Aura," Darius said after a while.

"No, thanks."

"We need to."

"The way you looked at me," Ronja said, her voice ratcheting up a decibel. A Kev Fairlan she did not recognize raised his head across from her, watching the exchange curiously. The Siren drew a breath and continued in a softer tone. "You looked at me like you were afraid of me, like I was some sort of freak. It was just like how people used to look at me when I was under a mutt Singer."

"You misunderstood me," Darius replied softly. "I was not afraid *of* you, I was afraid *for* you. I thought you might have injured yourself. I should have told you about the dangers of bending Auras, especially when you are just growing into your gift."

"Oh." Relief washed over Ronja. She wanted to say something, anything, but nothing seemed appropriate. Instead, she offered Darius a tiny smile, which he returned without hesitation.

"I told you that Auras exist without us, but I should have specified." Darius twisted in his seat to get a better look at her. She copied him, hanging on his every word. "We can bend the Auras of other songs, be it from a recording or an instrument or a vocalist, but they do not belong to us. Your personal Aura, from your own voice, is wholly yours. It is a part of you as much as your hand or your brain."

"Okay," Ronja said, bobbing her head slowly, though she only half understood.

"When you reach for it, try not to think of it as calling it to you. Think of it as moving a limb." Darius wet his lips, then let out a low whistle. Ronja sucked in an awestruck breath as a thin thread of rust colored light coiled in the air between them, casting its faint light across their faces. The king crooked his finger at it, and it fluttered toward him, spiraling around his finger once then fading into oblivion. "You try," he said.

Ronja swallowed, glancing around the cabin discreetly. No one was paying them any mind anymore, either asleep or absorbed in their own conversations. Rather than whistling, she began to hum a tune she had picked up from Iris, a lullaby. Before her eyes, her white Aura blossomed, a timid ball of light to match the gentle notes.

"Now, don't call it to you," Darius said quietly. "It's already with you. Just move it."

Ronja lifted a trembling hand and curled her fingers into a loose fist. The budding light shivered, then began to unfurl. It rolled over her knuckles, smooth as the belly of a snake, and wrapped around her wrist. Life pulsed in its luminous body, heating her skin. Or maybe the warmth was coming from her skin. She couldn't tell anymore. Shocked laughter burst from her mouth as her Aura faded. She looked up at Darius, beaming. "Skitz," she breathed. "That was . . . that was . . . "

"Well done," the king said.

"Tell me more about your gift," Ronja pressed him eagerly. "You said you can bring the truth out of people—how does that work?"

To her surprise, Darius winced. "I rarely use it, especially these days. It feels like an invasion of privacy." He rocked his head from side to side. "It *is* an invasion of privacy."

"Okay, but how does it work?"

"When you sing, it seems that you allow people to feel what they need to feel, if they've been bottling up their emotions on their own or if they've been under the influence of The Music," Darius explained. "When I sing or play an instrument, people spill their secrets. Secrets they're keeping from others and themselves."

"Why didn't I start spilling my guts when I heard you sing the other night?"

"I have learned to control my gift, so that it does not automatically affect everyone around me. Trust me, there is nothing worse than a room full of people straining to tell you a thousand things you did *not* need to know. "

"I see," Ronja said. She looked down at her knees, her brows knitting. "I guess what I do is an invasion of privacy, too." The thought made her skin crawl. Her fingers drifted up to the scar where her right ear used to be. Sometimes, if she listened hard enough, she thought she could still hear The Music pounding on her skull, begging to be let back in.

"You're not taking away their free will," Darius said with a shake of his head. "You're giving them the ability to make a choice, and to better understand themselves. In the case of the Revinians, you're giving them the chance to be human."

The Siren made a noncommittal noise at the back of her throat, her head still tilted forward.

"Ronja." The shift in his tone caused her to look up at Darius. His eyes were too bright in the red glow around them. "We're going into a war zone. One or both of us could die tonight." She nodded slowly, wondering where he was going with this. "Last night, you expressed some interest in learning more about your mother. Now might be the only chance I have to tell you what I remember."

Ronja stared at Darius for a long moment, a thousand words on her tongue, a million moments clashing in her mind. She swallowed the words and laid the memories to rest. "Yeah," she said. "Yeah, I'd like that."

54: TEN THOUSAND WORDS
Evie

The bang of her cell door slamming against the wall broke Evie from sleep. She stayed where she was, curled in a ball in the center of the room, while multiple pairs of hands dragged her to her feet and into the painfully bright hallway.

"What is this?" she demanded halfheartedly, blinking up at the Offs on either side of her. Neither of them paid her any mind, their dead eyes fixed straight ahead. "Where the hell are you taking me?" When it became clear that they were not going to answer her, Evie fell silent. They wove through the halls of the prison, past dozens of identical doors and gas lamps, past chemis in white coats and Offs in black uniforms. No one so much as glanced at her.

Eventually, they arrived at an unmarked iron door. One of the Offs, the bigger one with a blond ponytail, held onto her while the other unlocked the door. Evie was shoved into the room. She crashed to her hands and knees. The door slammed behind her. She looked up as the echo faded.

No.

Evie scrambled to her feet, a silent scream tearing from her lips. She flew at the glass separating her from The Amp, pressing her palms to it desperately.

No. No. No.

Just beyond the glass, wearing nothing but a thin white shift, was Iris. Her fiery hair was wild, her hazel eyes were round as moons in her wan face. Dried blood turned brown was still crusted on her ears and neck. She trembled visibly.

Maxwell stood at her side, his hand on her thin shoulder.

"Ms. Wick," he drawled, his voice crackling through the intercom. "I can hear you this time around, so you are welcome to speak." He giggled like a child, giving Iris a little shake. She squeezed her eyes shut, biting her lip until it bleached white. "In fact, I would prefer it if you did."

"Maxwell," Evie said, her voice quavering. "We had a deal."

"That we did," he replied with a somber nod. "But my men visited the cottage and found no sign that anyone had been there for months, much less Terra." He clucked his tongue admonishingly. "You have been a naughty girl indeed, Ms. Wick."

"I—I was wrong," she said. "I was wrong, but there are other places she could have gone! Safe houses, dozens of them, all over the city—"

"No, my dear, I think not. You had your chance. Now I intend to hold up my end of the bargain." He released Iris, prowling around her in a steady circle. "I was going to execute her with The Quiet Song, but that seemed too merciful. I thought I would go for something a little more old-fashioned." Maxwell grinned at Evie over his shoulder. "There is nothing quite like feeling the life pass through your fingers, wouldn't you agree?"

Before she could respond, The Conductor wound and backhanded Iris across the cheekbone. She went flying, skidding across the concrete. Evie screamed, slamming her fist against the glass wall. "MAXWELL! PLEASE!"

Iris got to her feet bleeding from a cut under her eye. She sprang into a fighting stance, breathing hard. Maxwell laughed, throwing his head back. The surgeon flew at him with a savage cry, delivering a solid sidekick to his chest. The breath went out of him with a whoosh, yet he continued to wheeze out a laugh.

"You have no idea how pleased I am to have someone who fights back, Ms. Harte!" Maxwell shouted, shaking his head and bouncing on the balls of his feet. Iris ignored him, lunging again. This time, he was ready for her. His long fingers clamped around her neck lifting her from the floor with ease.

"MAXWELL!" Evie shrieked, raking her fingers through her greasy, stiff hair. She slid to her knees before the glass, sobbing as Iris kicked helplessly. Her face had bled from white to pink to violet. Her eyes rolled back into her skull as Maxwell sneered up at her. "MAXWELL, I'LL DO ANYTHING, I'LL TELL YOU ANYTHING, I'LL—"

Maxwell let the girl crash to the ground. Iris sucked in a great rattling breath, coughing and wheezing at his feet. He began to kick her again and again in the stomach, the ribs. She curled in on herself like a pill bug, sobbing and clutching at her head to protect it.

Thousands of memories bloomed and shrank before Evie's eyes, overwhelming the nightmare before her. Iris, singing at the jam while Roark played the violin. Iris, dancing with flowers in her hair. Iris, her eyes sharp with determination and her hands slick with blood as she removed another Singer from another patient, freeing them from The Music. Iris, her warm body pressed to hers in the deepest part of the night. Iris, screaming at her. Iris, laughing at some ridiculous joke.

Iris.

Maxwell ceased his barrage, stepping back and letting out a savage whoop. "NOW THAT IS WHAT I AM TALKING ABOUT," he cried, circling the girl at his feet with the grin of a wolf. Iris twitched, spitting up blood. One of her eyes was swollen shut, her mouth hung open as she struggled for breath. He squatted next to her, brushing a lock of sweaty hair from her forehead. "You're beautiful, you know that? Especially like this. I almost wish I could keep you around."

Evie let out another savage cry, pounding on the unbreakable glass. "IRIS!"

The girl shifted slightly to look at Evie with her one working eye. Ten thousand unsaid words passed between them. Ten thousand moments. Ten thousand memories not yet made.

"I do have other business to attend to," Maxwell drawled, getting to his feet. He reached into his sleek jacket and drew out a palm-sized revolver. "Shall I make it quick, Ms. Wick, or shall I make it hurt?"

The shot went off before she could answer. Iris screamed in agony, clutching at her thigh. "Hurt, I think," Maxwell said.

"I AM GOING TO KILL YOU!" Evie screamed, the words hitting the glass along with her spit. "I SWEAR I AM GOING TO FUCKING KILL YOU!"

"I think not," The Conductor said sweetly. He raised his gun again, this time aiming at Iris's temple.

"Evie," Iris cried out. "Evie, I love you!"

"NO!" Evie screamed.

"No . . . " Maxwell said.

Evie froze in confusion. Her streaming eyes flicked to Maxwell, who had gone abruptly rigid. His free hand was pressed to his altered Singer. He stared into oblivion, his mouth askew. "NO!" he howled.

The gun slipped through his fingers. It clattered to the concrete. Without so much as a glance at his victim, he turned tail and raced from the room, slamming the iron door behind him.

Iris and Evie were left alone with a glass wall and a loaded gun.

55: REMNANTS

The next few hours were a blur. Darius spilled story after story of Layla and the original Anthem, of Revinia and his childhood at the palace. Ronja clung to every word, rocking back and forth between elation and devastation. Once Roark woke from his fitful sleep, he listened too. He was discreet about it, but they both knew he was tuned in.

"Let me get this straight," Ronja said with a disbelieving laugh. "You're telling me that my mother painted Atticus Bullon *naked* on the side of a building?"

"I swear to Entalia," Darius said, throwing up his hands. "She did it, and she spared absolutely *no* details."

"I wish I could have seen that." Ronja sighed.

"It was what she wrote that really took the cake, though."

"What?"

Darius laughed, his stomach heaving and his eyes streaming. Then he dissolved into a fit of coughs that wracked his whole body. He doubled forward, waving her off as she leaned toward him, concerned. "Nothing to worry about," he wheezed. "Just getting over a cold."

"Or the retch," Ronja said, her brow cinching. "Are you sure you're up for this?"

"Yes," he answered firmly, looking up at her through watery eyes. He righted his spine with a steadying breath. "I told you before, I owe it to you and I owe it to Layla."

"You really loved her."

"More than I can explain." Darius scanned the planes of her face thoughtfully. "But I understand that she was gone long before she died."

"She was a nightmare," Ronja said honestly. "She gave me half the scars on my body. But it wasn't her fault. It was the procedure, and her mutt Singer. It was The Music." Her fingers rolled into fists in her lap, her knuckles turning white. "I don't miss her," she said. "But I miss what she could have been. The Conductor, Victor Westervelt, they took that from me." She glanced over at Darius. "They took you from me."

"And you from me."

Ronja swallowed, looking around at the Kev Fairlans, who were mostly asleep. Her gaze landed on Roark. He was watching her with a softness that could not be found anywhere else. She took his hand. She knew that behind his eyes, the remnants of his own fractured family were swimming through his brain.

"We've all lost so much" she said, speaking to both of them. "We'll never get it back, but maybe we can build something new."

Before either of them could respond, a commanding voice filled the buzzing cabin. "We're approaching our first drop zone," Easton shouted, jolting the soldiers from sleep. "Ronja, Roark, Jonah, Darius, Paxton, with me. Everyone else, strap in tight."

"*Ai!*" came the resounding cry.

With one last look at Darius and Roark, Ronja undid her harness with trembling fingers and stood. Her legs groaned with relief. She rolled her shoulders and neck, shivering with pleasure as her stiff joints popped.

"Here."

The Siren looked around in time to catch the parachute Jonah had lobbed at her. She glared at him, then slipped the pack over her shoulders. It was fairly self-explanatory. It clipped around her chest in several places and had two straps that circled the tops of her thighs. She had herself done up in less than a minute.

"Here," Roark said, moving to stand in front of her, and purposefully blocking Darius from view. He leaned down and pressed his soft lips to hers. She reached up to palm his cheek, electricity shooting through her veins. "I just had to do that one more time," he breathed. "In case—"

"Shut up," Ronja cut him off sweetly, checking that his straps were locked in place properly. She tightened the one around his chest with a yank of the cord, chuckling when he let out a wheeze.

"Your turn." Roark tightened each of her buckles then planted one more kiss on her forehead.

"If you two are done making out, we're about to jump out of a plane," Jonah drawled.

"Skitz off," Ronja said, drawing a ripple of chuckles from the Kev Fairlans nearby.

"Anthemites, with me," Easton called again. They picked their way back up the narrow aisle between the soldiers and the mound of parachutes. As they approached the commander and Paxton, all traces of good humor withered in Ronja. Her pulse spiked beneath her skin, thundering in her ear. "*Zethas* in, everyone."

Ronja dug into her pants pocket and twisted her solitary *zetha* to life. Red light winked from its tip. She stuffed it in her ear, working her jaw as it settled against her cartilage.

"Do you know how to open your chute?" the commander asked, coming to a halt beside the Anthemites. His voice had a slight echoey quality through the communicator.

"I do," Roark answered with a nod. Ronja shot him a disbelieving look, tucking away her questions for later. If there *was* a later.

"Just pull this cord," Easton explained to her, tapping the tab on the left strap of his pack. "Pull either strap to steer right or left. The button on the right retracts the chute once you land."

"Be sure to bend your knees when you're about to hit the ground," Roark suggested. "Trust me, you'll regret it if you don't."

Ronja nodded a bit too enthusiastically, her nerves threatening to make her teeth chatter.

"I'll jump first," Easton said. "When I pull my chute, wait five seconds. Then pull yours."

"Okay," she said, her voice a few octaves higher than usual. Roark clapped a bracing hand to her shoulder. An alarm blared from somewhere inside the plane, making her skin crawl.

Then the belly of the aeroplane opened like a gaping jaw, spilling red light into the night sky.

Ronja ceased to breathe. She hooked her thumbs through the straps of her parachute as the frigid wind snapped at her curls. The engines rumbled beneath her feet, threatening to shatter her bones. Far below them, Revinia was laid out like the embers of a dying fire.

Someone tapped her on her free shoulder. She looked up, squinting through the sting of the air. Jonah beamed down at her cheekily. "You all right, princess?" he shouted.

"Shut up!" she screamed.

"We're approaching our drop zone," Paxton called. His short dreadlocks flopped back and forth in the gale. His eyes, radiating total tranquility, fell on Ronja. "Are you ready?"

"No!"

"Come on, love, it'll be fun," Roark encouraged.

She shot him a deathly glare.

He winked at her. "If we're going out, at least we'll do it in style."

"Splattered on the sidewalk is not what I would call style," she muttered, but the wind swept away her words.

"Sixty seconds!" Easton barked, his words crackling in her *zetha.*

"Ronja."

The Siren rounded on the voice, raking her hair out of her eyes. Darius stood before her. His goggles crowned his graying head, keeping his coarse hair from his eyes. Dressed in his black armor, two guns strapped to his thighs, he looked like an old solider.

Or an Anthemite.

"I have no idea what we're getting into here," he said, shouting over the roar of the wind. "But I want you to know that I—"

Ronja raised one hand to silence him, digging into her breast pocket with the other. Confusion rippled across his face, quickly morphing into joy when he saw what she had produced. The tin of black charcoal. "Hold still," she ordered, acutely aware of the seconds slipping through their grasp. "Close your eyes." Darius did as he was told, bowing his head slightly.

"Thirty seconds!" Easton shouted.

Ronja paid him no mind, drawing three fingers down the creased face before her. Through his brow, over his shuttered left eye, across his cheekbone, to the edge of his jaw. "There," she yelled. "Now you're ready!"

Darius opened his eyes, grinning ear to ear. Though the motion deepened the lines around his face, it made him look ten years younger. Ronja smiled back at him. Despite the unbearably cold air, despite the very real possibility that they could be dead in minutes, his impossibly broad grin widened.

Before Ronja could mirror him, Roark grasped her by the arm, whipping her around to face the hatch. "Heart to hearts later!" he yelled.

"Five!" Easton shouted from the edge of the sloping platform.

Steeling herself, Ronja brought her goggles down, settling the soft leather over the bridge of her nose. Revinia spilled out beneath her, the great clock tower like molten gold in the midst of the core. Only the streetlamps were lit, the roads luminous veins between the dark mansions. Just beneath them, the sprawling town square, ringed with lights to guide them home.

"GO!"

Jonah, Paxton, Larkin, and Easton all rushed forward, springing off the platform with cries of adrenaline.

"Come on!" Roark yelled, pulling Ronja toward the edge. Her brain was screaming at her to move, but her knees were frozen.

Then a gray and black blur shot past her. Darius let out a reverberating whoop as he launched himself over the edge, tumbling down toward their target like a spider on a string.

"RO!"

The Siren shut her eyes, snatched Roark by the hand, and dove forward. The cold arms of the gale hoisted her, tearing the breath from her lungs. She was too stunned to scream, but she heard Roark laughing maniacally. She forced her eyes open. Revinia pressed toward them with stunning speed, brass and brick and gold with a million rooftops to turn her bones to paste. In the distance, the white palace glared like a feather in a pool of oil. The stars wheeled overhead, their warplane nothing more than a shadow with a winking red eye.

Roark squeezed her frozen hand tighter as the atmosphere rushed past them. She looked at him and the world slowed. Somehow, through the wind and the dark, his face was perfectly clear. Brown eyes crinkled with blazing adrenaline, full lips laughing freely in the face of death. Endless tiny moments with him shot to the front of her mind, too many to focus on. She clung instead to the common thread between them.

Limitless, unyielding love.

"CHUTES!" Roark screamed over the roar of the wind. Ronja looked down. Beneath them, five black parachutes had popped open like full moons. She clutched at the cord on the left strap of her pack, zeroing in on the wide snowy target expanding below. "NOW!"

Ronja yanked her cord, a gasp tearing from her chest as she was pulled up like a rag doll by its hair. The rush of cold air slowed as she reached for the straps on either side of her harness to steer.

She focused on her target, the park several hundred feet below. Her chute fought her, dragging her toward the clock tower. *Not yet.* With a grunt of effort, Ronja tugged on the right strap and the chute begrudgingly began to glide back toward the open field. *Come on, come on.* The Tovairins and Darius had already landed, their chutes wilting on the frozen lawn. The blur of lights became individual lamp posts. The bare trees screamed into detail. She was level with the rooftops, with the windows. Ronja squeezed her eyes shut and . . .

"Ooof!"

She hit the ground hard, bending her knees to absorb the shock, then careening forward, but managing to stay on her feet. Swearing colorfully, she slammed the button on her strap. Her chute struck her back with such force she was launched face first into the snow. She heard a muted thump nearby, Roark hitting the ground. She looked up in time to see him stumble then fall forward like an axed tree.

"Smooth," Jonah chuckled from her left.

Ronja ignored him, clambering to her feet and wiping snow

from her front. It was disturbingly quiet in the blanketed park. The trees and gas lamps seemed to watch them from the edge of the field. Once the snow melted in the spring, white gravel paths would be revealed along with thousands of perennial flowers. She had never seen them herself—as if they would to allow a mutt into the core—but she had seen photographs in the library.

"That was fun," Roark said with a breathless laugh. Ronja looked at him sidelong shaking her head disparagingly. He clambered to his feet and slammed the button on his pack to retract his parachute. "One way to make an entrance, at least."

"Is everyone all right?" Easton called softly.

Ronja rounded on him as Roark padded over to stand at her side. The commander was the picture of poise, even after dropping out of the sky into the maw of a foreign city. Paxton knelt before a bag nearby, focused on whatever he was doing. Jonah and Larkin were peering around with suspicious curiosity. Darius . . .

Darius stood apart from the group facing the clock tower through the trees, his head tilted back. Passing Roark an uncertain glance, Ronja crossed to her father, her footfalls muffled by the snow. "You okay?" she asked. He jumped half a foot when he found her at his shoulder.

"Yes, yes, fine," he said, his voice as tight as the strings of a guitar. "I just . . . " He gestured around at the park, the opulent houses ringing it, the glowing clock tower only a quarter mile away.

Ronja nodded. "I know."

"Where is everyone?" Darius asked.

"Thankfully, not here," she replied. "The curfew must still be in effect." *Or they're already on the ships. Or they're just waiting to take us out.* The Siren crushed the thought beneath her heel.

"When I was a child, this park used to hold markets for the

winter solstice. Everyone was welcome. They lasted late into the night. They sold popcorn and candies and . . . " He trailed off his eyes glazing over. "They would play the most beautiful music. I can still hear it, if I listen."

"That sounds . . . beautiful." Even if they succeeded tonight, could Revinia ever be like that again? Could it bloom after such damage?

"Listen up," Easton said. Ronja and Darius turned to face him, their boots squeaking in the icy snow. The group converged into a tight knot, their breath fogging between them. "We have thirty-seven minutes to get to the top of that tower, set the charges, and get the Siren set up at the station. We move fast and stick together, no stragglers. Understood?" The group nodded collectively. Easton mirrored them. "All right. Move out."

56: ON YOUR FEET
Terra

When Terra opened the door to the guest bedroom, stinger in hand, she had expected Henry to attack her. The roar he had let out upon waking up was enough to shake even her to the core. But when she kicked it in and lunged inside, she found him on the floor, his knees pulled to his chest and his head bowed.

"Henry," she said cautiously, hovering near the door, still white knuckling the stinger. "Henry, do you know who I am?"

There was no response. He was so still he could have been carved from stone. Terra took a tiny step toward him. No response. The patter of lithe footsteps pricked her ear. She spun as Theo appeared in the doorway, shooing him away. He backed off, lingering in the hall with a small automatic in hand.

Terra turned back to Henry. He had not moved an inch. "Henry," she tried again. "I'm going to put my stinger down." She crouched low, setting the metal rod down with a hollow clang on the hardwood. He flinched at the sound. That was the only reaction she got out of him. "Henry, my name is—"

"Terra."

He said it so softly she thought for a second she might have imagined it. Then he lifted his head. His eyes were bloodshot, his face wan and slick. His handsome features were warped into a mask of horror, the kind that never really left a person. But his eyes were full. Fatally human.

"Henry," Terra whispered, a slow smile spreading across her mouth. "You're back."

"I—I killed him. I killed Samson," Henry breathed. Terra tensed. The words sent chills down her spine. "I hurt Ronja, tortured Iris. Maxwell—" His voice cracked, his dark hands flying to cradle his head. "He made me kill so many people. That girl, Valorie, he raped her and I let him—"

"Enough."

Henry dropped his trembling hands, looking up at her in shock. Terra got to her feet, advancing on the boy. He wilted in her shadow. "Nothing you did while under The New Music was your fault," she told him, her voice steady as a mountain. "You are not responsible for any of it. Maxwell is."

"Maxwell," Henry repeated. His swimming eyes hardened. "I'm going to kill him."

"Get in line." Terra stuck her hand out for him to take. "On your feet."

He stared at it for a long moment, then grasped it with weak fingers. She hauled him up. He swayed on the spot, clutching at his head.

"Skitz," he groaned. "My ear . . . I feel like my head is going to explode."

"That'll pass," Terra said dismissively. She looked over her shoulder at Theo. "Get him some water and food, something plain." The boy nodded briskly, then rushed off down the steps. She turned back to Henry. "I know you're hurting," she said. "But I need you to get ahold of yourself. I need you to tell me everything you know about the Vintian ships."

"Ronja, Roark . . . " Henry murmured. He sat back on the bed heavily, still holding his head as if it were going to burst. "They got out. Maxwell was furious, he was . . . "

"How did they get out? Where did they go?"

The boy shook his head, groaning at the movement. "No one knows for sure. The Tovairin was with them—they might have gone back there."

There was little left in the world that could shock Terra Vahl, but it took everything she had not to balk at those words. "Tovairin? Are you talking about Jonah? Big guy with the white tattoos?"

Henry nodded, his eyes squeezed shut as he massaged his temples through the gauze still wrapped around his head.

"Here," Theo called, hurrying back into the room. He leaned around Terra and offered Henry a tall glass of water and a fresh roll. He waved them off, but the girl snatched the cup up and forced him to take it.

"Drink," she commanded. "Ronja will murder me if you die under my watch."

Henry glared at her, then raised the glass to his lips. The water shivered as he did. One sip later, his instincts kicked in and he drained half the contents. He heaved a deep breath, allowing his head to droop forward again. "Ronja," he murmured. "The Siren."

"Yeah, she sort of made a name for herself after you supposedly died."

"That was her singing on the recorder, she freed me." Henry lifted his head again. "She must hate me. Roark must . . . "

"Shut up," Terra growled. "You killed Samson, and I was falling for his stupid dead ass. Guess what? I don't hate you. So shut up, stop wallowing, and eat your damn bread."

Henry opened and closed his mouth several times, gaping at her like a fish on deck. Then he raised the roll to his mouth and took a bite. Terra nodded approvingly as he chewed and swallowed, then took another sip of water.

"Excellent," she said briskly. She turned back to Theo. "Could you get him some painkillers? Cicada usually keeps them in the medicine cabinet."

Theo crossed his arms, his lips pressed into a pout. "You know, I came to help protect you, not be your butler."

Terra cocked her head to the side. "Did I ask for your protection, or did I ask for painkillers?"

Theo blushed pink, puffed up his chest, then marched away with all the dignity he could manage.

The girl turned back to Henry. The partially drained glass was trembling in his hand, the contents threatening to slosh over the brim. She snatched it back and set it on the nightstand. "Henry," she said. "Believe it or not, I'm glad to see you."

Henry glowered up at her, his nostrils flaring. *Good*, Terra thought grimly. *Get mad.* "I am," she insisted. "Believe it or not, I actually have a heart."

The briefest smile ghosted his lips. It faded so quickly she thought she might have imagined it. "Could have fooled me."

Terra huffed, sitting down on the springy mattress next to him. She left an inch of space between them, remembering how sensitive she was to touch after she was released from The Music. "We're screwed, H," she said, staring into the oblivion of the patterned rug at their feet. She felt him glance at her sidelong, surprise radiating from his every pore. "Ronja and Roark are gone; Evie, Iris, and Mouse are still in prison; the best the Anthem can do is escape through the sewer tunnels." She shook her head. "We're absolutely skitzed."

"I know my brain is a little fried," Henry said after a loaded pause. "But that doesn't sound like you."

Terra twisted her lips into a grim smile. "I said we were skitzed, not that we were giving up."

"Here."

Henry and Terra looked up to see Theo approaching with an amber jar of pills. She raised her hand, wiggling her fingers. He tossed it at her and she caught it single-handedly. "Take one now," she ordered the boy at her side, passing him the vial. "Finish that bread or you'll rot your stomach."

Something vaguely reminiscent of a laugh bubbled up on his cracked lips. Henry unscrewed the bottle and tapped a single white pill into his palm. "When did you turn into such a softy?" he asked. Before she could answer, he tipped the capsule into his mouth and swallowed it dry.

"I am *not* a softy," Terra shot back, glowering at him as he took a swig of water and tore into his roll again. "I just need you ready."

Henry swallowed, wincing as a too large lump of bread slid down his throat. "For what?"

"For our last mission."

57: RUNNING TO STAND STILL

They sprinted through the park, silent as wraiths in the night. The powdered snow muffled their quick footsteps. Ronja knew it was working in their favor, but it made her feel as if she were in a nightmare, running to stand still. When they shot out of the bare trees lining the park, she remembered that this *was* a nightmare.

The golden clock tower loomed above them, its northern face bright as the moons. The pools of light from the gas lamps scattered around the plaza like landmines. Everything was eerily still, from the mansions encircling the square to the tower itself. It was even quieter than it had been the first time they stormed it.

"Eyes open," Easton called softly as they approached the edge of the bright square. He drew the automatic at his hip, clicking the safety off.

The others copied him, arming themselves with their various weapons. Ronja drew one of the blades at her back with a ringing hiss, wishing not for the first time that she could get her hands on a stinger or a gun.

"Go," Easton said.

They started forward as a pack, their boots crunching
through slush and ice. Their shadows flickered in and out of
existence in the forest of streetlights. Ronja glanced around, her
nerves sparking. Roark was a comforting presence at her side, the
hard lines of his face exaggerated by his war paint. He had been
armed with a single curved blade wider than her own. Though she
had never seen him use one, he held it with the confidence of
someone who had been handling such blades all his life.

"Fan out," Easton ordered, gesturing left and right with his
gun. Jonah and Larkin peeled off to one side, their footsteps lithe
and sure. Paxton and the commander took the opposite direction.
"You three, go for the alley," he called over his shoulder. Darius
and the Anthemites nodded, jogging toward the narrow aisle
between two quiet mansions.

"I thought there'd be Offs," Ronja murmured as they pressed
toward the back of the side street. It was lined with snowcapped
trash bins and crates.

"Last time we were here, we thought we were alone," Roark
said, scanning the deserted square from their hiding place. "We
were wrong."

Ronja felt a chill slink down her spine. She gripped the hilt
of her blade ever tighter.

"I never thought I'd be back here," Darius whispered. The
Siren cut her eyes to her father, who was gazing at the tower again.
"They've perverted it."

"What was it, before The Conductor took over?"

The king pushed his salt and pepper hair out of his face,
dropping his attention to his daughter. "It originally belonged to
our family. It was a sacred space of sorts. Something about it
allowed us to access our gifts with ease." His gray brows
scrunched together. "I wish I could tell you more. I was young and
naïve, never paid attention to my lessons."

"I felt it pulling me, even when I was under The Music," Ronja said, tipping her head back to scan the looming tower. "I saw it in my head the day we did the broadcast."

Darius dipped his chin, as if he had expected this. "Not long before I was sent away, my father turned the top floor into a radio station—the same one you used to broadcast to the Singers." Nostalgia curved his lips into a vague smile. "The best musicians and poets in the world would come to share their work with the whole city."

"We'll make that happen again," Ronja said. "I promise."

Darius gave her a long pensive look, his eyes brimming with something foreign and kind. Pride. Before either of them could say more, movement near the base of the clock tower hooked her gaze. Jonah and Larkin emerged from around the bend, moving with the grace of thieves.

"Come on," Roark muttered, jerking his chin at their comrades. "Let's go."

The three Revinians hurried back through the swathes of light, arriving in the shadowy space where Larkin and Jonah had congregated.

"Nothing," the Kev Fairlan man said. "We're clear."

"For now," Roark said.

Larkin made a noise of agreement at the back of her throat, still scanning the flat landscape with her sharp eyes. She looked every inch a warrior in her armor, her midnight hair braided into a tight knot at the base of her skull. Booted footsteps approached. They turned to find Paxton and Easton jogging toward them, their breath mushrooming in the frigid air.

"Clear," Paxton told them as they approached. The commander said nothing, the muscles of his jaw clenching through his cheek as he peered around warily. The Sydonian rounded on Roark and Ronja. "Lead the way, Siren."

"Follow me," the Siren said, beckoning with a jerk of her chin. She began to jog toward the tower, her breath blooming around her. The others fell into step. Ronja pressed forward, ignoring the way the shadow of the tower seemed to swallow them alive. She skidded to a stop in a pile of gray slush at the entrance and sheathed her knife. Her heart climbed into her mouth as her eyes roved across the stone doors. They were just as she remembered, crosshatched with hypnotic spiraling patterns.

Deep from within came a distant, ancient hum.

"Do you hear it?"

Ronja almost jumped out of her skin. Darius had appeared at her side. His green-gray eyes trained on the engraved wall before them. The fine hairs on her arms stood up and goosebumps teased her skin.

"Yeah. Yeah, I do." It was low and bold, unmistakably organic. It was not beautiful, not exactly. It was as raw and powerful as the northern sea and as vivid as the winter moons. "What is that?"

"I believe," Darius answered in a low voice. "That is the Aura of the city."

Ronja felt the rest of the world fall away. There was only her and the tower. The air was yanked from her lungs, the sight from her eyes. She was trapped, falling endlessly through a suffocating void, she was—

Ronja.

The Siren sucked in a startled breath, stumbling backward. Roark caught her under her arms, their armor thumping together awkwardly. Her eyelids fluttered rapidly, grasping at vision. Every member of the team stared at her with a mixture of concern and curiosity—except for Darius, who was clutching his head as if it were about to fracture.

"Trapped," she whispered.

"Ronja," Roark murmured in her ear. He brushed a knuckle

against her cheek. "Skitz, you're burning up." He was right. It felt like someone was running hot coals over her skin. The frigid air did little to staunch the heat.

"Trapped," she repeated. Her voice sounded very far away, as if she were hearing herself speak through a long tube. "We have to free it."

"Free what?" Roark asked, looking around at the others desperately. He was met with helpless shrugs.

"Revinia's Aura," Darius spoke up, letting his hands fall from his temples with a visible wince, "has been trapped by The New Music."

Ronja nodded feverishly, whipping around to grip Roark by his forearms. He steadied her, scanning her face for signs of a breakdown. "Roark," she said, her voice hoarse. "We have to kill it, The New Music, now."

"What the *fiest* is she going on about?" Larkin demanded in her Tovairin lilt. "We're sitting geese out here."

"Ducks," Jonah corrected halfheartedly. Larkin socked him in the arm.

"She's right," Easton agreed solemnly. "We're wasting time." He locked eyes with Roark. "Get your girl together."

"She is not *mine*."

"Fine. Then get yourself together, Alezandri."

Ronja clutched at the frayed threads of sanity. She shrugged Roark off, stumbling forward. Darius caught her this time as the world spun out. The stars wheeled. The moons melted. The buildings and roads crumbled. The air twisted away from her lungs. "We have to free it," she said, but no words came out.

Deep beneath the city, she felt it move, reaching toward her with formless hands. *Siren. Siren. Siren.* It was calling her, dragging her down and lifting her up Blinding adrenaline shot through Ronja, igniting her bones and setting her blood on fire.

She launched forward and slammed her palm into the wall of the clock tower. Heat exploded beneath it, nearly blowing her back.

Stillness reigned. Silence washed over the square. Ronja looked over her shoulder at Roark as she shivered with uncaged energy. He was staring at her with his lips parted, his eyes wide with concern. Darius put his hand on her shoulder, calling her back to her body. She looked back to the tower as the doors began to grind open.

That was when the alarm went off.

58: A PARTY
Terra

Terra was passed out on the parlor sofa when the alarm sounded, rolling over the city like distant thunder. She scrambled to her feet, panting and reaching for a weapon that was not there. Theo, who had been lounging across from her with his feet on the coffee table, shot up as well. They looked at each other in the wash of the noise.

"What the hell is that?" he asked, wincing at the keening that bled through the walls.

Terra did not answer. Instead, she swept from the parlor, headed for the office at the front of the house. Theo trailed after her, jogging to keep up. She burst through the door, letting it slam against the wall with a crack. Cicada was at his desk again. He had cleaned the blood from his face and changed his shirt, but it did little to help his appearance. Branching bruises crawled up the bridge of his nose to his forehead.

"What is that?" she demanded, circling around his desk to peek out through the thick green drapes.

"Get back!" Cicada hissed. He snatched her by the wrist and tugged her away from the window.

Terra ripped it away from him with a snarl. "What the hell is happening out there?"

"I have no idea, but I would suggest staying away from the window. If you'll recall, you're a bloody fugitive."

"It means someone has broken into the clock tower."

Terra whipped around. Henry stood in the doorframe, still crowned with white gauze. He looked marginally better. Pain medicine, sleep, and food did wonders for the body. But a bone deep exhaustion clung to him, the kind that sleep could never fully chase away.

"The clock tower?" Theo asked, his brows cinching. "You mean—?"

"Yes," Henry cut him off with a terse nod. He locked eyes with Terra. "Someone is trying to get at the central mainframe. That means . . . "

"Ronja," Terra muttered. She did not give herself time to revel in hope. She stepped out from behind the desk and bolted over to the transmitter. Kneeling, she clamped the headphones over her ear, shutting out the keening alarm. She began to coax the machine to life, registering distantly that Theo and Henry were crouched behind her. Rippling static bloomed in her ear as she settled on the proper channel.

"This is Medusa," Terra said, her voice ringing clear. "Harpy, do you copy?"

There was a drawn-out pause filled with the wail of the alarm and the frantic hiss of static. Terra felt her muscles begin to bunch, made worse by the three pairs of eyes glued to her back. Then a voice returned: "Medusa, this is Harpy."

Terra blew out a relieved breath through her teeth. "Harpy," she said, wasting no time. "Has the Siren made contact with the Belly?"

"The Siren?" The bewilderment in her crackling voice was

answer enough.

"Can you hear the alarm?" Terra asked before Ito could question her further. "We think it's coming from the clock tower."

"We can't hear anything down here, but we got the hatch open. Everyone is preparing to leave tomorrow morning."

Terra shook her head, her blond locks rustling against her shoulders. "No. You need to get out now."

"But—"

"You're not going to get a better chance, Ito," she snapped. "The alarm is citywide. All the focus will be on the core, then the harbor."

"The harbor?"

"We're going to take out the ships tonight." Terra flinched when a firm hand grasped her shoulder. She twisted around to look at Henry. She had almost forgotten he and Theo were at her back.

"Terra," Henry warned her, his voice muffled by the pads of the headphones. "We're not prepared for that."

"Shut up."

"Excuse me?" Ito asked, sounding more surprised than offended.

"Not you," Terra said, smoothing over her outburst quickly. "Ito. You have to go. Even if by some miracle it is Ronja that triggered the alarm, there is no guarantee she'll be able to take down The New Music. One way or the other, we have to make sure Maxwell and his army never leave this place."

For a brief moment, Ito was quiet. In the absence of a response, Terra discovered she was breathing hard, her skin prickling with adrenaline. "Fine, we'll go," the older woman eventually said. "Be careful, Terra. I want you to know that I—"

"Good luck, Commander. May your song guide you home."

"Terra—"

She slammed the power button on the transmitter and knocked the bulky headphones from her head. Her knees knocked as she got to her feet. Beyond the walls of the row house, the alarm was still wailing. *That better be you, Ronja.*

"Terra, we don't have the resources to pull this off," Henry warned her. There was no anger in his voice, only logic.

"Sure we do." She jabbed a finger at the window. "That alarm has been going off for three minutes. Maxwell has the whole city on high alert to protect the tower. No one's going to be watching the ships."

"That might be a bit of an exaggeration," Theo cut in hesitantly.

Terra rolled her eyes at the ceiling. "Fine, so we have to neutralize a few Offs, big deal. Listen." She crossed her muscular arms over her chest, making eye contact with each of the boys in turn. Theo looked vaguely queasy. Henry looked like he was going to pass out. Not exactly a top-notch strike team. "Maxwell has taken something—or someone—from all of us. This is our chance to make him pay."

Charged silence greeted her speech. Theo bit his lip. Henry let his head droop forward. Beyond them, Cicada watched the exchange with a vindicated smirk. She fought the urge to fly at him again.

"All right."

Terra snapped her gaze back to Henry. He had lifted his head and set his jaw. "I am not sure how much help I'll be in my current state," he said, his voice gentle yet firm. She had always thought that his voice matched his personality, but had almost forgotten what it sounded like through the sheen of The New Music. "But I have a lot to atone for. I might as well start tonight."

The girl smiled, just a twitch of her lips, then reached up to clap a hand to his broad shoulder. "Welcome back, brother," she said.

Henry mirrored her, the corners of his full lips turning up slightly. "You've gotten nicer."

"Yeah well, don't get used to it," Terra muttered, taking her hand back and stuffing it into the pocket of the jacket Cicada had provided for her.

"I'll go, too," Theo spoke up, his blue eyes full and his fingers tucked into fists. "For Lawrence."

"If we're right, and it really is Ronja up there at the tower, she'll take down The New Music. When it falls, Maxwell will too." Terra lifted her chin, playing at confidence she did not possess. "We'll get Mouse back, and the others."

The trader nodded jerkily, flicking an escaped tear from his cheek. The Anthemites pretended not to notice.

"What exactly is your plan?" Henry asked, folding his burly arms over his chest.

"I'll tell you on the way there," Terra replied, slipping between the two boys and starting toward the door. She winked at Cicada as she passed him. He looked as if he had just swallowed a bug. "Gear up, then help me raid the liquor cabinets. We're going to have ourselves a party."

59: CAUTERIZED

Ronja stifled a scream as the piercing wail ripped through the gas-lit square, slamming her hand over her remaining ear.

Her comrades did the same, hunched over in agony as the blistering alarm tore the silence to shreds. The stone entryway continued to roll open lazily, the gap scarcely large enough to accommodate a single person. Movement to her left hooked her gaze. She squinted at it through the haze of her pain.

"DOWN!" Ronja roared. They dropped like stones just as a storm of bullets hissed over their heads. How had they not heard the Offs approaching? Where had they come from?

"Get her inside, now!" Easton screamed, whipping out the automatic at his hip and firing into the night. Jonah and the others with guns copied him as Roark grabbed Ronja around the waist and pulled her through the narrow gap. Once inside, Ronja spun reaching out to pull the closest person through. It was Paxton. He got off one more shot, then clasped her offered hand and allowed her to drag him through. Darius was close behind. He backed through the yawning door continuing to shoot with cold precision.

Only Easton and Larkin remained outside. Ronja could see

that the commander was shielding the girl with his body, firing over her head. Horror lanced through her as she saw the blood oozing onto the concrete. "*Ret la!*" Easton bellowed.

Roark tugged Ronja from the entrance, shielding her head and body with his arms as Jonah and Paxton began to fire again. She could not see, she could not move, but she heard scuffling as the commander dragged Larkin into the tower.

"Get her over there! Hold pressure," Easton commanded.

Instinct claimed Ronja. She twisted herself free of Roark and sprinted over to where she knew the lever that controlled the door waited. It was nearly pitch-black inside the tower. The only light came from the streetlamps outside, half of which had been shot out. She groped around for the lever, her pulse pounding erratically. Her fingers brushed something cold and metal. She gripped it with all her strength and pulled.

The stone door groaned over the shrill wail of the alarm and the hail of bullets, then began to close. Far too slowly. Dropping back into a crouch, Ronja peeked outside again. Her stomach vaulted. Dozens of men and women were marching toward them through the storm of returning fire. They were not Offs. They wore bathrobes and pajamas, house slippers and curlers. They shouldered automatics as long as her forearms.

These were the wealthy citizens of the core, dragged from their beds by The New Music to protect the clock tower.

"Keep firing!" Easton ordered. Ronja snapped back into her body. Jonah had given Roark his automatic and had taken over shielding the wounded Larkin around the corner. Paxton, Darius, and Easton all knelt at the lip of the slowly closing door, firing into the mob that was oozing toward them. *Think. Think. Think.* A glint of silver caught her eye, the second pistol Darius wore at his waist. Ronja darted over and yanked it from its holster before he could stop her. She dropped low, kneeling on one knee and firing off several shots in rapid succession through the narrowing gap.

Bodies dropped. Blood spurted on silk and velvet. The light from the streetlamps was squeezed into a sliver just as the first man stretched his hand out to reach for them.

The great stone portal sealed with an echoing thud, leaving them alone in the utter blackness.

The howling of the alarm had been snuffed out, only to be replaced with a new sound: the guttural hum and whir of the behemoth mainframe that loomed in the blackness behind them. Ronja blinked rapidly as someone turned on an electric lantern, bathing them in cold light.

"Was anyone else hit?" Paxton asked, holding the light aloft.

Everyone shook their heads. Ronja scanned the faces of her new band of comrades. Though most of them were hardened warriors, they looked shaken. Darius was trembling visibly, his knuckles white around the sole pistol she had left him with. It was not very often, she supposed, that an army of mindless drones came at them in their bathrobes. Her eyes found Roark. He was already looking at her.

You okay? she mouthed.

He gave a terse nod, his jaw clenched.

"Someone get the *fiesting* lights," Jonah barked. His voice was strained, as if he were holding a heavy burden. Roark hurried over to the wall next to the door, feeling around in the dimness for the switch. A moment later, they were bathed in jarring light.

Ronja turned slowly to face the pulsing beast of the mainframe. It was even more massive than she remembered. It climbed to the top of the tower, a dense mass of twisted metal, wire, and inorganic Song. She took a shuddering breath, letting her senses unfurl in search of the Aura that had reached out to her only minutes ago. But there was nothing. Nothing but clanking gears and sizzling electricity.

"They can still open the door with the keypad," Roark said, dragging her attention from the mainframe.

"On it," Ronja said. She popped open the cylinder, pleased to find there were still two bullets. "Get back," she said, shooing her comrades away as she took aim at the metal keypad mounted beside the ancient door. Shutting one eye, she aimed and fired. Sparks fizzled and cracked as the little machine died. She was about to ask how they were supposed to get out now when a pained cry sliced through the air.

Larkin. She hurried over to join the rest of the team, crouched around the wounded girl. She was flat on her back, her eyes scrunched with pain. Her armor had been removed to reveal an oozing wound in her lower abdomen. Jonah leaned over her, stroking her sweaty hair and whispering to her in Tovairin.

"Jonah, roll her on her side," Paxton ordered. Still whispering to the wounded girl, Jonah did as he was told. Larkin let out a scream of agony, her fingers contorting into claws. Ronja took one of them, massaging the cramped muscles until she felt them give. "The bullet went through," Paxton told them, gesturing for Jonah to set her down again. Larkin hissed in pain as she settled back onto the stone floor. Ronja fought a wince as Larkin's vice-like grip tightened around her fingers.

"That's good, right?" Jonah asked, desperation making his voice shake.

"Yes, but we need to cauterize it."

"With what?"

Paxton dug into the pack at his side and produced a black medical kit. "Someone give me their belt," he said, popping open the lid and pawing through the contents with nimble fingers. "Now," he snapped.

Darius got to his feet and whipped his leather belt out from around his waist, holding it out for Paxton to take. The Sydonian snatched it at once and passed it to Jonah. "Have her bite down on this."

Ronja inched closer to Roark as Jonah held the strip of leather taut before her. Larkin bit down hard, tears leaking from behind her eyelids. Paxton slammed the lid on the medical kit, looking down at his patient with a grim mouth. In his hand was a small metal tube. For a split second, she struggled to figure out what it was.

Then he flicked it on with the push of a button. A jet of white hot flame surged from its tip. "Hold her down," Paxton ordered.

Swallowing her horror, Ronja gripped Larkin by the wrist and pinned it to the stone floor. Across from her, Jonah did the same. Darius and Roark took her legs while Easton gripped her head. He said something to her in Tovairin, something that transcended language. Ronja shut her eyes. There was a pause, filled only by the constant rumbling of the mainframe behind them.

Then Larkin let out a bloodcurdling scream through her leather bit. Her arm fought against Ronja, her fingers shivering beneath her grip.

"Flip her," Paxton commanded. They did as they were told, working as a unit to turn the girl over with as much care as they could. Paxton did not skip a beat before pressing the searing flame to the wound in her back. Larkin screamed again, the horrible sound filling the entire tower. Then, Paxton snuffed the flame, tossing the miniature blowtorch aside.

Together, they eased Larkin onto her uninjured side. Her screams dissipated to sobs, then hiccuping gasps. Jonah eased her head onto his lap. She clung to him, her entire body wracked with chills.

"Jonah, stay with Larkin and set the charges," Easton ordered, getting to his feet swiftly. "We've got no time to waste."

Ronja was about to protest, but the mission overwhelmed her empathy.

Tonight, she was not Ronja. She was the Siren, and the Siren had a job to do. Sucking in a deep breath and forcing down her shame, she got to her feet and backed away from Larkin. Jonah looked up. His eyes were unusually bright in the glare of the lights above them. She gave him a slow nod. *Thank you.*

He mirrored her, a faint smile dusting his lips. Then, he returned his attention to Larkin, cupping her tear-slicked cheek with his callused palm.

"Come on," the Siren said, directing the words at Roark and Darius. "We're running out of time."

60: FIVE BULLETS
Evie

"Iris," Evie said weakly. "Iris, come on, look at me."

She was on her knees, her brow pressed to the thick glass that kept her from Iris. It was smeared with her sweat and tears. The intercom was still on; she could hear it buzzing above her. Iris could hear her, but she was not responding. Curled into a ball on the smooth floor of The Amp, she had not moved an inch since Maxwell stormed out. From this distance, Evie could not tell if she was breathing.

"Iris, please darling. Please, just look at me." The surgeon twitched. Relief unfurled in Evie. "Come on, love, sit up, I know you can."

Slowly, Iris began to move. Her fiery head lifted from the floor, revealing the awful mess Maxwell had made of her face. Her left eye was swallowed with a black bruise, her lip split in several places. The gash on her cheek was beginning to clot, but it would certainly scar. Groaning, Iris propped herself up on her elbow, raising herself into a sitting position. Her face contorted with agony as she caught sight of the oozing bullet wound in her thigh.

"Iris," Evie said loudly. "Look at me." Her solitary eye flashed to Evie, bloodshot and fevered. "You need to slow the bleeding," she said, enunciating each word carefully.

But Iris was way ahead of her. She had already set about tearing off a thick strip of her white shift. Pride spread through Evie like a shot of whiskey as Iris began to wind the cloth around the top of her thigh, just above her wound. She hissed in pain as she pulled the knot tight. With a shuddering breath, she heaved herself to her feet, transferring her weight to her good leg.

"Evie," Iris said, her voice crackling with pain and static. "What do we do?"

"The gun, behind you."

The surgeon turned laboriously and began to hobble toward the revolver Maxwell had dropped. *What had he heard?* Evie wondered, her thoughts spinning a thousand miles an hour. *What could have struck such fear into him that he would drop his own gun?*

Iris leaned down to pick it up, groaning and clutching her ribs. Pain reared within Evie. "There are five bullets left," she said, limping back over to stand before her. "What should we do?"

"I—"

Before she could get another word out, a piercing wail cut through the cell. Both girls clapped their hands to their ears, looking around wildly.

"What the hell is that?" Evie bellowed.

Iris just shook her head, her solitary eye wide with fear. She held the gun close to her breast, as if it were a child. Her ripped white shift was covered in her own blood. "Evie," Iris shouted over the alarm, plugging one of her ears with her finger. "I think that might be an escape alarm—someone got out!"

"Terra got out a day ago," Evie called back. "I think she has a plan!"

"Someone else, then." Hope shone through the puffy bruises

that dappled her face. "Who else would cause an uproar like this?"

Evie felt her lips split into a grin. "Ronja," she and Iris said at the same time.

The door behind Iris banged open. Despite her wounds, the surgeon whipped around, her revolver held out before her precisely. Two burly Offs in rumbled black uniforms stormed in, brandishing crackling stingers. Before Evie could so much as blink, Iris had fired off two shots, dropping both Offs like great trees. The surgeon peeked back at her girlfriend over her shoulder, her expression neutral beneath her bruising.

Evie felt her mouth go dry. "I love you," she managed to get out.

Iris smiled. "I know." With that, twisted back around and began to limp toward the fallen Offs. Groaning, she sank to her knees next to the closest one, yanking the automatic out of the holster at his side and setting it next to her gently. Her blood slick hands began to rove across his chest, hunting for something beneath his uniform. When she found it, she popped the silver clasps, reached inside, and produced a bulky set of keys. She held them high above her head for Evie to see.

"I think I'd like to be done with this place," Iris said. "What about you?"

61: AMBUSH

Riding the elevator to the top of the clock tower was a surreal experience. With each floor they slid past, a new memory slammed into Ronja, as solid as the men who stood around her.

Layla, dead at her feet. The Tovairin child, crushed by the hunk of debris. Revinia going dark in waves. Samson, a bullet in his brain on the white marble floor. Henry, his voice on the radio. Maybe the stars are alive after all.

In the end, it wasn't Maxwell she feared seeing tonight. It was Henry. She wasn't sure she could face him again, to meet his eyes with desperation and get nothing in return. The elevator ground to a halt. The Anthemites and Kev Fairlans drew their weapons. She copied them, cocking the gun she had lifted from Darius. The doors slid open with a polite peal of chimes.

Utter stillness greeted them in the clock chamber that was home to the radio station. Ronja breathed a temporary sigh of relief, letting the gun fall to her side. The station was dark this time; the only light came from the winter moons shining through the four glass faces of the clock. It spilled across the white marble floors like milk. The solitary piece of furniture, the huge leather chair which stood like a throne before the dark dashboard.

"Do what you need to do," Easton said, starting to pace the perimeter of the room, his gun still aloft. "We're down to twelve minutes."

Ronja nodded, determination sweeping away her relief. She hurried over to the chair, shrugging off her pack and letting it fall to the floor with a quiet thump. She slid the heavy armchair aside with a grunt of effort, then placed her hands on the cool dash. Dozens of buttons and dials winked at her in the moonlight, all shrouded in dust. Panic seized her. Nothing looked familiar. Without Evie and Terra, she wasn't sure she could work it—she was just the voice.

"If you would . . . "

She looked up. Darius stood behind her, a knowing smile on his weathered face. Understanding clicked into place in Ronja and a grin split her mouth. "Be my guest," she said, motioning at the dash.

The king cracked his knuckles. "Could someone get the lights?" he called.

Almost as soon as he spoke, bright light flared around them. Ronja blinked rapidly as her eyes adjusted. Darius's fingers flew across the dashboard, bringing it to life. It hummed beneath his touch.

"How did you learn to do this?" Ronja asked, leaning over the board.

"I watched my father do it many times," he replied, his eyes still latched to the machine. "And we used to have something similar in the original Kev Fairlan base. I worked it from time to time." He jabbed a large button near the center of the board with his index finger, then stepped back with a triumphant grin. "There, that should do it."

"Thank you," Ronja said, slipping behind the dash to stand

beside him. "I couldn't have done it without you."

"Sure you could. But I am glad to be here."

The Siren opened her mouth to say something else, but just then a massive shudder lanced through the room. Ronja swore, falling forward onto the dash and narrowly missing an important looking dial. She was not the only one. Around her, Roark and the others were righting themselves, glancing around wildly.

"What the hell was—?" she started to ask.

The glass panes of the clocks rattled, the dashboard trembled. Ronja locked eyes first with Darius, then with Roark. *Skitz.* Abandoning the radio, she dashed to the northern window, pressing her brow to it in order to look straight down.

"*Fiest*," she breathed. Bodies gathered around her, her comrades straining to see what she was looking at.

Hundreds of feet below them, the pack of empty citizens had scattered, making way for a hulking vehicle that Ronja had come to recognize during her stay in Tovaire. "Is that—a tank?"

"Yes," Easton cut her off grimly.

She rounded on him, her brow still cool from the frigid glass. "What are we going to do?"

"You will do nothing, little bird," came a disembodied voice.

Guns cocked. Blades hissed. The Anthemites and Tovairins pressed back to back, scanning the empty room for its owner. Ronja turned slowly, dread pooling in her middle. She knew they would find no one. "Maxwell," she called striding to the center of the room. "I should have known you would be too much of a coward to come here yourself."

"Ah, little bird, you're the one who ran." His creeping voice bled from the speaker on the dashboard. She approached it slowly, her lip curled in disgust. Chills born of adrenaline wracked her body. She set her blade down on the lip of the metal board and took a seat at the chair.

"What do you want, you bastard?" the Siren asked through her teeth.

"What do I want?" Maxwell hissed. "I *want* you to come home to me, little bird. I want you to sing for me."

"Oh, I'll sing," Ronja threatened, glaring at the gridded speaker as if it were his face. "I have everything I need to take you down."

The Conductor clicked his tongue admonishingly, the sound even more unnerving when laced with static. "Dear me, so confident," he said with a giggle. Ronja swallowed, glancing up at her comrades. They had gathered on the opposite side of the dashboard. Most of their eyes were fixed to the speaker. Only Roark looked at her, his brown eyes shivering with rage in the joint light of the moons and the electric fixture above them.

"Of course, I had to leave the station intact," Maxwell continued giddily. "How else would you inspire my loyal followers?"

"Loyal." Ronja barked a laugh. "You cannot possibly be that ignorant."

"I have *earned* their loyalty," Maxwell shot back. Static cracked as the volume shot up. Ronja white knuckled the edge of the dashboard. "I am *not* like my father, cowering behind The New Music. I will lead them on the front lines, I will—"

"Just like you're doing right now? You call this leadership?"

"Enough of this," The Conductor snapped. "Sing all you want, little bird. I dare you to try to pry my people from their savior."

"Are you sure you want to take that bet?" Ronja growled. She leaned toward the microphone, until it nearly brushed her lips. "I'll free them and then . . . I'm coming for you."

"That would be interesting," Maxwell said, his calm reinstated. "But I think you'll find it rather more difficult this time around."

Chills whistled down her spine. Ronja shook them off stubbornly. "I'll free them before your tank can put a dent in that door."

"Oh, little bird, I am not speaking of that brutish instrument, but something far more elegant." Ronja raised her eyes to Roark as understanding stirred within her. His jaw was clenched beneath his war paint, his dark eyes shivering. Her gaze snapped back to the humming dashboard. "While you were away, I had time to prepare. You see, when we patched you up after your little outburst, we collected some tissue samples."

Cold dread flooded Ronja. Her memory of those days in the prison was so hazy. She did not even remember them taking her out of the cell after she had attempted to smash the mirrored walls.

"Your DNA is so unusual, little bird. It makes you exquisitely sensitive to The Music. It's a wonder you were able to move, much less resist it all those years." She could hear the smile in his voice, and knew what he was going to say before he said it. "So, I spent some time engineering a Song born of a unique signal especially for you. I call it The Birdsong."

"You sick bastard!" Roark roared.

Ronja looked up through swimming eyes. Her stomach bottomed out. Wild desperation clashed with terror on his face, draining it of color.

"Mr. Westervelt, I thought you might be listening," Maxwell drawled. "Do you really have the right to call me sick? You are, after all, the one who brought her into this war."

Roark flinched.

"I have to go now, little bird," The Conductor went on. "But I look forward to seeing you soon. Please note that the Birdsong will begin when you start your little broadcast. I think you will find it most riveting."

Before Ronja could open her mouth, the line went dead.

62: IRIDESCENT

For an endless moment, no one spoke. Ronja stared at the dashboard that sprawled before her. Her mind turned over and over like the gears of the clocks that pressed in around them.

"No, DAMMIT!" Ronja jumped as Roark aimed a kick at the metal dash, sending a shudder rippling through it. "We have to get you out of here, we have to . . . "

"Roark," she broke in gently.

"We have to . . . " He raked a clawed hand through his jet black hair, staring at her with sparking eyes.

"The *zethas* may still help," Paxton spoke up. Ronja looked to him. The cautious confidence in his words did not match his expression.

"Thank you," she said. She switched her attention to Easton. Larkin's blood was crusted on the exposed skin of his neck and hands. His expression was as still and calm as a glass lake. She passed him a subtle nod, which he returned.

"There is no way in hell I am letting you do this."

Ronja turned to Roark slowly. "You can't stop me."

"Ro, *please.*" He grabbed her hands over the dashboard,

squeezing so hard it was almost painful. His eyes never strayed from her face. She maintained a calm mask.

"Let me go, Roark."

His teeth gnashed together. He gripped her harder, as if he could squeeze the resolve from her. "No."

"Let me go!" Ronja snapped. She yanked back, trying to free her hands from his, but he would not budge. She was about to shout at him when Darius stepped up and clapped a hand to Roark's shoulder.

"Let go of my daughter." His voice was quiet, but the blaze in his eyes told another story. Ronja felt her throat constrict as something swelled in her, an emotion she did not recognize. Roark gaped at Darius sidelong. His grip loosened. She slipped her hands from his as gently as she could. His arms fell to his sides, limp. The once king nodded his approval and retreated.

"I need room," Ronja said, casting her eyes around the room. "Everyone back up."

"We're down to nine minutes," Easton warned her as he and the others backed toward the windows. "Can you do it?"

The Siren nodded though every fiber in her body screamed *no*. She fixated her attention on the dashboard, on the gleaming brass switch that would connect her to the Singers. And the Birdsong. She took a breath, then reached for it.

"Ronja." The Siren looked up. Roark had joined the others on the outskirts of the room. The look on his face made her knees weak. Love and terror, the most desperate combination. "Please."

She smiled, steady as the rising sun. "Freedom is a state of mind," she reminded him. Tears bloomed in his eyes. She turned back to the dashboard. It seemed to expand before her, infinite as the stars above. "When I go in," she said, raising her voice to speak to the group as a whole. "I might not come out. If I die, blow the mainframes."

Ronja looked up again, her eyes roving across her comrades. "Some will survive, and Maxwell's conquest will be over." She settled on Easton. He offered a sharp nod. He would do what needed to be done.

The Siren reached for the switch. It felt as though her limbs were coated in honey, heavy and slow. Her body railed against her, begging her not to put it back in that awful cage. The one that had held her for most of her life. Drawing on the last shreds of her courage, she flipped the switch.

Nothing happened. Temporary relief wrapped around her. Maybe the *zetha* was working. She licked her lips, preparing to sing.

The world was snuffed, licked fingers pinching a wick. Her beating heart was petrified. Her blood ground to a halt in her veins. But somehow, she was able to let out a roar of agony as The Birdsong swarmed her. The *zetha* was no match. It was searing, white hot against her temples, unbearably bright through her closed lids. Nothing compared. Not The Day Song or The Night Song, not even The Quiet Song. In those days, she was comfortably numb.

Now, she was awake.

Someone laid a hand on her shoulder.

"NO!" she screamed, lashing out blindly. "GET BACK!"

She forced her eyes open. Horror engulfed her. The room was gone. Everything was gone. Even the sky had been ripped away. There was nothing but The Birdsong, black like thunderheads. It swallowed everything in its path, leaving a trail of decay in its wake. It was every stinger that had ever been pressed to her skin, every cut and every bruise she had ever received. Every person she had ever lost and everyone she would lose again.

Come to me, it whispered without words. *Come to me, sweet child. Little bird, you are so tired. You have worked for so long.*

Shut up! Ronja screamed.

Come to me, little bird. You will be rewarded. You can sleep. You can finally sleep.

Exhaustion like she had never felt enveloped Ronja. Somewhere far beyond her, her knees gave out. She felt them hit the marble floor of a room that did not exist.

Give yourself to me, little bird. You are so tired. You have done so much for so many people, and look where it has gotten you. Beaten. Mutilated. Scarred. Assaulted. Tortured. Killed.

Leave me alone!

Little bird, your wings are broken, but I can make you fly.

Infinity swirled around her, sinking its hooks into her skin.

Little bird, rest now. You are so tired. You have worked so hard. You deserve to sleep.

Yes . . .

You deserve to rest.

Yes . . .

Ronja!

The Siren shuddered. That name. Where had it come from? Not from the gentle blackness bearing her weight. It was attached to something warm and firm, pulsing with life.

Roark.

Leave him, little bird. He has caused you nothing but pain.

Ronja!

NO!

Ronja crashed back into her body, the force of her return rattling her bones and teeth. She was heaving before the dashboard, her pale skin dripping in icy sweat, her war paint running into her eyes. Roark was at her side—Roark. She reached out to him through the suffocating Aura of The Birdsong. He was there in an instant, her anchor. The Siren opened her mouth and began to sing.

When the day shakes
Beneath the hands of night

Each word was like a white hot blade in her skull. She forced herself to keep her eyes open, holding her screams of agony in her belly. She raised her chin, searching for her Aura among the black clouds that were eating her alive. There was not a thread of white anywhere. There was nothing. She was nothing. She kept singing anyway.

When your page is ripped
From the Book of Life

Someone else grabbed her free hand. She could not see them through the black Aura, but she knew who it was. She could feel the power sizzling between them. Darius. What had he said? Her Aura was an extension of the self, like her arm.

Ronja felt her eyes roll back into her head. Her back arched as wave after wave of agony rolled over her. A thousand memories poured from her, spilling into the black mass.

Layla. Dead at her feet. Georgie, crying after a classmate had broken her finger like a pencil. Cosmin, struggling to speak after being exposed to the prototype of The New Music. Henry, his voice on the radio. Henry, his eyes empty as drums as he pulled the trigger on Samson. Evie. Iris. Mouse. Imprisoned below the palace. Because of her. Terra, face down on the marble, dead or close to it. Darius, just a child when he was ripped from his home.

Roark. Chained to the wall by his father, the discoid scars on his arms glaring white in the fluorescents. Tears sliding down his cheeks as he spoke of Sigrun. Screaming as Maxwell dragged her limp body away. Under The New Music. Unfeeling. Uncaring. Unmade. No. Not again.

Sing my friend
Into the dark
Sing my friend
Into the black

Ronja got to her feet, staring up at the dark Aura. There was not a trace of white in its midst, not yet. She closed her eyes, curling each individual memory to her chest, crushing them into a knot of iridescent agony.

Sing my friend
There and back

With a roar that could topple mountains, Ronja released her Aura. It exploded from her chest, a deafening flash of the purest light. It shattered the faces of the clock tower, reducing the glass to dust. It poured over Revinia, bathing every street, every house, every tortured corner of the walled city in light that none could run from. It shredded the black Aura that choked them, until only shivering threads remained, slinking away into the night sky.

Then silence.

She crashed to her knees again, though she did not feel it. She was far beyond the realm of her body. She was in the stars. Only this time, they were warm. They were luminous. She was luminous. She was everything and she was nothing. She was the Siren.

She was song itself.

63: ALL FALL DOWN
Roark

Roark lunged, catching Ronja by the waist before she crashed forward. He might have been screaming, it was impossible to tell over the roar in his ears. Her body was hot to the touch, but the color had been drained from her cheeks, her wan skin stark against her war paint. The blood that leaked from her nose and remaining ear was already drying on her face. *No.* He pressed his fingers to her neck, hunting for a vital sign. Something. Anything.

Beat.

"Roark!"

Roark looked up. The world screamed back into focus. He knelt on the floor of the clock tower behind the dashboard, the limp form of the Siren cradled in his arms. Around him was chaos. The glass faces of the clock had been reduced to dust, the frigid winter winds pouring through them. Darius, Easton, and Paxton stood above them, struck dumb.

Then the commander shook himself free of shock. "We have to get out of here," he said. "Jonah should have set the charges by now."

Roark found his voice. "Jonah, Larkin, do you copy? The Siren has done it. If you can find your way out, the Revinians will be harmless."

"Copy that," came Jonah's breathless voice. "Rigged the first blast to blow the door, we'll meet you at the extraction point."

Easton nodded and began to speak in rapid Tovairin into his *zethas*. Darius took that time to crouch next to Roark and Ronja, laying his weathered hand on her wan cheek. Her head lolled to the side, her lips parting slightly.

"Will she be okay?" Roark asked, desperation making his voice crack.

"Yes," Darius replied, not taking his eyes off her. He shook his head in wonderment. "Never in my life have I seen anyone do anything like that, not even my father." He smiled, lifting his eyes to Roark. "You're lucky to have her in your life."

Roark opened his mouth to respond, but just then Ronja began to stir in his arms. "Ro, hey, Ronja. Look at me, love." He tapped her face lightly, giving her body a little shake. "Come on, love, look at me."

Her eyes peeled open like dawn peeking over the horizon. The whites were filled with red, burst capillaries. "Roark," she whispered, her voice scarcely more than a breath. "Did we do it?"

"You did it," he told her, bringing his brow down to hers. The touch burned his skin, but he barely felt it. "You did it, love. Now we just have to blow the mainframes."

"Darius, Roark." Both men looked up. Easton and Paxton stood at the edge of the north face. "Two minutes."

"How the hell are we going to get down in time?" Roark asked. As soon as he spoke, the answer came to him. "Oh, right." he said. He hooked his arms under Ronja's knees and neck, curling her to his chest. Even in her armor, she was light as a feather. She'd passed out again, but the pulse at her neck was still strong.

"Pull your chute the second you jump, understand?" Easton said, looking around at them all. They nodded in turn. The commander locked eyes with Roark. "Hold her tightly."

Roark flattened her back to his chest, holding her with one arm and gripping the chute release with his free hand. "Always."

Without another word, they leapt from the tower, leaving the remnants of the battle behind. The cold air rushed past them for a split second—then Roark yanked his chute. It pulled him back ferociously. He wrapped both arms around Ronja, clinging to her as they sank toward the ground. The city sprawled around them, an infinity of warm light and confusion. They landed a bit harder than he would have liked. He twisted and fell backward to protect the Siren.

Groaning, he deposited her on the ground and got to his feet. He hit the button that retracted his chute, stumbling slightly when it snapped back into its pack.

There were hundreds of bodies in the square, living and dead. The dead were strewn around haphazardly, blood and bone glinting in the city lights. The living wandered like lost children, silent and exhausted. Some touched their Singers, others cried. Some sat on the ground, staring at the dead.

"She all right?"

Roark rounded on the familiar voice, unprecedented relief cutting through him. "Jonah," he said. "You made it. Is Larkin—?"

"She'll live." He gave a pained smile. His hands and armor were coated in blood. He glanced down at Ronja, who had not moved since they landed. "Our girls are a hell of a lot tougher than we are."

"That they are," Roark agreed.

"We gotta move," Easton called, beckoning them with a gloved hand. "We have to—"

"ROARK!"

Roark stiffened. Time screamed to a halt. He turned slowly, as if his limbs were coated in honey. Before his brain could catch up with his body, someone slammed into him with the force of a steamer, tackling him to the slushy ground.

"YOU STUPID BASTARD!"

"EVIE!" Roark wrapped his arms around her, shocked laughter tearing from his lips. "You're not dead!"

"Not yet, mate." She rolled off him and shot to her feet, sticking her tattooed hand down for him to grasp. He let her pull him up, then roped her into another tight hug. She was filthy, her hair stiff with grease and her skin coated in grime. Somehow, she still managed to smell like home.

"Is anyone with you?" Roark asked, pulling away and sobering.

"Iris and Mouse," Evie said with a broad grin. If he had not known her so well, he might not have detected the flash of pain in her honey-brown eyes. "They're in an auto a block away. I came to see what all the fuss was about."

"What about Terra?"

Evie shook her head, her smile slipping. "Dunno. She supposedly got out a few days ago, but she's in the wind."

The ground shuddered. Evie clamped her hands over her ears. Roark scooped Ronja up as if she were made of feathers and took off toward the park.

"MOVE!" Easton shouted from ahead. "*Yessan!*" Snow shook free of the bare tree branches. The panes of the gas lamps rattled.

"What the hell is that?" Evie screamed as they ran.

"You're about to find out!"

Inferno blossomed behind them. The blast sent them flying forward, a tangle of bruised limbs and adrenaline. Roark rolled on to his back, spitting out a mouthful of dirty snow. Ronja was still unconscious next to him, her dark curls splayed against the white. Evie struggled to her feet, coughing profusely. Roark followed her. Together, they gazed up at the flaming clock tower. It was magnificent against the dark winter sky, rubble still raining down in deadly waves.

"Holy shit! You did it!" the techi exclaimed, punching him in the arm with a maniacal laugh. "You—"

More explosions shattered the night. Orange light washed over them. Roark began to count the eruptions. *Three . . . four . . . five . . . six. . .*

Seven . . .

The seventh was more of a rapid series, like the final burst of fireworks at a celebration.

"What was that last set?" Roark shouted, whipping around to find Easton. The commander was looking off into the city with a troubled expression.

"I have no idea," he said. "But we need to get to the extraction point."

"I can help you there," Evie said with a grin. She tapped her fist to her brow, then her chest. "*Perlo*, Tovairin."

A slow smile spread across the tense mouth of the commander as understanding clicked into place. He stood up straighter, then crossed his fingers over his heart. "*Eliest*, Arexian." Before either of them could say anything more, a sleek black truck with three doors came roaring into the park, skidding to a stop in the snow.

The Kev Fairlans all aimed at it, but Roark waved them off. The front window rolled down and an uncommonly pale head stuck out. "Need a ride?" Mouse asked cheekily.

"Mouse!" Roark shouted.

The other boy grinned. His face was considerably thinner than the last time they had seen each other, but he appeared to be unharmed. The back doors of the truck slid open, revealing Iris. Joy swelled in Roark, but it was quickly replaced with horror. She was covered in bruises, her left eye swollen shut and her thigh swaddled in a bloody bandage. Still, she smiled.

"Well, get going!" she ordered shrilly.

Roark did as he was told, scooping Ronja up and hurtling toward the truck. He carried her to the back of the auto, setting her on one of the leather seats gingerly. The rest of them filtered in after him and Iris slammed the door. "Go!" she shouted at Mouse. The boy stomped on the gas and they flew forward.

They were halfway down the block when Roark realized Darius was not with them.

64: LAST STAND
Darius

The walk to the palace went quicker than he had hoped it would. It was snowing by the time he arrived. He had passed many Revinians on his way. None of them paid him any mind. Some were passed out in the snow. Some wandered aimlessly, tears leaking down their faces. Their Singers clung to their ears, now nothing more than decorative metal.

Still, he walked on.

The gates were open when he arrived at the white wall. He paused at them, gazing up at his childhood home with tired eyes. It was just as he remembered. Bright and pure as the Aura Ronja had cast over the city, the palace sat proudly atop a rolling hill, an oasis. He started toward it, his footprints crunching in the snow.

Uniformed Offs wandered past him, blinking wearily in the gently falling snow. None of them even spared him a glance. They had no doubt done terrible things while under The New Music. Darius hoped for their sake they would not remember.

When he reached the palace steps, the king paused again. He had to crane his neck to see all the way up. The stark white pillars were brightly lit even in the deepest part of the night. They watched him silently, a solemn welcome home.

He started up the stairs, his footsteps echoing through the sprawling courtyard.

The golden front doors were unlocked, just as he had expected. He opened one with a groan of great hinges, spilling moonlight onto the smooth stone floor. The entry hall was otherwise dark. He lifted his eyes to the ceiling, where dozens of unlit crystal chandeliers still hung. They had always been too opulent for his taste. Slipping inside, he strode down the hall, running his hand along the cool wall until it found the lever. He pulled it sharply. The chandeliers ignited, bathing the stunning entry hall in warm light.

"I was expecting someone else."

Darius rounded on the voice slowly, leaving his weapons sheathed at his sides. Before him was a young man, perhaps in his late twenties, with a shock of black hair and glossy blue eyes. He was unusually pale and gaunt, dressed in what might have once been a beautiful suit. Now, it was rumpled and torn, stained with a dark substance Darius knew was blood. He held a gun in his hand, his fingers twitching around it anxiously.

"Maxwell, I assume," Darius said.

"How astute," Maxwell purred. His face fell. "My little bird has beaten me at my own game."

"She was never yours, boy," the king replied. "She was never mine."

Recognition sparked in Maxwell's pale gaze. "Darius Alezandri," he murmured. "The lost king of Revinia."

"Indeed."

"You're supposed to be dead." His tone was more curious than anything. He cocked his head to the side. "Where did you run off to?"

"My father sent me to Tovaire," Darius explained. "Though I

returned briefly when I was about your age."

"Ah, so that's when you met the mutt?" Maxwell sneered.

The king just looked at him, unruffled. "She will never be anything but Layla to me."

"Why have you come here, old man?" The Conductor snapped.

"I came here to die, and to take you with me." Darius placed a weathered hand on his chest, over his armor. "I'm on borrowed time as it is."

Maxwell raised his eyebrows. "Is that so?"

"Bad lungs."

"I see," Maxwell drawled. He raised his gun, aiming squarely at Darius's head. "Then you won't mind if I put you out of your misery."

Darius smiled. "You're a fool," he said. "You were in over your head the moment you tried to control the Siren. You should have known that an Alezandri in their prime cannot be contained."

"Shut up!" Maxwell barked, raising his other hand to his gun to steady it. "You are going to die. I'll string your body up over the palace."

The king wet his lips and began to whistle. Before his eyes, his coppery Aura bloomed, wavering in the frigid night air that was spilling in through the open doors. Maxwell's eyes popped. He stumbled backward, staring blankly at the writhing creature before him. Darius had allowed him to see it, just this once.

Every man deserved to see his death coming.

"You *freak*," Maxwell spat, raising his gun again and aiming at Darius's head. "I'll—"

Darius snapped his fingers. His Aura shot forward, a vicious spike straight through The Conductor's chest. Maxwell fell backward, landing on his side, the bolt of energy still sizzling in his ribs. The king crashed to his knees, the fight fleeing his bones.

Before him, the tyrant was choking on his own blood, his pale eyes flickering in their sockets.

Then, with a final twitch, he died.

Darius drew a deep shuddering breath, turning his gaze to the chandelier above him. His lungs rattled weakly; his heart beat sluggishly. He closed his eyes. Painted on the backs of his lids were the faces of his daughter and his love, smiling brightly in the late winter sun. They were walking through the outdoor market on the afternoon of the solstice, wrapped in warm furs, a song strung between them.

Darius was carried away on the wings of that song.

65: DAYBREAK
Three Days Later

Ronja awoke slowly, then all at once. Her body ached. She struggled against the weight pinning her eyelids shut. A moan escaped her lips. Then—pressure around her fingers. She opened her eyes. Leaning over her was the most beautiful face she had ever seen—golden brown skin, faint freckles like constellations, bottomless eyes as warm as the sun on her back.

"Roark," she rasped, struggling to sit up. He pushed her down as if she weighed nothing at all. She flopped back onto the feather pillow, blinking rapidly. "What happened?"

"You did it, Ronja," he said, reaching down to brush an escaped curl from her face. "You freed everyone."

"The mainframes?" she asked hoarsely.

"Here," Roark said. He slipped a warm hand behind her back, helping her sit up slowly. "There you go, drink this." He pressed the edge of a glass to her lower lip, tipping it back gently. She drank gratefully, though the cool water felt like a kick in the gut. He laid her back down with a sigh.

"Roark, the mainframes," Ronja asked again, her voice a bit stronger now.

He smiled. "Blown to bits."

Relief like she had never felt washed over her, giving her a slight burst of energy. "What about everyone else? Evie, Iris . . . ?"

Roark got to his feet swiftly. He swam in her vision, which was taking its time to return. "I'll be right back, stay here."

Ronja gave a hoarse laugh as he slipped out of her line of sight. She blinked up at the ceiling. It was eggshell white and smooth, with warm winter sunlight streaming across it. She struggled to sit up on her elbows, her curiosity overwhelming her exhaustion. She was in a large, fine bedroom with dark wooden furniture and wide windows with cream dressings. Her bed was huge, large enough to fit three people at least. A fire roared in the corner. She did not recognize any of it.

Then the door opened across from her.

"Ronja!"

A mousy blur shot at her, scrambling up onto the bed and bowling her back into her pillow. "Georgie," Ronja whispered, cradling her head to her chest and rocking her back and forth. "Georgie."

"And me." Ronja struggled to sit up, still clutching at Georgie with all her strength. Cosmin wheeled up to the edge of her bed, grinning at her lopsidedly, a new pair of glasses on his nose. Ronja stretched out her trembling hand, and he took it firmly. "Welcome back, sis."

"Ro!"

Ronja looked up as three more bodies tumbled onto her bed. She let out a noise that was half a laugh, half a sob as Evie, Iris, and Mouse all struggled get to her, gently pushing Georgie aside. Iris kissed her face, Evie tousled her hair, and Mouse hugged her around the middle with more affection than he had ever shown her in the time they had known each other.

"How did you get out?" Ronja asked breathlessly, leaning

back to look them all in the face. Her heart wilted when she caught sight of Iris. Her face was a patchwork of bruises, her right eye covered with a thick bandage.

"Long story," Evie said. "We'll tell you later."

"You did it, Ro," Iris squeaked, sounding just like herself despite her injuries. "You freed the city. You saved everyone."

Ronja shook her head, too overwhelmed to put a finger on any of her emotions.

"All right, let her breathe," Roark said in a voice close to a growl, shooing them away. Grumbling, all four of them slipped off the bed and joined Roark standing beside it.

"Where are we?" Ronja asked, looking around at them all with wide eyes.

"One of my apartments in the core," Roark said, folding his arms with a sly grin. "It took a while to get the heat up and running, but with my father gone, I am the sole proprietor."

"Don't let it go to your head," came a sarcastic voice from the hall.

Ronja cast her eyes to the door. Her jaw dropped. "Terra?"

The girl grinned, shaking her long blond hair over her muscled shoulder. "Hey there, Siren."

"How did you get out? How are you . . . ?"

"Alive?" Terra strode toward the edge of her bed. "I cut a deal with Bullon, and found my way to Cicada's place. Blew up the ships with his rather large collection of whiskey."

"That was the seventh explosion," Roark exclaimed with an approving nod.

"I had help, though," Terra said. She looked over her shoulder. Ronja followed her line of sight.

"Hey, Ro."

"Henry," Ronja whispered in a quavering voice. He filled the frame, just as solid as the others around him. He was dressed in a navy sweater, his broad shoulders hunched with shame, his brown eyes flooding. "Henry."

He started toward her slowly. The other Anthemites moved out of the way as he approached the edge of her bed. "I'm so sorry, Ronja, I . . . "

"Stop," she said, shaking her head. "Just stop."

Pain shot across Henry's expression. She shook her head again and beckoned him. "Come here."

The boy kneeled at the bedside slowly, never taking his eyes off her face. He looked haunted around the edges, exhausted. But alive. Whole. She opened her arms to him and he leaned into her, wrapping his thick arms around her skinny body. Ronja inhaled his familiar scent, tears pricking the corners of her eyes. Henry shuddered against her, silent sobs wracking his form. Over his shoulder, Ronja made eye contact with Roark. "Darius?" she asked hopefully.

Slowly, Roark shook his head.

Ronja buried her face in Henry's sweater and wept.

66: FORWARD

The days bled into weeks. The weeks into months. Slowly, Revinia crept back to life. The shops opened first. People needed groceries, supplies, medicine. Dozens were killed and hundreds had been wounded when the mainframes blew. They had everything from minor cuts and scrapes to broken bones. Then there was the withdrawal, of course.

The dead were buried beyond the northern edge of the great black wall, the gates of which had been thrown open to usher in the winds of change. When Ronja heard that mutts had been used for target practice, she insisted they be buried alongside the rest of the dead humans. She assumed she and her inner circle would be the only ones to load their bodies into the backs of the trucks, but to her surprise dozens of everyday citizens turned out to help.

Since the fall of The New Music, her story had spread like wildfire. It was twisted, as rumors always were, but at least the basics were accurate. The mutt princess from the outer ring had overcome The New Music, sending the shockwave of white light over the city. They had all seen it flash, momentarily washing out the stars and the moons. They had all felt the strange warmth that followed, and the sting of their waking brains.

The ache of life.

The hospitals reopened. Statues of The Conductors—Atticus and Maxwell both—were torn down to resounding cheers. The black and red flags were burned, the white eye of the original Conductor struck from the sides of buildings. The few who remained loyal to Maxwell even after their Singers were neutralized were arrested. Those who escaped were left to the wilderness. "They're not worth chasing," Terra had said.

Three weeks into the aftermath, Ronja heard Red Bay had been burned to the ground.

Most of the Tovairins, had been extracted by aeroplane in the immediate aftermath of the battle. The few who stayed behind after the fall of The Music had left a week later. To Ronja's great relief there had been no Tovairin fatalities. Hugging Jonah goodbye was harder than Ronja expected it to be. When she put her arms around him, he lifted her off her feet and twirled her around the living room, drawing a shriek from her.

"Put me down, *fiester!*"

"Anytime, princess," he said, setting her down with wink. Larkin rolled her eyes in the background. She had survived her wounds, but just barely. She still walked with a cane, but Iris said she would make a full recovery.

"*Perlo,*" Ronja said, locking eyes with her and tapping her fist to her brow and heart.

Larkin had raised her chin, the faintest smile drifting across her mouth. "*Pevra,*" she replied. "Good luck, Siren."

"Wait," Ronja called. She turned to Jonah. "Where's Easton? I need to talk to him."

Twenty minutes later, Jonah returned to the flat with the commander, who was still dressed in his armor. "Alezandri," he had greeted her with a dip of his chin. "The aeroplane is waiting—what do you want?"

"Do you have everything you need?" she asked.

"Yes, the weapons have been loaded." He gave a slight bow, making Ronja blush scarlet. "We are indebted to you, Queen Alezandri."

"I'll be dropping that title as soon as the Revinians choose their own leader," Ronja replied, her nose wrinkling with distaste. She stuck out her hand for him to shake. Easton took it firmly, not taking his eyes off her face. "Thank you for your help, Commander. We never could have done this without you."

"And now Tovaire will be free, because of your generosity."

Ronja let go of his hand, her smile slipping. "No one is free until everyone is," she said.

Easton looked at her for a long moment, his expression inscrutable. Then he gave the slightest nod and strode from the apartment. Larkin saluted them, Jonah winked, and they were gone. Back to their own home to fight their own wars.

The Anthemites, who had fled through the sewers at Terra's insistence, filtered back through the open gates. The Belly was pried open, allowing them to return and collect the belongings they had left behind. Some stayed in the subterranean tomb, too afraid to grace the surface just yet. Others threw themselves into the cleanup effort, most of all Ito.

The lieutenant—or commander, as Ronja often had to remind herself—quickly took charge of the organized chaos, dividing the remaining Anthemites into groups. Some went to the slums and outer ring to deliver food and supplies. Some helped the strapped hospitals care for the wounded. Others simply offered answers, standing on the edge of the demolished fountain at the center of the town square. People wondered what had happened while they were under The New Music. What were they to do, now? Why did their eyes leak when they were not in physical pain? Ito headed most of those events, or "Humanity 101" lessons, as Evie called them.

When Ronja was not aiding in the cleanup, her curly hair stuffed under a cap and her face partially obscured by a scarf, she was in the beautiful apartment Roark had claimed near the center of the core. The space was only large enough to comfortably house four—Ronja, Roark, Cosmin, and Georgie—but without anyone saying anything, it had been designated meetup point for their inner circle.

Their healing was slow. At times it stopped and sputtered like a rusty faucet. In the first days following the fall of The Conductor, there was mostly silence. Ronja spent the majority of her time sleeping, Roark at her side. They all slept scattered throughout the apartment, making beds out of the sofas and armchairs and plush rugs. Iris spent most of those days staring into oblivion while Evie read her poetry.

Henry and Charlotte were inseparable. The only times the boy left her side was to visit Ronja. Lapses occasionally occurred in his consciousness. Names and places temporarily forgotten, forks dropped as he swore at thin air. Like Cosmin, he had been exposed to The New Music before it was perfected. Like Cosmin, he would never fully recover.

Terra had rarely stopped pacing.

Mouse and Theo were the first to leave the apartment, after only five days. They retreated to the flat Theo had rented in the middle ring. Ronja understood. It had to be difficult to be around such a broken group, and neither of them had ever really been an Anthemite. "We'll visit," Mouse promised, squeezing Ronja on the shoulder as they bid her farewell at her bedside.

"You better," she said with a weak smile. Mouse hugged her. Theo shook her hand. Then they were gone. Moving forward. Moving on.

One week after the boys left, Iris and Evie moved into the

empty mansion across the street. No one knew where its owners were—if they had perished in the firefight outside the clock tower or if they had deserted the city. None of them particularly cared to ask. Soon after, Charlotte and Henry took over their basement, dividing it into two comfortable halves.

Terra remained in Ronja and Roark's living room, sleeping on the deep green couch. They did not ask her to leave, nor did they ask why she woke up with raw eyes and cheeks.

Slowly, surely, life found its way back into their eyes. Iris's bruises healed, revealing her lovely features. The bullet wound in her thigh scarred over. She still walked with a cane, but each day she moved a little faster.

Ronja's wounds healed, too. The ring of purple bruises around her neck faded. The scars left behind by Maxwell's bit smoothed over. Her cracked ribs healed. The pounding in her head faded to a distant drum, then to nothing at all. She and Roark spent every night together in the huge bed, tangled in each other's arms, so that when one of them woke up screaming, the other would be there to anchor them.

Healing came slowly.

Every night, the Anthemites gathered at the kitchen table at the apartment, squeezing in as many chairs as they could. Henry and Iris cooked, though the boy was not allowed near the knives. Georgie and Charlotte set the table. Sometimes, Roark played the violin. On those nights, Ronja sat on the rug at the center of the living room, coaxing her Aura into view, making the ribbons dance around her friends—her family. They did not feel foreign to her anymore. They were a part of her. When they danced, her soul followed.

Three months later, Ito was instated as president of the city state. Helping the election run smoothly was quite the undertaking, especially because half the population did not understand the concept of an election. There were several candidates on the ballot, but Ito won in a landslide. She refused to move into the palace, which had been empty since the fall, instead choosing a modest row house in the middle ring. On the first day of her governance, she selected Terra as Captain of her official guard.

And so Terra moved from their living room to a large room at the back of Ito's new house.

Spring spread like wildfire, ushering in foggy gray mornings and tentative blossoms. One such morning, Ronja slipped out of bed early, wrapping herself in one of the thick blankets and putting on her boots. Silent as a shadow, she left the apartment and climbed to the roof. The city sprawled around her, brass and gold and endless possibility.

She closed her eyes to it, leaning up against the edge of the guard rail. Listening. Waiting. It came to her almost at once, the murmur of the great Aura that wrapped around the metropolis. She opened her eyes to its wonder. A curling cloud of golden dust that arched above Revinia like thunderheads, fed by the music of the city. The symphony of three million voices, just learning to sing.

"Where are you, Siren?"

Ronja smiled as Roark appeared at her side, leaning up against the railing. She looked up at him. His hair had grown longer in the passing months. She liked it that way. Her own curls nearly brushed her shoulders now.

"Right where I want to be," she said, linking her arm with his and leaning into his shoulder.

Roark pressed a kiss to her temple, wrapping his arm around her shoulders. The damp wind rose around them, stirring their hair and clothes. "Do you miss him?" he asked after a while.

"Not exactly," Ronja replied, knowing who he was talking

about. "I miss what he could have been."

They had found Darius on the floor of the palace opposite Maxwell's rotting body when they arrived at the palace to take The Conductor into custody. The others were bewildered. The once king did not appear to be injured, and there was a gaping hole straight through Maxwell's sternum. Ronja understood perfectly, but she had not explained it to anyone. Some things were better left unsaid. She did not need them knowing that she could kill with her voice, too.

"Ito's going to be a great leader," Roark said after a while.

"Yeah," Ronja agreed. "She will be."

"Do you think they're gonna be okay?"

"Who?"

Roark gestured out at the city.

Ronja nodded. "Yeah, I do."

"Do you think they can do it without us, for a while?"

The Siren turned to her heart, her brow creasing. "What do you mean?"

He shifted to face her. "I want to get out of the city for a bit. I want to go . . . somewhere."

"Where?"

"Anywhere, everywhere." Roark spun her to face him, taking her cold hands in his. She gazed up at him, at his glowing excitement. "I want to see Sydon, where my mother was born. I want to see Arutia. I know we have people here and I know Ito might need our help but—"

"Yes."

Roark blinked. "Sorry?"

Ronja squeezed his hands, smiling up at him as if he hung the sun in the sky each morning. "Yes." She let out a startled laugh when he ripped his hands from hers and punched the air, letting out a whoop that arched over their neighborhood, startling a flock of pigeons roosting in a nearby tree.

Ronja watched him, tears pricking the corners of her eyes. Dawn was breaking across the horizon, smothering the gray haze and blending with the golden Aura of Revinia. It was full of agony and possibility, sorrow and laughter, but mostly, it was full of hope.

EPILOGUE: BACK AGAIN
One Year Later

A re you sure we're in the right place?"
        Roark frowned down at her, but the teasing spark in his golden brown eyes let her know he was just playing. "Yes, Ro, I am quite sure we're in the right place."

"Well, it has been awhile," she said defensively.

"I think I remember my own neighborhood, Alezandri."

Ronja rolled her eyes. The late spring air had whipped her curls into a frenzy, but at least the flowers she had braided into them were staying in place. *Mostly*, she thought dryly as a pale blue petal spiraled to the cobblestones.

"You look stunning."

She smiled up at Roark, her heart swelling the way it always did when he tried to flirt with her. Even over a year later, he still made her body sing. "You're one to talk." In the soft evening light, dressed in a high-necked black suit with silver clasps, he looked more beautiful than anyone she had ever seen.

"That dress suits you, I forgot to tell you that."

"You told me five minutes ago."

"Well, I'm telling you again."

Ronja glanced down at her dress. She had purchased it at an outdoor market in the northern reaches of Arutia. Even there the people knew her face, her name. Ronja Alezandri. The Siren. They whispered as she passed. It was not just her that drew their attention, though. Roark Westervelt. The Anthemite. The vendor selling the dresses had tried to give the garment to her for free, but she refused. It was the most beautiful thing she had ever owned—pale blue with skirts that flowed to her ankles and tiny white flowers stitched into its pinched waist. She wore a white shawl over it for when the sun went down.

"I still think you should have bought that scarf," she said, eyeing his bare neck.

"I look terrible in blue," he answered. He looked her up and down, his eyes lingering on her low neckline. "You look good in anything." Ronja swatted him on the arm, but before she could say anything they stepped around the corner.

There they were.

At least three hundred Anthemites, most of whom she recognized by face if not name, gathered around the fountain in the middle of the town square. The statue of Atticus Bullon had been felled over a year ago. All that remained were the living arcs of water that cascaded into the rippling pool. Lanterns dangled from the trees encircling the plaza, and white petals littered the bricks.

"Ronja! Roark!"

The crowd unzipped and Iris burst through, a streak of red and white. She slammed into Ronja, who let out a whoosh of startled breath. "Careful," the Siren wheezed, patting her on the back gingerly. "You'll tear your dress."

Iris stepped back, grinning ear to ear. Her red curls were pinned into an elegant bun ringed with white flowers to match her lace wedding dress. Her pale skin glowed through her dappled freckles, and her hazel eyes were framed with thick lashes. "You look beautiful," Ronja said with a smile.

"You call that a hug?"

The Siren looked up just in time to be enveloped by Evie, who lifted her off the ground. Iris skipped over to hug Roark, who kissed both her cheeks. "You look amazing," Ronja told Evie when they pulled apart. Her dark hair had grown since she'd last seen her and was twisted into an elegant braid at her crown. She wore a form-fitting white suit, a single silver clasp at its waist, accentuating her curves.

"Arexian tradition," the techi said, touching her braid lightly. Her face lit up. "I got more *reshkas*, too!" She rolled her left sleeve up to show off her expanded tattoos. "Dad is teaching me to read them."

Ronja grinned. "Congratulations."

"Georgie is going to lose her mind when she sees your dress," Iris said, eyeing Ronja appreciatively. "You look gorgeous."

"Now, now," Evie teased, slinging a strong arm over her bare shoulders.

The surgeon blinked up at her. "You know I'm about to marry you, right?"

"Where is Georgie, anyway?" Ronja asked, standing up on her tiptoes to see over the dense crowd.

"You can talk to her after," Iris said, shooing Evie back and taking Ronja by the hand. "Come on, you're late, as always." The Siren shrugged helplessly as she was dragged away from Roark and Evie, who both grinned mischievously. "We're about to get started. Do you remember your cue?"

"Yeah," Ronja nodded as Iris led her through the whispering crowd. *The Siren. Ronja. Alexandri.* "I remember."

"Perfect." The surgeon released her and pointed at a spot near the edge of the fountain, just out of reach of a stream of water. "Stand there and keep quiet until you hear your cue."

"Yes, ma'am," Ronja said, saluting her with two fingers. Iris beamed, then whipped around and hurried away, skirts rustling around her ankles. The Siren smiled after her, standing with her hands clasped. It was polite, she supposed.

"Ro."

Ronja felt her heart leap into her throat as she rounded on the familiar voice. "Henry," she gasped, opening her arms to him. He roped her into a bone-crushing hug, his musk enveloping her. "How have you been doing?" she asked as they pulled apart, still holding hands loosely.

"All right," he replied with a gentle shrug. "It gets easier."

"Yeah, it does."

"How is Charlotte doing?"

"Better," he said, his dark eyes lighting up. "She and Cosmin are pretty much inseparable. I gave them *the talk* a couple days ago."

Ronja winced. "Sorry about that."

"No worries, keeping them in line . . . it helps."

"How are you and Valorie?" she asked, changing the subject.

Only days after the fall of The Conductor, Henry had returned to the palace in search of the girl Maxwell had kept as his personal slave. He and Iris nursed her back to health, connecting her with other women who had faced abuse. Several months ago, as Henry explained in a letter, their relationship had progressed beyond friendship. "We're taking it slow," he said, a blush creeping into his face. "After everything she has been through . . . "

Ronja laid a loving hand on his broad shoulder, smiling up at him. "Just listen to her. She'll tell you when she's ready."

String music struck up from somewhere across the crowd. Ronja looked at Henry with a wince. "Iris will skin me if I am not focused. I'll talk to you later?"

"Always," he said. "I'll be here."

"I love you," Ronja said, letting her arm fall from his shoulder.

"And I you." With a little wave, Henry faded back into the audience.

Ronja smiled after him, peace stirring in her chest. Movement to her right caught her eye. Ito, dressed in an elegant cream dress that brushed the ground. Her orange hair was swept up into a tight knot, accentuating her long neck. She locked eyes with Ronja briefly, passing her a fond nod. The Siren returned it, scanning the area for Ito's shadow. Her lips quirked into a smile.

She stood at the edge of the throng, her arms crossed over her sleek black suit and thin tie. Her blond hair had grown longer; it nearly reached her waist. She looked rather pretty, now that she had relaxed a bit, Ronja thought. Their eyes locked.

Terra smiled, passing her the briefest of nods before returning her attention to the president. The tiny orchestra shifted music. Ronja stood up straighter, listening for her cue. The crowd parted as the cello began to play, casting ribbons of green into the spring air. Evie and Iris appeared, their hands clasped and their eyes bright.

The piano joined the fray. The Siren took a steadying breath and began to sing.

As the first threads of her voice washed over the crowd, her white Aura materialized. She reached out, coaxing it from the shadows of her mind. Gasps flew up as the shimmering entity materialized. Ronja smiled through the lyrics, sending her ribbons swirling down toward the brides.

Iris beamed as the lights swirled around her skirts, while Evie looked at her in quiet awe. As they approached Ito, who was holding a slip of paper in her hand, Ronja closed out the old rhyme.

Ronja sighed as her Aura dissolved, leaving a faint glow behind. Or maybe that was just Evie and Iris, standing before Ito with their fingers laced tight. The president smiled down at them fondly, then spoke. "We are gathered here today to join these two remarkable women in matrimony."

The Siren cast her eyes over the audience. Her heart jolted. Roark stood near the front, his hands in his pockets and his lips twisted into a knowing smile. *I love you,* her heart sang. *I love you.*

"Iris, do you take Evie to be your lawfully wedded wife? In sickness and in health, in—"

"Yes, yes," Iris cut her off, holding out her slim finger while the crowd laughed. Evie, grinned, pulling a thin silver band from her pocket and slipping it onto her ring finger.

"Evelyn," Ito went on, unruffled. "Do you take Iris to be your lawfully wedded wife? In sickness and in health, rich or poor, in war and peace? Do you swear to be faithful, kind, and loving as long as you both shall live?"

"You know it," Evie answered.

Iris trembled visibly as she slipped the band around Evie's tattooed finger. Ronja bit her lip as joyful tears pricked her eyes. "Then, by the power vested in me by the people of Revinia, I now pronounce you wedded. You may now kiss."

Before Evie could budge an inch, Iris threw her arms around her neck and kissed her passionately. Laughing against her mouth, Evie swept her off her feet, bending her backward. Laughter and applause burst from the audience. Shooting one last glance at the brides, Ronja hurried over to Roark, taking both his hands in hers. He leaned down to kiss her gently. The world swayed. "This is where I want to be," Ronja whispered against his mouth. "Right here."

She felt Roark smile. "It'll be hard. We still have a lot of work to do."

"I know." Ronja pulled back and turned around, leaning up against him as they watched Evie take Iris in her arms, the brides as different and as lovely as the winter moons. "But it will be worth it."

ACKNOWLEDGEMENTS:

When I first came up with the idea for *Vinyl* at sixteen, it was just a short story. I never thought I would share it with anyone, much less turn it into a series of books and publish it. Now at twenty-one, I am sitting in my apartment in New York typing up the acknowledgements for Book Three. To say this is unreal would be an understatement.

There are so many people to thank. I would like to start with my mother. None of this would have happened without her. She has been my biggest supporter. She took on the role of editor, designer, and agent in addition to being a physician, mother, wife, photographer, and advocate. She is my hero in every sense of the word. I have no idea what I would do without her.

Next, I want to thank my dad. Not only is he a fantastic father, he is one of my best friends. He is there for me through everything. Despite having zero interest in young adult fantasy, he has read every single word of this trilogy, which means more to me than I can possibly say. He is my rock. I am thankful for him every day.

My editor, Katherine Catmull of Yellow Bird Editors, gets the next shout out. I am so lucky I found her when I stumbled blind into the world of writing and publishing at eighteen. Not only is she an excellent editor with a knack for sensing the tiniest plot holes and continuity errors, she is an unfailingly kind human being. I would never have been comfortable releasing this trilogy without her assistance.

The next thank you goes to Jo Painter, the artist who drew the fabulous sketches that appear at the start of each book in this series. She is ridiculously talented and patient. It has been a joy to watch her grow as an artist over the past few years.

My family, friends, and loved ones. Allie Wolters, Maya Lippard, Mackenzie Shrieve, Sarah Maggard, Dani Hristev, Lucy Chen, Jillian Sloman, Cass Moskowitz, Alana Cohen, Kosyo Lafchis, Zoe Lewis, Evan Delgado, and Bryan Oliveira. Thank you so much for the light you have brought to my life and the support you have given me over the years. It is not forgotten.

My friends and colleagues in the world of writing and publishing. Amanda Lovelace, Cyrus Parker, Gretchen Gomez, Jennifer Wilson, Erin Summerill, Danika Stone, Elise Kova, Zóraida Cordova, Dela, Cheyenne Raine, C.B. Lee, E.J. Mellow, Sierra Abrams, J.S. Blair, Anne Chivon, Morgan Nikola-Wren, McKayla Debonis, K.Y. Robinson, Shelby Leigh, Jennae Cecelia, and Freedom Matthews. Thank you all for your love and support. You are all so insanely talented it makes my heart bloom. I am lucky to have each and every one of you in my life.

Next, I want to thank the Bookstagrammers, BookTubers, bloggers, and artists who have tirelessly supported this series. Hailee Bartz, Jenna Kilpinen, Sara Elena, Lindsay Keiller, Marlene Angelica Sjonsti Björnsen, Vari Siriruang, Stefanos Charalampous, Carlos Su´rez, Lindsey Robinson, Jay Gaunt, Lauren Crumly, Salome Totladze, Sofia Giappichini, Lissa Marshall, Rebekah Rose, and so many more. You helped make my very first series a success, and I will be forever grateful. I love all of you.

Lastly, I want to thank my readers. Every single one of you. Your comments, reviews, fan art, and love for this series and these characters is what kept me going on the hardest days. I am the luckiest author in the world. Thank you so much, and may your song guide you home.

Love,
Sophia

ABOUT THE AUTHOR

Sophia is the author of the #1 bestselling Vinyl Trilogy as well as *soul like thunder* and *hummingbird*, two books of poetry. She loves Star Wars and hates cantaloupe. She currently resides in New York City where she attends her dream school, NYU. Follow her on Twitter and Instagram @authorsehanson and on Tumblr as sophiaelainehanson. For book reviews, writing tips, and daily updates check out her blog, *May Your Books Guide You Home*.

Reviews are so important to indie authors. If you enjoyed *Siren*, please consider leaving an Amazon review today.

88462844R00239

Made in the USA
Middletown, DE
09 September 2018